The Absence of Complete Dark
Michelle Rivera

Copyright © 2024 by Michelle Rivera

All rights reserved.

No portion of this book may be reproduced in any form without written permission from the publisher or author, except as permitted by U.S. copyright law.

To all the lovely humans I work with, for fostering such a welcoming environment that I could be inspired to write something inspired by it.

To Luca, Miri, and Uniesia, for helping me elevate this book to its very best state with all of your insights, and again to Luca for helping me with the Romanian portions. This book wouldn't be what it is without all of your contributions.

This is a story dedicated to anyone whose parents raised them to feel they were unlovable. You, too, will be able to prove them wrong and find your happiness, someday, somewhere; I believe in you. Just keep looking.

Chapter One

Love: an ever-present presence, managing to weave its way through multiple facets of society.

Love, that which most accept readily; that which eludes a select few.

For many people, love– in all its forms– is the driving force behind the actions they pursue in their daily lives. Love from a family member, a close friend, a significant other, or even someone encountered in passing is often the push one needs to continue on with their day. In this way, it is not farfetched to say that love is what makes their lives worth continuing.

However, in the land of Basodin, love is even more essential; for without it, one will truly not survive.

In this world, as long as one is loved– whether that be from a romantic partner, familial figure, a friend, or anyone else– life continues on; with the power of love, one is protected from any strange maladies that would otherwise afflict them. It had been this way since the creation of this world: whenever a person did not receive any sort of love, the mysterious entity known as the Dark would latch on to them. The Dark, which everyone was familiar with from a young age due to school curriculum, has the ability to ravage the body of a person in many different ways; whether through physical decline or mental unrest, the affliction seems to always begin in that telltale way: the gradual decline of one's sight, starting as a dimming of light before progressing into complete sightlessness, and compounding with a multitude of other maladies, affecting every part of the person's body. Without intervention, everyone who is permanently afflicted by the Dark dies young; if one were to never feel any type of love, the Dark would probably consume them completely over a span of fifteen years.

However, as long as a person has not reached Complete Dark– a state where they are unable to perceive the world around them in any capacity– the affliction is not permanent, and can be fought; mitigated completely, even, if that person feels enough love.

None of the residents of Basodin knew for certain why this was, or how the Dark came to be, but the popular hypothesis was that it was because the world itself– according to the legends of its creation– was composed with the love of its creator: the Mother, an otherworldly goddess of a woman, spoken of in ancient mythology with words full of both admiration and awe. With a world literally made of love, it felt logical that feeling such an emotion would be imperative for the people who inhabited it. This, however, did not make life easier for the Basodinians that knew they were not receiving love, for there would always be that looming fear that someday, at some time, the Dark would find them.

The Dark was a complex force, though, and rarely– very rarely– it appeared to miss people; those who know they should have been afflicted a long time ago, but continue to live their lives as normal. Although this may sound positive at first, this is widely regarded as less of a benefit and more of a burden. For, what becomes of those people who are expecting the Dark to come for them, existing in a way that precedes the affliction of the Dark?

Will it come gradually? All at once? Or never at all?

And, in the meantime, how would a person in this position handle life?

★★★

"Oh, Mother! Girl! You have to tell me how it went!"

A long, pointed sigh of disappointment drifted through the air, followed quickly by the sounds of the bedsheets shifting as Yidarica turned from her stomach to her back. Yes, she would have to tell her best friend how everything had gone, wouldn't she? And that was the entire problem.

"What's with the sigh? Was it that bad?"

The two women had known each other for about four years now, having met at a shared interest gathering related to fashion. Four years was not a long time, in the grand scheme of everything, but even so, it had been enough time for Gracia to become the sole person that Yidarica could confide in; and over that amount of time, there had been a lot to confess, so the two were familiar with each other's mannerisms by now. The ever-so-familiar, drawn-out sigh meant that there was certainly bad news on the horizon.

Having arranged the words to what she wanted to say, Yidarica put the phone back up to her ear.

"It started out great. Hayden had some of the coolest vibes, and I really thought we were getting somewhere. I had a really fun time yesterday when we went out. But this morning, I woke up to a text message from him, telling me that I seem sweet, but he's not feeling any chemistry."

The line was silent for a few moments before Gracia replied, "Well, you *are* a sweet person." Usually, when people said things like that to Yidarica, she brushed them off as a formality; but it was not only easy to, but also somewhat reassuring to hear the sincerity in Gracia's voice.

A half-smile appeared on Yidarica's face. "I appreciate that, Gracia. I really do. But where is that getting me? All the sweetness in the world, on its own, won't save me when the Dark finally comes for me."

At thirty-one years of age, many a person was shocked to learn that Yidarica could see without glasses; and quite well. By all accounts, it didn't make sense; given how her life had transpired up to this point, she'd expected there to be at least a little bit of that trademark dullening in her vision by now, but no– there was none. There had been a period of her life where she'd gone through bouts of intense anxiety because of this, and it was only recently that she'd gained the ability to not worry about it so much that the sense of worry became debilitating. She could never understand why she of all people was "fortunate" to have the Dark miss her, and so, her plan recently was to ensure that she never *had* to understand. Her reasoning was that, once she found a person to love her, she would never have to look over her shoulder for the Dark again.

It was a pretty straightforward plan, she thought, but apparently not for any of the people with whom she'd gone on dates.

"I know, Yida. I know. I can't imagine how this must feel for you. But hey, if I can be practical for a second: would someone who blew you off like that ever be capable of loving you?" Gracia asked, in that tone that made it very clear she was intent on optimism. She brought out this tone a lot. Not just with Yidarica, with anyone in her life who she cared about. It wouldn't be farfetched to say that she had a natural talent for being a cheerleader for those she cared about.

"I guess you have a point," Yidarica admitted reluctantly.

"Damn right I do." Gracia laughed. "If I was at home, I'd offer to come by with ice cream. But we can make up for lost time when we see each other tomorrow."

"Tomorrow?" Yidarica shot up from her relaxed position. What was tomorrow?!

Another laugh from Gracia. "If I wasn't so familiar with how you are by now, I might be offended. Tomorrow's the day you give me the tour! Remember? I'm finally getting to see that big fancy building you work in!"

Oh– right, they'd been planning this for a while now. For the past two months, Gracia had been far away in the country of Dochram, helping tend to her great-aunt and uncle, and attending one of her many cousins' weddings. She was finally returning today, which meant that she would inevitably want to catch up with all of her friends. Not one to wait for a day off, Yidarica suggested she come visit her at work. After all, this would maximize the two's time together, and the industries they worked in were closely enough related that they were able to make it sound like a business visit on both ends. And so, the plan had been set for Gracia to visit the office, tomorrow.

"I didn't forget." This was not the entire truth. "It's just that we made plans so long ago that I didn't realize the day had already come, so soon. You know I struggle to perceive the passage of time."

The following sound of admonishment on Gracia's end made it clear that she didn't quite believe this explanation, but she didn't drag it out any farther. "I mean, you *are* the same girl who sent out our venue comms two weeks late that time, so I can't argue with that statement."

This was an incident that Yidarica still felt guilty about to this day, so she felt a tiny bit of hurt upon hearing this, but she told herself that Gracia still being in her life meant that she didn't view it too maliciously. "Oh, come on, that was one time!" Yidarica complained. "And what did you expect? In addition to all my other time and memory issues, I had just moved into a new position at work, so that was consuming all my brainpower. It was a valuable experience; now, you know to never entrust time-sensitive matters to me."

"It was valuable, all right," Gracia muttered. "Anyway, I need to get some sleep if I want to even think about being awake for my return trip. I'll text you when I make it home, okay?"

"And not a moment later," Yidarica insisted. "See you soon!"

With the phone call now over, and plenty of the day left, Yidarica decided that it would be nice to get out of bed at least once today. As she sat on the edge of her bed, the sun's rays cascaded upon her dark hair that faded into blonde and curled at the ends, as well as her bronze skin, highlighting it in brilliant tones of sparkling brown. She remained there for a minute or so, appreciating the sunlight, before she stood and walked to her closet. It had been raining for a few days now, and the sky was still visibly cloudy in a way that hinted more rain would be coming later. But for now? For now, she was grateful for the sunlight's fleeting warmth.

If she was leaving the house, clothes were necessary, but was leaving the house today worth the effort? After all, she'd be leaving the house again tomorrow for work.

Wasn't I supposed to be doing something today? I know I was supposed to be doing something today. What was it…

Being essentially dumped this morning had rearranged a lot of her mental space; last night, she had been filled with thoughts of the things she could text Hayden about today, but the tone of his most recent message had made it very clear that he had no intention of ever speaking to Yidarica again. And on some level, this was fine– preferred to the abrupt silence so many people seemed to love to give to others these days– but it also made her feel very small. Had it been such an unpleasant experience, going on these two dates with her, that he didn't even want to continue being friends? Was she that much of an insufferable person?

Insufferable. That had to be it, right? That was why she'd managed to get to this age without anyone ever having loved her.

Those thoughts would have to wait, though. There were more important things to do today than wallow.

The brain fog was heavy today as Yidarica walked over to her kitchen, determined now to try and remember what she was supposed to do today. Now that the sun was out, its light poured in through the small window over her sink, with the grape-adorned ivory curtains pulled to the sides. The kitchen was relatively small, so not much was in it aside from the sink and cabinets, and the tiny dining table and chair that Yidarica sometimes sat at to eat. The table was only big enough to fit one plate at a time, but considering that she was always the only person sitting there, there was never any need for more than that. The sink was mostly empty, apart from a few forks. She turned to the fridge and pantry, and after inspecting those, decided that they were of an appropriate stock level. Whatever needed to be done today, it wasn't located in the kitchen.

Her bedroom had been pretty normal when she had left it. Hadn't it? Sure, there had been some articles of clothing on the floor, but that was a normal Yidarica thing to do. It was so normal, in fact, that those few hours where she managed to get her room completely clean felt strange. There was something about her bedroom looking and feeling lived in, that made it as cozy a place as it was. She would defend her messy room with her life.

At this rate, she'd never remember what today's plan had been.

"Oh! Wait, I know what I was going to do today," she said to no one in particular, since she lived alone. "I wanted to get a new houseplant or two. To the nursery, then."

It was as good a reason as ever to get out of the house, and the nursery was right around the corner, so she headed back to her bedroom to get dressed. Yidarica's closet was overflowing with colorful, frilly dresses, skirts, and shirts; some with the most ornate designs she could ever imagine, some with simple prints, and some still with solid colors, most of them pastels. Whenever it was time for her to be seen by another person, she made certain that she was first dressed in attire that emulated the most elaborate of cakes. She was not always successful at this, especially if the day ahead would be full of manual labor, or if she hadn't gotten a lot of sleep or time to prepare what she was going to wear; but even her lower-maintenance attire was adorned with frills and bows.

This small one-bedroom apartment that she called home was far from special, but it was hers– the living room, decorated with vibrant furniture and art pieces, and the bathroom, which was uncharacteristically monochromatic, completed the layout. There was the smallest of back porches on this building, and sometimes, Yidarica would stand at the railing and watch the stars. But it was not large enough to place any seating or much of anything else there, so she didn't spend a lot of time in the area unless she wanted a little fresh air.

Yidarica lived on the third floor of a three-floor apartment building; down one flight, she passed the apartment of the quiet old lady she'd seen maybe twice, in the three years she'd been living here. Down another flight, she passed the married couple that had just recently brought home a baby. She saw them a lot, but never spoke to them unless they spoke first. From the interactions she'd had with them, she could tell that they were not exactly kind people, and the father in particular seemed to always be short with her. She was fine with keeping communications brief with them; it wasn't as if they had ever contributed anything meaningful to her stay here.

After leaving the front door, there were a few more stairs before heading out completely.

The walkways were still wet as Yidarica made her way to the nursery, which would take her about seven minutes to walk to. The puddles that remained on the pavement were small and shallow, reflecting the sky. When the wind blew, it would cause drops of water to fall from the leaves of the trees dotting the path. She walked at a leisurely pace, taking moments to look up at the sky and survey the clouds, and allowing herself to get lost in her thoughts.

They're so fluffy and white. It's been raining for so long now that it's nice to see the signs of us finally earning a reprieve. According to the most recent time I looked at the forecast, I think we were due for one more brief shower because of the impending cold front blowing into the city, but that shouldn't have us in the same situation as we've been in the past few days. Even so, it's probably in my best interest to make this a quick trip.

Ever since she was a young girl, Yidarica had taken an interest in the weather, which caused her to be observant of the skies and the forecast like this. It was something that she could only rarely put to practical use, but this didn't lessen her enthusiasm. Learning that a rare weather event was happening soon, or watching the sun's position, or even measuring how much rain had fallen even now filled her with a sense of joy. It was not uncommon for her to go off on weather-related tangents that lasted longer than a radio show, whenever something only slightly related had reminded her of some random weather occurrence that happened to be floating around in her mind. She had, of late, become increasingly conscious that this was not something other people did; and so, she had been working on keeping her anecdotes to herself, but it wasn't at all easy to. Sometimes she would slip up, but so far, she had been fortunate enough to not have anyone deride her for it– at least, not yet.

The nursery was in a building that was the same size as the houses on that block, and from the outside, it was difficult to tell that it wasn't just a house, to the unfamiliar. However, the porch was often adorned with assorted plants, giving it a greenhouse aesthetic. There was no limit to the types of plants one could find here; the selection rotated depending on availability, so one could never predict what exactly would be there at any given time. This (and the proximity to her building) was the main reason Yidarica liked shopping here; she never knew what she would find, adding a sort of thrill to the occasion. It helped that the place was run by a friendly old man who had seemingly endless knowledge about plants and how to care for him; combined with Yidarica's love for the weather, sometimes they'd talk in excess of an hour.

Stopping just outside of the doors to peruse the offerings that had been placed on the porch, Yidarica pondered the current situation, weather-wise. *We're still in the rainy season, but referencing the past few years' trend of when it ends, we don't have many weeks of it left. I wonder if there's any plants here that initially require a lot of water and then don't... then again, does it really matter what the outside climate is going to be like, if there's an almost definite chance of this plant spending its entire lifespan inside my apartment?*

The doors to the nursery opened then, and one of the employees walked onto the porch, carrying a potted plant and a mist bottle made of pink-tinted glass. Yidarica instantly recognized her as the daughter of the man who owned this place, who had only begun working here a few months prior; the two had never spoken, but Yidarica had been speaking to the owner one day when he'd mentioned his daughter had just moved into town and was helping out until she was able to find a job in her field here. Most of the reason they had never spoken was on Yidarica's part, because she was too shy to approach her. She was too shy to approach most people, but she felt it impossible to come up with words around this specific person. There was something about her presence… or maybe it was her dark hair that seemed to always be impeccably curled, or her surprisingly dainty hands, or perhaps even her chocolate-brown eyes, which caught the light in a perfect way when she smiled. It could be any of those, really.

"You're here often, aren't you?" When Yidarica heard her voice, as velvety smooth as soft-serve ice cream, she could only hope she hadn't been staring.

"Yeah, I, uh…" Yidarica shrugged. "I come here a lot for plants, and yet, I don't seem to be learning how to keep them alive too well, so I have to keep coming back. That is way more embarrassing when I say it out loud. Please don't judge me."

She smiled, and her eyes sparkled as they always did; so captivating. "I won't. My father and I speak to a lot of our customers, all at various skill levels, so don't feel guilty for not having a green thumb; you'd be far from the only one we know who doesn't. It has to be learned often; it's a skill that only very rarely happens innately."

Yidarica nodded. "Yeah."

"That being said, there are plants that are better suited to beginners. And I'm pretty sure that my father has probably already had that talk with you, so if those are still dying, it just means we have to go even easier. Do you have time for a little discussion, uh…"

"Yidarica. And yes. Of course I do." *I can always make time for such a pretty girl.*

"Zaya. Pleased to meet you, Yidarica; that's a pretty name."

At this, Yidarica paused. Was it? She had been named as such, as a combination of the names of her paternal grandmother, Yira, who had passed before she was born; and Dalicia, the city where she had been born. She wasn't quite sure what made her parents rearrange the letters enough to get to her name, and she had never asked. Mother forbid the woman who gave birth to her ever have to "explain herself," but Yidarica decided quickly she wouldn't let that woman occupy any space in her head today. That space was better occupied by the plants that would hopefully live longer than a month this time… or Zaya herself.

"So if I may ask, do you know what's been happening to your plants that causes them to die?" Zaya asked. "Are they too dry, or maybe too wet? Are they getting enough sunlight?"

"I think they get as much sunlight as they can in my apartment," Yidarica replied. "I make sure they're by the windows, or on my back porch, and if they are outside, I bring them in if we're having any inclement weather, like the way this past week has been, or the big flood we had a couple of years ago that was actually not caused solely by rainfall; there was a… that's not the point, sorry. In conclusion, I have no idea what's killing them off."

Zaya nodded. "Do you ever tend to them with any flora spells? Maybe watering them, or creating light when we've had a slew of gloomy rainy days like this one?"

"Oh, I've never been very good at those," Yidarica confessed. "Something about the specific way you need to call the energy forth doesn't compute in my brain, so I've been trying to raise my plants without using magic. That's possible, isn't it?"

"Of course. Why don't we start you off with the easiest plant I know?" Zaya picked up a pot with a plant in it that had very long, slender dark green leaves, with a few curly vines as well. Because of its small features, it was easy to tell that this was a baby plant, and would grow larger over time. As the wind blew softly onto the porch, Zaya gently traced the edges of one of the leaves with her fingers. "Now, care for this plant is a standard 'water every three days or so,' but as soon as you see it begin to grow a bulb, you need to put it in a bigger pot so it won't become pot bound, and its roots can expand and continue to grow. But until then, all it will need is water and light. If I remember correctly, the forecast says it should be clearing up for a few days soon, so maybe you can leave it outside for a while?"

Yidarica studied the plant. It didn't look very exciting, but if it was a baby plant, she had to remind herself that baby humans were also not very exciting before they grew into their personalities. "I'll give it a shot," she replied, accepting the plant. "Might as well. How much do I owe you?"

Upon being asked this, Zaya smirked just a little, before surveying Yidarica's entire body with a quick look. "How about, instead of paying us for it, you send me updates on how it's going? If you're okay with sharing your number, of course, and maybe stopping by a few times so I can see her progress."

"Sure. Where's your phone? I can put my number in." As Yidarica was busy doing that, she completely missed Zaya's smile as she observed her doing so.

"And there you go." Yidarica handed the phone back to her. "Thank you for all your help, Zaya. I'll come back and visit in a few weeks or so, so we can talk about if I'm able to keep this little one alive. See ya!"

As Yidarica walked home, past the familiar houses, she felt a stray raindrop touch her arm. She'd have to pick up the pace if she wanted to stay dry, and so, she began to walk faster. Past the general store, past the mailbox, and up to her front door with– thankfully– only two other stray raindrops touching her.

By the time she got up the stairs to her apartment and took off her jacket and shoes, it was officially pouring rain outside. Just in time, indeed.

"We made it," she said to her newly procured plant, placing it on her coffee table for the time being, while she had a mind to go and get something to eat. "It's raining so hard, this kind of precipitation could drown a poor little baby plant like you I'm sure. After all, there was that storm seventeen years ago that… never mind, that's not the point. I should let Zaya know that we made it before you got drowned."

Midway through typing the message Yidarica was smacked with a realization. *Wait a minute. Was she flirting with me that whole time? Is that why the plant was free– and why the stipulation is to come back and talk to her again?*

Am I somehow the most oblivious person on the planet?

For many years now, Yidarica had believed that she was, in fact, the most oblivious person on the planet; which led her to begin studying other people, in an attempt to perhaps understand what it was she lacked when it came to human interaction. While she still, to this day, didn't really understand the answer to that, her studies had led her to curate what she believed was a rather trustworthy compendium of human social conventions. Whenever she was faced with an unfamiliar interaction, or one she didn't quite understand, mentally referencing her studies of human interaction had a pretty good track record for keeping her afloat in the situations she found herself in. "Pretty good track record" was probably overly generous; it had worked at least half of the times it had been referenced, though, and that was good enough for Yidarica.

She'd be using this when it came to trying to figure out what Zaya's intentions may have been earlier today. She had been very kind, and smiled more than twice, so maybe it had been flirting—but strong indicators like this always got muddy if the person in question was working in customer service. It would be difficult, if not impossible, to discern whether the kindness given was flirtation or a woman doing her job really well.

Wait. I need to send the message.

Looking back down at her phone, Yidarica noticed that she'd somehow typed an entire paragraph about the weather conditions that had caused her to worry about the plant. This, too, was typical of her. She often worried that her propensity for talking about the weather at length was part of what was getting in her way of her social life. It was a well-established fact that there was a general dislike of "small talk" in her age group, and weather was often cited as a "small talk" topic. At the same time, though, she felt it a shame that so many people didn't realize how interesting weather could be, if looked at on a deeper level. Their loss, truly.

"The plant is saved, and my message is sent," Yidarica said to herself as she placed her phone on the coffee table in her living room, beside her new plant. "I've got the rest of the day left to do things… but what things do I do?"

She sat on the couch, with its vibrant orange, purple, and pink floral pattern, noticing that there was a stack of books on the side table. She picked them all up, deciding that reading would be a welcome diversion until it was time for her to go to bed for work tomorrow.

Chapter Two

It had been raining, more or less, for a week straight– but when Yidarica woke up for work the next day, the sun was shining in all its glory. She chose to believe this was a good thing.

She got dressed, deciding the brightest colors were appropriate for the miraculous return of the sun, and pulled on a long-sleeved, knee-length chiffon dress with a Peter Pan ruffled collar, in pastel rainbow hues. It wasn't common for people in her line of work to consistently wear such bright colors, or clothing that was so ornate, so it did often earn Yidarica plenty of attention. She wasn't sure if all the attention was positive or sincere, but this was one of the few things she could make herself not get too caught up on before it sent her into a spiral of despair. Even amidst her social anxiety, nothing could take away the joy she felt when being dressed in the most frilly and feminine clothing she could find.

After pinning some of her hair back with some golden, flower-shaped hair pins, she was right on schedule for leaving her apartment.

Transportation in Basodin was mostly facilitated by walking in its larger cities, but larger cities meant large distances to cover, at times. Sonusia, the city that Yidarica lived in, was no exception to this, and to walk to work would require an excess of time allotted. Some seventy or so years ago, the government recognized this was an issue, and created a solution: the communal transportation system. Called the Comtran for short, and operated via cable trolleys on land and ferries over the water, all one needed to do was register for the service, and look up the schedules for when the nearest station was being served. A rather convenient institution.

Historically, one could also travel via the piloting of large transportation leaves, which floated upon the air as whimsically as their smaller counterparts. The aptitude tests to obtain a license to own one of these were notoriously difficult and laborious, though, so many people never bothered with them, and as a result the skies were never congested with people traveling, which was nice. Learning to use them required a level of balance, sturdiness, and generally low levels of anxiety that Yidarica could never reach, so she had accepted a long time ago that this would not be something she would ever utilize.

As the Comtran traveled on to its next stop, Yidarica gazed at the scenery around her. She'd moved into this apartment about three years ago now, but even so, the commute had yet to lose its magic; she loved to watch the scenery, especially on days like today where minor detours were needed (this time, it had to be because of the past week's weather; there was a nearby hill that always made the surrounding avenues a muddy, non-traversable mess if it rained enough). Today, they were passing by one of the small parks near Yidarica's building, one she often passed by to get groceries or to visit any of her friends. Since it was so early in the morning, it wasn't very busy, but she could still see a couple of people jogging along the pathways.

It's a good day to jog. All that rain brought refreshingly cool breezes to the area. Plus, the clouds aren't going to completely clear up until late afternoon, so they'll give a brief relief from the sun. If I was more of a jogger, I'd have chosen this morning to do it.

Gracia would be coming by to visit around lunchtime, so the two would still have plenty of time to enjoy the day after Yidarica gave her the tour. They could venture around the park, but with as much as they needed to catch up on, they'd probably settle in somewhere more stationary.

Approaching the city center, Yidarica reminded herself that even if she lived in constant fear of the Dark, she had been very fortunate to have gotten a position at a very prestigious company without completing all of the schooling that was usually required to do so. Her position itself wasn't glamorous, but she was grateful that she didn't have to spend her days miserable in the name of earning a living, which seemed to be the fate that befell many of her fellow non-graduates. She often felt like she didn't belong at her job, but knowing how much worse it could be, she'd rather feel like she didn't belong than worry about a high stress, low pay job that drained her of her will to live at all.

Thanking the conductor of the Comtran, as always, Yidarica waved before heading into the huge skyscraper that housed her place of employment.

In this day and age, it was almost impossible to meet someone who had never heard of Mega Flare Industries, and for good reason. There were a lot of intricacies that came with life in Basodin, and this was one of many companies that aimed to make these intricacies more navigable. Whether it be weather prediction, travel, food sources, or anything in between, Mega Flare Industries was there trying to figure out the most efficient way to make life easier for the average citizen via technological advances. Or so they said, anyway. Often, Yidarica wondered if the company's meddling made things more complicated than they had to be in some ways, but she never thought about that for long. After all, if they didn't meddle, she'd be out of a job.

Arriving at the area of the office that she worked out of, Yidarica immediately noticed that no one else was seated at any of the desks nearby, which never felt good to discover– not that it was impossible to work on her own, but it did get a little lonely if she did. It was unfortunate. Maybe it was a good thing that she wouldn't be staying the whole day.

Logging into the tablet with which she did all her work, and taking a bite from her apple cinnamon muffin, she immediately noticed a new meeting on her calendar that hadn't been there before.

> **Yidarica/Shiori 1:1**
> *Discussion of a new project with the company's weather department. This project is to be executed by the Project Garden c/o Yidarica Verbestel*

Shiori was Yidarica's manager, which was something she often had to actively remind herself of because Shiori was both smaller and younger than most of the people who worked in the Project Garden. Despite her age, she was a no-nonsense woman who even still was able to deliver news and updates in a way that made her fairly approachable. So, meetings with her were not uncommon, but what was uncommon was the last part of the meeting description. Yidarica had never been the person heading a project. As far as she knew, none of their projects ever had been headed by anyone; the work was divided evenly among the team, and then presented to their manager, to give to whatever person in higher management had requested the project.

Despite her confusion, though, there was a part of her that was excited. Yidarica had always been curious about the Weather Department's work, but it had rarely– if ever– overlapped with her own. This could finally be her chance to learn more about them and what they did!

The meeting was in an hour and 15 minutes; she'd need to keep herself together until then.

***

The one positive to teammates not being in that day was the necessity of using the meeting rooms. From the outside, they appeared to be pitch-black rooms with no windows or furniture. And that was what they were on the inside as well, until someone began the meeting via their work tablet; then, the room would come to life with vivid magical projections of everyone present in the meeting as well as any of the materials and/or presentations being referenced. It was something that continued to amaze Yidarica no matter how many times she attended meetings (which was a lot)– and so, she was eager to begin on this day.

After typing in the code for the meeting, it wasn't long before the room lit up with the backdrop of an area much like the park that Yidarica had passed on her way to work. Almost immediately after, a cloud of firefly-like creatures congregated beside her before materializing into a glowing, perfect duplication of one Shiori Montalban. Her deep black, shoulder-length hair as straight as always, she was dressed in a sensible gray blouse and black pencil skirt, with black stockings and a pair of white heels; even so, she still didn't quite reach Yidarica's height. Yidarica had often thought that one of the reasons Shiori took no shit from anyone, was because she was so small. One had to be that way, especially as a woman, if they didn't want to be infantilized.

"Good morning, Yidarica," Shiori– or, rather, her projection– spoke. "Hope you got to the office okay."

"Yeah. Pleasant Comtran ride. Today's weather forecast was accurate, so no surprises there. Nothing's on fire," she replied with a shrug. "I can't ask for more, except for the rest of the team to be here maybe."

Shiori nodded. The Project Garden currently had four employees in its rank, but one of them was currently on leave, so really, it was more like three. "That's understandable. It's easier to collaborate with someone when they're in front of you in real time, right? I'm going to have to have a talk with Muiren and Hadiza about better coordinating our days in office. But don't forget that they're still online, and you all can still schedule meetings like this one; something that you'll probably have more of an inclination to do with this new project we've been given. Let's get into it. Walk with me?"

The two began to walk then, the fabricated park greeting them with the patter of their footsteps and wind caressing the boughs of the trees. "So, as you may have realized, this is the first time the Weather Department has reached out to us with assistance on a project. There's a part of their operations that overlaps with the Sustenance Department, and an aspect of that area has fallen between the cracks... you know, like how most of our projects come to be."

Shiori stopped in front of one of the trees, which appeared to have a nice selection of oranges within its branches.

"When we have days like the entirety of last week, where it rained nonstop, there are areas of the city that are less safe to travel to, due to infrastructure or environmental hazards; and, thus, less safe to get food from. This project was drafted and given to us in record time, after a few reports of bodily injury while our couriers were en route to their pickup destination."

The tree in front of Shiori was enveloped by rain clouds, pouring nonstop. Then, a shadowy figure of a person walked under it with the intent to harvest the oranges from it. Before they could begin, they slipped and fell.

"I'm sure Legal is going through hell with that, but we'll let them deal with that aspect on their own. The part of this situation that concerns us is helping to ensure that this doesn't become a regular thing. You know, so Legal doesn't have to *keep* going through hell."

Yidarica had been of the mind that Legal was always in hell regardless, but that was beside the point.

"If you took a good look at the details of this meeting," Shiori continued, "you'll have noticed that I named you as the POC for this project. That isn't usually how we take on work here, but there are a few reasons I'm doing this. The main reason is because we still have other minor projects going on, so we can't wholly dedicate the Project Garden to this, as much as we'd like to. After taking some time to evaluate the strengths of the team, I chose you to take on this responsibility because, in addition to how analytical you are, I know you have an interest in the weather." Shiori smiled here. "I've also noticed how eloquent you are in your emails and messaging, which will be something you'll need for this task. You and Muiren will be the two doing the heavy lifting here; Hadiza can lean in when you need something tested or looked over for a third opinion or fresh set of eyes, but she'll mostly be maintaining our other projects until the two of you are free again."

"Okay." Yidarica nodded.

"Now, let's get to what you'll actually be doing."

Two display screens materialized then. One displayed the interface for MFI's weather service, and the other, the interface for the market service.

"As they are now, the integration between these two services is minimal to nonexistent. What we want to do is have them work together in a way that forewarns people about the possibility of injuries from treacherous food gathering, if not eliminate them completely. The benefit here is that we already have the two services; we just need to find a way to connect them in a way that best serves our needs."

After a pensive silence, Yidarica asked, "But… *why* do we need to do that? If it's been raining for five days straight, wouldn't it be common sense that travel is gonna be harder and more hazardous?"

The two women stared at each other before Yidarica sighed. "Never mind." She knew as well as anyone else that the concept of "common sense" was a misnomer.

"Well, for the rest of the day, continue to work on our other projects while I work on getting everyone the permissions they need to start working on this. I'm meeting with the rest of the Project Garden later today to explain how our duties will be shifting. We'll have another quick sync in the morning tomorrow, and then I'll be able to send you all the resources you'll need."

"Thanks, Shiori." Yidarica smiled.

"If you have any questions, I'll be online all day." With a wave, Shiori's projection disappeared, and with her, followed all of the fancy projections. It wasn't long before the room was back to its regular, dark state. No longer were there lights or sounds; it was a foreboding, desolate place; almost a little scary.

A pitch-black room. Lovely. Beautiful. The type of environment everyone covets, I'm sure.

The echoes of Yidarica's footsteps as she walked to the door bounced off of the walls that she couldn't see, no matter how hard she squinted, and tried to make them out. When she slowed her pace, wondering if smaller steps would make the area less scary, she was met with the tiniest scrunches of the leather of her shoes. She looked down, recognizing where the sound was coming from, but found that in such profound darkness, she wasn't able to see the things close to her, either, like her hands and feet.

This is what life in all aspects will be like if I don't find someone who loves me soon, won't it?

But Yidarica picked up the pace, hurrying out of the room and back to her desk, before those thoughts could overtake her.

★★★

No one could have possibly stopped Yidarica and Gracia from hugging each other once the latter made it to the office.

At first, for a split second, Yidarica almost didn't recognize her friend, and it was mostly because of her hair. Gracia, who had always had hip-length dark, straight hair, now stood in this office with ash blonde hair that reached the middle of her back, styled into loose curls, and also had bangs. She'd never even mentioned wanting bangs! In addition, the plain gray cardigan and simple, short-sleeved sundress in a dusty blue felt unusual; she usually dressed in a similar manner to Yidarica, but today, she looked more like the average salarywoman.

"I cannot believe this place, Yida!" Gracia said once they had let go of each other. "I mean, you always said it was extravagant, but this is not what I was expecting at all. I'm amazed!"

Yidarica shrugged bashfully. "Yeah, it really is something. So, are you all checked in? Can we start the tour?"

Gracia pointed to the visitor's badge stuck to her cardigan, which read: *Gracia Fidelia Budiawan, Business Partner*. "VIP and all-access, I'm hoping."

"Nothing but the best for you, of course," Yidarica smiled as she began to walk past the front desk, ready to show her best friend where she spent most of her time away from home. "Since it's close by, we can go to my favorite place first."

That favorite place was the office's library, which Yidarica had spent copious time in, mostly during her breaks and on the days where the thought of lunch didn't readily entice her. It was a simple space, with four rectangular desks arranged in the center of the room, and bookshelves adorning the walls. Usually, when she came here, she would immediately make for the weather books; the weather section wasn't very big, though, and she was certain that she'd already read through every book on that shelf at least twice.

"This is the library. There's a lot of information here about the specific lines of business we work in, but there's also some leisurely reads too. With these resources, I supplement my ability to never shut up about the weather with reading about the weather." Yidarica held an arm out to show off the many shelves full of books in the room. "But sometimes, I like doing my work in here, too.

The silence makes it easier to concentrate on our projects that are a little more mathematical."

Gracia nodded. "It sounds like you come here a lot."

"Pretty regularly. My favorite book is this one over here, which details the start of the Weather Department and its operations." Yidarica didn't know if it was truly her favorite, but it was definitely the one she had read the most. She'd committed a lot of time to not only memorizing the timeline to the establishment of the Weather Department, but the branches of the department and the people that had been responsible for its inception, researching if they still worked here and what positions they held. After all, whenever a position opened over there that she was interested in, that knowledge would undoubtedly score her brownie points, wouldn't it?

"Speaking of my favorite places, we're near another of those."

The two women left the library and made an immediate right to access a tall stairwell. There was a set of glass doors at the top of it, and the sun shone through them, lighting the hallway in an almost poetic way. Ascending the stairs here was always bothersome, but reaching those doors was always worth it, because on the other side of them was the office's garden, filled with so much life and fresh air that one could almost forget about the corporate world as long as they were here. There was one main walkway which was lined with benches and small side tables, and at the opposite end, there was a dry bar; although there never seemed to be anyone working at it.

"Oh, this is beautiful!" Gracia whispered, clearly amazed with all the greenery. "Does anyone maintain this?"

Yidarica had actually never asked this question. "I'm not sure. But I do know that there have been a few times where I've gotten to work really early, and some of the building staff were here. One time I noticed a few of them casting a regeneration spell, but I don't know if that was out of obligation or kindness." She shrugged. "I would imagine somebody has to, and they do a great job of it, whoever they are. Wanna continue on?"

Heading back into the building, they were now walking through the less exciting parts of the office: the workstations. "I work in the Project Garden, which is a team dedicated to maintenance and experimental procedures related to the Sustenance Department. Each department has a project team, and then they're all given cute little names like that. Like, the Weather Department has the Project Biome, and the Entertainment Department has the Project Theater, and so on. I like to think that these areas here are where the magic happens.

"Unfortunately, I was explicitly told that I can't show you the meeting rooms, which is sad because they're really cool. We utilize the latest in magical projection to make presentations that are brought to life in them. It's hard to explain it to a person without them seeing it, but hopefully you at least get the general idea."

"Yeah." Gracia nodded. "I'm jealous. At my office, we're still doing meetings the traditional way, with projection screens and sitting at a table."

"Oh, we have those too. Sometimes the subject matter doesn't need a lot of fanfare, and that kind of thing is the better option. It's nice to have multiple options. Something else I really like about this office is that all of our meeting rooms, regardless of which type they are, were given names based on pastries! Isn't that adorable?"

Gracia smiled. "Really? That's so cute!"

"Yeah!" Yidarica looked around, attempting to locate the nearest meeting room. "Oh, there's a room right over there. Let's go see which one that is."

Approaching the door to the room, there was a plaque beside the door with a sign that had a room number and its name on it. "305, Trifle," Yidarica read. "My desk is right by Profiterole. Why don't we head over there so I can clock out for the day and we can go get lunch? It's about that time."

At this, Gracia's eyes lit up. Mentions of food were always the key to boosting her already usually high mood even higher. "Absolutely! Let's go!"

On the way to the appropriate cluster of cubicles, the two passed someone that Yidarica knew she'd seen before: a man assumedly around her age, but much taller than her, with dark hair and usually dressed in some combination of blue, red, khaki, and/or black. Today, since there was still some residual chilliness from all of the rain, he was wearing a fluffy blue sweater and dark gray pants. The first time she had ever noticed him, it was because he wore glasses; many people here did, but that wasn't surprising. This office had a fair amount of older people, and listening to them talk, it felt normal for them to be trapped in loveless marriages, so it made sense that the Dark had started to come for them at some point. On the other hand, this man was someone not much older than Yidarica herself; possibly the same age or younger even, but it was difficult to tell because he would periodically let his facial hair grow in, which aged him enough that she was fairly certain he was older. It had broken her heart to see someone around her age needing glasses, and it almost made her want to talk to him about it. At the same time, though, she knew that if things had happened as expected– if she had been as afflicted by the Dark as she expected– she probably wouldn't want random people coming up to her and asking about it. So, she always left this man alone, but the intrigue never left her mind. She wondered, what kind of stories could he tell? How similar were they to her own?

"Yida? You okay?" Gracia was gently poking her in her side, worried that her friend may have forgotten where they were.

She looked up again, but the man was nowhere to be found.

"What? Oh, I'm sorry, Gracia. I was caught up in thinking about something, but it's not important. Right over here."

Chapter Three

After leaving the Mega Flare Industries building and walking to a nearby restaurant for lunch, Yidarica and Gracia began catching each other up on the past couple of months. Even though they'd kept in touch the entire time Gracia had been away, things were different now that they were actually seeing each other. There were some stories that simply could be told in no other way than in person!

"Please tell me you have close-up pictures of your cousin's wedding dress," Yidarica said after the waiter had taken their orders and left the table. "It looked so stunning from far away, I just know it was even more breathtaking up close!"

"Oh, it was," Gracia agreed, nodding eagerly and picking her phone up. "I know I took a lot of pictures though, so this might take a while. In the meantime, what did I miss while I was gone? What crazy antics did you get yourself into, besides giving the time of day to some guy who didn't appreciate it?"

"Yeah, funny story about that," Yidarica said, nervously kneading her hands under the table. "That, uh… that wasn't the only time recently that I had a prospective partner decide they weren't vibing with me."

Gracia slightly tilted her head. "Did you keep those to yourself, or am I that bad at remembering things?"

"I didn't tell anybody." Yidarica found it impossible to make eye contact at this point, deciding it was more comfortable to stare at a stray piece of plastic on the table, left from when she had opened her straw. "It's embarrassing, so it was hard to admit. Basically, I chatted up this guy at one of the bars near work and, as usual, I thought things were going well. I slid him my number before I was about to leave and do you know this man gave it right back? How do you ever recover from that? Looking back, I don't know how I did, but somehow, miraculously, I did."

"Well, that's good." Gracia smiled.

"But was it really?" Yidarica asked. "A few weeks later, I met a girl named Marguerite– beautiful name for a beautiful girl, as the sentiment often goes– and we hung out a lot. Pretty frequently, but... things didn't work out there either. We were, uh, looking for different things I guess."

Yidarica neglected to mention that the "different things" that she and Marguerite didn't agree on was the level of intimacy required for the relationship to progress. When Marguerite had made it expressly clear that she wouldn't be able to decide if this relationship was worthwhile until after the two had slept together, Yidarica found herself instantly feeling not only disgust, but also fear. It wasn't a situation she had felt comfortable being put in, and that had been enough for her to realize the situation wouldn't go anywhere she wanted it to.

But I can't tell Gracia about that. I can't tell anyone about that. I can only imagine the reactions I'd get when I tell people I still haven't met anyone that I'm comfortable thinking about sex with. People made fun of me for it when I was only twenty-one years old. I don't want to think about what they'd say ten years later.

"At any rate, that led to me meeting Hayden, which I thought was a good thing," Yidarica finished. "Just another swing and a miss, it turns out."

It was easy to tell, based on the look on Gracia's face, that she sympathized. "So much in such a short time. I wish there was something I could say or do to make this easier, Yida. I really do."

"Eh." She shrugged. "It can't be helped. Our ancestors had thoughts about spilled milk and crying over it."

"Yeah," Gracia agreed as the waiter came back around, placing two plates of pasta dishes on the table. Yidarica had opted for a relatively simple dish with spinach and bacon in a creamy sauce; the large piece of blackened salmon with diced tomatoes, onions, and peppers on Gracia's plate made hers look boring in comparison. This wasn't something that made Yidarica feel ashamed, though. Especially after work, even if her time there today had been short, a simple meal felt like the perfect end to the day. "By the way… what were you, of all people, doing in a bar? It's unfathomable that some guy would ever turn down somebody as cute as you, but it's even more unbelievable that you'd ever show your face in that kind of environment."

"It was more of a lounge than a bar, but I did sit at the bar," Yidarica explained as she tried to remember why she had ended up there. Gracia was right– it was very unlike her, and she remembered that it hadn't been her idea, but that was all she could recall at the moment. "Why can't I remember why I was there? I think somebody recommended something on the menu to me, but I can't remember who it was. I do remember what they recommended, though: their garlic parmesan fries, which were amazing. There were little bits of chicken in them, very tasty."

Gracia gasped. "Please take me there sometime. I *need* to experience this." She then placed her phone on the table and pushed it toward Yidarica. "I organized all my photos into folders while I was on my return trip home, so you can swipe through; that's my dress folder."

As Yidarica admired the design of the wedding dress Gracia's cousin had worn to the ceremony, in all its embroidered and beaded cream, red, pink, and green glory, she also took a moment to once again admire how organized Gracia always was. This was, she was sure, the reason she had been able to get her job at a quite accomplished design firm, one which had worked with a few prestigious clients in the past. Yidarica always hoped that, someday, if she was lucky, that skill with organization would rub off on her. The problem was that she was very aware that she was not a lucky person.

"The applique is so ornate, right?" Gracia asked. "It's what caught my eye most often during the ceremony. It's hard to tell with still photos, but there were small beads woven into the embroidery that caught the light at the right angles so that it looked like glitter. It was so cool! I wonder if I could afford something like that for the next time we're able to book a show. What do you think? Nice? A bit much? Although I guess we'd probably need to get everybody else's opinion there too."

The "everybody else" Gracia was referring to was the band that she and Yidarica were in; they were a group of vastly varying tastes, so there was a certain level of democracy required in order for them to make any decisions, which meant they ended up voting on almost everything dealing with the band, including what they would wear on stage. This could possibly be why they had very rarely played any shows, but there were other factors going into that as well, so the democratic system appeared to work.

"Oh, right, I should tell everybody I'm back," Gracia said then, reaching for her phone. "I'll give it back after I do this. I need to dive into everyone's calendars and see when the next time we can meet is. Yida, there's nothing too crazy happening with you at your fancy job, is there?"

"I *did* just get a new project today, so... I hope not," she replied.

Gracia glanced at her for a moment before returning to texting. "Sure. Let me know how that goes, then, and I'll check with everybody else too."

Of the band, if not Gracia, the person Yidarica looked forward to seeing the most was the person she'd known the longest: their drummer, Cérilda. Yidarica had been friends with Cérilda's older sister way back when they were teenagers, and even though that friendship had faded because of distance (physical distance, she'd moved far away to a different country for work) she and Cérilda had kept in touch, and gradually became friends of their own accord.

Yidarica didn't know the other two members as well as she knew the girls. Walchelin, their rhythm guitarist, was a longtime friend of Gracia's, but she always seemed to forget how exactly they knew each other. Still, Yidarica liked him. He frequently brought baked goods to meetings that were very clearly going to run long, and always made sure everyone was accommodated well. The final member of the band, Landen, had been found via the ad the group had posted looking for another guitarist, and was notoriously difficult to read. Neither Yidarica nor Gracia would call him mean or unpleasant, but both would agree that there was always this feeling in the air, whenever he was around, that felt as though he didn't want to be there. This never transferred to his playing though– the man was a damn good guitarist– so nobody ever complained. Not out loud or in the band's group chat, anyway.

"There. That's taken care of." Gracia put her phone back on the table, feeling accomplished. "So, what are the plans once we leave here? Wanna walk around, go shopping? Maybe scout out the area for another very cute potential suitor?"

"I'm cool on that, I think." Yidarica shook her head. "I think what's really gonna be best for me is if I take a step back and try to evaluate what's happening that makes people so sure I'm not a suitable partner. I mean, these were all three very different people. I'm the only common denominator, so it has to be something about me." She shrugged. "I'm gonna head home. I'm getting tired."

Gracia signaled to the waiter behind Yidarica that they were ready for the check, before she stood. "Come on, I'll take you."

"Are you sure?" Yidarica asked, not one to impose.

"Yeah. If you're tired, better for me to be able to personally see that you make it home okay. I don't want you passing out on your way up the stairs, all right?"

Yidarica couldn't pinpoint exactly when this had happened, but it had to be no more recent than a decade ago when she noticed a decline in her stamina; where she could formerly walk more than a mile with no difficulty, she found herself getting winded sooner and sooner; standing began to be more difficult; naps became more frequent. She'd spoken to so many people about these issues– doctors, magic masters, therapists, healers– but none were able to give her conclusive answers as to why she was experiencing this; until recently, when the new doctor she was seeing finally explained to her what was happening. Her bloodstream was lacking essential nutrients, and after a litany of tests, it had been determined that her body was unable to absorb them. This was a complicated issue, because it could be caused by such a large number of things that she'd probably be in her late forties before the cause was able to be pinpointed.

She'd let her predisposition to defeatism convince her there was no point in going down that road, considering the Dark would probably be coming for her any day now. Until then, she'd just have to deal with this weakening body of hers. She could still withstand her commute to work and the grocery store, so she wasn't down and out yet– even if these duties were often supplemented by nap time.

And honestly? Yidarica could live with this. She was perfectly fine with the fact that she'd never be an athlete. Since she lived alone, it wasn't like she'd upset anyone with her habits, so she could live with her space not always being tidy. She'd learned to have an emergency stockpile of ready-made food for the days where she was too tired to cook. But what she couldn't live with was the idea that her weak body was disappointing the people in her life. A good example of this was right before Gracia had gone on her trip; Yidarica had planned to go see a limited-time exhibit with her, but ultimately had to cancel when she didn't have the strength to leave her bed. She sometimes had to use sick days at work when commuting would be too much. And she'd had to cancel on band practices at least twice. How many more times was she going to be able to let people down before they cut her out of their lives? She always felt the threat looming over her.

"Let's get a move on, then," Gracia said as she put her wallet into her purse. "I haven't finished unpacking, and my place is a mess right now because of it, so I'd like to get it in some type of order before our next band meeting."

After being gone for two months, Yidarica could only imagine how much needed to be done. "Of course. Lead the way."

***

It had been a long time since Yidarica had been a passenger on one of Basodin's commuting leaves, because she didn't know many people who owned one; Gracia was one of the few, and even then, she didn't particularly like using it, only bringing it out when she had a lot of stuff to bring with her, or was pressed for time. Since it was a calm day, the breeze was gentle as it brushed upon Yidarica's face, flowing through her hair. It was always nice to be able to travel like this, once in a while.

There's something about the first clear day after extreme weather that feels so serene, so perfect. I'm glad that I'm getting to enjoy some of the sun on a day like this, especially with us technically still being in the rainy season. I should check the forecast again when I get home to see how many days we have before it starts pouring again.

"So what's going on with the new project?" Gracia asked. "As much as you're able to share, I mean. As far as I recall, it's been a while since you've gotten a big one, right?"

It had, hadn't it? For a while now, the norm had been lower impact, longer projects, which was yet another part of why Yidarica was looking forward to this one. Things had almost begun to get boring. "Yeah, it's been a minute," she agreed. "How do I tell you without making it sound like a boring corporate meeting, though? Basically, we're trying to absolve ourselves of legal responsibility should someone eat shit during inclement weather."

"Oh! Fun." Gracia's tone made this feel like a sarcastic statement, but Yidarica was not the best at picking those out. "Legal stuff is always at least a little stressful, though. Please remember to take care of yourself, bestie."

A reminder that Yidarica definitely needed. "Yeah."

"If it starts to feel like too much, just call me, and we can make plans. You know I am always down for a spa day." Gracia glanced back at her, smiling. "Work is important, but you yourself are the most important."

"Yeah, absolutely," Yidarica agreed. "It's been a while since we had a spa day. And I can think of a few fun restaurants that I don't think I've taken you to yet. A new dessert parlor opened near me since you've been gone, and I know you're probably interested in that. I haven't been inside, but I've been past it. The exterior is really cute."

"Cute dessert shop? It's like it has my name on it!" Gracia grinned. "I'd love to go! Okay, we're getting close to your place. Is it all right if I drop you off in front?"

"If my neighbors give you grief over it, I can look the other way when you fight them," Yidarica replied with a smirk.

Slowly losing altitude as they proceeded down the lane of houses that would eventually lead to Yidarica's building, her fatigue began to settle into her bones all over again. She was confident in her ability to get in without falling over, but nap time was sounding more and more enticing the closer she got to home.

This was always a fear that lived in the back of Yidarica's mind: while she'd been doing great at not falling down the stairs of her building yet, she never wanted to tempt fate, and so, she always tried to make sure she had enough energy before conquering them. She had never considered what to do if she was faced with the stairs while dealing with low energy. Hopefully, she could remember how that one pain mitigation spell went, just in case she did take a tumble.

"There we are. Safe and sound!" Gracia beamed. "I'll text you when I get home."

"Please do," Yidarica told her. "I had a great time today, Gracia. I'm so glad you're back!"

She smiled and waved, before starting on her journey home.

While on her way up the stairs, Yidarica felt her phone vibrate, but waited until she was in her apartment and kicked off her shoes. It was obviously too soon for it to have been Gracia, so she was curious as to who it could be. Once she was finally able to fish her phone out of her pocket, she took a look at her screen and smiled. She'd received a message from Zaya!

> **Hey, you at home right now?**

Technically, yes, but…

> **I just got in, but I'm absolutely wiped, so I'm going to take a nap. I'm sorry if this leads to the decline of potential plans.**

Truly, she was sorry. If there was a single thing she resented about chronic fatigue, it was the possibility of needing to cancel plans with cute people.

> **Nah, no prob. I was gonna ask if you were willing to swing by though. It's kind of slow in the nursery, and at the moment it's just me and my dad here. Which, you know I love the old man, but he's veering into some really uncomfortable topics and I can't just leave the room when no one else is here.**

There was something to be said about that generation and their inclination to making people uncomfortable– and refusing to stop when told as much. This was something Yidarica didn't really have the words to empathize with, even though she was familiar with that kind of predicament; before she could try to reference what other people usually said in this situation, Zaya sent a second text.

> **By the way, you've met my dad, but I don't know what your family dynamic is like.**

Chapter Four

Yidarica's family life was… complicated. When asked for a word to describe it, that was always the word she ended up settling on.

Her parents had had two other children before her, years ago. They were much older than she was, and didn't keep contact with her for reasons she was fuzzy on since most of those reasons happened when she was a toddler. She couldn't remember the last time either of her older siblings had spoken to her, and considering how her relationship with their parents was, she didn't see that changing for a long time, if ever. This was something she had accepted at a relatively young age.

She also had a younger sister, Runiala, who– similarly to their older siblings– was born more than a decade after Yidarica had been. Even so, they were as close as one would reasonably expect a thirty-one-year-old and a twenty-year-old to be; they didn't spend a ton of time together because of work and school taking up most of their time, but tried to get together once a month for a fun activity and to catch up.

Those meetings had been a lot more infrequent, lately. In fact, the two hadn't spoken in… almost a month, Yidarica noticed when she checked their string of text messages. She wasn't sure why. She didn't remember her sister doing anything that upset her, so she'd been going along under the assumption that it was Runiala who had either been upset by her, or she was having such a busy, fulfilling time away at school that she'd rather surround herself with people who weren't her loser of an older sister.

Yidarica didn't think of her parents often these days, and preferred to keep it that way, but they crept into her mind as soon as she thought to herself, "loser of an older sister."

Gracia had always chastised her whenever she referred to herself that way, but Yidarica could never form her thoughts into sentences effective enough to convey why she felt that way, which was strongly because of her parents.

If asked, Yidarica would probably say she had no thoughts when it came to her father. Despite having always been there, and still being at home as far as she knew, it had been very rare for her father to actually speak to her. As a child, the only time she could remember hearing his voice was if he was reprimanding her. As a teenager and adult, she heard him speak slightly more often, but by then she'd had no interest in having conversations with him. He had always been a quiet and stoic person to everyone, though, so at the very least, she knew his behavior wasn't targeted to her. This would never be something she could say about her mother, at any point in her life.

Her earliest memories were of school days, studying hard and reading well. It hadn't taken long for her teachers to notice, and within a couple of years, they gave the feedback that Yidarica was undoubtedly gifted and should be in a special program, levels ahead of her current age group. To most parents, this sort of feedback would be a source of pride. To Yidarica's mother, it was a direct attack.

She had dismissed all of the positive feedback. She had argued to keep Yidarica down in a grade that was so elementary to her that it became boring. She saw her child miserable for missing out on such an enticing opportunity and her only words were, "do you think you're better than us? You need to stay in a child's place."

This, Yidarica was unfortunately bound to learn, was just the beginning in a series of ways in which her mother would seemingly fight to keep her "in her place." If anyone were to ask, she loved Yidarica, as long as she never surpassed her in any way. She could never be too smart, too intuitive, too beautiful, because doing so was a sign of disrespect. How dare she try to be better than her mother? She should be grateful to her forever for giving her life! For a child like Yidarica, who was both stubborn enough to do what she liked and unaware enough of social cues to not understand why this could be a problem, it was difficult to get her to dull her shine. When her mother realized this, her antagonization went from passive to active. And so, the attacks started.

The one not beamingly positive feedback Yidarica ever got at school was that she wasn't social with her classmates, so her mother capitalized on that. She made a strict set of rules that basically shut off any possibilities for her daughter to socialize with anyone outside of school, and then berated her for having no social skills. Knowing that she read a lot of books, she criticized her for speaking robotically. The criticisms only increased as she got older. The unkind things that were said to her when she went through puberty and gained some weight, or when her body began to become more frail and her hair began to thin, were things that still kept her up at night.

The final straw, for Yidarica, was when she'd failed out of university (for no academic reason; this was around when her health had begun to decline) and found out that her mother had been taking all the credit for her being able to go in the first place. She found this out because of the phone call she received after her dismissal, screaming at her and asking how she was supposed to explain to people that she raised a lazy piece of shit for a daughter.

That was nine years ago now. They hadn't spoken since.

It wasn't the first time I was suicidal, but it was the closest I ever got to the edge.

That night had been the moment with the most clarity in Yidarica's life, to the point that it felt uncanny. She had gone to the beach, late at night when no one else was around, and stood at the edge of the boardwalk, gazing out at the ocean.

My parents never taught me to swim, but my mother always said I should've taught myself if I was so smart.

The moon had made a perfect crescent shape that night, with the slightest warm pink tint.

I remember feeling like I had nothing left. I wasn't going to be able to finish school. My parents hated me. My body was getting weaker and weaker, and I didn't have any friends. Even though I had decided that I was never going to speak to the woman who gave birth to me again, I struggled to fight her words. What was I doing? I was failing at everything I had set out to do. I didn't want to have to keep giving up on my dreams. I didn't want to keep failing. I didn't want to keep disappointing everyone.

She remembered how clear the sky had been before she took that final step off of the boardwalk. The stars sparkled brighter than she had ever seen. It had been so beautiful.

The water was so cold. It didn't take long before I started shivering. I could feel myself getting lightheaded, and my eyes started to sting even though I kept them closed. The water in my nose went from feeling unpleasant to feeling painful. My chest hurt. Everything hurt. But then

I started to feel warm. I started to feel warm, and there was this… this blinding bright light.

And then, the next thing she remembered was waking up in the crappy apartment that she was about to be evicted from soon, now that she didn't have her passive student income.

My memories of stepping off of the boardwalk are too clear and real for it to have been a dream. I know I was out there. But I've never been able to understand what happened after I fell into the water, and why I didn't die that day.

So much had happened since then. She'd moved a few times, and picked up an assortment of jobs before striking gold with this one. It had helped her find the apartment she lived in now which, while certainly not glamorous or luxury, was the most comfortable living space she'd ever had. But there was always the feeling in the back of Yidarica's mind that said she didn't deserve this. That someday, someone would find out she was some type of impostor, and it would all be taken away.

And then where would she be?

The alarm from her phone pulled her away from these thoughts, serving as a reminder: it was time to get ready for practice. Had that much time passed already?

Today, practice was being held at Gracia's place: a ground-level apartment in a two-flat building, in which her upstairs neighbors were barely ever home. Yidarica had never asked why, but based on a conversation that she'd overheard Gracia have with one of the other band members, she didn't know either. Her running theory was that this was their retreat home, and their permanent home was somewhere else. It would make sense, but the idea of having enough money to be able to have something like that was astounding.

It was also on the other side of town, which meant a Comtran ride was in order.

Today was yet another lovely day, with even less clouds than the previous day; while temperatures were similar, the lack of clouds meant that there was less refuge from the heat of the sun, so it felt comparably hotter than yesterday. These kinds of days always made Yidarica think of how much she loved bright, sunny days, but hated the inherent heat of them. She would always hope that someday, magic or science– or both, even– would someday conceive a way for humans to expel excess heat without the gross feeling of sweating. She was also aware that not many people would consider that necessary, which explained why no one seemed to be working on it yet.

As Yidarica sat in the cable car, holding her bass guitar upright, her arms securely around it, she wondered what today would have in store. Not just at practice– although she obviously wondered that too– but the entire day. She wondered if she'd still have the energy to do laundry and cook dinner today, or if she'd need to choose between the two again. It had been a while since she had gotten one of those days where she'd suddenly get the strength to do multiple tasks, so that meant she was due for one soon… right?

Needless to say, because of her inability to regularly keep a perfectly clean house, practice was never held at Yidarica's. Well, that and the multiple flights of stairs. She couldn't in good conscience ask her friends to get a drum set up those stairs, and that was before considering the issue of her neighbors complaining. She knew for a fact that those crotchety people on the first floor would have a lot to say about the amount of noise that band practice created.

Stepping off at the station closest to Gracia's place of residence, Yidarica hadn't walked far before she crossed paths with Walchelin;

as usual, his long brown hair was tied up into a bun to keep it out of his face, his guitar was securely strapped to his back, and he was holding a basket with some type of food inside. Today, he was dressed in a simple t-shirt and jeans, both of the dark blue variety. There was a dark gray shirt underneath his blue one, which appeared to be plain.

"Fancy seeing you here," he said, when Yidarica had ventured close enough to hear him speak. "Would it be an imposition if I requested your company for this walk?"

"I could think of no better way to spend the afternoon," replied Yidarica, as they set off.

Yidarica's overall sentiment of Walchelin was that she liked him, but she could also admit that arriving to that conclusion was based more on vibes than anything else. He was always kind and gentle, his speaking voice being that kind of soft, nurturing tone one would typically expect of a primary school teacher, which was fitting since that was what he did for a living. Even so, and even after being in a band with him for almost two years now, she didn't feel as close to him as she expected to. She figured this was why she could never be completely sure that he liked her. She was always open to the opportunity to get to know him better, but the opportunity never seemed to present itself; they never spoke to each other outside of the band's group chat, and never spent time together unless (at the very least) Gracia was present. She was sure that, if asked, Walchelin would happily agree to a friendly outing together… but there was always the chance that he wouldn't, and she wouldn't want to make him uncomfortable by proposing something he wouldn't want to do.

"What's in the basket this time?" Yidarica asked, noticing they'd been quiet for almost the whole walk.

"This time, we just have a plain loaf. Nothing fancy," Walchelin replied. "I made this specifically because Gracia said she found some gourmet butter at the specialty store that she goes to sometimes. The way she's been talking about it makes it sound like it's life-changing, so I thought it would be best to make the plainest bread I know how to make so that it wouldn't interfere with the flavors of the butter."

Gourmet butter? I didn't know something like that even existed.

"Then again... it's Gracia. The probability of her having over-hyped it is high," Walchelin laughed, making Yidarica laugh with him, because it was true. Gracia's excitable nature did have a tendency to oversell things.

They had arrived at the building now, its alternating brown and red bricks feeling like home at this point. After ringing the doorbell, it wasn't long before Gracia arrived at the door, today wearing a bright yellow sundress with daisies on it. "Oh! Glad to see you guys found the place okay! Come on in, me and Ceri were just setting everything up."

If there was one thing Gracia was good at, it was making her apartment feel like home; this was something that all the band members agreed on. It was difficult to tell exactly what made it feel that way; maybe it was all of the vintage rugs she had placed throughout the place, or the knitted afghan on her couch with all its bright colors. It could also be the lace doilies on the arms of the loveseat and couch, or the cream-colored sheer curtains and the way the sunlight lazily burst through. Or maybe, perhaps, it was an amalgamation of all of these things, coupled with the welcoming, sunny personality of Gracia herself.

In the living room, Cérilda was sitting on the couch, reading the book of sheet music that she and Yidarica had worked on at the previous practice session. It was a work in progress, but even so, considerable progress had been made. At this point, there were about six completed songs in the book, with seven in progress. Of course, the six that were considered "complete" could probably also use some workshopping, so who was to say if they were truly done?

"Morning," Walchelin said as he sat beside her. "I hope we didn't keep you waiting."

Cérilda smiled and turned to him, her brown curly hair bouncing with the motion. "No, it's fine. After all, we still have one more missing, don't we?"

"Nope, we don't," Gracia replied, entering the room while she held her phone. "The official communication from Landen is that he won't be able to make it today, and to go on without him; so with that, it looks like we have a full house. I hereby call this, Week Seventeen of Half Past Haberdash practice: to order!"

Yidarica was silent as she sat on one of the chairs surrounding the coffee table. *Seventeen? I missed weeks fifteen and nine. I used projection for ten, eleven, twelve…*

"So! I came up with an agenda for the day." Gracia's voice drew everyone's attention to her. "Knowing that we won't be able to practice full sets because of Ceri not having her drum set today, and now Landen not being here either, I've blocked out some time for us to discuss choice pieces of our yet-unfinished songs. But before we get into that, I thought it would be best if we discussed the overarching lyricism in our EP, to decide if any of the lyrics need to be amended, and/or to come up with new ones. What do we think, does this sound like a suitable itinerary?"

Everyone present began to affirm. "Yeah, sounds pretty reasonable to me," agreed Walchelin. "Am I slicing up this bread now, or are we waiting a while?"

Gracia's face lit up. "Oh! Right! Slice it up immediately, Wally! I'll be right back with the freshest and most flavorful butter that any of you have ever experienced. I promise you!"

She hurried off, leaving Cérilda to look at her other bandmates. "Butter?"

"Yeah, it's–" Walchelin chuckled. "The more I end up having to explain it to people, the more ridiculous it sounds. It's butter. Gourmet butter. Allegedly."

"Gourmet... butter." Cérilda nodded slowly.

It does sound a little silly, but maybe it is as amazing as Gracia says. She knows her food.

"When I went to the store, I made sure to pick up a few assorted flavors just in case you guys don't like the original one. So here!" As Gracia sat each jar on the table, she explained: "We've got the original... and then this one's a smoky one. I'm not sure what they put in it to give it that smoky taste, but it ends up making everything taste like it just got off the grill! This has a subtle sweet pineapple infusion, and the sweet-salty mixture is amazing. And then this one has a sweet onion flavor; I haven't tried this one yet, but it sounds good enough. I think I'm gonna go for that one. Go ahead, pick something out!"

After a moment of contemplation, Yidarica decided to also taste the sweet onion flavor. *I don't want to eat just butter, and this one sounds the safest out of all the flavors. I should like this one.*

When she bit into the bread– at about the same time as everyone else bit into theirs– she knew they were all feeling the same way.

Why would we ever doubt Gracia when it comes to food? This is amazing!

"Can we, like... spend the rest of the day just eating this?" Walchelin asked. "And where did you find it? This is amazing! I need details."

"Oh, *now* you're interested?" Gracia asked smugly. "Luckily for you, I believe in whatever the opposite of gatekeeping is. Now, I found this stuff at the specialty store that's a bit due north of here, but when I was doing my research into all the different flavors and whatnot, I read that the creators also sell at various farmer's markets. You have a market near you, right, Wally? Checking there the next time you have the ability to go will probably be the best way for you to get your own. By the way, I definitely recommend you check out their flavors on their website before you go. This is merely a sample!"

"Still, this is such a cool thing for you to share with us, Gracia," Cérilda said, finishing up the piece of bread she had prepared for herself. "Now, shall we get started?"

Everyone hesitated to move.

"By the way, how did your visit with your family end up going, Gracia?" Walchelin asked. "I know about all of the big things that happened, but overall, did you have fun? Did you have a good time, or was it frustrating?"

Gracia sighed. "The wedding was beautiful, but you know how it is. I'm always happy to see family, but you know how they are once you reach a certain age. I'm twenty-six years old now, so the fact that I'm still unmarried, to them, sounds outrageous and even a little dangerous."

This was something that had been transpiring in Gracia's life for a little while now. Her parents worried about how long she could go before the Dark began coming for her, but they also had no idea just how loved their daughter was. However, Gracia was unable to tell them not to worry about her in a way that didn't reveal to them that she was a lesbian. She knew her parents well enough to know this was not a development they would approve of, and would potentially resort to arranging a marriage to a man in retaliation. So far, she had been able to dodge her family's prying questions about her love life, but she also knew it would get more difficult to do so the more it went on.

"Is there anything we can do to help make the whole situation easier?" Yidarica asked.

Gracia shrugged. "I don't know. I always appreciate you guys offering to help me with stuff, but the issue is that I don't really know what I *can* do. So I guess if any of you have any bright ideas, I'll gladly take them."

Whenever the topic of ideas was abound in this group, it was borderline instinctual to assume Cérilda would be the person to contribute the most of them. Indeed, by the time Yidarica and Walchelin turned to her, she was already ready with a notepad and pencil. "What are we if not a vehicle of ideas, Gracia? Now, to start: what have you tried so far, in this situation?"

Yidarica was willing to bet that this was the quietest Gracia's apartment had ever been, while she was still awake.

"Okay. So, nothing." Cérilda wrote this down. "Let's phrase that a different way. You're twenty-six years old now, right? So the topic has to have come up before. How have you been handling it so far?"

"Oh! I am so glad you asked!" Gracia clapped her hands together. "Do you remember... wait. No. I didn't know you guys back then, except for Wally of course. So, when I was about to graduate high school, I had this thing with a guy; I don't really know if I can call it a relationship, because looking back, that kinda feels like a stretch. Anyway, my parents found out about us because my sister is a snitch, but they were like, *really* happy about it. And I mean, happy to the point where it felt so out of character for them that I asked what the deal was, at that point. The explanation I got is that they were just *so* happy that I was 'only a late bloomer' and 'were so worried that the big city kids convinced me I liked girls instead.' It felt shitty to hear, but if I got one positive thing out of that, it's that since he broke things off the day I started my university courses, I've always been able to use that as a fallback. Sorry, benevolent Mother and Father. I am simply still too depressed about Bradlan leaving me high and dry."

"His name was Bradlan?" Yidarica asked in disbelief. "That name just screams fuckboy."

"It really does!" Walchelin agreed. "I always wondered why you bothered with someone like that."

Gracia shrugged. "High school is brutal, but it isn't complicated; the best way to dodge lesbian allegations is to pull the bro-iest bro in the land. It worked, didn't it?"

Walchelin grumbled before replying, "Yeah, well, it worked a little *too* well. For the rest of the year, my DMs were full of casual acquaintances trying to get me to put in a good word for them with you. It's all so silly, now that I look back on it. I'm surprised more people didn't realize you're into skirts; it's really obvious."

"Really? Half my team at work was surprised when I mentioned it in a meeting once," Gracia pointed out. "Maybe it just feels obvious because we've been friends for so long."

At this, Cérilda crossed her legs. "That's right. You guys have known each other the longest of any of us here, right? Which is impressive, considering I've known Yidarica since I was nine years old."

"Yeah, but you two have a pretty substantial age gap," Gracia pointed out. "Wally was nine when we met, but since I was six... hey, we've been friends for two decades now!"

Sometimes, Yidarica forgot that Gracia and Walchelin weren't the exact same age, but when she realized why it was so hard for her to remember that, she suddenly was able to recall why they had become friends in the first place.

Twenty years ago, when the Budiawan family had newly moved here to Sonusia from Dochram, and Gracia's mother struggled to learn the language, she worked as a caretaker for particularly wealthy families; her magic prowess was astounding, which garnered her a fair amount of attention. In the beginning, she struggled to have a consistent client. Many dropped her because of the language barrier, until one day, it was as though her feet had been Mother-guided to run into the somewhat wealthy heiress of the Gallifrey family, who had only dared to venture to a grocery store on her own because her sickly son was running a high fever and nothing on hand seemed to be effective in treating it. Gracia's mother had shared a home remedy that broke the fever in record time, and the rest– as they said– was history.

To hear Gracia's mother describe Walchelin as a child always felt like peering into a window few had access to. He had been weak and low-energy because of his propensity to running fevers and overheating, but it was also easy to see that he was a gentle, sweet boy. Even more obvious to her, though, was how lonely he was. His siblings seemed to want nothing to do with him, even after being reassured his sickness wasn't transmissible. He'd been out of traditional school for two years at that point, and had to be kept inside, so chances of meeting friends were nonexistent.

It hadn't been planned for Gracia and Walchelin to meet, but one day when flooding paths meant school closures, Gracia's mother was left with no one to care for Gracia and her younger sister while she worked. Immediately, Mrs. Gallifrey remedied the situation with a, "just bring them with you and everything will be fine." But she would not accept not having someone present to care for her son. And so, the friendship happened almost immediately; it worked out that Walchelin had some developmental delays for his age, because it didn't bore him to play with a six-year-old. Even when Gracia had to be told to slow down so he could keep up, the smile had never left Walchelin's face.

Twenty years later, even when the two teased each other, it wasn't hard to see that happiness still there.

"Is there a reason you two never, you know, fake-dated to get your parents off your back?" Cérilda asked.

At the mere suggestion, Walchelin held his hands up. "Nope! Not right now, right now would be a horrible time to do that. I've finally gotten to the 'bring them into your home' stage with a very cute gentleman, and I would hate for anything outside of the two of us to make things go wrong somehow. Sorry, Gracia. I am here for support in literally any other way."

"You won't be receiving any complaints from me; I'm just glad you've finally found someone who isn't a weirdo," Gracia replied. "I'll never forget the guy who tried to argue that your hoodie, which obviously was fitted to you and has your family's crest on it, was his. Like, at that point, just steal it."

"Or that really jealous girl who ate all of his students' cookies he made the night before," Yidarica stifled a laugh. This was one of the first things she had learned about Walchelin, when they first met. At least, when it came to how unlucky she was when it came to the dating world, she didn't attract the colorful characters that seemed to be drawn to Walchelin like ants to honey. A small grace, but a valuable one.

Now that I think about it, it's probably his family's money that attracts the odd people. I never thought I'd be grateful to be broke, but I guess I am, in that way.

As discussions continued, getting on topic again, Yidarica received a text message from Zaya.

> **Hey! Was wondering how your plant's doing. She's still alive I hope?**

Yidarica smiled as she typed her response.

> **Alive? Yep. But some of the leaves are wilting and drying even though I know I've been keeping up with watering. Here, I'm gonna send you the best picture I could get**

"…which makes it stand out that much more," Gracia was saying. "How do we feel about on-stage stunts?"

"No, Gracia," Yidarica and Walchelin said in unison.

"We have to consider how quickly things could go wrong if the stunts don't work out," added Cérilda. "Especially for Yida and Walchelin, one fall could mean a hospital stay."

Gracia sighed. "Yeah. That's why we're a team; thanks for reminding me, guys."

Zaya's next message came through then:

> **That doesn't look great but it's also kinda hard to see.**
> **Are you at home? Can you stop by the nursery so I can take a look?**

Of course she'd done so badly that her plant already needed intervention. Yidarica wasn't sure what to say; she knew that, once she did get home, she wouldn't have the strength to go back out to the nursery. And even if she did, that would absolutely be her limit, and then she could forget about being able to cook dinner. It was time, yet again, to try and shuffle her obligations around in a way that her fatigue wouldn't get in the way of.

Suddenly, she had an amazing idea.

> I'm not at home, but if you're able to come over in like 3 hours that'd be great.

★★★

"Oh, well, she's just being a little moody," Zaya said this in the same way a parent would about their infant child, holding the plant in a similar way as well. "Don't stress yourself out, Yidarica; you're doing everything right. But sometimes you can do everything right, and be faced with a diva of a plant like this one."

"Okay." Yidarica nodded. "Sure, but what exactly should I do when a plant is, uh, a diva?"

Zaya turned to her and smiled. "There are *so* many ways to deal with that. Even with you not wanting to use any plant-related spells, I've found a lot of success with moving moody plants to another section of the house. Even if it's not quite as good of a spot for air or sunlight, they seem to like the change in environment. Now, Dad swears by withholding water for a couple of cycles, but I haven't tried that myself."

"A couple of cycles..." Yidarica repeated.

"Yeah. So, for example: this plant is being watered once every three days, right? The way Dad explains it– or at least how I understand it– you'd initially wait nine days, and then water it," Zaya explained. "He's explained it as giving the plants a little shock to get them to behave, but I'm not so sure I like the implications of that."

Yidarica couldn't stop the odd noise of disapproval that came from her. "We're still in that really weird transitional period when it comes to shock therapy; where it's incredibly unpopular with the general population, but it's still technically not illegal. Personally, I'm forever grateful that the woman who gave birth to me was too stupid to get it to work."

The way that Zaya turned to Yidarica set off sirens in her head.

Oh, no. I know that look perfectly well. That's the look people give me when I say something that feels completely normal for me, but it turns out it's actually not a common thing to talk about, and I've succeeded in weirding them out.

"Uh, sorry about that," Yidarica nervously pushed a piece of hair behind her ear. "It is, unfortunately, very easy for me to forget that not everyone's mothers declare them public enemy number one."

"I wouldn't be able to tell whether they do or not," Zaya shrugged. "I never got to meet mine."

And now I've stepped in it. "Oh, I'm so sorry," Yidarica replied. "Sincerely. If there's one thing I struggle with, it's mother talk; I have so many emotions surrounding the one that I was given that I admit I can be a little tactless about the topic."

"You don't have to apologize," Zaya told her. "While, yes, I'll always be sad that I never got to meet my mother, this might be weird to say, but… I really like meeting people who absolutely hate their mothers. I think, in some really strange roundabout way, it grounds me. Like, sure, I can spend my days agonizing over how lovely a person she could have been, and that we never got those cute mother-daughter interactions that I see all the time, everywhere I go. But it's equally as possible that she was an awful person, someone I'm better off never having met. Am I making sense?"

"I follow," Yidarica agreed. "And while I'm sure I have enough childhood trauma to make you feel great about things, I'd rather our interactions be positive. You know, because I like you."

Shit. Too forward. Humans don't like forwardness, especially from women! Why did I just say that?

It was relieving to see Zaya's expression morph into a smile. "I couldn't agree more. As much as I'd like to stay longer and hear about how much you like me, though, I did kind of sneak out from the shop. I should get going. It was nice getting to see you, though!"

"Yeah!" Yidarica agreed. "Now that you know where I live, we could maybe configure some time to spend together?"

"I'd like that." Zaya smiled again, and her hand gently brushed Yidarica's as she handed the plant back before heading out.

She's so lovely. I look forward to the next time I get to see her.

Chapter Five

The amount of emails that greeted Yidarica the next day at work were a pretty good indication that things were about to get funky.

Sifting through them, the majority appeared to be notifications that she'd been granted access to the many new programs and spreadsheets she'd need for what was being dubbed the Weather Project. One of them was also nice enough to send a tutorial on how to use it, which wasn't the standard, but always appreciated. There were two emails from Shiori: one to just her explaining the extent of what had been explained to the other members of the Project Garden and where to pick up in today's sync, and one to both she and Muiren with a list of contacts that would be useful.

There was also a message from Shiori in Slapdash:

I've scheduled the sync with Muiren in Beignet. It's defaulted to 30 minutes, but now that it's on your calendar you can adjust that either way you need to.

Yidarica didn't see Muiren at the desk they usually sat at, but when she thought about it, it had been a long time since she had seen Muiren at all. They had been granted complete remote work permissions for… had it been a year? One of their relatives far away had fallen sick, and apparently, Muiren had been the only person in their family able to go and care for them. When that relative sadly passed, they'd then gone on bereavement, and then they had finally returned maybe two or three weeks ago. Yidarica was quite fond of Muiren, and had missed their bright red fluffy hair and freckles around the office, as well as their kindness. She'd always felt that Muiren's presence was like that of an older sibling, which was odd because Muiren was younger than her. Suffice it to say, she was excited to work on this project with them; she liked Hadiza too, but found that she was less… approachable? Relatable? It was difficult to put words to it. While Hadiza had never been mean to her, or even slightly unpleasant, Yidarica always got the feeling that she was on thin ice whenever the two spoke.

Or is it me imagining things to be that way?

The sync was in ten minutes, and Beignet was on the other side of the building. Best to start heading there now.

★★★

"Yidarica! Why, it's been ages since we've seen one another, hasn't it?"

There was the fluffy red hair, the pale, freckled skin, and the green eyes Yidarica was used to seeing. The familiar lilt in Muiren's voice, somehow, felt like a warm blanket being wrapped around her shoulders as the two quickly embraced. "It certainly feels that way, Muiren. But I'm glad to be seeing you again. How have you been adjusting to your return?"

"It's been a time, but I think I appreciate life here in the city much more than before, now. I'm living with my parents for a little while, and that has its own challenges, but it's nice to be cohabiting again; I didn't realize how lonely I had been on my own. I've also started taking the Comtran again lately because of the move, and it's nice to be able to sit for a little while, rather than having to walk the entire way. How have you been? You must have been putting in exceptional work here if you've been named the leader of a project."

"Less exceptional work and more not shutting up about weather, probably," Yidarica replied as she started the sync's projection. "Speaking of which, did you happen to see the sunrise this morning? The cirrus clouds that were around at the time created some really beautiful color variance in the sky. I guess we have that warm front to thank for that; the warm air rising must have…" she trailed off then. *And there I am, doing it again.*

Muiren gave her a curious look. "What were you doing up so early that you saw the sunrise?"

"I couldn't sleep," Yidarica gave the control tablet a few more taps. Had she configured everything correctly? "As excited as I am for this project, I'm still nervous about it. Okay, I'm pretty sure everything is set now. We just need to wait for Shiori. Like you, I was only just told about this project yesterday, but she's done some of the groundwork for us, at least. We still have some foundations to place, but I think I at least know where we'll be starting."

"Ah, I see," Muiren hummed in thought. "Always good to hear that we won't be left in the middle of the ocean, so to speak. Although, even though I know I haven't been given the complete rundown on what this project is and how it'll go, I can't help but ask: what the hell has been going on to make it necessary for us to be implementing this kind of feature? You'd think people would be smart enough to know that if they're treading on muddy ground, they're going to eat shit eventually."

"Maybe so."

Both immediately turned to see Shiori's projection materializing in the room, somewhere behind them. The room didn't transform into a scene as elaborate as yesterday's meeting, but the light coming from overhead, simulating sunlight, was calming; and the few trees gave the space a more authentic feeling.

"You know, Yidarica said something very similar in our meeting yesterday. And while I'd remind you that the gift of foresight is not as widespread as we'd like to believe, there's another side to it we need to consider." Now fully materialized, Shiori walked up to her team. "And feel free to tell me if I'm just being an obnoxious twenty-four-year-old by saying this; but my life experience thus far has led me to believe that people, by nature, seem to *really like* pushing responsibility onto others. It leads them to, among other qualities, be extremely litigious. We're in a position where it could possibly be argued we're at fault for someone's hurt or misfortune– and you can't really say, 'Your Honor, this person is a fucking idiot' in court, so the next best thing we can do is play the legal game well enough that we're left out of the whole ordeal."

Mitigation in place of prevention was indeed a wise tactic, in cases like these.

"Something I don't think I did the greatest job at expressing yesterday is that it isn't our concern *how* we're informing people of the risk they're assuming; we're working on the most user-intuitive way to give them that information," Shiori continued. "Legal will give us the correct verbiage soon, so we just need to put it in both of our applications in a way that's likely to actually be read."

"Right, because if we just T&C it, I think there's a legal defense for it not being obvious enough, right?" Muiren asked.

"Exactly," Shiori agreed. "That would be the Clause of Recognition. I was a little too young when this happened to remember it, but you two might: there was a very famous class action lawsuit about this very issue. Actually, fun fact: one of my titas and my older sister got settlements out of that one. That was one of the first times I was genuinely upset at being too young for something," she laughed. "Well, you have your mission. Until we get the official verbiage from Legal, it'd probably be a good idea to look into the backend of both our weather and market applications; you know, get a good understanding of the technical aspects of the 'how' we're working to achieve."

"Got it." With this, Yidarica felt that she understood the project a lot better than she had yesterday.

Shiori didn't miss a beat upon Yidarica agreeing with her. "Yidarica, I'm handing the rest of the day's itinerary off to you, since you're leading the project. I'll be in the office all of next week, so we can go over first impressions then. For today, you know I'm always a message away."

As their manager disappeared, Muiren sighed. "Of *course* we're starting with the most technical part."

Muiren was brilliant when it came to aesthetics and design, which is why they had been with the Project Garden the longest out of everyone currently there, but this brilliance came at the cost of being almost completely tech illiterate. It was a strange thing to do, work for a company that was probably one of the most technical in the entirety of Basodin, but they at least had enough knowledge to, say, use their phone and tablet, and know how to operate a select few online programs. That was usually enough. Usually.

"Well, it's…" Yidarica thought. How to start this project in a way that didn't feel hostile to Muiren's needs? If it got complicated later that was a different thing, but having a new project seem impossibly difficult in the very beginning was a fast track to burnout. She had personal experience with that. "We don't have to start by diving right in. Yesterday, Shiori sent me a list of contacts that will be helpful as we work on this project. Let's have a seat right outside of this room, and we can familiarize ourselves with our resources."

As the two took a seat at one of the empty tables nearby, Yidarica opened the email with all of the contacts listed, studying it for a moment. "Hmm. Well, whenever we start a new project, one of the first things Shiori does is have us meet with the person who's responsible for looping us in, right? In this case, that person also happens to be our Weather Department POC, Iris Guantian."

I… I have to be the one to approach her. I– usually it's Shiori. But she explicitly said I was in charge of setting up meetings related to this project, because I'm the… the primary contact. I have to reach out. Me.

Will anyone even read messages from somebody as lowly as me?

"Oh, Iris!" Muiren said then. "I know her! We got hired around the same time, we were in the same training class. I didn't realize she still worked here."

This is a blessing in disguise. "Do… you want to be the one to reach out to her, then?" Yidarica asked.

"Really?! That'd be awesome!" Muiren was already typing away on their tablet. "What's our angle? Are we trying to just set up a brief meeting?"

"Yeah, we- you can say that we're trying to gain some more perspective on the project, or something along those lines," replied Yidarica. "No more than fifteen minutes, almost definitely less."

"And sent." Muiren smiled. "Flattered that you'd trust me with responsibilities this early on in the project, Chief."

On one hand, I feel bad that I've already chickened out of a responsibility I should have taken on, but those big shot business people always say to make wise use of your resources, right? It's an objective fact that Muiren is more social than I am. It makes sense to entrust them with some of the interpersonal obligations.

Or am I just making excuses for myself again?

The sound of a Slapdash notification caught both of their attention. "Iris says that she's booked solid in meetings and other obligations for the next ten business days; *but*, she also says that she can always make time for an old friend, and suggested we meet for a quick chat at noon during her lunch."

"Oh! Really?" Yidarica asked in disbelief. "In that case… we should both take our lunch then too. That way, none of us are distracted."

***

Lunchtime couldn't come soon enough.

Making their way to the cafeteria, Yidarica didn't find herself feeling incredibly hungry, but she was well aware that it was because of her nerves. If she didn't grab something to eat, she knew she'd regret it later, so she took her place in line with Muiren, reading the menu posted over the kitchen window to see what was being offered today. There were usually around four different entrees, each thematically different, and it was sometimes a struggle to pick just one. Today's meatloaf and mashed potatoes certainly did look delicious, though.

"Oh! The noodle dish is vegetarian today!" Muiren pointed out. "Finally! I don't know what it is about noodles that makes the kitchen always pair them with meat, but I finally have my chance today. I know what I'm getting!"

"You always know what you're getting, there's only ever one vegetarian option," Yidarica said with a laugh.

Muiren laughed with her. "Hey, there's the salad bar. You never know. Someday, maybe they'll finally add spinach to it, and I'll be able to stomach the idea of eating a salad here."

This only made Yidarica laugh harder. "You are possibly the only vegetarian I've ever heard of that hates lettuce."

"I get that a lot," Muiren agreed. "Think about it. In a world where we have the peppery taste of arugula, the sweet tones of kohlrabi, the slight buttery tones in spinach, the delightful texture of bok choy, or even whatever the hell kale has going on… why would you ever choose something as bland and watery as lettuce?"

"I can't imagine being so passionate about leafy greens, but I admire the dedication you've put into studying them." Now at the window, Yidarica stood slightly on her toes to ensure the chef could hear her. "Meatloaf entree, please."

After the two grabbed their bowls, they walked over to the side table where all the silverware and condiments sat; currently, there was only one fork left. "Take it," Muiren handed it to Yidarica. "I've got noodles, so I can use chopsticks. The… chopsticks that we seem to also be out of right now. Oh."

Both stared at the empty container that the chopsticks were usually in for a moment, before being approached by someone. Yidarica looked up, and the sight made her knees go slightly weak; it was the man with the glasses she always saw, but this was her first time seeing him close up. His dark brown hair was swept to the side as usual, and he was dressed in a plain light blue button-up shirt and khakis. Her knees had gone weak because, this close, it was more evident than it ever had been: he was *cute*.

I need to talk to him. I've been putting it off, but Mother, give me strength to finally talk to him now. I don't know what I'm going to say, but I have to say… something. What if I ask him about the weather?

"Oh, Muiren. Doing okay?" he asked, his hand up in a waving gesture.

Wait! Does Muiren know him? This is an opening!

"Debatable. I was looking for a set of chopsticks to eat my food with, but it looks like we're out for the day," they replied.

"Really? Did you check right over there with the plasticware?" The man pointed to a counter on the far end of the room. "I think there are still some over there. If there are no chopsticks, there should at least still be more forks."

"Are there? Awesome, thanks!" Muiren waved as he walked away.

Wait, he's gone? He didn't say a word to me! He didn't even look at me! I wasn't introduced! What the hell just happened?!

"Come on, Yidarica. If we don't get settled soon, we might miss our meeting with Iris," Muiren said, bringing her out of her trance.

"Oh! Right. Let's find a suitable place to sit."

***

Before beginning this project, Yidarica had never heard Iris' name, so she hadn't been sure what to expect for this meeting. She soon found herself faced with a thin woman, a bit taller than average, with slightly tanned skin and mostly dark hair, pieces of blue, indigo, and purple poking out at random times. Seeing her walk up to the table and then take a seat, it was obvious that she was someone who was confident in herself; her posture and gaze commanded attention in a way that a person only could if they were certain of their every move. It would not be entirely incorrect for Yidarica to consider herself in awe of her.

"Thanks for making some time to meet with us," Muiren said once Iris had settled in her seat.

"Well, it's like I said: I can always make time for an old friend," Iris replied. Usually, one would expect a person to smile when saying something like that; the tiny smile that barely moved the curvature of her lips didn't seem to match the sentiment of what she had said. Because of this, it was difficult to tell if she had meant it sincerely. "What have you been up to, Muiren? It's been so long that I had no idea you still worked here."

Muiren smirked, "It's funny you say that, because I just said that exact same thing about you, before I sent you that message. I'm still part of the Project Garden, but I've actually just recently come back to the office after handling some family affairs. This is Yidarica, who's heading the project we're currently working on."

"Oh! I've seen you around before, but I didn't realize you were the same person that Shiori was telling me I'd be contacting for updates on this project. It's nice to be able to put a name to the face, now. Or a face to the name." Again, it was impossible to tell if Iris was saying this in an amicable or demeaning way, because her expression barely changed, and even then, it did so in a very neutral way. "Now, what is it you two need from me?"

Muiren immediately turned to Yidarica, wordlessly indicating that she would have to be the one to explain their angle. Which was expected, being the head of the project and all, but she was not mentally prepared for this. How would she get through it without sounding grossly incompetent?

"We, uh…" Yidarica started. "We've already met with Shiori and discussed the baseline expectations for what we'll be doing, but it's always good to personally meet with the requester of a project to get a clearer picture on what it is they're aiming to get out of the whole thing. There has to be a reason you came to our team to take this on, rather than any other, right?"

"Indeed." Iris nodded, taking a sip from her water bottle. "I was faced with the choice of approaching either you all, or the Project Biome, and in the end, I ended up going with the Project Garden for a few reasons. For one thing, I took a look at all the previous work of the two project teams, and found that the Garden has a more aesthetically pleasing tendency, which suits this undertaking better than the more analytical output of the Biome. After checking with the managers of both teams, you all also seemed to have a lighter workload at this time. And finally, at its core: this project seems to affect the Sustenance Department more than the Weather Department, so it would need people working on it with an express knowledge of the department."

Yidarica was taking notes diligently. "Got it. Okay, I think that, based on that, I've got a pretty good idea of what kind of output you're expecting. Lastly, is there anything else you think we should know, as we're working on this?"

This gave Iris pause before she answered. "If Shiori hasn't already hammered in the legal implications of this whole thing…"

"Oh, she has. She definitely has," Muiren confirmed.

"The sooner this can be done, the better. We don't want to be embroiled in too many legal claims; if that line gets crossed, then regardless of the rulings, our reputation as a company would be tanked," Iris said then. "I'm sure none of us want that, which is why I'm committed to doing everything I can to ensure it doesn't; by extension, doing anything I can to help you two. Well, this has been lovely, but I need to be across the building in five minutes if you'll excuse me. If you have any other questions, you know how to get in touch," she smiled, fully, as she stood and waved.

Iris is… I can't tell if she enjoyed or hated this meeting. It's so difficult to get a read on her. It makes it hard to decide what I should say to her, or what kind of tone I should use when I speak to her, and write emails to her. I don't want to overstep any boundaries– but even consulting my studies of human behavior, she didn't give me anything that helps me determine where that boundary is.

When Iris left, and while the remaining two continued to eat, Yidarica pondered what had just transpired. There was never a point that this meeting had felt hostile, and Iris had even said that she would do everything she could to help their project along. So then, why was she feeling a feeling close to rejection?

"Speaking of the gravity of the situation…" Muiren said suddenly, picking up one of the napkins on the table before summoning a pen into their left hand. *Muiren is left-handed? I can't believe I never noticed that.*

"Here. I think you might need this. As much as I know we're both hoping for it to not be the case, we might need a way to keep in touch with one another outside of work hours, in case this whole thing goes off the rails."

Yidarica looked down at the napkin; Muiren had written their phone number.

"Thanks. I'll text you so you'll have mine." Yidarica pulled her phone out.

"And let's pray to the Mother that we won't need these for work purposes," Muiren replied, standing. "I'll be at our work area, but there's no rush for you to finish eating; just come by whenever you're done."

Muiren is right; I can only hope that things don't get so drastic that we need to start pulling overtime.

As she finished up her lunch, Yidarica had a sudden realization.

I have Muiren's phone number. Muiren knows the cute guy. Muiren might even have the cute guy's number. What if I just asked them...

Chapter Six

Yidarica couldn't believe she was doing this. Muiren had only just entrusted her with their phone number, and she was already back to being that same overfamiliar weirdo she'd been as a teenager, which was one of the reasons why she couldn't make friends. Was she trying to speedrun being blocked and making the workplace more awkward than it had to be? This was a horrible idea! This was…

This was, admittedly, not the worst thing Yidarica could do. Her studies of interaction had shown that, although people tended to be turned off by overfamiliarity, there also seemed to be more leeway when it came to coworkers. Coworkers, she had noticed, existed in this strange space where it seemed to be socially acceptable to become friends because of the amount of time spent together– similar to school settings– but equally as acceptable to never speak to each other outside of necessity, like the coworkers she'd had before she moved to the Project Garden. Muiren had spoken to her before about plenty of things that weren't related to work at all, so this slightly related to work thing should be fine, right? With that in mind, she picked her phone up and began to compose a message.

> Hi, Muiren. Was curious and didn't know if this was the type of thing to ask on Slapdash: do you know that gentleman with the dark brown hair and glasses that walks past our area sometimes?

This message was very good at being neutral, right? But Yidarica still couldn't possibly send it. She'd never be able to explain herself when Muiren inevitably asked why she was asking about him. Maybe she needed a few minutes away from her phone, in order to be more rational. Maybe standing on the back porch for a few minutes would help her regain her wits.

As she tried to sit her phone down, it fell and landed face down; picking it up, Yidarica was horrified to see the "send" button had been pressed. Her heart felt as if it had plummeted into her stomach.

Well. I guess this is my life now.

It would be impossible for her to focus on any other task as long as the question was in the air, but thankfully, it didn't take too long for Muiren to respond.

> The one who helped me find the extra sets of chopsticks today, right? Can't say I'm super familiar, but we've spoken upon various occasions. His name's August.

"August? Like the month? Huh." Yidarica nodded. A name that one recognized *could* be a name, but not one that was encountered often. Just the right amount of obscurity. She immediately wanted to know more about this August, but Muiren had said that they weren't super familiar with him. And to ask anything along the lines of "tell me everything you do know about him," would be incriminating. If Yidarica wanted this information, she'd have to get it from someone who wasn't Muiren– and, preferably, not anyone else at work, either, mostly because Yidarica didn't know anyone outside of her team well enough to be asking these kinds of questions.

No, if she wanted any more information, she had to do this the old-fashioned way: through independent research.

***

Doing my own research is going to be hard partly because I don't know where this August guy sits. I only ever see him when he walks past our section, but I never see him sit down anywhere. I guess I can start by determining which direction he sits in, which, to do that I just need to pay attention to the first time he goes past today.

As Yidarica set up her workstation for the day, she tried to think of the best way to do that. If today's workload got heavy, it would be very easy to get sucked into it and not realize who was going where and when. Getting sucked into work, to that extent, was something she'd had to work hard to learn to do in the first place; it strongly went against her natural instinct to look up at every single thing that passed through her peripheral vision, which had partially contributed to her struggle when she had first started in this position. Maybe there was a way to find a midway point between the two?

"Morning." Shiori had arrived, placing her work bag in the chair of her desk, across from Yidarica. "Did you get up here okay? I think one of the other businesses here must be having some sort of event or something, because there was almost no space in transportation storage when I got here."

"Oh, really?" Yidarica asked. "I didn't notice, but I– I do also take the Comtran, so I guess I wasn't in a position to."

"Right. I forgot that about you." Shiori took a moment to turn on her work tablet before turning back to Yidarica. "Maybe I should start doing that more. It would save me a lot of trouble. Well, anyway, I see you have breakfast there; what's looking good today?"

On Yidarica's small breakfast plate was a tiny pile of scrambled eggs and diced potatoes, alongside a banana nut muffin. "You know. The usuals. It fulfills the needs well enough. They were out of orange juice when I got there, but I'm gonna grab some water before the day officially starts."

After getting that water and settling in, ready to start the day, a Slapdash notification distracted Yidarica from her breakfast.

```
New message from Muiren Tierney
hey, wanna work on the deck today? saved you a
seat if so
```

Deck? What deck? Aside from the garden and the courts... were there any other outdoor areas?

```
Sure, but where is it? I can come over after I'm
done eating my breakfast.
```

And with that she went back to her muffin. Fortunately, the next message came through right as she finished eating.

> **New message from Muiren Tierney**
> **easternmost side of this floor, go up a few steps to where the other drink bar is and make a right**

Other drink bar?! How was it that Yidarica had worked at this company for four years and still had no idea what was in this building? Had her tunnel vision with work gotten that intense?

"Shiori, if it's all right with you, Muiren and I are going to be working in a different area today," Yidarica said as she stood. "I… told them to choose the place this time, and they just let me know they found the perfect spot for us to take on the day."

Shiori looked up, a vague look of intrigue in her eyes before waving her direct report off. "Have fun. I'll be here with all my other reports, so if you need anything, you can always come back or send me a Slapdash."

"Got it." She nodded, and was on her way.

***

There were two reasons Yidarica had been so lost when Muiren had mentioned this area. Partly, it was because she hadn't ever been on this side of the office, because she'd never needed to be. But it was also because this technically wasn't a deck. It was more like an indoor balcony; a small, wooden area that overlooked the rest of that part of the office somewhat like a deck, but completely indoors. There was a certain amount of privacy that came with the way it was positioned, though, so not a bad place to set up for the day.

"It feels good to gain a new perspective, doesn't it?" Muiren asked, charitably pulling out a chair for Yidarica to sit. "In all seriousness, though, thank you for indulging me. I've grown quite fond of this area. I can't quite explain why, but something about this place feels calming."

"Yeah, for sure," Yidarica replied. "Is everything all right, Muiren? I've noticed you haven't sat in our area at all since you've been back."

The air became notably tense then. *Should I have not said anything?*

Muiren placed their hands in their lap, and let out a long, drawn-out sigh. "It's nothing to do with you or Hadiza or Shiori. You're all wonderful people. I can't believe I'm about to say this: the last time I sat at my desk, my grandmother was still alive, and sitting there again reminds me of… everything. How I got the news at work that she was so far gone. How I had to drop everything and be the one to go and care for her, because no one else in our family could be bothered to. How she continued to decline no matter what I did, and having to see her become a shadow of the woman she once was. How, despite my best efforts, she still ended up dying. She was one of the first people I felt comfortable confiding in about my gender, and was the main person to defend me from other family when arguments started because of it. I think all the time about how she supported me going into tech, even though I still needed help working tablets at that point. She did so much for me, and would always say how proud she was of me, but I can't help but feel as though, in the time where she needed me… I failed her."

This hadn't been an answer Yidarica was expecting– and even more so, not an answer she knew how to address. She hadn't had anyone in her family pass that she had established a relationship with. Announcements from her parents that some relative she'd never met had died felt functionally the same as when she'd see bad news emails: regret on a level of human decency, but with no real impact to her mental state. What was she supposed to say to this type of thing? She hadn't studied enough grieving people to understand how this kind of interaction went.

"Sorry. It's silly, I know," Muiren said then.

"I don't know that I'd call it silly," Yidarica replied. "Listen, my silence is only because I've never had to grieve anyone. So, you can feel free to think that anything I say next is absolute horseradish and toss it out of your head immediately, but I get it. What you said makes a lot of sense to me. And I don't think it's the place of anyone in this building to tell you there's any correct way for you to handle your grief. You just… do what you need to do, all right?"

"I can do that." Muiren nodded. "Can we try to set up shop here from now until the project's conclusion, then? I should be able to pull myself together by then."

"This is a pretty nice area, so I won't say no," agreed Yidarica. "Now let's get started on whatever today's damage is."

As both began shuffling through emails and other notifications, Muiren asked, "So what made you ask about August?"

Yidarica was sure she'd never looked at someone so fast. "What?"

"Just curious since it kind of came out of nowhere," they explained.

How in the world am I gonna talk my way out of this one?

"Well. You know." Yidarica wracked her brain before she miraculously thought of the perfect explanation. "When you mentioned that you knew Iris, you explained how: that you trained together, but I don't remember if you'd done the same for him. As reluctant as I am to admit it, I'm a little envious of how easily getting to know people comes to you. I think it's something I can stand to get better at, and what better way than to learn how you do it?"

"I see." Muiren took a moment to think. "Now that you raise the subject, though, how *did* I end up meeting August? I know that he walks past our area sometimes, but I can't recall what compelled us to speak to one another. If I had to guess, it was probably– wait, no, I remember now! A couple of years ago, I signed up for the mentorship program for new hires, and he was one of the mentors too, so we had a few days where we talked to pass the time. We didn't speak much, but through the communications we did have, he always struck me as a kind person."

Kind people are good. We love kind people.

"By the way, my emails are concerningly quiet," Muiren said then. "Have you gotten anything that I perhaps wasn't copied on?"

This compelled Yidarica to look at her own emails. "No, nothing here either. This makes me worry a little, honestly. Where did we leave off, again? I think we have enough context to do some light legwork on our own until… well, until something happens, I guess."

"Right." Muiren shifted into a pensive position. "I read the initial proposition for the project, the one that was written by Iris, and in there she said that we can consider this project complete when, at the very least, there's a warning and/or disclaimer in the food application about the weather and the user assuming the risk. That means– in addition to how it functions– we're also going to have to design how that's going to look."

"And I know that's all you," Yidarica agreed. "If you could come up with a bunch of possibilities, that would be excellent. In the meantime…"

"Yeah?" Muiren asked.

"I know we need to wait for Legal to give us the official verbiage of the disclaimer and all, but something I think we also need to keep in mind is *how* this information is presented. Like we said in our meeting with Shiori, we can't just slap it in the shadows. It needs to be somewhere noticeable– but from my time in Triage, I know that it can't be obnoxious, or else it'll deter people from using the application at all. I wonder…" Yidarica began to look through her emails. "Of all the new programs Shiori was able to get me access for, I wonder if I have the ability to run polls? If I do, we can assess which kinds of in-application notifications are most likely to be read. And also the least intrusive, too."

Muiren nodded. "I didn't even think of that, but that's a great idea! There's a pretty notable difference between the two of us coming up with solutions we think are a good idea, and making a decision based on the most popular response. We'll never be able to please everyone, but we'll at least have some sort of intuitive guidance. How do you find out if you can do that?"

"It would be in the recap email that Shiori sent me, and if I don't have it, I can always ask her to look into it for me," Yidarica explained. "I certainly hope that it doesn't take twenty years like a lot of other permission-based things do. Okay, so looking at all of my emails, that's not on the list of programs I was given access to, so I'll have to ask. I think it'll be more effective if I go ask her physically. Mind holding down the fort for me until I get back?"

"Yeah, sure; I'll do my best to not drown," Muiren replied, with a wave. "Safe travels."

Yidarica was fairly confident that she could remember how to get back to the Project Garden's area, so she set off in that direction. This walk required her to pass the juice bar that she had no idea existed until today, and judging by how well-stocked it appeared to be, not many other people knew of its existence, either. She decided that on her way back, she'd make a stop to familiarize herself with this bar and how its tools functioned, and maybe make herself a drink in the process.

Continuing on her way, Yidarica decided to read the names of the meeting rooms she passed so that she could remember the way back; she'd just need to recall them backward to know that she was going the right way. There was Doughnut, followed closely by Choux, and then there was a gap before she arrived at the next one, named Mille-Feuille. After this one, she noticed that there were a group of people seated around one of the tables in this area, and stopped for about two seconds when she noticed one of them was August, the person who had been consuming her thoughts for at least the last twenty-four hours.

She could only assume that the other people he was seated with were his team, because from what she could hear from this distance, they were discussing a system glitch that was prompting random clients to provide results of a magic aptitude test, something usually given to a person when they were about six years old. As she was beginning to pass the group, in her peripheral she noticed August talking excitedly, his hands gesturing in a similar manner to the way elders moved when they told their exaggerated tales of childhood to their grandchildren.

He seems to be full of ideas.

As she continued on, drawing close enough to Shiori's desk that she could see her, Yidarica noticed one unfortunate truth: she didn't remember any of the names of the meeting rooms she had passed anymore.

Approaching Shiori's desk, Yidarica noticed that Hadiza was also seated in the area today, which hadn't happened in a little while.

Although the invisible distance between them could always be felt–this time being no exception– if there was one thing Yidarica always admired about Hadiza, it was her braids and how perfect they always seemed to be. This time, they were a dark red color, of medium thickness, and long enough that it felt reasonable to assume they reached her waist. The warm undertones matched well with her skin, an earthen shade that felt as familiar to Yidarica as her own. Hadiza usually dressed in a way that was full of neutrals and loose, plain clothing; there was something about this that gave her a calming appearance, like a person who always had advice.

Despite this, Yidarica had never been in a position where she asked Hadiza for advice. She'd sooner struggle on her own.

"You're back," Shiori noted as Yidarica arrived to her space. "Is everything going well?"

"Hm?" For the briefest of moments, Yidarica forgot why she'd come over here in the first place. "Yeah, things are going fine so far. Muiren and I were discussing how we want to go about this project, and I thought it'd be really helpful if I had the ability to run polls via Slapdash, for when we need the general public's opinion. I'm not sure if that was one of the things you got me permission for, though, so can we look through that together?"

Shiori affirmed, and turned back to her tablet. "Sure, because I don't remember if you can do that yet, either; which is on me as a manager, because now that I think about it, that'd be a really useful ability for all of you to have. Let me check and see how you can get those permissions. I know it's through a different program that integrates with Slapdash, I just need to remind myself of which one it is. Give me a moment, and I'll be able to figure that out."

"Of course," Yidarica agreed, and with Shiori busy, she turned to her teammate. "Good morning, Hadiza."

She looked up, a nondescript look on her face. "Good morning, Yidarica. I heard you and Muiren were the ones who got picked to be yelled at by those Legal people."

Yidarica couldn't help but smile a little at that. "Yeah, we're the lucky ones."

"Well, y'all have fun with that." Hadiza chuckled. "If I get time to, though, I do want to see what you end up building. We don't get a lot of work that goes that high up."

"It is a rarity," agreed Shiori. "I think the only time I worked on a high profile project like this was around when we first hired Muiren, which ended up becoming one of the Food & Goods application's biggest overhauls up to that point. Our manager wasn't going to let them work on it with us because they were so new, but they advocated for themself so strongly that I knew they'd do great here in the future."

"Oh. You know, because I filled your spot, I guess I never thought about the fact that you worked alongside Muiren and Hadiza at one point," Yidarica admitted.

Shiori nodded. "Yep, we were a dream team for a little while. Me being so young, Muiren was the first non-binary person I'd ever met, actually. I thought they'd hate me because I'd constantly fudge their pronouns in the beginning, but I'm at least fairly confident now that they won't poison my coffee if I leave it out," she smirked.

"Can any of us ever *really* be sure Muiren won't do something to our coffee if we leave it out, though?" Hadiza asked, clearly being humorous.

The chances are low, but never zero. I like Muiren, but they do kind of have this embodiment of chaos within them that makes me feel like my life would be in danger if I ever got on their bad side.

Thankfully, I have no intention of ever getting on their bad side.

"There we go. Yidarica, you and Muiren– and you too, Hadiza– should now be able to run polls in Slapdash. I sent a tutorial and troubleshooting document to our team chat, and as always, you can ask me about anything you don't understand. If I don't have the answer, I can find you the person that does."

"You're the best, Shiori." Yidarica waved, and started to leave before having to stop.

Wait… which way did I come from, again?

Chapter Seven

As Yidarica was remiss to admit, the more she learned, the more she realized there weren't really any reasons for her to strike up a conversation with August that were related to work. Although they both assumedly worked under the same department, their specific positions didn't seem to touch each other unless it was in very abstract ways that she couldn't figure out. This was fine, but inconvenient because that left her with one option, if she ever wanted to sate her curiosity about this man: she'd have to approach him socially.

There were many layers as to why this was not what she wanted to do.

At the foundation: there was not a single soul in this world that would ever claim that Yidarica Verbestel was a social creature. Beginning conversations with unfamiliar people was a thing she never did; in fact, every friend she currently had was the result of either being introduced by a mutual friend, or of an extrovert finding her interesting enough to take her under their wing.

Furthermore: it was always difficult to tell the appropriate level of casual conversations in the workplace because of how dubiously social workplaces were. Sure, she was cordial enough with Shiori, and she and Muiren were practically on their way to being friends, but that didn't mean this would be the case with everyone. After all, she reminded herself, there was that "walking on thin ice" feeling she always got around Hadiza, and the fact that she couldn't tell if Iris had loved or hated her during their meeting.

Additionally: she had no idea what kind of person August was. Who was to say he would even be open to having a conversation with her? Just because everyone in the Project Garden was kind, didn't mean everyone in the office was. And while Muiren had mentioned that he had been kind to *them*, that didn't mean he'd be kind to *her*. She'd lived long enough to know that she wasn't always afforded the same graces as everyone else, for reasons she didn't understand.

I should just do it. I should go up to him one day and talk to him in the cafeteria. He seems too demure to cause a scene.

Then again, this wouldn't be the first time Yidarica misread someone's temperament. There was a nonzero chance that he was *not* too demure to cause a scene, and that he certainly *would* yell at her for daring to speak to him.

Yeah, these are very healthy thoughts I'm having here.

Holding her hand up in the air, Yidarica concentrated until the object she was trying to conjure appeared: a transparent board, divided down the middle. "Okay, board. The comparison we're making today is: the pros and cons of speaking to a cute guy at work."

There was a barely audible hum before the title appeared on the board: "Speaking To Cute Gentleman At Work." One side labeled itself, "Pros," and was colored green. The other labeled itself, "Cons," and was colored red.

"Beautiful. Now let's think about this." It was a silly statement to make, given that the board was only semi-sentient and didn't have the capacity for independent thought; Yidarica knew this, but felt more comfortable framing things as if this were a group project. That way, she didn't have to consider the implications that came with the fact that she was talking to herself.

Reasons to, or not to, talk to someone who she had never spoken to before…

Well, there is my track record.

"It's probably a little silly to have my history preclude my potential getting to know someone new, but…" Yidarica sighed. "Humans are creatures of very specific behavioral patterns. All you have to do is study them long enough, and you recognize those patterns. And a pattern that surrounds me, for better or worse, is cute people not being interested in me. Let's put it up, board."

Sparkling lights scrawled the words: *Yidarica's track record with attractive people.*

Without her saying anything, the board added: *Worries surrounding the work environment.*

That wasn't wrong. How tense would things be if they went badly? Would a complaint be filed? Would Shiori take this project away from her? Would she be moved to a different department? Maybe even fired?

"There has to be some potential good in this situation, right?"

The board hummed again for a second before writing on the Pros side: *Silencing the negative voices in Yidarica's mind.*

She chuckled. "Yeah, those guys do get pretty loud, huh. Not to jump the gun or anything, but: if the initial talk goes well, we could maybe end up being friends, kinda, like me and Muiren are."

The board wrote: *Potential new friendship.* Then, again, the board wrote without prompting: *Potential for more than solely friendship.*

"Let's not get ahead of ourselves," Yidarica said when she saw that. "Maybe we should give it some time before we suspend our disbelief *that* far."

The board obeyed, and erased that entry.

"Everything looks pretty even as it is," Yidarica noticed as she sat up. "Okay. Then, maybe I'll let things happen as they may. If he never speaks to me of his own accord, I'll leave it be. And if we do end up speaking to one another, I'll let that play out on its own without being too defeatist about it. Or I'll try to, at least. Thanks, board. You've done well."

The board sparkled a bit before it disappeared.

"Now, just because I'm absolving to let this happen as it will…" Yidarica summoned all of her strength to flop out of her bed, and turned to her closet. "I'm not above a little silent influence."

It was time to select the outfit she would wear to the office, and so, she walked over to her closet and flung the doors open. Hanging dresses, sweaters, outerwear, and dress shirts greeted her. This would be the workshop from which she would construct a compliment-worthy ensemble; one that would be sure to gain the attention of August (and probably a bunch of other people in the building, too).

"What color are we going to be working with?" Yidarica asked herself as she filed through all of her hanging articles of clothing. This was usually the first question she asked herself, if she wasn't particular about a specific clothing item to wear. "I feel like I wear blue a lot, so maybe I can venture away from that. What is the opposite of blue on the color wheel? Isn't it orange?"

Upon saying this, Yidarica remembered that she had a tiered skirt with an orange print, one which she hadn't worn in a long time; some of the lace trim had been torn, so she had needed to take it to a tailor to get fixed but dragged it out due to constantly forgetting, or not having enough energy to make the stop; by the time she had gotten it tailored, months had passed. It would be great to wear it again!

But where did she leave it?

That's the million-dollar question.

"Until I find that skirt, I need to find some attire to go with it, and I already know the perfect pair of tights and a cardigan to pair with it," Yidarica reached for the only orange cardigan she owned, which was a very vibrant shade, and was cropped, with ruffles on all of its hems. From there, she placed it on her bed before heading to one of her dresser drawers, sifting through the hosiery before finding what she was looking for: a pair of white striped lace tights.

Now, what was a suitable shirt to go with all of this? The body of the skirt she had yet to find was a cream color, so maybe she'd have a shirt that matched it? She knew that she had plenty of cream-toned tops, but would one of them be suitable for the rest of the coord?

"Oh! Here's the skirt!" Yidarica smiled as she pulled her coveted skirt out of the closet: a cream-colored, two-tiered circle skirt with burnt orange ruffle trim on both tiers. The print on the skirt was made up of oranges in both sliced and whole forms, as well as orange blossoms, seemingly painted with oil paints. It was a lovely piece, and after seeing it, Yidarica immediately knew she needed to find her cream silk blouse to go with it, the one that had ribbons at the rounded collar to tie into a bow.

There it was. If this outfit didn't entice August to speak to her, she didn't know what would.

***

"You know, I just realized. And pardon me for taking so long to do so, but I don't think I've ever asked what it is you do for work."

Zaya was seated on Yidarica's couch, with a glass of ice water in one of her hands. Today, she was wearing a long-sleeved floral-print dress, adorned with an assortment of purple flowers. It was a beautiful dress, but every now and then, Yidarica would have thoughts about how perfectly the dark blue of the background of the dress perfectly contrasted Zaya's fair skin, and the way the cut of the dress gave her the most tasteful cleavage.

"Really? I thought I mentioned it already, but maybe I didn't. I work at a tech company in one of the offices downtown, on a project team." Yidarica was always purposefully vague about her work until she knew how the person she was talking to would react to her working for a large company. There were people who had less than positive opinions of MFI... and then there were people who could seek to use her because of her connection to the company.

And as much as I like Zaya, I can't let that blind me to the reality. I'm too old to be getting played like that.

"Oh, okay. Big important corporate stuff." Zaya nodded. "Respect. I don't know if I'd ever be able to survive in that kind of workspace. Though I guess being in communications won't be too much better, once I break into that."

This was a reaction Yidarica never knew how to perceive. Sure, her company was corporate, but fortunately they were also pretty relaxed about pretty much everything: she was shocked at the nature of some of the conversations she'd overheard at work, it wasn't at all common in the industry to have lunch spreads that were as lavish as the ones she commonly ate there, and Yidarica was personally extremely aware that she wouldn't be able to dress the way she did in any other corporate setting. She knew her workspace was unconventional to its industry, but it was hard to explain that to people who weren't familiar with it.

"Both stressful environments, to be sure," was what she decided to say.

"Mm." Zaya nodded again, placing her water on the table. "Even if I'm not currently working in my industry, I know how things are going to be once I do. Sometimes, even the thought stresses me out. But even so, I'm not too worried; I wouldn't have studied communications if I wasn't prepared to deal with everything that comes with it. I'm sure I'll learn ways to de-stress."

At this, Zaya turned to Yidarica, hesitating before moving so that she could sit right beside her, and brush her bangs aside. "It'd be nice if I could spend some time with a pretty girl like you to do that."

Okay. Even I'm not that oblivious. "You are *definitely* flirting with me, huh?" Yidarica asked, just to be sure.

"I am if you want me to be," Zaya replied with a smirk.

Oh, Mother, finally something is turning out the way I want it to.

Too afraid that she'd say something to ruin the moment, Yidarica opted to instead lean in and initiate a kiss, one which Zaya eagerly reciprocated. It was a much more sultry kiss than either expected, quickly but naturally progressing to the usage of tongues, and lasting until both women needed to catch their breath, smiling at one another.

When they kissed again, Zaya's hands eagerly reaching for the buttons to Yidarica's shirt, she asked, "You okay with messing around a little?"

Was she? Her initial instinct was to always say no, but there was a growing part of her that wanted to go a little further; she couldn't tell if it was desire or just curiosity. After all, the idea of opening up just a few more of those buttons felt just as exciting as it did nerve-wracking. Plus, she couldn't pretend that she hadn't been sneaking glances at those beautiful milky white breasts peeking out of that dress. There had to be a reason that she was willing to even entertain the thought, for once, and she had never felt unsafe around Zaya. But was feeling safe enough to take such a large leap?

Noticing the extended pause, Zaya hummed in thought, glancing down at the buttons she had already undone. "This doesn't have to be anything you don't want it to be. If you want, we can stop right now; I just need to know what it is you want from me."

"What if I'm not really sure?" Yidarica asked.

"Not sure? Well…" Zaya thought again. "We can wait until you are. Or, we can try some things out, test the boundaries a little."

The idea of "trying things out" was what excited Yidarica in this moment. She'd never thought she'd have a choice in this sort of thing; that any potential partners would sense her trepidation, and either force her or be completely turned off.

A nod was all that was needed, before Zaya gently grasped one of her hands, holding it with both of hers before placing it onto her chest, encouraging her to touch before nudging it under her dress.

"Is this your first experience with a woman?" Zaya asked softly.

"Kind of." Yidarica wasn't sure how to classify the things that had transpired while she had been away at school. They were curious touches like this, enthusiastically agreed upon between her and a couple of other girls, but she still wasn't sure how she felt about the self-proclaimed straight girls on campus doing that type of thing with no (admitted) attraction behind it. Were they exploring, or were they exploiting? The answer was impossible to tell.

"If you don't mind, I can show you what feels good," Zaya replied, slipping one of her own hands between the opening of buttons she'd created; moving past all of Yidarica's layers of undershirts and a bra, to grasp her breast. A few lingering kisses on her neck ensued as she felt fingers swirling around her nipple in the most enticing way, trying her best to repeat what she was feeling.

It's good. It's so good.

"Come here," Zaya gently patted her lap. "I can tell you like that. Let me make it even better."

Curiously, Yidarica did as asked; and hadn't been sitting for long before Zaya lifted her shirt completely, wasting no time in holding one breast and taking the other into her mouth, sucking as her tongue teased the nipple. Before Yidarica could react, though, the clattering of a vibrating phone on wood interrupted the moment.

Zaya sighed. "It's my dad. Do you mind if I take this?"

"Far be it for me to interrupt," Yidarica shrugged.

As Zaya spoke to her father on the phone in a tone very indicative of someone trying to end the conversation as quickly as possible, Yidarica sat on the couch, in a sudden state of discomfort.

I shouldn't have let things go so far. Why did I..? I feel disgusting. I know I wanted it at the time, but now, I feel so used. And I don't blame Zaya for any of these feelings. I just…

She pulled her shirt back on.

No messing around with people I'm not dating. That has to be why I'm repulsed. Right? And that's why the things that happened in college also had that sense of ickiness that came with it. I need to get a hold of myself. Just because I want something doesn't mean I should always agree to it.

When Zaya returned to the room, she reached for her keys. "I'm sorry, I know the moment has passed anyway; but I need to go. Dad was on one of the ladders, hanging some planters, and fell. He isn't doing great."

Yidarica gasped. "Oh, no. How bad is it, if you're willing to say?"

"He's awake, at least, but my aunt who's with him now was telling me that there's no way around him having surgery. I'm heading to the hospital where he was taken, and I'll let him know you send your best wishes," she replied, smiling in a slightly mischievous way.

"Okay. I hope his surgery goes well," Yidarica knew her voice sounded pitiful at this point, but she was quite fond of Mr. Linyi at this point given all the times she'd had to visit his nursery when one of her plants died. The thought of anything bad happening to him made her inexplicably sad.

Zaya was at the door now, her hand on the doorknob before turning back to Yidarica. "When this is all settled, we'll have to pick up where we left off sometime."

When the door shut, Yidarica had one thought:

Or don't. Not picking up is perfectly fine too.

Chapter Eight

The rain was back today.

Many, many years ago, a relative of Yidarica's had given her a hat to wear in the rain; one of those special hats that had been imbued by magic to keep its wearer safe from the assault of rain and humidity. She had kept the hat to this day, but it didn't always fit on her head anymore. If her hair was pulled up or too fluffy, it wouldn't stay; and, unfortunately, the previous night, she'd put considerable time into ensuring her hair would be nice and fluffy.

Someday, she'd gain foresight. But today was not that day.

The one drawback to riding the Comtran was that it required a moderate level of walking to, which meant there would be considerable time spent outside, exposed to the elements. And, sure, there was always an opportunity to dry herself off once she got to the office, but the problem with that was, Yidarica hated being involuntarily wet. Her feelings toward unwelcome moisture passed the realm from unpleasant into downright painful, almost. If she was made to go more than three minutes at maximum wearing soaked clothes, her mind would yell at her to claw off her skin until those damn clothes were no longer touching her body. Her commute to work was much longer than three minutes, and the last thing she wanted to do was draw attention to herself in a public space.

To her credit, she was usually able to resist any actual clawing, but it was never easy, and got progressively more difficult the longer she remained wet.

She could attempt to cast a spell of dryness over herself before she left home, but she didn't remember any by heart, nor did she remember which of her magic study books they were listed in. Her brain fog had been exceptionally annoying lately, getting in the way of remembering anything that wasn't top of mind.

There was always walking, but in addition to needing to first cast a spell she didn't remember, and requiring stamina she didn't have, walking would have required her to have woken up much earlier than she had. If she walked to the office now, she'd be late.

Sighing, she decided that squishing her hair under her hat was the most efficient way to go with this. A part of her died inside seeing how badly she was ruining all of the styling she'd done the previous night, but her hope was that if she got her hair into the hat in a specific way, she'd be able to fluff it back up once she got to work.

***

The hair was not fluffing back up at work.

Even with the added advantage of getting to work earlier than usual because many people hadn't left their houses today (which meant the Comtran didn't stop as often), this was clearly not going to go the intended way with enough time to grab breakfast and start the day. With a resigned sigh, Yidarica settled for the bare minimum of not looking like she had hat hair, and continued on to the cafeteria for breakfast. A nice omelet with spinach would surely lift her spirits, and stopping by the drink bar near where she and Muiren sat didn't sound like too bad of an idea, either. After the disappointment that was her hair, a consolation juice sounded amazing.

When she got to the drink bar, Yidarica was pleased to see that there were still plenty of fresh fruits available, and no one was at the bar at all. This wasn't uncommon on rainy days. It was like once those drops of rain hit the pavement, there was a collective consensus among most people to not brave the outdoors until they were dry again.

As she was busy slicing her oranges and strawberries into juicer-friendly pieces, Yidarica didn't notice another person had come to the bar until she picked up her plate of fruit and turned toward where the juicer was. Abruptly, she was face-to-face (or more like face-to-chest) with the very man she'd been wanting to speak to for the past month– August, today wearing black jeans and still wearing his raincoat, which was dark blue with gray and green plaid stripes.

Yep. He's just as cute as the last time I saw him.

"Oh, it's you!" she said before she realized she was speaking aloud.

The slightly confused look she got in return meant that she'd have to try and recover this fumble somehow. "You... no, it's just, I notice you walk past where my team sits a lot, but I don't... I never... I don't think we've ever spoken, I just recognize you because of that. Um, hi. I'm Yidarica."

How many seconds passed between them before either of them moved? Realistically, probably no more than three, but in that moment it certainly felt closer to three *hundred*. And with each passing second, Yidarica could feel her stomach dropping– plummeting to the very bottom of the earth this building was built upon, until she saw the progression from confusion to a half-smile upon this man's face.

She wasn't imagining things, right? That was a smile?

"August. Pleased to meet you. I see you all the time around the office too– you're probably the most memorable person in this building, by the way. Very bright."

Immediately, she knew he was referring to her clothes. "Oh, well, you know. I like… highly feminine clothing and all its accoutrements," Yidarica's hands would have been flaring out her skirt if she hadn't already been holding something, because that was her habit whenever her clothes were being called into question, but this time she settled for turning her hips in a way that would flare the skirt a bit.

"Well, they're fun." August gave her a full smile now, and she feared she may melt. "I don't think I've ever seen where you sit, though. What kind of work do you do here?"

"The…" for a moment there, Yidarica completely forgot what she did for a living, but she was fortunately able to quickly recall it. "Gar– the– I'm in the Project Garden, we do… projects and stuff."

"For the Sustenance Department, right?" August asked as he turned and reached into the nearby refrigerator to retrieve the orange juice. "No wonder you see me pass by, then. I'm under the same department, but my team works on technical glitches related to food providers; things of the, 'instead of being paid in currency I was paid in bananas' variety."

"Oh, my condolences." Yidarica said this before she could think about it, and panicked, before she heard August laugh; a light, airy, jovial laugh that sent a sensation of warmth through her body.

His laugh is just as cute as the rest of him.

"Definitely not a team for everyone," he replied once he had calmed down. "But it's not the worst job a person could have, either, so I can't complain too much." He shrugged as he twisted the cap back onto the orange juice, and took a quick sip from his cup. In the process, he noticed the clock on the wall behind Yidarica. "Oh, is it that time already? I'm gonna need to start the walk back to my desk if I want to get started on time. Nice finally meeting you, Yidarica."

"Of course! You as well!" She waved, feeling as though she was now slowly descending from the cloud she'd been floating on this entire time.

***

"Are we having a good day so far, then?"

Yidarica had never understood the expression "shit-eating grin," but she was pretty sure that when people used that expression, they were referring to an expression not unlike the one Muiren currently had on their face. She had never seen them with such a simultaneously happy and smug look on their face, so something had to have happened.

"I mean, I guess? No complaints on my commute; despite the rain, it went pretty smoothly. Why, did something interesting happen before I got here?"

"You ought to know." Muiren pulled out their work tablet, and gave it a few taps with their finger to turn the display on. "Despite the day's weather being so gloomy, I don't think I've ever seen you as sunny as just now, when you were talking to August."

Oh, dear Mother. Muiren had seen them talking? Now that Yidarica was trying to recall, she supposed she may have seen a flash of red go by her peripheral vision at one point, but Muiren wasn't the only person here with red hair. How was she supposed to have known that she was being watched?

"The last thing I'm here to do is judge you, Yidarica. But you'd think we've known each other long enough for you to have been straightforward about why you asked me about him in the first place," Muiren laughed. "Would that I knew anything else about him other than what I already told you, I'd let you know, though. I know it's none of my business, *but,* the two of you certainly do look nice beside each other."

Suddenly, Yidarica was overtaken by a foreign feeling. The unsteady knees of bashfulness, combined with shyness and... some third thing. This was a type of compliment she'd never heard directed at her. She didn't have the script in her head for how to respond. What was she supposed to say? Would Muiren hate her if she didn't say anything?

Both were then distracted by the unmistakable sound of a Slapdash notification. It had gone solely to Yidarica.

```
New message from Shiori Montalban
Just got notified of a family emergency, so I'll
be leaving at 10. I had a meeting with Dahlia
that I had to cancel, so I told her to email
you the information we were going to discuss
instead. If you have any questions reach out to
Henley
```

Now here was a name that wasn't familiar. "Muiren, do you know of a... Henley?"

Almost immediately, Muiren turned to their tablet and began typing. "I think that's the manager for another of the teams under the Sustenance Department, if memory serves. Hmm... oh, it's *that* guy. Yeah, he manages one of the client relations teams."

"Okay. Shiori has to leave early, so she's directing us to him if we need anything, and at least one of us should be getting an email from Dahlia today too," Yidarica explained.

At this, Muiren's expression shifted to one of discontent. "I hope that won't be the case. He's not the most pleasant person to deal with."

"Oh?" Maybe it was a good thing Yidarica had never heard of him. "How so?"

"Typical man in corporate: aggressive, apprehensive, condescends to anyone who appears feminine. Nothing unheard of, but never a good experience to be required to speak to someone like that."

As one of the most feminine people in this building, to the point that it probably bordered on obnoxious, Yidarica was inclined to agree. "Bad experiences with him?" she asked.

"You betcha. In the three and a half years I've worked here, only three people here have ever misgendered me. Want to take a guess as to who the third asshole is?" Muiren frowned. "I'd say that I don't understand why they keep him around, but unfortunately, he just so happens to be good at what he does. There's a reason Shiori directed us to him, after all."

"Well, hopefully we won't need to talk to him at all," Yidarica said then, pulling up her emails.

Muiren nodded in agreement, and was going to turn to their work as well, but then turned to Yidarica again. "By the way, where is Nanda? I just realized I haven't seen her at all since I've been back."

They were speaking of the fourth and final member of the Project Garden, Nanda, who was the youngest of the team; Yidarica didn't know exactly how old she was, but knew she was the only person here she could think of who was younger than Shiori. "Oh, Nanda's on maternity leave," she explained. "She should be back soon, actually. It's been a little while now."

"Is that so? Well, that's exciting! I'm told that starting a family– as long as that's what the person carrying the child is intending to do– is fulfilling. I hope she's doing well," Muiren said. "Does that sound weird? I never know what to say whenever the topic of children is brought up. It's such a foreign topic to me that it's hard to construct words in a way that makes sense."

"Makes two of us then," Yidarica replied. "I'm not a person who aspires to parenthood, and the few close friends I have aren't either, so at this point it feels weird whenever I remember that it's a really important thing for some people. When Nanda broke the news to us, though, she seemed very happy about it, so I'm happy for her."

"I think we can both manage to be happy for her in that way, then," Muiren said. "I didn't realize you also live the childfree life, but it's really reassuring to meet someone older than me that's stayed true to that belief despite outside pressure. My grandpa– the one that's currently living– sends me a card every year for my birthday asking when I'm going to find a nice man to settle down with and give him some grandchildren. He's senile, so I always wonder if it's frowned upon to tell him 'absolutely fucking never' if he's going to forget I said it in a week."

Yidarica frowned. "It's especially weird given that, respectfully, I never would have thought you were into men."

"That's because I'm not." Muiren laughed, but stopped when they turned to their tablet. "This damn thing is refusing to load any of our programs. It can't be a company-wide issue, because I was able to use it a few moments ago, and you got that message from Shiori. What's happening here?"

"Do you think you might need to go to maintenance?" Yidarica suggested. "Everything is still working fine for me; okay, the one spreadsheet is lagging, but I mean, it always does that."

"As I recall, maintenance only handles hardware issues, and I think the tablet itself is fine; it's the software that's the issue. Who do we go to for software issues, again?"

Whenever a program of mine doesn't work, I usually tell Shiori and she gets it fixed, so software probably falls somewhere under managerial duties. It's a shame that our manager just left. "I have an answer, but you're not going to like it."

"And I was dreading that it was the solution." Muiren sighed. "Fine, I'll go and get it over with."

"*We'll* go." Yidarica corrected them, and stood. "There's no reason you need to go alone to speak to someone that you've already had issues with. Plus, I'm pretty sure that me being able to pull rank as the leader of this project will be helpful. Where are we heading?"

★★★

When Muiren had mentioned Henley being a typical man in corporate, Yidarica had imagined a specific type of appearance for him. And, when the two of them got to the area where he presided over his team, she was not surprised at all to see that she had been mostly correct. His dark blond hair was cut short, and the silhouette of it– coupled with the full beard around his round face– gave his head a sort of oval shape. He was standing when the two had approached, so it easy to see that he was about average height and just a bit on the heavy side, something that would perhaps be less obvious if the white polo he was wearing had been fitted correctly.

She had practiced what she was going to say on the way here, but actually getting to where her destination was made it more difficult to want to do it. Her legs began to feel weak. Her stomach twisted.

I can do this. I have to do this. Muiren is counting on me, and after I already unloaded some of my responsibilities on them when I had them set up that meeting, I can't do anything else that might have them call into question my effectiveness as a leader.

And as anxious a person as Yidarica tended to be, she was also very aware that her desire to protect the people she was fond of often superseded her anxiety. She'd seen this in practice in many aspects of her life, including at work, so she'd just have to do it again. Easy, right? She tried to convince herself as much.

She arrived at Henley's desk, and stood up straight. Her studies of human interaction said that helped, even for someone as small as her. She could feel that Muiren wasn't behind her, which was probably better at this point. Better that they didn't see what a quivering mess she was.

"Excuse me," she said, proud of her voice for not wavering. "You are Henley, correct?"

He looked down at her, his gaze of disdain immediately obvious. "What are you gonna do if I'm not?"

Before she could think, Yidarica said, "Apologize and go find who I really am looking for? It's never that serious." She knew that was slightly rude, but upon a brief reflection, decided it wasn't so bad that she needed to apologize for it. "But if you are, you probably got a message in Slapdash earlier from Shiori Montalban telling you that she diverted her direct reports to you for the remainder of the day if they run into any issues."

He frowned in a way that let Yidarica know that he knew exactly what she was talking about. "Yeah. What about it?"

"Now would be the time that those issues occurred," Yidarica replied. "We haven't met: Yidarica Verbestel, POC for the current Weather Project. My teammate Muiren Tierney– they're here with me somewhere, I think they got pulled aside by someone for a brief chat– is having a software loading issue; as of about ten minutes ago, nothing except the search engine on their tablet is responsive, and we both know maintenance will only fix hardware issues. With us unable to consult with our manager, I thought it would be reasonable to consult with you; either for direct assistance, or to redirect us to someone who's better suited to that kind of task."

It had been impossible to miss the change in expression on Henley's face when Yidarica had said Muiren's name, but she wasn't able to read it. It had seemed neither disapproving nor approving, but if she had to guess, it leaned more toward the latter; which was strange, considering she knew the two's previous interactions hadn't been amiable.

"Let me know if you want to take a look," Muiren said from behind Yidarica. She had no idea they had arrived, so hearing their voice startled her just a bit. "I know that you have to look through your own programs for software troubleshooting, but I think that may only be visible to the people who are listed directly under you."

"Well, maybe you should leave the speculation to the managers before you go thinking," Henley said as he sat down, beginning to type on his external keyboard. "What's your issue?"

"Nothing on my tablet is loading, as Yidarica *just* explained to you," Muiren replied. "We know the internet is working because we tested the search engine, which is functioning as normal and at its expected speed, but nothing else will load at all."

"And we're up to date on all of our certifications, aren't we?" asked Henley.

When it was clear that Muiren faltered because they weren't sure how to answer this, Yidarica picked up. "Yes. All of the programs that Muiren is trying to access, we were just given access to those when this project started, which was less than a month ago. The certificate would never have expired that fast."

Henley was quiet then, reading whatever was on his screen. "Did you check and see if there are any reported outages? You should know how to do that."

"I assure you that I do," Yidarica replied. "It was the very first thing I checked, but in addition to having no reported outages, all of my programs are running fine. It's just Muiren that's having the issues."

"Well, if all of that is running normally, the last resort I have for you *ladies* is to do a hard reinstall of all of the programs that are being problematic," Henley said, making sure to emphasize "ladies" in his speech. "It's probably some kind of missing obscure folder that got skipped during installation, that you've never touched until now. If that doesn't work, you can go bother maintenance about a replacement tablet, as sometimes it's the hardware refusing to cooperate, and let them handle it."

Yidarica nodded. "Noted. Your assistance is appreciated. What is *not* appreciated is your disregard of Muiren's identity. Please do better."

With that, she turned on her heel and walked away, leaving Muiren equally surprised and impressed with how she'd handled the entire interaction.

If Yidarica hadn't been as wrapped up in what she needed to say and processing her emotions that she was literally unable to notice anything else around her, she would have noticed that this area of the office was also where August's team sat. She would have also noticed that Muiren wasn't with her, because August had called them aside.

"Hey, is Yidarica all right?" he asked them. "I just saw her walk by, and I don't think I've ever seen her look so intense."

"Ah, I wouldn't worry about it. It was just her first encounter with the asshole in chief over there, but she handled it extremely well," they replied, but then realized who had asked this question, and realized this was an excellent opening. "Wait a minute. Since when are you and Yidarica acquainted?"

"Well, she…" August had clearly been flustered by this question. "We've spoken. I spoke with her for the first time this morning."

Muiren nodded. "Yeah. And yet, the turn of phrase, 'I don't think I've ever seen her look so intense' makes it sound as though you have more experience than that with seeing her."

"Yes. Even before we'd spoken, there would be times where I would notice her around the office," August explained. "It would be kind of hard not to. Her clothes stand out from everyone's here. I really admire her commitment to frills and pastels, and it's like she always chooses the best palettes to complement the ombre of her hair, as well as the lovely brown shade of her skin."

Muiren smirked. "So she does. Well, at any rate, I need to get back to the grind. She's gonna be fine, August– but if you're that worried, I'm sure she wouldn't object to some positive reinforcement, especially from you."

August waved, completely missing the implication of Muiren's last statement.

Back in the work area they had claimed, Muiren sat beside Yidarica, who was clearly having a moment where she needed to regulate her breathing.

That was horrible. That was awful. I hope I never have to do that again. I don't know if I can do that again.

Whenever she tried to move past it, her mind would immediately recall Henley's condescending tone and glares of disapproval, and pull them to the forefront, causing her to become distressed all over again.

I should have handled that better. I don't know how I could've done better, but I should have. There should never have been an opportunity for that man to have misgendered Muiren again, or for him to have been so mean. What did Shiori do to have him agree to help us in the first place? Why didn't I ask her? I guess I didn't know the guy we were being directed to was a jerk until she was already gone, but I still should have asked questions.

Wait. I recognize this. This is that thing I do where I hold myself to unrealistic expectations. I need to not do that. But how?

I need to breathe, before anything else. I can do that, right? Inhale… exhale…

Now that Yidarica appeared to have calmed down some, Muiren put an arm around her shoulders. "Hey."

Yidarica looked up, startled by the sensation. "Yeah?"

"I get the feeling you had to do a lot of mental work to be able to handle that conversation, but you did great," Muiren said. "I mean it. With the exception of Shiori, I don't think anyone's ever stood up for me so firmly. You know me– you know I'm not afraid to be a ballbuster when I need to, but it's always nice to have someone else defend my honor, so to speak."

"It just irritates me," Yidarica replied. "It's not hard to listen when someone tells you how to refer to them. If he could remember your name and face, he could remember your pronouns and gender identity."

"Still." Muiren smiled. "I appreciate it. You did great otherwise too. You've always been so quiet, ever since you joined the Garden at least, but it's also been really obvious to me from day one that you know your stuff. So, it's nice seeing you in a role where you also know that about yourself, and confidently convey as much."

That's probably the biggest compliment I've ever gotten on my work here. I don't know what to say.

"Well, at any rate, I don't know how to reinstall programs so I'm gonna go bother the guys over in maintenance," they said then. "Take it easy for now. I'll bring back snacks."

Chapter Nine

"Wow, you've been here for a while now, huh?"

Somehow, the most perfect chain of events had transpired: Yidarica got to work early enough to sit and eat her breakfast somewhere that wasn't her desk, so she settled on the garden– the garden where, almost as soon as she sat down, she'd been joined by August. He didn't have any food with him, but had asked if he could sit with her. And now, they were talking to one another about work.

"Oh, yeah," Yidarica agreed. "But I wasn't always part of the Project Garden. I actually started out in Triage, which is something that's really difficult to actually get good at, because you're constantly being hit by all of these different and unique situations, and you have to use your best discernment to decide where they should go. Nevertheless, I think I got fairly good at it, and that helped when I interviewed for this position. Shiori, my manager, had just taken on the role she's in now, so they needed someone to retroactively fill her spot. The hiring committee seemed to think I was it."

August nodded. "So, Triage is being done by actual people. I didn't know that. It's– back at the job I had before this one, we had this really big mailroom; we were intrinsically tied to the postal service, so the mailroom was a big deal. By the time I was hired, though, most of the main operations were done with magic. I asked about it once, because I was curious, but my supervisor didn't explain it very well. He just said they wanted to be sure human hands didn't ruin everything."

"Oh." Yidarica didn't know how she felt about that sentiment. On one hand, she'd been able to personally experience how the hands of man were often underhanded; working with the sole goal of furthering their own means, with a complete disregard for who or what could be hurt in the process. But so too had she been able to see the beauty that man could create with their hands.

"I can understand why someone would feel that way, but I still find myself feeling a bit... crestfallen over how cynical the whole train of thought is." August rested a hand under his chin, indicating he was thinking about something.

"For sure," Yidarica agreed softly. Louder, she asked, "So no breakfast?"

When she said that, it was as if a lightbulb had lit over August's head. "Oh! Thank you for reminding me," he said, picking up his work bag, and rummaging through it for a few moments before pulling out what could have possibly been the most boring-looking trail mix bar that had ever existed.

"Seriously? This sad beige nutrient bar is your breakfast?"

"Hey. It's got raisins," August defended himself, obviously amused. "I'm not usually hungry this early, but breakfast *is* the most important meal of the day, so I like to try and eat at least a little something, you know?"

Yidarica gave him a look that made it clear she wasn't convinced. "Whole ass breakfast buffet and this is what you decide is quality eats. So, your questionable breakfast habits aside, we've talked about what I do here. Your turn! Although I can assume there's probably a lot of unpleasant interactions involved with your day-to-day life here."

"I'll put it this way: I've learned a lot of new ways to curse someone, both verbally and magically," August replied. "But even with that, as I mentioned the day we met: this is one of the better jobs I've had in my life, so I can't complain too much. Sometimes I get to speak to some genuinely kind people, which is grounding; but at the same time, I doubt it's a surprise that I'm actively looking for openings on other teams, too."

"Very much not surprising," agreed Yidarica. "I hope that's going well."

"It's going." August laughed a little. "I've managed to get a few interviews recently, which are welcome. I can't remember the last time I got to that stage. The other day, I was able to speak with… uh… darn it. I forgot their name, but the interview was for a position in the Project Biome–"

"The Project Biome was hiring?!" When? How had Yidarica missed that? Even if it was essentially the same role, she had missed her opportunity to finally get into the Weather Department?! This was disappointing. This was more than disappointing!

Meanwhile, August looked more than a little confused at her outburst. "Yeah, but for some reason, it took them a really long time to begin the interview process. I think they may have initially chosen someone who didn't work out, so they had to do the interview process again. I don't know the specifics, but at any rate, the person I spoke with seemed to really like me, which makes me feel horrible for forgetting their name."

"Oh! That's good news, that the interview went well!" Yidarica clasped her hands together. "I am hoping for only the best news for you!"

This made August smile. "Thanks, I appreciate it. It means a lot to hear that from someone I haven't known for a long time. I've really enjoyed speaking with you this morning, but I did want to get some errands out of the way before work, so I should get going; see you around."

Yidarica, meanwhile, was still in a trance brought on by August and his smile. *Does he know? Does he know that he has a smile that's so cute and amazing that it has the ability to make me weak in the knees while I'm sitting down?! I wonder if he ever uses that to his advantage.*

She continued to eat her breakfast, but it was no surprise that she wasn't able to concentrate on it like before.

***

A few days later, on a day where Yidarica was alone in the office because Muiren had specifically asked for this day to be a day they worked from home, she decided it would be a good day to revisit the library. It would give her a nice, quiet environment to analyze the results of the poll they had run. However, immediately after clocking in, she noticed a message from Shiori:

Come to my desk as soon as you read this.

Shiori had never been one for hyperbole, so Yidarica felt she was extremely justified in having this message strike the fear of the Mother into her. This was the first time she'd ever been summoned like this, with such curt language. What was so dire that she couldn't explain herself over Slapdash? Needless to say, Yidarica wasted no time in packing her things up and heading to the Project Garden's seating area.

When she arrived, Shiori and Hadiza were both seated at their desks, both working. Yidarica had been hoping that getting closer to the area would give her some clues as to what was happening, but no– everything appeared identical to a normal day in the office. This partially made everything feel even more tense and foreboding, as if the surrounding environs were being held together with a fraying thread.

"Yidarica." Shiori stood up as soon as she saw her, a hand tapping the surface of her desk. "Why is it that things seem to happen to this team at the worst times?"

This certainly didn't make her feel any better. "Because… the nature of our work is that we touch so many other aspects of the company that we're at an increased risk of being put into situations?"

"I got an email from HR today," Shiori explained. "I'm told that *someone* complained to them about both you and Muiren. What did you all get into, that day I had to leave early?"

The day Shiori had left early, and directed them to the most unpleasant person Yidarica had met so far in the entire building? That day? "Do you mean the day I was forced to communicate with a man who condescended to me with almost every sentence he spoke to me, and purposely misgendered Muiren? Because all I said to him in retaliation was that I didn't appreciate him disregarding their identity and to do better. I didn't even defend myself and my competency."

Shiori sighed. "I understand, but you have to be careful when you begin speaking with people at a certain level, especially those who are particularly high-strung. If you're not, you get put into situations like these. If the both of you end up getting suspended, who's going to work on your project?" She folded her arms and sat back in her seat, facing Yidarica. "Tell me how I'm supposed to fight this."

"I wasn't wrong!" Yidarica regretted saying this the moment it left her mouth, feeling that it made her sound immature, but knowing she couldn't take it back. "MFI prides itself on not standing for discrimination or prejudice on any fronts, which means we shouldn't abide by it happening in our own company. Also, I'm sorry, this feels incredibly frivolous to be bothering HR with. What kind of grown-ass man can't handle being told to do better? I had worse things yelled at me every day back in Triage. And also, why is the complaint about me *and* Muiren? They barely said anything the entire time we were over there."

Shiori turned back to her screen, but after reading what was on it for a few minutes, she frowned. "Actually, that's a really good question. I've read this email at least ten times now, but the body only mentions things you did."

Great. I don't know if that makes me feel better or worse.

"Shiori..?" Hadiza's voice floated over the wall of the cubicle that separated their desks. "I know I'm eavesdropping, but this can't be the same man that Muiren had to report to HR that time?"

Yidarica immediately turned to her. "When did this happen?" Shiori asked quickly.

"I think it was around the time I first got put onto the team," Hadiza replied. "Two years ago? It was definitely before you became our manager. I remember because they had asked me where HR sat, and then left. When they got back later that day, they mentioned there was a man here that made them feel unsafe because of the aggressive way he was hitting on them."

Wait a minute.

Yidarica suddenly remembered the odd look that Henley had given Muiren when they had joined the conversation; a pointed look of visual approval. *Was that because he's attracted to them? My studies of human behavior don't cover this, but I do have a wealth of secondhand knowledge about what men can be like when they're rejected. Could this be retaliation? Is this even about me, or did he see an opportunity to get back at Muiren just because he was slightly annoyed with me?*

"I have a few reasons to think we're talking about the same person," Yidarica said aloud. "Muiren mentioned that the previous interactions they'd had with this man weren't pleasant. They didn't say why, but I'm pretty sure they'd have no problem explaining why, if asked."

"I tell you to give me a way to fight this, and both of you do it with flying colors. That's why I love this team," Shiori picked up her tablet. "I have to go talk to Muiren. Wait here for me, Yidarica."

Sitting at her desk, Yidarica looked over at the photos she had pinned to the wall between her and Nanda's desks; two pictures taken at different events hosted by the fashion community where she'd met Gracia, a band picture taken after Half Past Haberdash's first show, and one picture of Runiala with her cat, Mithica.

I wonder how Mithica is doing. It's been a while. She must be an old lady now.

"I never thought you would get reported to HR before I did," she heard Hadiza say to her then.

"Yeah, I know, right?" Yidarica agreed. "Wait. That sounds mean. I didn't mean that you deserve to get reported or anything, it's just that—"

"It's okay, I know what you meant; that's what I meant too," Hadiza clarified. "You're one of the few people I know here that sits down, does their work, and minds their business. I wouldn't worry. From the sound of things, this is probably gonna get thrown out anyway."

Even so, I worry that it'll stay on my record. I hope it doesn't get in the way when I apply for a new position eventually. "We can only hope, right?"

Yidarica felt her phone vibrate then, and saw that she'd gotten a text message from Zaya.

> **Dad's going in for the big surgery today. I'll be with him all day. I'll tell him you send your best.**

Work had been busy lately, and Yidarica felt guilty that it had taken its toll on her ability to hold regular conversations with Zaya. Part of her wondered if it was because she didn't want to delve into the complicated situation of what would happen the next time they saw each other, but she knew part of it was also because she was worried about her father. She knew it was unhealthy, but her thought process was that, if she didn't speak to Zaya, she didn't have to know whether or not her father was doing worse.

Knowing that Shiori would be gone for a while, she quickly texted back:

> **Thanks. Hope the surgery goes perfectly.**

As long as she had to stay put, Yidarica decided she could at least get a head start on the day's work. She pulled up the poll dashboard, reading through the responses. It appeared that most people were concerned with warning notifications being invasive, to the point where a couple of them mentioned they'd uninstalled applications that gave them too many notifications. There was also a trend of people saying they disliked notifications that required an action, for similar reasons.

So, something that didn't require action, but was recognizable enough that they wouldn't be skirting the law. How would they accomplish that?

Yidarica's attention was diverted from her phone when she heard two women talking, passing behind her desk. "...which really is a shame, you know. They say life begins at forty years old, and here she is, with her life beginning to end. At least her new glasses are stylish."

"Well, it's not Complete Dark, right? She still has time to reverse it."

"I don't think she will. After her husband cheated on her, I doubt she's able to trust anyone anymore."

"Oh, that's right. I forgot about that part. Hm, what a pity."

Yidarica's mood turned somber at hearing this exchange. *I wonder, is this how people speak of me when I'm not around? Or how they're going to in the relatively near future? I guess I have the advantage of not being cheated on, but still, I'm closer to forty than twenty.*

Time is running out.

"We are cooking with gas," Shiori said before she could even get back to her seat. "Yidarica, don't worry about this; Muiren and I can take it from here. This is very clearly a case of someone scorned trying to retaliate, and I will not have a single person in this building bringing anyone from my team into some mess that doesn't have anything to do with it. I might need to borrow Muiren a few more times today depending on what HR says and does, but otherwise, the two of you can get back to work."

"Thanks, Shiori." Yidarica stood. "Sorry for the trouble."

"Eh. Now that I know the whole situation, I can see that you weren't in the wrong," Shiori waved it off. "Remember what I told you about choosing your words carefully; but at the same time, I am also *very* proud to see you gaining confidence. You're going to do great things here, I can tell."

Yidarica smiled bashfully. "Um, thanks."

As she walked back toward the library, Yidarica heard a notification go off, but decided it could wait until she sat down, since she wasn't going far. The message she received, fortunately, made her laugh at what this morning had been.

New message from Muiren Tierney
dude what the hell was that.

***

Today's lunch offerings didn't look amazing, but there was flatbread pizza, which seemed hard to mess up; Yidarica chose to take her chances with that. Realistically, how could the combination of bread, tomato sauce, and cheese ever be bad? She sat, hoping her logic wasn't flawed.

Is this how I've always taken lunch? It hasn't been that long since we started this project, and yet, compared to eating lunch with Muiren, this feels so lonely.

A bite into the crust shooed away any fears Yidarica could have possibly had. There were echoes of an unfamiliar herb somewhere in there. Did the cooks post a recipe log anywhere? Maybe a cookbook in the library? It would be useful; she pondered stopping by the library sometime today to check.

Speaking of recipes, I never made my grocery list... I should probably do that now, while it's on my mind.

Yidarica silently summoned a checklist, using the same trusty checklist spell she'd learned when she first started college. It worked amazingly... whenever she remembered that it was an option. All she needed to do was dictate her grocery list to it, and give it a time to reappear so that she could reference it. She preferred going to get groceries on her off days, so she could devote all of her energy to the task; that was in two days, so she set the time for then.

Why doesn't magic simply let us summon the groceries to our refrigerators? That would make everything so easy. But then that would get rid of her entire department here, or at least make it a lot smaller.

As she continued to ponder this, she was distracted by the sound of someone placing a bowl on the table, beside her. She looked up, and saw August pulling up a chair.

"I hope it's okay if I sit here," he said. "We had such a nice breakfast together that I assumed you'd want to replicate that feeling for lunch. Wait. Now that I say that out loud, that is *really* forward. Should I– should I go? I'll go."

"No, August, it's okay!" Yidarica reassured him. "It's fine. I was just thinking about how quiet lunch is without having Muiren with me, so it'd be nice to have some company. What's in the bowl?"

August looked down at his bowl, confused for a moment. "It's some kind of noodle broth dish. It looked good in the pictures on the menu, so I figured it wouldn't hurt to try," he explained. "How is the flatbread?"

"Delicious." Yidarica grinned as she took a bite. "How's the day been treating you?"

"It's treating me," August replied, and when he said this, Yidarica could feel every bit of resignation in his voice. "In the few hours since we last saw each other, my team has discovered a major glitch in the input fields for client information. We don't yet know enough about it to know the extent of the damage, but the whole reason we found out about it was because I had to call someone who was clearly not in the mood to talk to anyone here, because the glitch has caused their standing with their clientele to take a nosedive. Days like this are hard. They're hard and they're exhausting. I wish I had somewhere to take a nap."

At the mention of a nap, Yidarica wondered if she should tell August about the secret nook in the library that she'd curled up in before on her lowest energy days. But at this point, she didn't know him well enough to be able to discern how he'd react to the information. How could she be sure he wouldn't tell other people? She'd already been reported to HR once today, and really didn't need the stress of that happening again. Besides, this was information that would probably be of no use to him; he'd never be able to get those legs to fit in there.

"A nap would be heavenly," was what she decided to say.

"I might just check with my manager to see if I can call it a day early. I spent so much energy dealing with the fiasco that was this morning, she should understand if I do. So, how about you? How are things with that project?"

"We've only just recently started it, so we're still in that phase where we have to gather as much information as we can," Yidarica replied. "There's a component of this project that needs to be sanctioned by Legal, so there's a certain level of, uh, what do you call that? When you don't completely know what you're going to be doing, it creates a level of unfamiliarity. You know?"

"I'm familiar with the concept." August nodded.

"The project itself is going fine, so it's a shame that I got reported to HR today because some men are children in adult bodies," Yidarica continued. "My manager told me not to worry about it, so I'll try my best not to, but the long and short of it is that I was a little curt in my interaction with someone here and they used that as ammunition to complain about someone they've had… issues with in the past, I guess. If the issue is what I'm told it is, it feels wrong to even call it that, but it kind of has nothing to do with me so I'm being told to just wait."

The expression on August's face was one of intrigue. "I can't imagine you being curt enough to anyone to warrant a complaint to your manager, let alone HR. That's ridiculous. I hope that you get the best outcome you can receive in this situation."

"Yeah, I hope so too," she agreed.

August picked up his soup spoon then. It was easy to tell he was trying his best to not make any noise as he slurped it into his mouth, and he did manage to at least be quieter than people usually were when they slurped soup.

He's being so considerate. And cute. Wait, am I watching him eat? And am I being obvious about it?!

Fortunately, August was busy looking down at his bowl, moving its contents around with his chopsticks. "There's a really good selection of vegetables in here, wow. I didn't expect to see potatoes in here, and I'm really loving the thinly sliced cabbage leaves. I'm no cook, but I feel like this would be even better with the inclusion of something crispy. Onions are always good."

"I do love a nice crispy onion," agreed Yidarica. "But hear me out: caramelized onions."

August gasped, pointing a finger at her. "That would actually be really good, too! Although not fulfilling the crispy requirement, the slight sweetness would add another dimension to the whole thing!"

Somehow, he's even cuter when he's excited.

In the following moment, when conversation subsided as the two focused on eating, Yidarica would occasionally steal a glance at August. This was the first time she had time to study him– the added advantage of having gotten here first meant she finished eating first– and she was beginning to become of the mind that he was even more attractive than previously thought. Obviously he was cute when he smiled, but she was now noticing how cute it was when he ate. Whether it be his eyes so intently fixed on his bowl, or the slightly awkward way he fiddled with his chopsticks, it was like he was purposely being adorable; and Yidarica was eating it up with the same level of eagerness as she'd eaten her meal.

The end of her lunch break came far too soon.

"I need to get going," she said as she stood, pushing her chair in. "It was lovely getting a chance to have lunch with you, August, but the grind continues. I hope the day starts getting better for you."

"Well, one of my teammates said she was going to cast a spell of protection once we all got back from lunch, so at least things shouldn't be getting any worse," August replied, sounding very weary of the day. "But I appreciate you saying that. My day became immensely better when I was able to spend time with you," he smiled sweetly, before waving. "See you around!"

As Yidarica walked away, she could only wonder: *Did August just… did he just flirt with me?*

Chapter Ten

Why is it so unnerving to get emails from people in management that aren't Shiori?

Even though she'd been working with Iris for a few weeks now, seeing her name in the inbox was still too new to not elicit a reaction. After everything that had been going on, unfamiliar names in her inbox always set Yidarica on edge.

```
Hello Yidarica, Muiren, and Shiori,
I am writing you all this email to inform you
of organizational changes within the Weather
Department, as we've undergone a restructuring
over the past few days. As of today, I will
no longer be your main point of contact for
the Weather Project. For further consultation on
the Weather Project, please contact Eira Daschen
(@eiradee, she/they). She's been studying the
project for about two weeks now, so she has a
comprehensive understanding of where we current-
ly are.
Legal doesn't seem to be happy with our current
pace, so they're now requesting weekly updates
for the project. Until Eira's permissions clear,
```

**you should send those updates to the manager of
the Project Biome, Celosia Ramura (@rcelosia,
she/her).**
**Lastly, and speaking of the Project Biome, we've
all agreed that the project will move faster if
we have people on both sides working together to
find those solutions we need. The Biome was the
most recently restructured, but we decided that
it was best to have the newest member of our
team work alongside Yidarica and Muiren— August
Sostrin (@sostie, he/him), who also needs time
for his permissions to clear. We believe this
will take about two days.**
**If any of you have any questions, I will still
be working within and seated with the Weather
Department, and will try to help as best I can.**

**Yours,
Iris Guantian
Senior Weather Research
she/her/hers**

"Oh, that's so nice that Iris got promoted, she's been working so hard on this project," Yidarica said as she placed her tablet on the table. "Okay, Muiren. According to the email we just got, Legal is being Legal. Today we need to–"

It clicked then, what she had read. Yidarica quickly picked her tablet back up.

THE ABSENCE OF COMPLETE DARK 129

we decided that it was best to have the newest member of our team work alongside Yidarica and Muiren— August Sostrin.

That was actually in the email, right? This wasn't one of those tricky deception spells? Was this the opening she'd been hoping for?!

Before she could speak anymore, a second email came through from Celosia. This email had been sent to August, but Yidarica and Muiren had been CC'ed.

```
Hi August,
I have your first official project ready, so I
hope you're eager to get started!
For the past month, the Weather Department has
been working with the Sustenance Department's
Project Garden on a project to mitigate the
chance of bodily harm that occurs while food
deliveries are being made. We think having
someone on our side working with them will
be effective in many ways. I've CC'd the two
people who have been working on the project thus
far: Yidarica Verbestel (@verbestely, she/her)
and Muiren Tierney (@muirent, they/them) who
I believe sit in the area between Profiterole
and Tartine. I'm told that they're both very
approachable, so don't hold back on the many
questions I know you'll have for them!
If you need help with Project Biome-specific
```

```
matters, you can always reach out to me or any
of your new teammates.

<3 Bună ziua,
Celosia Ramura
Manager, Project Biome (she/her)
```

Muiren was the first to finish reading the email. "Interesting. It appears this duo has become a threesome."

That mix of exasperation and disgust– the one that Yidarica felt whenever she was around crude humor– was back in full force. "Muiren. Do you have to say it that way?"

"Just an attempt to keep the mood light," Muiren replied, smiling at first, but then their face went blank. "I'll stop. Please don't call HR on me. I've had enough of them."

This, of all things, was what got Yidarica to laugh. "No worries. But I'd better let August know that we're not sitting where we usually do; don't want the guy getting lost."

"Wait a minute." Referencing their tablet first, Muiren asked, "How do we feel about going over to where the Project Biome is situated, instead? The first email says that August is waiting for access to all of his programs and probably will for two days, so he wouldn't be getting any work done with us right now; plus, I don't recall us ever meeting Eira or Celosia, so if either of them are in the office today, it'd be nice to build that social bond."

Yidarica had never met or even heard of Eira. She did, however, recall seeing Celosia's name a lot of times in her obsession with weather and everything the Weather Department did; she evidently had been around since its inception. The more she thought about it, Muiren was right– there had never been a time where they'd spoken. Attempting to recall a face for her only brought up the still photo attached to her emails, which was so tiny that one could only ever make out her fair skin and dark brown hair. It was a good idea to go make themselves known in person, furthering Yidarica's belief that the two of them made the perfect team.

"Let's go, then. Most of the Weather Department is seated at the very southeast end of the building; the closest meeting room to it is Eclair."

***

The most familiar face in the Weather Department, at this point, would have been Iris– but she wasn't at her desk when the two Project Garden members arrived. A quick cursory check of her calendar said she was currently in a meeting, and it was one that had just started. She'd be gone for 25 more minutes. Not a lot of time, but what was a person to do until she got back?

"Hi! Are you looking for Iris? She just left for a meeting." A voice with a vague, but noticeable accent sounded off behind the two.

Two heads turned to see an average-height woman standing on the other side of Iris's desk; her brown hair, currently pulled into curly twintails, fell past her shoulders, and her bangs stopped just before her sparkling, light blue eyes. It would not be wrong to compare her clothing style to Yidarica's, with one key difference: the colors. Where Yidarica was almost always bright and pastel, this woman's wardrobe consisted of warmer, cozier colors; the red crocheted shawl, which was the perfect shade to match her long, layered skirt, the cream-colored blouse… it all evoked a sense of warmth, one only augmented by the mug she was holding, full of an indistinguishable hot beverage.

"We were," Muiren was the first to speak. "But since she'll be occupied, would you happen to know who else we could speak with regarding the Weather Project?"

At this, the woman's eyes lit up. "Oh! You can certainly speak with me! We haven't met in person; I'm the manager of our project team, Celosia. You must be Yidarica and Muiren, then?"

"That's what we've been going by," Muiren agreed. "I'm Muiren, she's Yidarica."

"It is a pleasure to be meeting you in person! I'm not sure how diligent you are with your emails, but if you haven't yet seen, I've entrusted you with my newest team member. Try not to scare him off too badly, okay?" Celosia winked, before beckoning for the two to follow her. "Let me introduce you all! My team sits right over here."

The three began to walk, but didn't get far before a brunet man in jeans and a blue T-shirt approached. "Celosia! Just the person I needed to see. Do you have a minute?"

"My minutes are in short supply, but my ears are always listening," she replied. "Please, walk with me. What's happening?"

"How much do you know about the frequency we use for our weather predictions?"

"It's changed multiple times since I was in a position to be knowledgeable about it, so not much," she explained. "That question is better suited to someone in Weather Study. You know Iris Guantian, correct? If it is not urgent, she was just promoted to their board; you can send her your inquiry on Slapdash and she'll probably get back to you after her meeting."

The man grinned. "Excellent, that works. Thanks!"

Both Yidarica and Muiren took notice of the fact that many people here said hello or good morning to Celosia as she walked past. Of course, most people here were friendly and were inclined to greet one another as they went about their days, but something about the way everyone in this department approached her indicated a certain level of either respect or admiration. Yidarica would never be able to tell which.

"Apologies for all of the interruptions; we're going into our busy season, and with the restructuring, everything is more frenzied than usual," Celosia explained to Yidarica and Muiren. "When the time approaches for the rainy season to end, we receive our highest traffic. People obsessively check the weather forecast, seek counsel regarding the best days to travel or plan outdoor activities. There is not a single portion of the Weather Department that doesn't feel the effects of it all; and so, there are many issues we come across that—"

"Miss Ramura! Can I borrow you for a—" a young person, very clearly an intern based on the tray of coffee orders they were holding, approached the trio, but stopped when they saw Yidarica and Muiren. "Are you occupied at the moment?"

If Yidarica hadn't already had her eyes on Celosia, she may have missed the way her hands tensed around the cup she was holding, when she had been called by her last name. "Yes, I am occupied at the moment." She said this in an impossibly kind way; Yidarica found herself thinking that Shiori would have been much more curt. "Also, please, just Celosia. I know it's hard to adjust, but you are an adult just as I am. This is a casual setting. There's no need to be formal. Please find me in about an hour and a half, okay?"

The intern sighed just a little. "Roger."

Passing a few more desks occupied by (assumedly) people who worked on different Weather Department-related teams, and turning a corner, they finally arrived at the target area. From here, Yidarica could only see the top of August's head over the cubicles, but the sight nevertheless caused her heart rate to increase just a little bit.

Celosia stopped at what was assumedly her desk to sit her mug down, almost dropping it at one point, before sliding over to where August was seated. "Sostie! Ce faci? I hope you've read your emails for the day."

"I've been clocked in for a maximum of seven minutes, Celosia." August had a neutral expression on his face when he said this, but quickly shifted to a smile. "Of course I have."

"That's great! Then, this visit will not be surprising to you at all," Celosia replied. "Have you met Yidarica and Muiren yet? They both came over to speak to our department about…" she trailed off then, realizing she didn't know the specifics of this visit.

"Actually, this is exactly it," Yidarica explained. "Iris sent us an email with a bunch of new names, so we decided it'd be a good idea to come over and see who we've been directed to."

"Right." Celosia took a look around the immediate area, at one point standing on her toes for extra visibility. "Eira won't be in for a few more weeks, so I cannot introduce you to them, but you do get to meet August and myself, so at least you didn't…" she timidly raised a hand to excuse herself, and turned away from the group for a brief moment, beginning to speak softly to herself. "Nu ai venit aici degeaba. How to say… you didn't… arrive here in vain! Yes, that's it. I think we can schedule a quick recap meeting, I have some time. Let me just check which meeting rooms are available. It looks like there are vacancies at the small tables over by Macaron, so let's head there!"

There was a table with exactly four empty chairs, so Celosia hurried over to claim it before anyone else managed to sit there. Once seated, she began to configure the projector so that she could use it. "I don't think I'll need this, but it never hurts to set it up just in case. Now, before we get started, I would like to emphasize that this is only August's second day on my team, so there are a few things he does not know about our department yet. How familiar are you with projects, August?"

"Not very," he replied. "This is the first time I've ever been on a project team, and I know I have a lot to learn, so thanks for putting this meeting together. Hopefully, it'll help me get my footing."

"Well, you know," Celosia twirled a piece of hair between her fingers in an almost nervous way. "The Biome hadn't been called into this particular project until today, so I don't know very much about it either. If you are thankful to me for calling this meeting, I am just as thankful that these two decided to make their way over here."

This was a very informal meeting, one that Yidarica would be hard-pressed to remember anything that happened at it, aside from the very beginning. At a certain point, she had suddenly realized that August was very cute when he was being attentive, and she couldn't help but gaze at him– discreetly, of course. She was fortunate enough to be able to answer the questions that Celosia would occasionally ask, or defer to Muiren if she didn't know how to answer, so it was her hope that she didn't come off as a complete airhead.

"Um, Celosia–" Yidarica knew, if this meeting went on for too long, and she continued to not be able to pay attention, she'd end up getting lost at some point. "Sorry to interrupt. I think that's good enough, to cover the basics. We can pick up on the floor, and you can get back to your team. I'm sure you have other pressing matters to attend to, with everything going on."

Celosia nodded. "Of course, that's a great idea! No wonder Shiori has so much faith in you. Well, if that's all for now, I'll get back to my desk. August, if you have any questions, you know I'm only a quick message away, right?"

"As any good manager should be," he replied, saluting.

He's such a dork, but he's cute, so I'll allow it.

***

"Let's start from the top, then," Yidarica said when the group had settled in on their balcony area. "August, how well would you say you understand this project so far? Would you be able to summarize it for someone who hasn't been made aware of it yet?"

"Probably, but it'd be a pretty elementary summary," he replied. "Basically, we're implementing a user-friendly warning about inclement weather that absolves us of legal liability, right?"

Yidarica and Muiren exchanged a look. "Yeah, that's the long and short of it, basically," the latter agreed.

"Now, let's determine how you fit into the machine," Yidarica said then. "So far, I've been dealing with reaching out to contacts for assistance, because I'm good at writing comms, and Muiren has been designing the disclaimer's appearance, because that's what they're good at. What are you good at, August? Let's find something you can contribute to the team."

"Well…" August thought about it for a moment. "Oh! So, relating to Muiren designing the disclaimer, is it our responsibility to bear in mind how it's coded into the application? I can do that."

"What exactly do you mean by 'coded,' could you explain?" Muiren asked.

"Sure. There are a bunch of different ways this disclaimer can be incorporated into our application, right? They could bring up a new screen, redirect to existing ones, create a pop-up window, use environmental magic; that sort of thing. Each effect requires a specific set of computing language to take into consideration, which I suppose would also influence your designs, somewhat."

Muiren nodded stiffly; it was easy to tell that this was out of their field of knowledge.

"That's great! You'll fit in perfectly," Yidarica said. "Neither of us know much of anything about that side of things, so you will only be making our team stronger. Now, Muiren and I did already have some thoughts about the different ways to implement the disclaimer, based on the results we got from polling people about application design."

"Basically, we're inclined to not go the route of the pop-up for two reasons: one, people are so used to them by now that they mindlessly click through them, which means we skirt a bit closer to the Clause of Recognition than we'd like, and we all know that Legal wouldn't be a fan of that. Two, if the pop-up gets too obnoxious, it alienates the user base, which is also something we don't want." Muiren thought then, "But when you think about it, there's really no way around that, is there? How else would we present the information?"

The area was quiet as everyone thought.

"I have a practical idea, and an unhinged idea; which do you want to hear first?" August was the first to speak.

"You can't just say you have an unhinged idea and then expect us to listen to anything else," Muiren answered with a laugh. "Let's hear it."

August laughed as well. "You've got a point," he replied. "Not many applications do this– and, arguably, for good reason– but have either of you ever experienced one that creates an external magical reaction?"

"Oh! I've been using one of those for years!" Yidarica replied. "It's an application for reminders. I've set it up so it gives me cute magical confetti and streamers to celebrate my birthday."

She did not realize until she'd said it, how sad that made her life sound. *But confetti makes everything feel happier, so that's fine.*

"That's…" August smiled. "That's kinda cute. I worry about the possibility of scares if we did that though, especially with our older user base."

"Right, and the last thing we need is to create more problems for Legal," Yidarica agreed. "So, as cool as it would be, I guess that idea is out. What was your more practical idea, August?"

"My more practical idea is to implement a… what's the word…" He sat, trying to recall the word before giving up and pulling out his phone. He swiped on the screen a few times, tapping some buttons, before showing his screen to Yidarica and Muiren. "See, I have this fun little vocabulary database application that provides a quiz a day. When you get a question right, these stars shoot across the screen."

I've never seen this before, but it looks very cool.

Muiren turned to Yidarica and asked, "What is this called? Didn't we have a project with one of these right after you came to our team? Or was it before?"

"It had to be before. I have no recollection." Yidarica shrugged.

"Damn it all, it's on the tip of my tongue. I– wait! I can ask Hadiza." Muiren picked up their tablet. "She should know. We worked on it together."

"It sounds like going that route is the best way to go, then," Yidarica said then. "It doesn't interrupt the flow of using the application, but it's also impossible to miss. I think it would be ideal if we could combine that with a menu that pops up, but doesn't take up the entire screen; maybe just a strip on the bottom, which has details about the assumption of the risk. That way, we aren't skirting the Clause of Recognition. What do you all think?"

Muiren and August exchanged a look, but were interrupted by a notification sound. "An overlay! That's what this thing is called," Muiren said, reading the message that had come through.

"An overlay. Do you know how they work?" Yidarica asked. "Since I wasn't on the team when you guys built it, I wouldn't know."

Muiren shrugged. "Hell if I do, either. I didn't touch any of the building when we had that project, but it did require me to draw and animate some graphics to put into the program. I don't mind doing that again; I think it'd be fun to draw some weather stuff."

August slightly raised his hand, indicating he had something to add. "If I do some research on overlays, I'm fairly confident I could take care of the code building. I'd just need to know where to start."

"Do you think it would be helpful if you got to examine the file from our old project?" Muiren asked. "Shiori should have a copy of it."

"Oh, that would be lovely!" August agreed, nodding. "If she's willing to share it, that would give me a ton of insight on how to begin my part of this process."

"This is good. This is great, even. This gives us at least a vague idea of how we're going to tackle this. Muiren, we can start with you; doing some research on what weather conditions this company calls 'inclement,' deciding the best ways to depict them, and a general hold on UI sounds about right. Right?" Yidarica tacked the last part on quickly, hoping her teammates didn't perceive it as overbearing. *According to my studies of humans, being in charge is often met with hostility. Therefore, the best action is to behave so that they forget I'm in charge at all.*

"Makes perfect sense," agreed Muiren. "I'll remember to be in drawing mode tomorrow."

"August, you'll be taking control of the buildout," Yidarica said next. "While we don't have an exact idea how that'll look just yet, I'm sure we will by the time you're done learning the basics, and probably still before all our designs are done. After that, we'll need a few more days to test everything and be sure it works. And then we turn it in."

"A plan if I ever heard one," Muiren nodded. "You on board with all this, August?"

"Of course," he agreed. "It's a pretty intuitive schedule, one that gives us the space we need to modify it if something comes up. I look forward to all of this."

Hearing this filled Yidarica with pride. *This is my first time leading a project, so I'm really glad my thoughts and ideas are making sense. Before, I thought I'd confuse everybody with my rambling if they ever had to listen to me.*

"I'm glad we have an itinerary now," Yidarica replied, with a smile. "This is what we'll be following from now on, then. Now, let's call a vote: what do we do for the rest of the day?"

"We can do that weather research today, maybe?" Muiren suggested. "I already know the really obvious inclement weather, like tornadoes or floods, but if we could build a compendium of all of the possible weather occurrences we need to warn about, that would be great."

Yidarica immediately got excited about this idea, bouncing in her chair just a little. "Yeah, we totally could do that! The library has some of that information, but I think this may be one of those things we should ask Celosia about. She's been here a long time, so she should have some wisdom to impart upon us."

"I'll ask her," August volunteered, preparing to compose a message to her.

As he began to do that, Muiren turned to Yidarica. "How do you know that? Wasn't today your first time meeting Celosia?"

"First time meeting, yes, but I may have spent a little too much time reading about the inception of the Weather Department," Yidarica admitted. She explained, "The department was founded just shy of a decade ago, and if you read the retrospectives of the early days, a few of them are written by Celosia. Her sections are really short compared to the others, but now that I've met her, I think I know why: there was probably a language barrier. She clearly knew her terminology in her entries I've read, but in the really, really old ones where they were still handwritten, I noticed she had a lot of issues with spelling that got better as time went on. Even today, when we had that brief meeting with her, it's easy to tell that she knows her stuff."

"Yeah, for sure," Muiren concurred. "I'm shocked to know she's been here that long; she must look younger than she is. She's cute, though."

"Very." Yidarica nodded.

August stood then, and stretched. "May I excuse myself for a minute? Celosia says she has some notes to share with me, related to what we asked about inclement weather."

"Dude, we all get paid the same wage. Have fun," Yidarica waved him off. "Just come back before lunch so we can discuss those notes."

"I make no promises." August's facial expression clearly conveyed that he was joking.

When he left, Muiren looked over at where he'd left his things. "How are we feeling about having a new person added to this adventure? Personally, I'm glad it's someone that has a lot of tech knowledge. If that had fallen to just us, I'd feel awful about putting that all on you, but I genuinely cannot wrap my head around the concept of putting a bunch of letters and numbers into a piece of tech and having that translate into it doing things."

I know a few things about coding and how we do it here, but if it's expected for us to code the whole thing, Legal would be even more unhappy with us than they are now, with how long it would take me to learn how to do it. August's addition to this team is a miracle.

"Do you think I should ask Shiori if coding is our responsibility?" Yidarica asked. "I'm realizing we don't know that. With our past projects, we haven't gotten that far into the details, but with this one being so unprecedented… okay, yeah. I'm asking her."

"Excellent idea." Muiren looked at their tablet. "While you're doing that, I'll see if there's something else I can do."

At this moment, August returned, taking his seat nearest the door. "Okay, team. Thank you for waiting for me. Celosia shared with me a definitive list of inclement weather occurrences, but I've never heard of some of these words. Are either of you really good at weather terms?"

Immediately, Muiren turned to Yidarica. "We are fortunate enough to have this project led by someone who's *really* passionate about weather. It would be an honor to have you guide us through this list, Yidarica."

Chapter Eleven

Door open, shoes off, work bag on the chair that sat beside the front door.

When August returned home from work, every day, he followed that same routine. He struggled to explain why he did this; he just knew that if he ever did things in a different order, the rest of the evening would feel wrong somehow. After that, though, what was to happen was anyone's guess. He could sit on the couch and get lost in reading a novel or practicing magic, or go to the kitchen to scrounge up dinner. If he was tired enough, he could even go straight to bed; this only happened when the day had thoroughly exhausted him, though, which hadn't happened in a while.

August lived in an apartment complex not far from the MFI building, accessed via an artistic spiral staircase that was attended to by a doorman. The apartment itself was graced with plenty of space and high ceilings, but he'd always thought the place felt a little sterile because of that. Consequently, he'd quickly filled the space with greenery, including the plants he'd inherited from his father, and they gave the living room this sort of living, breathing life that only plants could.

He sighed in relief as he sat on the couch, glad to finally be off his feet. Before doing anything else, he sat up straight and began to cast the water spell he used to water all of his plants.

Gotta make sure the little guys are nourished.

While August wouldn't say that he loved plants, he'd always been fond of them because his father had been a botanist. His memories of childhood were decorated with plant life, whether it be the plentiful clay pots scattered through the home he grew up in; the beautiful rose trellis in the backyard, adorned with vibrant roses in shades of white, yellow, and peach; or the magnificent apple tree that sat on the border of their house and the neighbor's, which grew the same inedible and quite ugly green apples every year. His father had been extremely passionate about plants, and his enthusiasm had been so infectious that even now, his absence was felt profoundly in the Sostrin family.

It had been three years, now, since August had gotten the call. His father had died in his sleep; gone peacefully, but so suddenly.

He missed him so much that he could never conceive words that were of an adequate gravity to convey that sense of longing. Not only because they had been close– which they absolutely had– but because soon after his passing, everything changed.

August was the youngest in his immediate family, but his two older sisters were, well, sisters. With their father gone, it was a surreal and almost immediate shift to everyone insisting that he "take on his father's legacy" and "further the family name;" and this was done without knowledge, or care, that August himself didn't have the desire to do either of those things. He had always been forthcoming about the fact that he didn't aspire to wealth or fatherhood. Growing up, his father had always emphasized that he should be himself, and stay true to himself. Now, it was like his family was pushing the opposite: to be what they wanted him to be.

Needless to say, his contact with family had become limited these days.

"Dinner. I should eat dinner." August said this to himself, but made no effort to get off of the couch. It had already claimed him, with all of its comfiness.

One of August's biggest insecurities was that he didn't know how to cook. It wasn't entirely his fault; there were a number of circumstances that had made it this way. For a long time, he had lived with other people– his family, dorm mates, partners– so there always had been someone else around to pitch in for food. Additionally, his mother had insisted he didn't need to learn to cook when he was "destined for greatness" and "would have people dying to cook for him," whatever that meant. He just knew that as an adult he'd tried to cook once, and the resulting fire caused his mother to flip out at him. It was partially why he knew that water spell so well… and why stovetops made him so anxious.

Dinner. Hungry. Should eat something. But still he remained on the couch. Would it be so horrible if he didn't eat dinner today?

I suppose I could also grab something from a place nearby, if I'm not feeling up to whatever I have here.

***

After a courteous wave to the doorman, August set out to find dinner. It didn't take him long to realize he was hungry enough that walking too far sounded like an insurmountable task, so he settled for the nearest restaurant at that time, which promptly had him seated with a bowl of chips and three dipping sauces. He'd never been to this place, but so far, they were making a good impression.

As he popped yet another chip into his mouth, he checked his messages for the day and saw that, at some point, his mother had sent him something.

> **Work's having a picnic next Saturday. Would love to see you there. Coworker has a gorgeous niece that's around your age**

This was how most, if not all, messages from August's mother looked these days. It was almost as if she didn't have an interest in reaching out to him unless it had to do with setting him up with somebody's daughter. He harbored no resentment toward her, but he was starting to wonder if she cared about him anymore, and not just the person she wanted him to be.

"What can I get you, sweetheart?" The waitress asked, a pen and notepad in hand. Her dark red hair was clipped into a bun, and the fine lines within her tan skin implied that she was about in her fifties. She regarded August with a look of curiosity, if not pity.

"Um, I… steak sandwich is fine. No tomatoes, please," he replied.

"Mm-hmm." The waitress nodded. "That all? No drink?"

Right. I should probably drink something. "A drink. Yeah. Um… surprise me?"

At this, the woman put a hand on her hip. "Now, what is a handsome young man like you doing in here, so distraught that you can't decide what you want to drink?"

It was a good question, one that he wished he had the answer to. He settled on, "Disappointing my parents."

This made the waitress laugh; a loud, hearty laugh that filled the half-empty restaurant with color and life. As she walked away, she gave August a pat on the back. "It'll get better, hon. In the meantime, let me get that steak sandwich for ya."

I can't decide if that was hilarious or embarrassing.

August picked his phone back up then, wondering if he should respond to his mother, and if so, what he should say. He didn't like not responding; he still loved his mother, but all of their conversations had been so consistently frustrating ever since his father had passed. What was he supposed to say to her?

I wonder if Yidarica has this problem.

He blinked, then. *Why did I just think that?*

To say that the frilly, pastel-adorned woman he worked with had not captivated him would be the very essence of a lie. Even before they had spoken, he'd found her interesting. Her clothes always caught his eye, because he'd never seen anyone dress so boldly. He admired the way she seemingly marched to the beat of her own drum, partially because he envied that she was able to do so, when he struggled to do so himself. But now that they had spoken, he couldn't deny that he also found her attractive, both physically and mentally. Whenever the two spoke, he found himself looking forward to listening to what she had to say– and this wasn't limited to work topics, either. She could be a little awkward, but it was endearing in a way.

What should I do? I'd love to let her know that I'm interested in being friends outside of work, but how do I do that? I don't want her to think I'm coming on to her. Although…

This was where August stopped himself. Yes, Yidarica was pretty. Yes, he enjoyed speaking with her. But he'd been down this road before, and if he had learned one thing from the last few times he'd been down it, it was that he needed to be more cautious than that when it came to prospective relationships. After the last time, he was a little afraid of the idea of a relationship, even.

But I'm getting ahead of myself. What if I just, very platonically, asked for her number? How do you platonically ask for a coworker's number? Can you do that, is that possible?

The sound of a plate being placed on the table distracted him from that line of thought. "Here's your steak sandwich and your lemonade. Take it easy, young man."

"Thanks, I'll try," August waved as he picked up his sandwich. As he ate, he tried to mentally compose the message he'd send to his mother– for that was what he had been trying to do before he got sidetracked– and, by the time he'd gotten halfway through his meal, he hit a point where he was sure his ideas wouldn't get better, so he took a break from his sandwich to type it up.

> Hi Mom. Not particularly busy Saturday, but not free enough to make the trip back home. You know how long the trip gets. I miss you and everyone else, though. Would love to hear from you sometimes without the added pressure of you potentially playing matchmaker; it's been a while.

He knew it sounded a bit pointed, but that was the point. He'd been trying to play nice with the idea, but August's mother as a person– not just toward him, toward everyone– was the type who refused to acknowledge boundaries unless the person in question was firm enough with her. He'd wanted to be kind because that was his nature, and he knew that she, too, was still reeling from the loss of her husband. But it could not be at the cost of his own sanity.

Everything would be so much more simple if you were still here, Dad.
But, of course, he wasn't; and he never would be again.

Finishing his sandwich, August placed all of his dishes together before paying at the payment center in front, making sure to leave compliments for the lovely waitress who had attended to him. Back outside, he was shocked (but also pleased) to notice that it was still quite mild out; a gentle breeze was blowing, and the air was just dry enough that humidity wasn't a problem.

He decided then to take the scenic route home.

It was a little worrying that his mother hadn't yet gotten back to him, because she usually was able to respond to messages with the expected quickness of someone who was retired, but this was also a sort of grace, in its own way. He wasn't sure if he had the wherewithal to deal with her insistence on settling down with someone. It was also not lost on him that, every time she'd do this, she would make sure it was always a woman she was trying to set him up with. But it made sense; after all, how else would he create the grandchildren she and the rest of the family were clamoring for? Never mind that his oldest sister already had two children; those didn't bear the family name, so they didn't count.

For a moment, and for the first time, August felt very sad for his niblings. They were small now, so they probably never heard or understood what the adults were saying about them, but the idea that they didn't matter in the grand scheme of things was something no child should have to grow up believing.

There's plenty of time in adulthood for that, after all.

August, in regards to his family, mattered in the sense that he was the vehicle to further the Sostrin lineage. But sometimes– often, even– he would venture to believe that August the person didn't matter to them at all. When he really thought about it, he could recall a large number of childhood memories peppered with disapproval of the adults in his life over his gentle nature. Even more so as a teenager, for his love of fashion design; he'd never wear high fashion himself, but he owned multiple photo books and resources about costume design and historical clothing styles. This honestly may have influenced his tendency to dress in clothing on the plainer side; but that was neither here nor there.

Actually, now that I'm on my own and far away from anyone who would have any strong opinions of my inclination to fashion... I should pick it back up. There are probably so many new books I can buy on the subject. And, naturally, it would be fun to discuss them with Yidarica, completely platonically. Considering the way she dresses, she'd probably find the topic mentally stimulating if nothing else.

It was always nice to find a common interest with a prospective friend; but even knowing this, August found himself getting more excited than usual about this idea of having a non-work-related conversation with Yidarica. He would be able to pick her brain about the clothes she wore, which he'd been admiring from afar for a long time now.

I'll even have an opportunity to tell her how pretty her wardrobe makes her look.

He sighed to himself then. *No, August, we are not doing that.*

As he waved to the doorman, he continued to battle with his internal monologue. If he let things happen, and they led to something other than friendship, that would be lovely. But he could also possibly be beaten by his trepidation regarding ever dating another person again... especially another small, cute woman.

Whenever he thought of *that woman*, the scar on the left side of his stomach always seemed to prickle in a very uncomfortable way. This time was no different. He squirmed, trying to think of something else to take his mind off of the event; he opened his door, intent on going to bed early now that this was happening, knowing that he'd struggle to do anything else.

Even though the event currently plaguing August's mind had happened years ago, he could unfortunately still recall it in his memories with a shocking amount of clarity. He had been in the kitchen, preparing to assemble some kind of lunch. He'd been grabbing the newly washed limes out of their bath in the sink, excited to try the new limeade recipe he'd read in one of his cookbooks; while cooking wasn't his forte, August did at least have the competency to make pretty tasty drinks. He remembered slowly cutting the limes into fours, trying his hardest to make them all equal sized; he wasn't sure why this mattered so much to him when they'd just get blended anyway, but in the moment, he had devoted his entire attention to this one single task.

He never heard *her* coming into the kitchen.

What had she asked for? One of the mugs, probably. Maybe the sugar? But his hands had been full when she had asked, so he had wanted to let her know he couldn't get whatever she'd asked for immediately.

Did you just tell me to wait? Who do you think you're talking to?! Didn't I tell you, you drop everything if I want something?

You're sorry? Not nearly sorry enough!

The scar on his stomach began to burn then. August curled up into the fetal position in his bed, a soft whimper escaping his lips. Wasn't having to live through that experience once enough? Why did he have to keep reliving it?

But… as horrible as this is, that was her. She was a horrible person. To many people, not just me; it just took me too long to realize that.

On the other hand, Yidarica is one of the loveliest people I've ever met. Granted, I haven't known her long, but she's so kind to everyone I see her interact with, not just me. She and Muiren seem like good friends. I was shocked when I found out she'd only just met Celosia the day I was put onto the project we're doing, because it seemed like they'd known each other for years the way they got along. She was even happy for me when she found out I was interviewing for a job she wanted. That other woman would've never done that.

This helped to alleviate some of August's distress. He was, at least, able to unfurl his body some, where before, it had felt too tight and nerve-wracked to do so.

He wasn't sure what his feelings for Yidarica were just yet, but he knew that they were comforting. That, if she had been here, she'd have probably helped him through that episode. The idea of her comforting him made him feel warm inside, while simultaneously, finally, calming down the discomfort near his scar.

The next time he was in the office, he told himself, he'd try to gather the courage to ask for her contact information.

Chapter Twelve

At this point, progress on the Weather Project felt slow. Simultaneously, August began working on the code to add their overlays and menu to the Food & Goods application, and Muiren worked on the designs for those overlays. Today, Yidarica was helping with the latter: providing feedback and advice for everything Muiren had designed so far.

"Here's a change I made yesterday," Muiren was saying as they navigated to their folder of graphics for this project. "I really liked the old snowstorm overlay I designed, but I realized that it would be incredibly difficult to see if someone is using light mode. I don't know why anyone would choose to use light mode, but at any rate, I redesigned it so that it's a little bit more emblematic of ice than snow. Do you think it still gets the point across, or should I make more changes?"

Yidarica watched the animation for the overlay, which had a few snowflakes blow across the screen before they began to accumulate in the bottom corner. The two biggest changes were that the snowflakes were now elaborately drawn instead of being orbs of various sizes, and that all of the snow was given an ice-blue tint. This did indeed make it more visible on a white background, so it did what it needed to do.

"I think this is fine. If I were to see it on my phone, I'd immediately know it's a snowstorm," Yidarica told them. "If we have any doubts, we can always run another poll about it. How goes the list? Making good progress on getting all of these depicted?"

"I'm glad you asked," Muiren replied. "There are a few things I wanted to run by you. I know that you know a lot about the weather, so I figured you were the perfect person to ask."

Muiren hesitated for a moment before casting the same board spell that Yidarica used often. "I created a checklist to keep up with everything I've completed, but there's some that I needed to come back to, and I left notes about them. For example, what the hell is a downburst?"

Yidarica's eyes lit up at the question. "Oh, a downburst! The easiest way I can describe it is, you know how you can cast a water spell that allows you to throw this orb-like entity of water, and when it collides with something, the water splatters every which way? That is what a downburst does with wind that comes from above the clouds. It hits the ground and goes in all directions."

It was easy to tell that Muiren was still confused. "Okay. Cool. How do I depict that on a screen?"

"That's..." Yidarica hesitated. "That is a question I don't really know how to answer. Maybe we can watch a few videos of the occurrence so that you can get an idea?"

"You are so astute." Muiren regarded her with a look of admiration. "Not that it surprises me, but you've been especially on a roll with this project." They cleared their throat then, loudly, in an attempt to get the third person's attention. "August! Is everything okay over there? You're really quiet today."

August, meanwhile, was seated across the room, scrunched in his chair as much as he could, almost mimicking the fetal position. "Suffering," he said softly. "Starting new code is suffering."

"Well, alrighty then." Muiren turned back to Yidarica. "My other concerns are all about how to make screen graphics for some of these. It's tricky for some of them since, on a phone screen, we lose a dimension in which people would be accustomed to seeing them. The one I'm struggling with the most is the tropical storm; not because I don't know what it looks like, but because I haven't been able to visually differentiate it from either a regular severe thunderstorm, or a hurricane. Everything I draw ends up looking like one of those."

Oh, yeah, I guess they would all look similar two-dimensionally. More rain gets you closer to severe thunderstorms, more wind makes it like a hurricane. Too much wind, and it could look like a tornado. Yidarica was stumped by this one. She knew that tropical storms were a notable problem in the more southern areas of Basodin, so they'd definitely need a graphic for them. What could they do?

"Although…" Yidarica turned to Muiren, as she crossed her legs. "The sliding menu that accompanies the overlay will have a dialogue about the weather, right? If we mention the weather hazard being a tropical storm, do we really need it to be super distinct? The explanation, plus some wind and water, should drive the point home well enough, shouldn't it?"

Muiren was very clearly thinking about this. "That is a good point. I think this is one of those things where I make the animation and then ask other people if they can tell what it is, like I just did you and some other people today about the snowstorm. I can use that fancy poll feature for that. Mind if I take a walk while I do that?"

"Not at all. Have fun." Yidarica smirked just a bit before turning to the email she had open. Today was recap email day, the first one she would be sending. It was difficult to tell what level of detail to include, because no one had ever told her that. *If it's too short, Legal will think we're not taking the project seriously, and the last thing I want is to give them that impression. But if it's too long, they're very busy people who will likely not have time to read the whole thing, and then they'll get mad at me for that. I really cannot win here.*

She looked up at where August was agonizing over writing the code he was working on; he'd been typing this whole time, but he stopped a second after Yidarica had looked at him, resting his head in his hands and sighing heavily.

I know this is hardly the time, but the way he runs his hands through his hair is really cute.

"Are we doing okay over there?" she asked gently.

The room was silent for at least five seconds before August softly replied, "No."

"Oh." *That is not what I expected him to say.* "Um, okay. I… can I help somehow?"

Another few seconds passed. "I honestly don't know," August admitted. "Maybe? The thing is, as difficult as starting code is, I finally was able to get the basic functions down at least. I was finally hitting a groove, but then I realized. I cannot stylize a single thing until I know how the rest of the application is stylized, so it doesn't stick out too much. I have no idea where I would find that out. I asked Celosia over Slapdash, but she hasn't responded to me yet. She's probably been pulled aside by somebody who's talking her ear off."

"That seems to happen a lot," Yidarica noted.

"It's mostly because the Weather Department is the smallest of all of MFI's areas of expertise," August explained. "The higher-ups who do really technical stuff aren't very accessible, like the rest of the departments here, and without them, there's really only about four manager types around at any given time. And especially now when Eira isn't in office, Iris is busy acclimating to her new duties, and Lexiea– who I haven't yet met– has a reputation for being rude and unapproachable, everything's kinda falling on Celosia at the moment. I learned all of this from one of my new teammates my first day."

"Oh." *That's a lot for one person to deal with, but if anyone could, it would probably be the person who's been with the Weather Department for nine years.*

The door creaked slightly as Muiren peeked their head back into the room. "Hey, Yidarica? Could I enlist your help in something really quick? August, we'll only be a moment, I promise."

"Sure. Take your time," August was the first to respond. "I can't do much of anything until Celosia gets back to me, anyway."

"Huh." Muiren placed a hand on their hip. "Yeah. Be back in a wee jiffy, then."

Now intrigued by that reaction, Yidarica followed them out of the room. She could barely make it out of the room before the door closed and Muiren pulled her aside.

"Dude, what the hell goes on over in the Weather Department?" Muiren asked, in a hushed voice, but one that still conveyed a certain level of urgency. "While I was walking around, I noticed that a few of them were in an open-air meeting. There were these guys in suits that looked like they've had sticks up their asses for longer than either of us have been alive, and one of them was talking at Celosia– not to her, *at* her– with no regard for the fact that she was as pale as a ghost, looking about two seconds away from fainting. I went over and yelled at him, but she still isn't doing so hot; I figured her being out of commission would have some ramifications for our work, because we've had to rely on her a lot so far, so that's why I came back to check on you all. Then August said the thing he said, and now I have no idea where to go from here."

This is so much information that I feel a little dizzy. What's the first thing I should say? I have so many questions. My studies of humans say, in situations like these, that it's more meritable to inquire about humans than work.

"Is Celosia feeling stable, at least?" Yidarica asked.

"Stable enough. I left her in the library with a bowl of ice and some small snacks, assuming the quiet would help her, and some of the color was returning to her by the time I left," Muiren replied. "I do worry about how it seems like that department puts a lot of responsibility on one woman. That can't be good for them or her in the long run."

"Yeah, tell me about it," Yidarica agreed. "Want to go check on her? I think August might need something from the library anyway, so I don't mind picking it up for him." *I haven't actually checked to see if we have coding books in the library... but if we have them at all, they'd be there, logically.*

"Good idea. Let's head there."

***

The library was as quiet as it always was; at this time, the only person in the room was Celosia. On the desk in front of her was a plate of crackers, grapes, and sliced bananas. Yidarica noticed that she reached for one of the banana slices, her hand unable to grasp it the first two tries before finally getting it the third time, and she ate it slowly. By the time this had happened, Muiren and Yidarica had gotten close enough to her that she noticed them.

"Hey. Doing better?" Muiren asked, taking a seat beside her.

Celosia took a moment to respond, as if she hadn't understood the question at first. "I can hear my thoughts again, if that is what you mean."

"Assuming you couldn't before, that's what I meant, yeah," Muiren replied. "What happened to make that guy be such a jackass toward you, anyway? It seemed so uncalled for. Even the other men in suits looked appalled at him."

The question was met with a blank stare. If she wasn't able to share the backstory for confidentiality reasons, that would be one thing, but it genuinely appeared as though Celosia had no idea what Muiren had just asked her; she was looking straight at them, but the look in her blue eyes was distant, as if she wasn't entirely in the room at the moment.

"I think she needs some more time, Muiren," Yidarica said, placing a hand on their shoulder. "I'm gonna go look around to see if we have any books here that can help August with what he was going to ask her. There's no way she's in good enough shape to give him a definitive answer anytime soon."

"Okay." This was the shakiest Yidarica had ever heard Muiren's voice be. "Is it all right if I don't help you? It's just, Celosia, she–" Muiren waved a hand in front of her face, but she didn't move at all. "I'm worried."

"I know. I am too." Yidarica gave them a nod. "Take care of her. Leave the day's work to me and August."

Approaching the bookshelves, Yidarica wasn't entirely sure of what she should be looking for. She could surmise that she'd be looking in the section that pertained to work, rather than the leisure reads, but that was where her knowledge ended. *There aren't any notes about the Weather Department's application design, and the more that I think about it, if something like that exists it's probably for the entire company. All of our applications look similar, so they probably use the same UI.*

Wait a minute. If we're working on something that shows up on the Food & Goods application, and pulls from the Weather one, would it not be more intuitive to research the base code for the former? That would be the one we need to stay in line with.

And if anyone would be able to help this team find out the inner intricacies of the Food & Goods application, it would be Shiori "if I don't know, I'll find out who does" Montalban.

Even so, it's probably a good idea to sift through these books to see if that information is already here. If I don't have to bother Shiori, that'll make things all the better.

While searching through all of the books on the shelves dedicated to books pertinent to MFI, Yidarica noticed that there weren't many books here that got too explicitly technical. Even that book she liked to read about the Weather Department focused more on weather events and the personnel that had inaugurated the department than any technical aspects of the application. She briefly wondered if this was by design– to keep the secret sauce of the company a secret– before her eyes fell upon a book in the wrong area. This wasn't uncommon, so she simply scooped it up and put it on the correct shelf before returning to see how things were going over by the desks.

"...had gone through so much together. So, from experience, I know that's how he is. I can't be too upset at him, although I can also admit that me being unable to remember what he said is probably doing a lot of heavy lifting in making that possible," Celosia was saying as Yidarica rounded the corner. *It's good to hear her being able to speak sentences. She had me worried.*

"Okay, I guess. But I still hate the way that happened," Muiren replied. Now that Yidarica was close enough, she could see that the two had split the fruit that had been on the plate.

"Yidarica!" Celosia waved excitedly. "Hello! I didn't know you were here."

"I just told you she was here with me, Celosia," Muiren reminded her, in a tone so gentle that Yidarica was surprised it had come from Muiren, of all people. "What's up? How is everything going?"

"Swell. I have to bug Shiori about something," she replied. "After that, I'm gonna let August know what she tells me, so I won't be coming back here. Can you two hold down the fort here in my place?"

At hearing "hold down the fort," Celosia mimicked holding something over her head, like a blanket or newspaper, looking particularly pleased with herself. Muiren sighed just a little, but it was easy to tell they were amused by the action. "Yeah. We'll be here until lunchtime, probably," Muiren was the one to confirm. "I get the feeling there's at least three people over in the appropriate area waiting to bother this one with questions, so it's probably best that we hide out here until she's ready to answer them. We can meet up at lunch."

Yidarica smiled. "See you then. The macaroni looks immaculate today."

***

The next day was one of what Yidarica liked to refer to as "decomposition days."

Having the day off of work usually meant that she'd devote time to getting things done around the house; cleaning, organizing, replenishing things she was running low on. There would be times, though, where she didn't have the energy to do any of that. She'd be so low on energy, in fact, that it would be all she could do to take care of her online and magical tasks while lying in her bed, seemingly decomposing. Ergo, decomposition days.

A large, disgruntled sigh echoed around the room as she clicked the button to pay her rent, the largest and most burdensome of her bills. *It's manageable; I know rent could be a lot worse, but wouldn't it be wonderful if we came up with a better way to ensure people have places to call home?*

A text message interrupted her thoughts. She looked down at her phone, and noticed it was from Zaya.

> **Hey quick question, what's your favorite color?**

It was a question that Yidarica had to give considerable thought to. It wasn't so much that she had a favorite color as it was that she simply liked *colors*; every single hue of the rainbow, and the ways they could combine to make aesthetically pleasing palettes.

It was something she felt especially passionate about at this point of her life, fear of the Dark afflicting her notwithstanding, because she was at the age where many of her contemporaries surrounded themselves in boring grays and neutral tones. But that was neither here nor there.

> That's a little hard for me to answer. Maybe if I had some context?

Wait, was that too mean? Should I have said that a little more gently?

> Well, I wanted it to be a surprise, but maybe it'll be better if you have a visual. I'm going through my clothes, and was wondering if anything I have here will be suitable for the next time I'm able to come over and see you– if you know what I mean ;)

> What do you think of these?

Following that set of messages was a collection of photos, each of Zaya wearing a different set of lacy lingerie. Yidarica wondered, for a moment, why she had so many of these– but she soon became engrossed in typing up her response.

> I think the red one is a bit too harsh; it does no service to the undertones of your skin. On the other hand, the dark green set is really pretty. I love the ornate rose designs in the lace! However, my absolute favorite is that black one-piece. Not only does it contrast your skin amazingly, the addition of frills around your legs adds a feminine flair that I'm always a fan of. If there was a negative, I'd worry about how comfortable it is, which is personally one of my biggest qualms with these types of sets–

> they tend to be made for aesthetics more than practicality, which always makes me wonder: what's the point of making something to wear on your body if it's not comfortable while it's on your body?

...

The whole point is to not have it on for long, Yidarica.

> So, for photography reasons?

That's... one reason. Look, don't worry about it. I'll circle back when I've decided on something.

For reasons she couldn't explain, Yidarica knew she had said something wrong– but she would never be able to tell what it was. Before she could spiral about it, she received another text message, this time from Gracia.

Yida! Look at this place I found while I was coming home from my magical meditation class! The decor there is sooo cute, and they have doughnuts that are almost as big as my head!

> Really? That big? That could practically account for a whole meal!

> **I know, right? Let me know the next time you're free, and I can show you where it is- my treat!**
>
> **It looks like it could be a really cute date spot too! Has there been any luck for you there, or are you still taking it easy?**

Although she hadn't actively done anything, Yidarica wouldn't classify her current state in regards to dating under "taking it easy." On one hand, she had the girl she'd been admiring for months wanting to come back over to her house and have more one-on-one time with her. On the other hand, she had the man she'd been mystified by finally communicating with her, and even possibly flirting with her. She hadn't been this conflicted between a man and a woman since she first realized she was bisexual, fifteen years ago.

Amazing how it hadn't gotten easier to navigate since then.

> **I'd much rather tell you about things in person, Gracia. Maybe we could meet up this weekend?**

***

The next day, when Yidarica got to her project trio's base and didn't see Muiren, she was confused. Muiren was almost always at work early, even before they had left for that extended period. To not have them here, especially on a day when Yidarica herself was cutting it close on time, felt strange; unnerving, almost.

August was seated in the area, though, reading a book. From what Yidarica could see, the shades of blue on the cover kind of reminded her of toothpaste, but she couldn't make out the title from where she was. *He seems really engrossed in whatever's in that book. Maybe later I'll ask him about it, if we end up having time.*

"Good morning," she said, noticing that her voice startled August. "Sorry I'm later than usual. During my Comtran ride, our route was intercepted by the cutest little family of ducks crossing the road. I know, it sounds like the most cliche thing ever, but those little guys were adorable," Yidarica grinned. The baby ducks had been so fluffy and yellow; she was sure she'd remember the sight for a long time.

"No need to apologize. We're all sharing the same world, so it's nice to hear of someone being considerate of the smaller beings we share it with," August replied. "Glad you made it, even so. Muiren is here, but they said we may not see them very much today. Something about an official summons."

Today must be the day that HR is concluding their investigation. "Oh, okay. I was wondering where they were. That does put us in an interesting spot though, in regards to what we're going to do today. If my memory is correct, today was the day we were actually going to start putting the overlays into the code. It's gonna be hard to do that without the files for the overlays, which Muiren has, because they're the one who made them."

"Ah, I didn't even think of that." August set his book aside. "So… now what?"

Your guess is as good as mine.

Yidarica knew she couldn't say that, though, and so she leaned on the table nearest her as she tried to think. "Well, I suppose there's the possibility that everything Muiren has worked on was saved in the folder that everyone in the Project Garden uses to retain our files. If that's the case, I'd be able to grab everything they prepared for the project."

"And if that's not the case, then what?"

Can he not ask me the hard questions in succession? "Then, we do what we always do: ask our managers for help. Shiori would probably be more helpful here, since if I'm not mistaken, she would know some details about that whole thing Muiren is dealing with. In general, she seems to always have some idea about the best way to deal with things, so she's always my go-to for whenever I'm in a pickle."

"Really?" August asked. "And she's– she's okay with it? I haven't had many interactions with Shiori, but every time I have spoken with her, it's given me the impression that she hates me."

"I doubt it." Yidarica shook her head. "Even if we disregard the fact that the two of you have only spoken rarely, Shiori's too busy to hate anyone here. She's just very direct."

"Direct," August repeated. He was clearly thinking now.

I wonder what it is he's thinking about. I can empathize with what he said, because when I first joined the Project Garden, I thought Shiori hated me too. But that's just the way she communicates, and over time, I've grown to like her communication style for what it is. She's one of the few people I've ever met that I don't have to constantly guess what it is she means or is implying. Shiori says what Shiori means, and it makes her much easier to understand.

Now, if only I could learn to do the same, without worrying about if I'm upsetting people or confusing them, or anything.

"I think," August said then, "that a nice, brief walk around the garden would only benefit the two of us. If we have to determine what we're going to do with our day, we could at least do so with sunlight and fresh air surrounding us, right? Plus, it's usually pretty quiet this time of day. Even with this being one of the more remote areas of the office, you can't beat the scenery in the garden, especially the area near the birdbath."

There was also the iron bench Yidarica loved to sit on whenever she went there, because the balance of all the different sounds around the garden seemed to converge in the perfect ratios when she sat there. But before she could agree to the idea, the door to their area opened and Muiren walked– almost ran– inside.

"Oh, you guys are here, great," they said, winded. "I'm back! I'll be back for the rest of the day. I won, bitches!"

August was clearly lost. "You… won?" he asked.

"For the second time in a row!" Muiren continued. "People here have really got to learn to not run to HR with complaints about me. I might be a little galling at times, but never so much that we need to get the professionals involved– and if I need to keep proving it… well, I'd actually prefer I didn't because that would get really annoying, because I hate talking to HR. But I will *never* go down without a fight!"

"That's… favorable, Muiren." Yidarica wasn't sure if she could consider anything surrounding the situation good, so she'd had to think of a different word to use. "I'm glad they were willing to listen to and believe you. I'd hope they're putting some initiatives in place so that you don't have to go through this again."

"You'd think." Muiren rolled their eyes. "But we all know there's no stronger bond than that of a multimillion-dollar company and their toxic corporate-brained men. No offense, August."

He shrugged. "No harm. I wouldn't consider myself corporate-brained, anyway. I have too much of a conscience for that."

Muiren laughed, a borderline cackle that filled the room. "I'm inclined to agree with that! Now, what do we say about getting down to business and hopefully giving Legal what they need so they can get off our backs, too?"

Chapter Thirteen

Aside from the social aspect of the thing– or perhaps because of it– this was kind of a dream team.

Yidarica was observant, and analytical. Muiren was creative, and had many connections. August was technical, and had the added advantage of appearing male in a corporate setting. There'd never be a team more perfect than this to take on any other problem in this building, Yidarica was certain.

Today, after a few weeks of trial and error, it was time to check on how the prototype interface had held up over the weekend.

"All right, you know I'm the least techy out of the three of us. What's the damage?" Muiren asked.

"Well, the basic menu seems to be appearing at the appropriate time…" The way August started this sentence made it very clear that there was going to be a "but" coming soon. "But the visual cues are missing from the screencaps. It is possible that all the screencaps were taken on bad frames, though; I'll have to look at the videos that were recorded. If they're not showing up, I'll have to dive into the code and see what's missing."

Dive into the code? That sounds… laborious, for lack of a better word. "Would you need some help with that, the 'diving in' part?" Yidarica asked. "It sounds like a lot."

August was busy watching the videos that had been recorded over the weekend, but took a moment to glance up at her. It was difficult to tell if the brief smile he gave her was to reassure her, or if it was the result of observing her. "It usually is, but now that I think about it: if we have permission to, it would be a lot easier to use one of the meeting rooms to try and suss out what's wrong here."

"That we do. Shiori got me those permissions when I was named head of the project," Yidarica said, excited to be using a meeting room again. And without a manager this time! It was so exciting!

"Great. Well, it looks like we're going to need to go down that road, because none of these videos are showing any of the overlays," he said, sighing just a little bit. "It's fine. If the three of us are in the room, I'm sure at least one of us will catch the issue. When should we do this?"

"Now, probably," Muiren spoke up. "Correct me if I'm wrong, but I don't think we can do anything else until we establish what was missing here, right?"

"Precisely," August pointed a finger in Muiren's direction. "Yidarica, how soon can we have access to a meeting room?"

"Immediately, probably. I just need to check what rooms are available."

While checking the office's database for available rooms, Yidarica ran into a problem she hadn't foreseen: if August was the one who created the code, he'd have to be the one who controlled the room, but he likely didn't have the permissions to do so; and with Legal making it clear they wanted this project done yesterday, they didn't have the grace of waiting at least a day for him to obtain that.

"Everything okay?" Muiren asked.

"It's fine! Everything is fine!" Yidarica replied quickly. *Why did I just lie? I'm making it worse!*

She stared at the form to request a room and noticed there was a section that said: *Projection Access (people who will be accessing the room's environmental control)*

This field had the ability to enter more than one name, so she typed all three of their names and silently prayed to the Mother that she wasn't stopped because of it. When she got to the bottom of the page, and was able to confirm the reservation, she heaved a heavy sigh of relief.

"That's taken care of," she said proudly. "I booked us a half-hour in Strudel, which becomes available in about five minutes. Shall we head over there now?"

***

Yidarica's knowledge of the back end of her employer's applications was minimal; while knowing more about it than Muiren, who knew nothing about coding, she would never call herself an expert on the matter. And so, when she stood just inside the meeting room she'd booked, watching August type in some codes to get the projection going, she could only be amazed.

I wonder where he learned all of this? It's impressive.

"We are good to go," August said as he tapped the "Enter" button.

Not long after, the room quickly populated with all the various pages of the Food & Goods and Weather apps, hovering in the air like tangible touch screens one after the other, illuminating the area. Strewn throughout the room were lines of coding, in an electric blue color; random letters, numbers, and symbols, as far as the eye could see, that made both of these applications function.

It was mesmerizing, even if August was the only person who would understand it fully.

"This looks great in here!" he noted, smiling. "I wasn't sure how everything would appear in real time, but this makes it easier to parse than if we were looking at it on a screen. If I'm right, in order to find out where the issue is, we'll need to find the end page simulator. I don't know exactly *where* we would find that, though."

"And I don't even know what an end page simulator *is*," added Muiren. "Yidarica? Any words of wisdom?"

Meanwhile, Yidarica was busy still taking everything in, mesmerized by all of the colors and lights. She hadn't been expecting such a technical display, because all of the meetings she'd attended so far leaned more heavily on the visual output of the rooms. This was one of the instances where she was glad to be learning something new about her workplace. "I think..." she started. "The end page simulator isn't actually a page itself, right? So it wouldn't be displayed on one of these bigger windows. August, when you wrote the code in, where did you put it– like, on what line? We need to find that area."

"Oh! Right. I created a conditional for it, but it's pretty far down on the document," August explained. "I had to move it that far down, so that the overlay wouldn't accidentally display on days where there's no inclement weather. But are we going to have to walk all the way to it? I wore my dress shoes today."

Muiren raised their hand. "I've got an idea."

August smiled at them. "Of course, Muiren. What's up?"

"I can't believe today is finally the day where I get to use one of the tricks I have stored in the back of my mind, but..." Muiren trailed off as they began to cast a spell, summoning bright yellow-tinted light to the area in a ring-shaped formation before it all settled on the floor, just in front of where the three were standing. It simmered there for a few seconds before an indescribable sound whooshed through the area, and wind began to blow. Muiren walked up to the newly created hole, and then waved, before leaping into it with a yelp.

"We have to… jump… down that hole," August realized. "I wish Muiren had stuck around for the reasons why I *really* don't want to do that."

"Oh, August. Are you afraid of heights?" Truthfully, Yidarica was extremely afraid of heights herself, but it helped that the room was mostly dark except for the light displays. Even so, if she thought too much about how unpleasant it would be to land on the ground– wherever the ground was– she could understand why he was less than excited about the idea.

"It's not heights so much as it is the falling sensation. I wouldn't call it pleasant. It's not something I want to experience."

August held out a hand, then. "I think I'll feel a lot more at ease about the whole thing if we go together, though."

I want to be cautious about this, but at the same time– holy hell, it's like my dreams just came true in a span of five seconds. There is nothing more I'd like right now than to hold your hand, August Sostrin. I'm probably gonna squeeze it, too. Maybe even yell directly into your ear, if I'm feeling funky.

"Yeah, let's go," Yidarica agreed, reaching for August's hand. His skin was so soft, but it was impossible to ignore that it was also very warm, and just a tad sweaty, most likely because of his nerves. With each of them nodding to one another to confirm they were ready, they leapt together, into the magic hole.

As soon as the ground under her feet was no longer solid, Yidarica instantly felt dread, as if she was free-falling. It was as if her stomach dropped farther than however deep this hole was, but as frazzled as this fall had her, she would bet that it was affecting August even more; they hadn't been falling for long before he progressed from squeezing her hand to holding onto her arm tightly. And not long after that, he must have decided that this still wasn't enough, because by the time they reached the ground– with a much softer landing than either expected– Yidarica was enveloped completely in his arms.

This is not how I ever imagined August would be holding me, but… I would never complain about it.

She felt dizzy– for more than one reason.

I don't want him to let me go. I want to stay here, in his arms. Can't we forget about work, just for a little while? Stay here, and remain in each other's arms forever? Confess our undying devotion to each other, maybe?

"Hey! It's about time you got down here. We need to–" Muiren had caught up to where the two had landed, but stopped when they saw how close they were. "Or I can give you some privacy. Whichever works best."

This clearly flustered August, as he hurried to place Yidarica on the ground and let go of her, turning away so quickly that it was almost impossible to see the blush encompassing his face. "You really ought to tell people when we'll be jumping off things. Some of us need to be prepared for that."

"It wasn't so much jumping off of something as it was jumping into something, but noted," Muiren replied. "Anyway, the important thing is: did it work? Are we where we need to be?"

Now mostly recovered, August looked up and around. In this area, there were multiple depictions of gradually shifting weather;

the area the trio was currently standing in was sunny and beachlike, but a few feet away, an area with sparse trees and plenty of mud was pouring rain. Farther away still, an area densely populated with trees was experiencing high winds; these were the types of visuals Yidarica was used to seeing in meeting rooms, but they had never been so chaotic.

"It certainly looks as though we're in the right area. This is where the visuals for weather depictions are stored. I had no idea it would be this beautiful."

He started off, leaving his coworkers to follow behind, and it was easy to tell he was mesmerized by everything going on. The look on his face as he sifted through floating lines of code reminded Yidarica of her face upon the rare occasions she would receive birthday gifts as a child: a face of unbridled joy, and equally as adorable.

Everything he does just makes him even cuter.

"I think this is it," August slowed to a stop in front of some particularly colorful lines of code. "At a glance, it does look like everything here is correct. It's not even the case of me forgetting any semicolons, which is the usual culprit. It looks as though everything is mirrored correctly in both applications. Maybe it has to do with this line placement? Maybe I placed it too far down."

He scrolled through a few lines, thinking, while Muiren and Yidarica watched, waiting for him to have some sort of epiphany about the code.

"Wait! I think I know what's happening!" August turned toward his teammates. "The lines that complete the integration between the two applications, they may not be in the correct order. I didn't think that mattered, but I could be wrong; let's move some lines around and see if that fixes the issue. That should go right over… here, that one can go here… and this at the beginning. There we are. I bet everything will work perfectly once we confirm that's been fixed." He immediately pulled up the notepad on his tablet and began to type.

"Glad to hear it's a minor issue," Muiren said, in the type of tone one took when they were still lost, but supportive. "So... what do we do from here?"

"In a couple of seconds, we can give the entire thing a test drive," August replied, putting the final touches on whatever he was typing. "There it is. Now let me just go into the backend of the weather forecasting service and manually create a situation that would ideally require one of the overlays and pop-ups to appear. If we were to say it was going to snow in about ten minutes, how does that affect the Food & Goods order page–"

Before August could finish that statement, the environment around the three began to snow heavily, the flakes coming down hard and quickly accumulating. Yidarica immediately shivered, and Muiren didn't look very comfortable either, but August's face was filled with glee; he was too excited to pay much attention to how drastically the environment had shifted.

"That's it! It works!" He laughed, grinning so hard his face trembled just a little bit, as he bounced in place. It was easy to tell that he was trying to restrain himself from jumping with joy. "I can't believe it! I didn't think I had the appropriate knowledge to pull something this monumental off, but I... I did it. No, *we* did it, together. This is amazing!"

"It is amazing, isn't it?" agreed Yidarica.

"As amazing as it is, can we get back to our perfectly climate-controlled office environment?" Muiren asked.

"Oh! Yeah, of course. Sorry about that. I'll end the projection now." August pulled out his tablet again. "I'll have to delete the code I put into the Weather Application too, so I don't accidentally make people believe it's going to snow anytime soon." As he typed, the room began to wind down, returning to its normal dark state, as the three began to leave, walking back to the area they had claimed as their base.

"When we get back, I have to do a write-up of the revisions I made for the report, Yidarica, and then I can give it to you," August explained as they walked. "If something doesn't make sense, I'll be happy to revise it until it does."

"You're the best, August," she said, hoping it didn't sound too much like flirting. *But it would be the opposite of a bad thing if he interpreted it that way.* "Do you think you'll need our help with that?"

"Almost definitely. It'll be a good idea to use all of our perspectives to create a comprehensive report," he replied. "Especially from the view of someone who isn't familiar with the coding aspects of things. Right, Muiren?"

They looked over, surprised. "Me? Uh, yeah. Sure, but why?"

"Because you're a part of this whole adventure, silly," August laughed. "But to be more specific: the report we submit is going to be read by a great many people in both of our departments and beyond, all with differing strengths and skill levels. Inevitably, some of those people will be like you: those more inclined to the graphic and visual design aspects of our work, who won't be as well-versed in tech. A good report will ensure that they can understand its contents, as well."

He's right. If for no other reason, Legal will absolutely be looking over our work, and I'm inclined to believe none of the people over there would know anything about the work August just did. Your input is so valuable, Muiren. I hope you understand that.

"That makes sense," Muiren admitted. "I'll help as best as I can. Is anyone thirsty? I think a monumental success like this should be celebrated with fresh juice. Wouldn't you all agree?"

I don't think there's ever been a time where I said no to a fun little drink. August and Yidarica agreed immediately. "Oh, just– I'm extremely allergic to starfruit, so if we have any here, could you please forgo it?" August asked.

"Of course. After you saved our project from infinitely dragging on, it'd be in horrible form to kill you," Muiren laughed. "I'll take a detour, then. Meet you guys there?"

They split up then, Muiren heading to the nearby juice bar while the other two continued on to their work area. "August, I'm curious. Where did you learn so much about code?" Yidarica asked as they settled back into their seats. "Usually, people who are that well-versed in it are older."

"I think my confidence may have fooled you into thinking I'm more knowledgeable than I am," August laughed. "I promise I don't know as much as you think I do; I'm just *really* certain of what I do know. To answer your question, I was close to someone a long time ago whose mother was really into tech. It's a long story to get into, but when she took a liking to me, she began teaching me what she knew. Technology has always fascinated me, especially when it works directly alongside magic, so I was always eager to learn. I strongly believe that it was her tutelage that helped me get a job here, so I'll always be immensely grateful for that."

"For sure," Yidarica couldn't argue with that. "I suppose I should be grateful to this woman, too. It's because of her that we work together, and that you've been able to be this much help– but also, that I got to meet you at all. Part of the reason it's such a pleasure to work with you is because of your kindness and your accommodating nature, which is always refreshing to have around."

Am I laying it on a little thick here? Maybe, but I mean every bit of it.

"Well, thank you. It's really nice to hear that," August bashfully smiled. "But I think you should give yourself some credit as well. You're also very pleasant to work with. I can think of a hundred different ways this project could have been a disaster, especially considering I joined when it was already in progress, but from the beginning you made sure I was included. I appreciate that a lot. You're an incredible person, Yidarica, and I hope you realize that."

Yidarica's immediate response was to squeak a little. She had wanted to say something, but no words arrived at her mind before her mouth was ready to speak. Compliments from August frequently affected her in this way, but this time, her mind had gone especially blank because she had noticed that, with the way the two were sitting, their knees were touching.

I should not be losing my mind like this over something as minor as our knees touching... and yet, here we are. I need to say something before this gets weird! But what can I say?

Fortunately, she was saved from needing to speak when Muiren arrived at the door, having to slowly push it open with their back since their hands were full. "I did not take into account how there'd be a lot less fruits available in the late morning," Muiren pulled the door closed behind themself. "I did my best to make a drink that evokes the imagery of summer, to signify the change in seasons that we're due for any moment now. No starfruit, so don't worry, August. You kids didn't get into any trouble with me gone, did you?"

Yidarica laughed as Muiren poured everyone some juice. It was funny to have the youngest person in the room call everyone else "kids."

"We were on our best behavior, I assure you," August said as he sipped his juice. "Mm. Tasty. So, do you guys have plans for lunch today? We could make some, if you don't."

"Ah, well, you know me: eating the one vegetarian dish that's offered, picking around any lettuce, same as always," Muiren replied. "But... I... *think* I may have made plans with a friend for today, actually. Why don't you and Yidarica eat together without me? You can talk about all that really cool techy stuff you just pulled off somehow. I'll catch up with you after lunch!"

Muiren left the room quickly, but not so quickly that Yidarica didn't see the wink aimed at her. *So they're trying to play matchmaker, huh?* "Lunch with you sounds lovely, if you'll have me." August stood, offering a hand. "Want to go see what's on the menu today? I think I may have overheard some talk about strawberry lemonade cake."

Yidarica quickly grabbed August's hand so she could stand. "Let's go," she said. Nothing in this world was going to keep her from strawberry lemonade cake.

Chapter Fourteen

Yidarica was working from home today, and she hadn't been on the clock for more than ten minutes when she got a text message from Gracia.

> I swear to the Mother, Yida, you will not believe the email I got while I was asleep

Gracia was never one for understating things, that was for sure. It was what made it so hard to resist immediately responding to her texts.

> I'm working, but I can spare a little time. What's going on?

While she waited for Gracia's response, she continued to review the draft of the week's progress email to send to Celosia. It was strange– it was like so much and, at the same time, so little had been done. They had the majority of the project taken care of at this point, but there had been so many setbacks getting here...

Silently, Yidarica hoped that Legal wouldn't chastise any of them when the project was finally done. Especially not her, but she'd be lying if she said she didn't experience intense sadness at the idea of anyone yelling at Celosia. She was much too soft for that. And she was sure that Muiren and August could take it, but didn't particularly like the idea of them experiencing confrontation, either.

This was her team. She cared about all of them, which meant she wanted the best for them, which extended to not wanting any of them to experience any undue hardship.

Gracia's response came in then:

> **My cousin just texted me. He's got an in for our group to perform at the Firefly Migration festival!**

Yidarica almost dropped her phone.

> **He what?!**

The aforementioned festival was one of, if not the, biggest attractions in Sonusia; people from all over usually came to see it, and only the coolest and most prolific people were ever invited as performers. There had never been anyone on that stage who wasn't a household name, so needless to say, this news came as a shock.

What would we even do with an audience like that? Our music doesn't exactly appeal to the masses. A crowd like the one the Migration Festival pulls wouldn't want to hear us... would they?

It was still amazing to think of, though: the idea of performing in front of that many people, having that much attention put onto the band...

As long as we don't mess things up, it would be monumental. And of course, that was when all of the feelings of inadequacy began to pour in.

I'd mess everything up. And as the bassist, if I mess up, I'm messing everybody else up, too. Would it even be worth it? What would be the point in me bringing everyone out just to embarrass us and ruin our reputation like that?

Yidarica wanted to be excited for this, but all she could do was be nervous. And of course, whenever she got nervous, it was only a matter of time before her feelings became defeatist. That was how things always were.

She messaged Gracia:

> have you told anyone else in the band yet?

> Of course I did, but you're the first to reply. Wally and Ceri are both at work. Landen probably is too.

Today was Thursday, which were usually lab days for Cérilda; which meant it would be a while before she would be anywhere near her phone. As she had explained to the band once, lab days meant that for hours on hand, she was either looking at things through a microscope, or updating her job's database with new findings, with a side of asking her coworkers for assistance. Whenever the topic of Cérilda's work was at hand, Yidarica pictured her in her pristine white lab coat, seated at a table with who knows how many new specimens, taking notes about each one as she went along. Yidarica would never be able to conceptualize what exactly those notes would be, but even when she'd first met Cérilda, she had accepted that she was simply more intellectual than most other people. After all, not many people were able to work in biology labs at the age of twenty-two.

Conversely, imagining Walchelin at work conjured thoughts of brightly colored displays, of small humans full of energy, and a generally higher than normal noise level. He had mentioned teaching a first grade class this year, which was an adjustment because he'd taught third grade for the previous two school years, but with this came a certain level of both whimsy and patience. It was always interesting to hear Walchelin talk about his students; he clearly cared about them, and they mostly seemed to be rather fond of him as well, but he'd sometimes mention getting the (oftentimes, unsolicited) feedback that he'd be an excellent father, and this was something that he clearly didn't like to hear. It was easy to tell that he enjoyed being able to give his students back to their parents at the end of the school day.

Yidarica was distracted then by the sound of a Slapdash message.

New message from August Sostrin
Hey, good morning. I'm going over the code again to be sure we've crossed all our Ts - do you know what this is? It seems to be blocking the Food & Goods display from coming up, specifically whenever we're expecting high winds.

Attached was a screenshot, with an arrow pointing to what appeared to be a pop-up conditional menu. Conditional...

Yidarica typed:

That's one of the optional menus that pops up under certain conditions within the application. I assume that, like the code you wrote, it's also coded with a conditional, so maybe it and the overlay are interfering with one another?

While she waited, she checked her phone again. The band chat hadn't moved. She wasn't sure what she wanted to say to Gracia, so she wanted to feel out how everyone else felt to see if that would help her form an opinion.

In the meantime, a Slapdash message sounded off.

```
New message from August Sostrin
Yidarica, you're amazing. That's exactly what's
happening! That kind of conflict is out of my
wheelhouse, but I'm going to go run this over
to Shiori to see if she knows who's familiar
enough with this code to know if I can move it
without breaking anything else, since I at least
know where to start now. Much appreciated!
```

Yidarica, you're amazing. This line repeated itself in her mind, making her feel warmer and fuzzier with each repetition. She wasn't sure if she agreed, but the fact that August thought so— August, of all people! It made her feel like everything up until now had been worth it; not just at work, but in life in general.

An unreal opportunity for the band, and more one-on-one communications with August. Life is good sometimes.

***

As Yidarica slumped onto her couch after work, it became very obvious to her that she'd been slacking on home maintenance again.

I know I need to be better about keeping this place tidy, but between work and commuting, it's been so hard to reserve the energy I need to give this place a good cleaning. I hate this. I put all of that work into cleaning just for it to get dirty again eventually. It never ends.

Whenever she spoke to anyone she trusted about having difficulty with keeping up with cleaning, at some point, the advice to "take it a little bit at a time" always seemed to come up. It made a lot of sense, but when Yidarica tried to put it into practice, she found herself struggling with the concept. For example, her living room at the moment: she had a few empty boxes that needed to be broken down and taken to the dumpster, some assorted trash on the coffee table, her vinyls were out of place, there were still dead leaves from the last plant she'd killed, and then, there were also a few small articles of clothing she needed to put away. Of course, the place could always use a good sweeping and mopping too, and cleaning of the windows. Where she struggled was trying to decide which of these needed to be done first. Of course the boxes would be taken out last because other stuff also needed to be thrown out, so she could take the trash and boxes out in one go. But the leaves? The table? How could anyone decide what order these tasks needed to be done?

She was alerted to a phone call then, which pushed aside all of the overwhelming thoughts of her living room and its need for a cleaning. It turned out to be a call from Zaya, which she happily answered.

"Hey, Yidarica! I wanted to call and talk to you since I know it's been a little while, and the last time I saw you in person, things were a bit hectic. Do you have time for that?"

Boy, did she. "Yeah, of course. What's been happening? Is your dad doing better?"

"That's a big part of the reason I wanted to talk to you," Zaya replied.

Yidarica noticed the shift in her tone; she didn't sound as though she was about to deliver the worst outcome, but it was easy to tell that something bad was about to happen. Her stomach tightened, unsure of what other bad news could be on the horizon. "O-of course. What's going on?"

"Where to start… well, as you've probably been able to infer, after Dad fell and was sent to the hospital, they ended up finding a lot of underlying health conditions we never knew about, 'cause getting the old man to go to the hospital has always been like pulling teeth. The good thing is that it was easy to get him in stable condition again after the big surgery, but his recovery will be long, and this does call into question how we're going to maintain the nursery while that happens. Selling it is not an option, because he's put so much work and so much love into it, and we're all sure he'll want to take over again once he's fully recovered. But it does leave us with a lot of time to account for, and our family has been debating it for days to try to find an optimal solution in the meantime.

"There is something that complicated the whole debate, too. Currently, I'm the only person in the family who lives near the nursery. A week ago, I would've had no problem taking over operations, but… I ended up having to tell them all not to consider me an option as an owner or store runner. You know that I've been applying to jobs in the communications field the entire time I've lived here, while I've been working at the nursery. It's been a long, grueling process, but I was recently offered a position."

Yidarica gasped. "Zaya, that's amazing!"

"Yeah, it is. But the less amazing part is, it will require me to move away immediately."

And there it was. Immediately, it was like Yidarica's spirits plunged to the first floor of her building. She had a mildly amusing thought about how pissed that would make the people who lived there, but that emotion was fleeting. Her thoughts were consumed with how sad she was to possibly never be able to see Zaya again. She was lost for words.

"You're quiet," Zaya noted.

"I am," Yidarica agreed. "What am I supposed to say? Am I ever going to see you again, Zaya?"

There was a brief silence. "Yes, of this I am sure. I will still visit occasionally. My cousins will be running the nursery. Dad will still be here too, checking in as much as his health will allow him to, which means I'll always be tied to Sonusia. But I think... considering everything that's happening, I think that friends will be the extent of our relationship, Yidarica."

Of course it will. That's how it always is.

"I understand," she said, trying her best to conceal her disappointment. "When do you leave?"

"Tonight, actually. I have to meet one of my aunts at the city border so she can take me the rest of the way to the city I'll be working in, which is why the constraint is so tight. I start my job next week."

So soon. "I guess this means you don't have time to stop by for one last hug, then."

"Don't be ridiculous, I always have time for another hug. I'm at the nursery now, so I can be there in less than ten minutes."

That means I need to keep it together for ten minutes.

Yidarica surprised herself with how stoically she sat on her couch as she awaited Zaya's arrival. The exact opposite of a surprise, though, was how quickly the floodgates opened once the two women hugged.

I know it hasn't been a long time since Zaya and I actually began speaking to one another, and I know that my emotions when it comes to her are a mess, after what happened between us that time. But I like to think that she's my friend, too, and it'll always hurt to have to say goodbye to a friend.

"Okay, okay. Let's try to cry a little less. I don't want my memories of you to be a sniffling mess," Zaya gently scolded Yidarica.

"Sorry. I can't help it. I'm an emotional baby," she admitted.

"I wouldn't say you're a baby. You're very aware of your emotions, and I admire that about you." Zaya took one of Yidarica's hands and held it tightly. "I know that things got complicated between us for a while, but still, I'm so happy that I got to meet you."

"You are?" Yidarica sniffled.

"I am." Zaya smiled. "You're truly one of a kind. I'll never forget you, Yidarica, and I can only hope you find someone soon that's better for you than me."

This was something Yidarica wanted to refute, but she wasn't sure why. It wasn't irrational to think that, in the long run, she and Zaya would have run into problems if they had pursued a relationship. And that was fine. Yidarica had known that for years: not every person she was attracted to would be compatible with her dating-wise, and that was okay. *But would it kill me if at least one of them was?*

"I hope you find someone of your own, as well," was what she decided to say.

"I'm sure we both will."

The two shared one last kiss before Zaya left to continue packing.

***

The next day at work, Yidarica sat alone, letting Muiren and August know that she was "emotionally distressed" and couldn't handle much socialization. Everything had been too short-notice for her to ask Shiori if she could work from home today, so she'd gone into the office and tucked herself away in one of the quieter corners of the building.

Even if I already had an inclination that things wouldn't work out between me and Zaya, getting confirmation of that… it hurts. Who will I talk to about plants now? And how much closer am I to the point where I know for sure my days are numbered? I imagine that each subsequent heartbreak I've experienced in my lifetime has only brought me closer.

She sighed aloud, the sound bouncing back to her. It had been so quiet in the area that it startled her. The only other sound she'd heard all day, aside from her own typing, was the occasional distant rumble of thunder. At least today's scheduled downpour would wash away any tears that fell on her way home.

The day was ending now, at least, so she could go home and have a good cry. As she was packing up to leave work, August approached her, clearly intending to strike up a conversation.

"How did you know I was here?" she asked before he could make it all the way to where she had been stationed.

"I didn't. This isn't far from Celosia's desk, and I needed to go see her so she could approve some time off for me in a couple of months so I can attend a friend's wedding," he explained. "With that taken care of, I was on my way out when I noticed you. It's hard not to, I'm sorry," he gestured toward her rainbow-colored vest.

Yidarica nodded. She certainly hadn't dressed the part of someone who didn't want to be perceived today, she could admit.

"So, um, not to ask about work when you've clearly already clocked out, but what are we doing from here?" he asked. "I'm just a little curious."

Yidarica stood, looking up at August. *Maybe work talk is what I need to distract me from my feelings. I can indulge him for a little while.* "Yeah. Now, I have to arrange all of the notes we took while the project has been in process, and formulate them into a neat and tidy… almost like a postmortem, for archival purposes. That'll be our final report. We do this for every project when it ends, but this one is gonna need to be super detailed given how big and urgent of a request it was; but the three of us have discussed that before, so I'm sure you already know that."

"I see. You're not taking that on alone, are you?" August asked.

Yidarica looked up at him again, confused. "Why wouldn't I? You did so much of the legwork when it came to coding our solution, and Muiren was an absolute monarch when it came to designing all of those overlays. It makes sense for me to be the one doing this part, especially since being extremely analytical is my greatest strength."

"That makes sense, I suppose. But it doesn't feel right to leave you with all of that responsibility," August explained. "When Muiren was creating the designs for our overlays, they deferred to the both of us for guidance and feedback. When I needed to correct the code I'd written, I wanted the two of you there, even knowing you might not be as well versed in the intricacies in coding, because it's always helpful to have fresh eyes. To have you work on our final report all on your own... not only does it feel wrong, but it also feels extremely tonally different to how we've done literally everything else for this project. Even when you send our recap emails to Celosia, we compose those as a team."

Damn it, he's right. I just want to pick up the slack I've left from barely doing anything this whole time, but I admit he's got a point.

Yidarica wondered how she should handle the dilemma this posed, before deciding that she could simply tell August why she was hesitant. He seemed to be empathetic enough that she felt no reason to believe he'd be difficult here.

"You're absolutely correct," she said. "But you have to understand that for the duration of this project, the heavy lifting has been you and Muiren. Which, I don't mind that at all, but it does leave me feeling like I haven't pulled my weight enough; and so, since writing emails and communications and stuff is the one thing I can contribute to this whole thing, I just... I need to do this."

August gave her a curious look. "Do you seriously think that's all you've contributed to this whole thing?"

"Yeah. Isn't it?" Yidarica pulled her work bag over her shoulder as she and August began to walk.

"So all of the knowledge you have of how our applications work and the overall hierarchy of the Weather Department was nothing?" he asked. "I've only just started working with them, so I don't know a whole lot just yet. And while Muiren has been with you guys' team forever, they'll be the first to admit they know jack squat about the inner intricacies of you guys' department. You've contributed so much. You literally just helped me with coding a couple of days ago."

Why does he have to make so much sense?

"Listen, I understand what it's like to inhabit a space and feel as though you have nothing to offer to it, so I'm okay with you taking it on alone if that's what you need to prove to yourself that you're valuable," August said then. "But please also understand that no one else involved agrees with that sentiment. It isn't– I would feel horrible knowing that you shouldered such an important part of this project alone. If you truly refuse to let anyone help you, then… then, can I treat you to lunch tomorrow?"

Yidarica froze in place, in the middle of the entrance to the MFI office. The only thing that caused her to move was the door hitting her in the back. "Ow! Uh, what?" she asked.

"And feel free to refuse, of course, but I've been meaning to check out The Spinning Top for months now, and I hear it's immensely more enjoyable with company," August elaborated.

"I've heard of that place!" Yidarica nodded. "Um, I… that sounds really fun. I guess that would be all right. Are you sure, though?"

"Absolutely. Outside of any obligations, it's always nice to get an opportunity to hang out with a friend, right?" August smiled bashfully. "I look forward to it. Oh! Hold on, I should probably make sure we can keep in touch with each other, just in case one of us has something come up that's out of our control. Could I put my number into your phone?"

At least there's no door here to whack me this time. "Uh, yeah, of course," Yidarica replied, reaching into her pocket for her phone, before handing it over. "Go nuts."

Curse my predisposition to either be a stuttering mess or the most bland person in the world when I'm trying to keep it cool.

They'd reached the outside of the building now, where indeed, rain was pouring from the sky. Yidarica reached into her bag and was horrified that she didn't feel her umbrella. *Wait. That's right. It's in a different bag. I was carrying a different bag last time it rained. Darn it, not again!*

Judging by the seemingly never-ending expanse of dark gray stratus clouds, the downpour wouldn't be stopping anytime soon, so it wouldn't be wise to try and wait out the storm. What could she do to prevent herself from becoming a wet, sopping mess on her way home?

August looked back, realizing Yidarica was no longer at his side; when he saw her still standing under the building entry, he walked back to where she was. "What's wrong?" he asked.

"Left my umbrella in a different bag." Yidarica sighed. "Excellent day I'm having."

"Oh." August looked at his umbrella, which was decorated in a stunning blue, purple, and pink ombre. He then looked at Yidarica, and then at the umbrella again, before holding it out toward her. "Here. This suits you."

Yidarica gasped. "But then you'll…"

"I'll be fine. I live nearby, so I can make it home before this wears off." August paused for a moment, summoning warm golden magic particles into his hands. They simmered there for a moment before he placed his hands over his head, and sparkles cascaded down through his hair and on his clothes: a dryness spell. With that taken care of, the two set off in the same direction, away from the building, and were silent for a few moments before August spoke again. "All I ask is that you give that back eventually. Oh, and here you go." He handed her phone back to her. "So that settles it, then. I'll see you tomorrow?"

Yidarica nodded. "Tomorrow!"

She waved, having reached the point where she needed to turn to get to her station, as August continued walking down the street.

I can't believe it. I have August's phone number. Should I send him something so that he knows it's me? I should, right? I think I should, but what should I send him? I don't want to freak him out. I guess I could always send him the same thing I send everyone when they first give me their number. That's pretty neutral.

The thing in question was a very cute magical projection that would toss an armful of glitter once the message was opened. People tended to respond positively to it because it didn't leave physical glitter, which was always a positive. She combined it with a short message reaffirming it was her, and sent it, continuing to wait for her rail car.

Just when she was about to step onto the rail car, a reply from August came through.

> **Haha, this was really cute. Thanks for confirming. Can't wait for tomorrow.**

Chapter Fifteen

Yidarica would, upon introspection about the subject, consider herself a fashionista. Every time she left her house, to enter a situation in which she knew she'd be perceived, deliberation and care went into the process of choosing her outfit for the day. The same, if not more, effort went into styling and accessorizing her hair. All this to say: when the day came around for her and August to meet at the Spinning Top, she still had no idea what she was going to wear.

It was a little silly, wasn't it? This was a man who had seen her countless times before, at work, so he had to be familiar with her whole deal by now. And neither had explicitly called it a date, even, so why was she being so meticulous when it came to what she wore? Maybe they were just hanging out for a few hours. Hangout time was always fun.

That's what I should do. I should dress for fun.

And in that moment, her eyes fell on the one cardigan in her possession that she'd never worn– partly because she had no idea what else to wear it with. It was meant to be oversized, and was dyed in a sherbet-colored ombre, with white buttons shaped like flowers. Very cute, but the issue was that when it was combined with many of Yidarica's other clothing, it was like all the colors were competing for dominance. She always told herself she'd need to get around to more neutral and boring clothing for times like these. As of yet, she had not done so.

"I have got to have *something* in this damn closet that's able to neutralize this cardigan," she muttered to herself, pushing hanging pieces of clothing aside in pursuit of the one thing that fit the description. "I know there's got to be something in here. I remember buying at least one dress that I never wear because it's too boring. Or was that in a dream?"

And then, as if by a conscious spell, she found it: a beige A-line dress with short sleeves and a Peter Pan collar. So neutral, so plain... so salivatingly boring that it was the perfect piece to accompany the pastel cardigan.

From there, all that was left was to spend a minute or two in the hairstyling area before heading out. This was her favorite part of getting ready to leave the house. Stepping in front of the mechanism, Yidarica tapped a few screen prompts before stepping in, placing the head attachment over her hair. Before long, a small sprite appeared in front of her.

"We have successfully loaded the history and saved favorite hairstyles of Yidarica Verbestel. What will we be doing to your hair today?"

Yidarica looked over at the orange-shaped clock on her wall, to see how much time she was working with; she was due to meet August in an hour, but she also had to block out half of that to allow for the commute. With thirty minutes open, it was best to not get too elaborate. "May I see my history?" she asked.

"Certainly." The sprite conjured four projection images of the last time Yidarica had stepped into this contraption.

"Okay." Yidarica studied the photos, recalling that these were all hairstyles she'd worn to work. All fairly simple, but a little boring.

Also, considering that she and August knew each other through work, she didn't want him thinking she always looked the same. "Can I browse through my favorites now?"

"As you wish." Now, a feed of every hairstyle Yidarica had ever given a heart to appeared in front of her. She had a sizable collection, so it took a little time before she was able to make a decision.

"Okay. I think it's gonna be this one."

After a little thought, she had decided on the one with loose braids on the sides, pulled together by a bow, and with loose curls. It was a hairstyle that always struck her as being highly feminine, which was exactly what she was going for. As she sat, feeling the tiny sprites use their magic to curl and twist her hair, she felt her phone vibrate. It was a message from August!

> **Looking forward to seeing you. I am running a little late, but I'll be there, I promise. I didn't want you to think I was standing you up when I showed up late.**

Well, that was kind of him.

> **I haven't left yet, if you want me to wait for you?**

After all, being at the mercy of communal transportation meant she was personally a little *too* familiar with the concept of running late.

> **I appreciate it, but I don't think I'm running quite that late. If you want to leave out a few minutes later, though, I think you'd be golden.**

This was fine, since she wanted to be sure she looked perfect before she left the house; she'd take enough extra time to put some finishing touches onto her look for the day.

★★★

The Spinning Top had been named as such because it was a restaurant with completely randomized food options, which all arrived to their customers via a large, open spinning table that spanned the entirety of the restaurant. Yidarica had heard of it, but had never been; she could never quite grasp the concept of the place, and whenever anyone tried to explain it to her, she always ended up more overwhelmed than before. But this was the place that August had chosen, so here she was. Besides, she was pretty sure she'd be too focused on his cute face to get too overwhelmed by how overly complicated this place seemed to be.

Stepping into the restaurant, she noticed that there was a check-in counter, which appeared to also be where customers paid. Very little of the place could be accessed immediately upon entry, because not far behind the counter was what Yidarica first assumed to be a gate, until she realized it had to be part of the spinning table mechanism; now that she was seeing it in person, it made a lot more sense to her. The spinning mechanism was more akin to a conveyor belt than a table, which meant that eventually, food would travel down that path to the tables further inside. She couldn't see the tables from here, but they couldn't be too far away, since the restaurant itself wasn't very large.

"Welcome to the Spinning Top!" One of the hostesses, with bright pink hair, greeted her with a very sunny disposition. "Just one today?"

"I, um..." this caught her off guard. She'd been so busy studying the interior of this place that she'd forgotten about needing to speak to the staff... or anyone, really. "Two, actually. I'm waiting for the other person to get here."

"Oh, okay." The hostess nodded in understanding. "Do you want to be seated right away, or would you like to wait here for them?"

That is an excellent question. I probably should've asked August which one he preferred, but I was sure he'd get here first with my commute being longer. Wait, is he already here? He might already be here.

Before Yidarica could ask, though, the door behind her opened. With the slightest gust of wind, August had arrived, dressed only slightly more casually than he did at work. It was a surprise to see him in dark blue denim jeans, but the green, purple, and blue plaid long-sleeved shirt was very much his brand. Once his eyes adjusted to the lower light in the restaurant, and caught sight of Yidarica, he immediately smiled.

"I hope I didn't keep you waiting too long," were the first words out of his mouth.

Oh, August. I'd wait for you forever. ...actually, maybe not forever. Definitely slightly to moderately longer than normal, though.

"No problem!" Yidarica responded, practically beaming. "I was just now speaking to one of our lovely hostesses about our seating arrangement."

"Looks like I arrived just in time, then," August replied, giving a smile to the hostess before adding, "A table for two, please."

The two were taken through the gate portion of the table into the main body of the restaurant, which housed about fourteen tables situated on the walls of the room, each with the spinning, conveyor-like portion intercepting them in the middle. At this time of day, the restaurant was fairly busy, but not so much so that it was difficult to find seating. They were promptly seated at a table on the opposite side of the building from the entrance.

"It makes so much sense now," Yidarica murmured to herself as she took her seat.

"What makes sense?" August asked. Apparently, she hadn't been as quiet as she'd thought.

"Oh, the…" she started, being taken off guard. She hadn't been prepared to verbally answer this question. "Before, when I'd only heard of this place, it was difficult for me to mentally conceptualize how it worked. Now that I'm seeing it in real time, the pieces connect a lot easier."

"Ah, yeah. I admit, I didn't really understand it either, but I've overheard some of the other people in my building talking about this place enough times that it sounded like a big deal. I hope I wasn't wrong to assume that."

"I don't know, the smells from the kitchen are leading me to believe that you weren't," Yidarica replied. "But the one thing I'm not clear on is: when exactly can we expect the food to–"

Before she could finish that sentence, a plate of wings approached on the conveyor belt. They looked presentable enough, but the fact that Yidarica could already smell a hint of how spicy they were meant that she'd be passing on this round. August, on the other hand, made sure to grab one of the sauce-coated pieces of meat.

"None for you?" He asked.

She shook her head. Now that August had one of the wings on his plate, the spicy scent was bordering on uncomfortable.

"Consider me surprised if you still have your nose hairs after you're done eating that."

This made August laugh. "Don't worry about me. I like the occasional food with a little bit of spice," he said as he took a bite from the wing.

Less than five seconds later he began to cough, looking around almost frantically before noticing an unattended pitcher of ice water on the adjacent table, and pouring himself a cup. After he downed the entire thing, he coughed and said, "Bad idea."

"Really? You don't say?" Yidarica teased him.

He gave her a look before pouring another cup of water.

I was so nervous about this whole thing, but I'm not even the first to embarrass myself today. Things are going surprisingly well. I should let myself enjoy it.

***

After a few more platters had passed, and both August and Yidarica had been able to grab a few pieces to their liking, the latter noticed the table across from them, at which two swankily-dressed women were sharing an impressive-looking milkshake. Amidst her jealousy over currently not having a milkshake of her own, Yidarica realized that they must be on a date. A date… that thing that she could possibly, maybe, potentially be on herself.

This is my chance at clarity; I have to take it.

"Oh, those two look like they're on a date. That's so cute!" she said, making sure to make her voice sound sweet and free of expectations.

"Hm?" August looked up, and over at the table that Yidarica had pointed out. "Yeah, and it looks like it's a good one, if that milkshake is of any indication. This is a good date spot. If we'd been living here back then, I'd imagine this would be one of the places I'd continuously badger my ex-boyfriend into taking me to."

Boyfriend? Back then?!

There were now two questions Yidarica had to get answers to: how old August was, and if he was attracted to women at all. Excellent. Now she just needed to think of a way to get that information out of him.

"You've dated…" Yidarica started, but paused; not sure if she wanted to complete her sentence with "for a while" or "men." Which one did she want to know more?

Before she could decide, August nodded, as if the question had already been asked. "Mm-hmm."

Nailed it.

"Yeah, I mean, I'm thirty-two years old. It would be weird if I hadn't dated anyone yet, wouldn't it?"

Hearing this, Yidarica placed her hands in her lap, her gaze downcast. She had seven months until she reached the thirty-two year mark. And she had accepted long before now that she was weird (for many reasons, some unrelated to this), but there was a difference between her existing in that reality, and someone she liked using the term almost pejoratively.

I knew there would be something about me that August would find undesirable. I just wish it wasn't something as minimal as the combination of my dating experience and my age. I mean, it's not like I can help that no one seems to be interested in me. Would that I could, I would absolutely change that!

"Are you...? Oh, dear Mother, I'm so sorry," August apologized when he realized how quiet she'd gotten. "I didn't mean that— you—" he leaned in closer and whispered, "Are you not, like, twenty-eight years old? Somewhere around there?"

Yidarica blinked. "No. I'm thirty-one years old, August."

It was a reaction she had witnessed many times before, and probably would still in the future. She always figured it was because of the combination of her round face, short stature, and the colorful, whimsical clothes she wore. She didn't think this line of thought extended to people at work, but apparently, she'd been wrong.

"Huh." August regarded her curiously now. "Good genes? Took a trip to the Fountain of Youth? Anti-aging magic?"

"I don't know." Yidarica shrugged. "I just wake up every day, and my face is still like this."

"That's neat." August said then. "I wish I had that quality. So, you've never dated anyone? Really? I find that hard to believe."

She shrugged again. "Believe it."

"If it's any consolation, it's really difficult to find someone that makes it worth it," August added. "In fact, as I get older, I become more convinced that it's too much work for very little payoff."

According to my studies of people, this is the type of thing people say when they have personal experience with the subject matter. "How so?" Yidarica asked, proud of herself for getting the whole question out this time.

"Well..." the way August sighed was indicative of weariness. Yidarica almost regretted asking, but before she could rescind the question, he began to speak.

"You know how it is sometimes with the older generation: a lot of them are so preoccupied with maintaining the perfect family image— which, for many, extends to the ideal of creating a legacy—

that they don't take kindly to any circumstances that might threaten that ideal. My first boyfriend was part of such a family, so we had to keep anything alluding to our relationship a secret. Things were great, for a long time. When I told you that I learned about code from an older woman, it was actually his mother that taught me; his parents loved me, because they thought we were simply best friends, and they loved the way I always supported him and was kind to him. I thought I didn't mind this, but… you start to wonder why, after a while. Why, knowing that the relationship will always have to be secret, would you engage with it? After a while, I got frustrated. He got frustrated right back, saying I didn't understand. Which, yeah, that was the whole point– I *didn't* understand! And so, rather than explain to me why I should be okay with being a skeleton in his closet, he called it quits.

"After that, I absolved to never again be with anyone who behaved as if they were ashamed of me. So, a couple of years later, when I fell for a man who was very obvious and intentional with his feelings for me, it felt as though everything made sense. I think… I think that I was so relieved to have someone in my life who was so loud and forthcoming about their adoration of me, that I allowed myself to become dependent on that. That, as long as he told me he loved me, and was grandiose in displays of affection, I could overlook when he'd get angry and yell at me for forgetting something on the grocery list, or if I said something he didn't like and he hit me. It took me needing my glasses for me to understand that, even if I was being told I was loved, I wasn't receiving any of it.

"Since we'd begun living together at one point, when I left, I was on my own. I'd never been on my own before; I was scared. Months later, I regained contact with an old acquaintance from high school, and found myself falling for her beauty and wit. But... as I unfortunately got to learn firsthand, she wasn't a kind person, to me or anyone else. She hit me sometimes, too, but she was small, so she didn't usually leave bruises. Sometimes it was worse than hitting. I don't remember what made me decide I'd had enough, but I know that a major contribution was me telling her I got the job where we work. When I learned I would be interviewing at MFI, it felt like a dream come true, since I had always been enthusiastic about the idea of magic and technology coming together to create grand things. And when I learned I got the job, I was ecstatic, but she wasn't so enthused. She asked me, 'of all people, they picked *you*?' It hurt me deeply that someone who was supposed to love me thought I wasn't worthy of a job I had been very clear about wanting. So, I left. I didn't tell her I was leaving until I was already on the train back to my parents' house, with all of my things accounted for so she couldn't destroy them in retaliation, which was a large fear of mine."

Yidarica was silent. Even if she had covertly discovered that August liked both men and women, she couldn't bring herself to react in any way. *He's so sweet, and yet, he's been through so much.*

"I've never told anyone about that last one, by the way," August added as he sipped his drink. "Just that we broke up. It hurt a lot to stay silent, but I knew that I couldn't tell anyone. The reactions I knew I'd get if I said that cute, tiny woman hurt someone who looks like me..."

Yidarica nodded solemnly. "I'm very flattered that you feel comfortable enough with me to share this."

"I can't describe it, but there's something about you that puts me at ease," he explained. "There's a certain... aura surrounding you. It's very calming. Enticing, in that way; it's why I enjoy your company. Part of why, anyway."

"I'm glad." She smiled. "The fact that you aren't permanently put off by cute tiny women is reassuring."

Yikes. That was probably the worst thing I could've said as an attempted flirt. Where are the forgetfulness spells when I need them?

"Yeah, it's– it was a learning experience, since she was the first woman I ever dated. There are certain social aspects that are different from dating men. It was fascinating to learn," August smiled as he reminisced. "Fortunately, it wasn't the worst experience I could have had. Women do cute things like curl their hair and ask me to grab things off of high shelves for them. And your bodies have a completely different magnificence to them than men do. I wouldn't consider myself a person who relishes in nudity, but I was stunned to discover the beauty of a woman's breasts, whether clothed or not."

The most complicated feeling bubbled into Yidarica's stomach then. There was the usual discomfort at a topic that veered toward a sexual nature– but very vaguely, because she immediately recalled the second-to-last time she had seen Zaya in person. The sensations from sucking each other's nipples was probably the most beautiful thing she'd experienced up to that point in her life; marked only more beautiful by the fact that things hadn't gotten to a point where the further removal of clothes was necessary.

And then there was the curiosity. *Would I like it if August did that to–*

She cleared her throat then. "Agreed, honestly, as a person who's seen a decent amount of breasts in their time. There's something aesthetically pleasing about them."

August raised an eyebrow, but not for long. "Huh."

"Don't tell me you thought I was straight."

"No, I didn't assume that. There's something inherently queer about you that I could never quite place, but what *does* surprise me is that you can be so straightforward about it. I hadn't gotten that impression of you before now."

"Well, yeah. Every other time we've been able to talk to each other has been at work," Yidarica pointed out. "I might be tragically unable to notice most social norms, but even I know you can't just blurt out how much you love boobs at your place of employment."

August laughed then, loudly, and Yidarica found herself feeling both proud, and grateful that she'd brought him out of the somber mood his memories had placed him in. This was the most joyful she'd ever seen him, and she couldn't be happier.

"You've got a point there," he said, once he was able to catch his breath. "I think the office would foster a completely different environment, if we did things like that."

"One that I'm not entirely sure I'd like. Ooh, mozzarella sticks!" Yidarica gleefully picked them up from the rotating table, so preoccupied that she missed the brief moment that August gazed at her, adoration in his eyes.

"Can I ask you something?" she said then.

He nodded. "Sure. What's on your mind?"

"Your glasses. You mentioned there being a certain point when you were with your ex where you started to need them, so this is something that happened when you were already an adult, then, right? What was that experience like?"

"Oh." August ruminated on the topic for a moment before explaining. "To start, I'd like to clarify something a lot of people don't realize: sometimes, people are born with vision issues that are unrelated to Dark affliction. We're all familiar with how the Dark affects us if it takes hold– the dimming of light in our vision, the random black-toned obstruction of sight– but there are also people who don't have good eyes. I bring this up because ever since I was a kid, I've had issues with random blurriness in my sight; where I could be doing absolutely nothing, and then, my vision would be cloudy for a few minutes. Honestly, I never brought it up to my parents back then because I thought that happened to everyone. But when I started being affected by the Dark, my vision issues were exacerbated. My vision, as it is now, is not as dim as someone who had perfect vision before their affliction; but the blurriness is constant now, so it's at the cost of not being able to see much of *anything* without these. If I'm not wearing my glasses, everything is just badly lit blobs. The only way I'd be able to tell you and Muiren apart, for example, is because of the height difference."

Considering Muiren and I look nothing alike, that really hammers in how bad it is.

"It's not all bad. I can always just take my glasses off when I've decided I've seen enough," August smirked.

Yidarica laughed loud enough that the people at the next table over noticed– and she immediately stopped, embarrassed. For a moment, she noticed August's expression change slightly as he looked from the other table to her, but she couldn't quite understand the emotion that the change had conveyed. Sympathy? Pity?

"It's getting a little late," she said then, more than anything wanting to get away from the people beside them, who were now glaring at her intensely enough that she could feel it under her skin, crawling under it like the most unwelcome of insects intent on upsetting her. And by the Mother, they were doing a great job of it. "Should we go? I can go– I should go home."

"Whoa, hey." August gently grasped her arm to stop her. "Are you in a hurry? I can walk you home."

"Are you sure?" Yidarica asked. "It's a ways away. You don't have to go to the trouble."

"I insist; if you don't want me to walk you all the way home, I can at least take you part of the way," August replied. "Let me just pay for the check and we'll go."

"Okay." Her voice was soft. More than anything, she just wanted to be away from those judging eyes.

The sun was beginning to set when the two began to walk toward Yidarica's apartment building. "I, um, I hope you had a good time today," August said. "I did."

"You did?" She looked up at him.

"Yeah. It's always nice to get out and spend quality time with good people," he explained. "I noticed, though, that at a certain point something seemed to have upset you. I'm sorry if I played a part in that somehow; I know that the conversation got heavy for a little while there."

"It wasn't you." Yidarica shook her head. "It was those people near us. I laughed a little too loud, and because of that, they looked over at me with venom in their gaze. Once I saw it, I couldn't unsee it. It was as if they were staring into my very soul. Oh, how I wish I was better at ignoring people."

August was silent for a moment, staring down at his hands. "I can tell there's a part of you that feels you were partially in the wrong. The fact that those people were able to make you feel guilt for experiencing joy… I wish there was something I could have done to make that not be the case."

"I appreciate that," Yidarica replied. "Don't worry about it. Hopefully, that whole debacle will disappear from my mind the next time my brain fog rolls through."

They were now approaching the nearest Comtran station. "Well, this is it," Yidarica said, gesturing to the station sign. "I'll see you at work, then?"

"Count on it," August replied. "I really did have a wonderful day today, Yidarica. I hope you did too."

She nodded. "I did. Thank you for having me."

"It was my pleasure." August smiled before turning to begin his walk home. "Get home safe, all right?"

That smile… I will never get tired of seeing it.

Chapter Sixteen

Today would be one of those days where Yidarica pondered her existence.

The previous day with August had been amazing. There had scarcely been a moment in which she didn't feel like she was walking on air. But she had also been hyper-aware of the fact that he didn't seem to be returning her enthusiasm, and was now convinced that she was sliding headfirst into a dead end.

Or maybe he's just shy. He's always seemed quiet at work, before we were put together for this project.

But at the same time, it would be perfectly reasonable if he wasn't into her.

I mean, that's how it goes, right? I fall for a person who's filled to the brim with buts. I'm sweet, but. I'm kind, but. We've been having fun, but. I try and I try and I try. And yet, even the most positive traits of my personality are never enough.

Yidarica sighed. *Thirty-one.*

If the Dark was silently affecting her, how much more time did she have left? Those who were afflicted and went down a similar path that she was going down usually died a lot sooner than thirty-one. She'd felt like she was on borrowed time for the past two years at the very least.

It's not fair.

It wasn't, was it?

Why is our existence so heavily dependent on the emotions of others? Why is it that I can try my hardest to be good, to be kind, to be all of these positive things and still have it not be enough? I can't make August reciprocate my feelings. I couldn't make Zaya feel the same way about me as I felt about her. I can't make my friends admit that they're just putting up with me. There's nothing I can do to make anyone in this world love me. Hell, I couldn't even get my parents to love me. But– and pardon my transgression, Mother– I don't think it's fair that someday, I'm going to fucking die because of it.

And, honestly? Knowing that this is the way things have to be– what's even the point of living out the rest of however many days I have left? I lay here, and I can't help but wonder: would it even truly matter if I were to kill myself today?

There was a soft, almost unnoticeable twinkle tone right outside of Yidarica's window, which caused her to whip her head toward it. When she got to the window, though, she didn't see anything out of the ordinary. Even though it had been faint, she was certain she'd heard it– what could it have been?

Just as she was about to go back to her bed and continue to wallow, she heard it again– and felt the urge to look down this time. Standing on the path right outside of her building, there was a girl on a bike, no older than twelve. She wore green denim overalls with a bright yellow shirt, and her blonde hair was braided into two plaits.

She was speaking now, but her voice wasn't reaching this high. Yidarica lifted the window then.

"Are you Faerin?" the girl asked, sounding confused.

"No, I'm Yidarica," she replied. "Sorry to disappoint."

The girl shrugged, dejectedly. "It's fine. I guess she really did move away."

More than twenty years ago, Yidarica had been put into almost this exact same situation– she had been becoming close to a girl in her class, just to find out that she moved away one day, abruptly, with no warning. She never saw or heard from her again.

"Well, since she's not here, do you want these flowers?" the girl asked then.

Hard to say no to flowers. "Maybe. Whatcha got there?"

"I've got some, uh… roses and lilies of the valley."

"Interesting combination."

"Will you people shut your traps?!" someone on the first floor yelled. "I'm trying to put my son to sleep!"

Yidarica sighed, making a grand gesture of pointing toward the ground to signal to the girl that she was coming downstairs. Grabbing her phone, wallet, and slipping into a pair of shoes, she hurried down the flights of stairs to the front door to meet the girl outside.

"Sorry about that. The family on the first floor is the opposite of kind," Yidarica apologized. "Wow, your flowers are even more beautiful up close; the colors are so vivid, and they're full of life. Where did you get these?"

"They're mine," the girl replied proudly. "I spent the entire summer break practicing the spells I would need to get them this perfect, because I wanted to give them to Faerin. But I guess I took too long to finally get it right."

"Oh…" Yidarica pitied this small human, but she was also full of intrigue, so she sat on the steps to her building, and beckoned the girl to do so as well. "So, Faerin was a friend of yours?"

"She was the most beautiful girl I ever met." The girl smiled wistfully. "We've known each other since we were six years old, but she's always been sick. I don't think her parents like her very much. Sometimes when we were in class together, or during cheer practice, I'd see bruises. But what could I do about it? I'm just a kid! So I tried to make her time away from her parents happy and full of warmth. Last year, I told her I loved her, and that someday we could get her away from her home life. The next day her parents screamed at me and said I would never see her again, and… I guess… I won't. I just wish I could've said goodbye."

This is heartbreaking. Yidarica couldn't find the words to console this young girl, one she'd only met a maximum of ten minutes ago, but she felt her heart aching so much for her.

"I thought you were her for a minute, because of your pretty brown skin. But then I realized it was the wrong floor. Faerin lived on the second floor."

The second floor? That couldn't be right. The only person who lived on the second floor was that old lady that kept to herself, and she'd been in this building longer than Yidarica had.

Meanwhile, the girl was holding out some of the flowers now. "Take them. You look like you could use 'em."

"Thanks, um…"

"Ashelia."

Yidarica nodded. "Thank you, Ashelia. You know, I think I did need these. Maybe it's fate that we met each other today."

"Yeah." Ashelia nodded as well, a faint smile on her face. "Maybe so. I'm gonna go now. Take care of yourself, okay, Yidarica? A lot of people would miss you if you didn't."

As Ashelia mounted her bike, Yidarica felt her phone vibrate. A text from Muiren. On a Saturday? Why would they be texting her on a Saturday?

A lot of people would miss you if you didn't.

When Yidarica looked back up, there was no trace of Ashelia. Even the tracks from her bike had vanished.

The text from Muiren read:

> **Not sure why, but I feel like I need to text you this. My dad cooked a huge meal for the family today, a quantity we couldn't possibly all eat in one sitting. If you're hungry, why don't you come on by? Let me know if you're interested and I'll send ya my address.**

Well, the fridge in Yidarica's apartment had seen more food in the past than it currently had stocked, for sure.

> Sure, and thanks for the invite; I'd love to. Where am I headed?

***

Fortunately, Muiren's home was close enough that Yidarica felt comfortable walking there. Close enough that they probably shopped at the same grocery, and it was interesting that they didn't have the same Comtran route. But far enough that, by the time she stepped up the stairs to the door, she was fairly winded.

The doorbell tinkled with tones reminiscent of a ballet tune. Somewhere in the distance, she heard the unmistakable sound of children running and playing. It was the same sound she'd always hear from her bedroom as a child, forbidden to go out and play with other children.

Just short of enough time for Yidarica to catch her breath completely, a man answered the door: obviously at least in his mid-fifties, his brown hair peppered with strands of gray and silver tones. His skin bore the appearance of the passage of time, the wrinkles forming most obviously around his eyes and mouth. He had to have experienced a life of joy.

If I'm allowed to live so long, I hope people have similar assessments of me.

"Can I help ya?" were his first words.

"Uh, yeah, probably. Definitely. I don't know why I said–" Yidarica exhaled shortly. "I was invited here, uh, by Muiren. I think I'm in the right place..?"

At this, the man's brown eyes lit up. "Oh aye, you are! She said she'd have company. Come in!"

The man spoke so fast that Yidarica didn't have the opportunity to correct him.

Walking into the house, the first room visible was the living room, with its navy blue walls decorated with framed photos; there were black faux-leather couches that weren't dilapidated, but had definitely seen better days; but in a strangely comforting way, as if they had been lived in. Muiren was seated on one of these, with a large bowl on their lap, dressed in a dark green and black checkered sleeveless blouse, a black tank top, and gray denim shorts; the outfit was similar to how they dressed in the office, but in a more relaxed way. They sprung up at the sight of their coworker.

"Welcome! Found the place all right, I see," they smirked. "Dad, this is my friend Yidarica. We work together."

Yidarica's heart soared at her ears receiving the sound of Muiren referring to her as a friend. She'd made it! She was good enough at being a friend to be considered one!

"Ah, a pleasure to meet ya, Yidarica. Don't think Muiren's ever had a friend over, but she's always been a little awkward when it comes to—"

"Dad." Muiren nudged him.

"What? Oh, sorry. They've always been a little awkward when it comes to interacting with others. A shame it's taken this long for them to find people who appreciate the charm in that."

"Well, you know what they say." Yidarica shrugged. "To be weird is to challenge yourself to find somebody weirder than you and call them 'friend,' et cetera, et cetera."

The room went silent. "Who… says that, exactly?" Muiren asked.

"Nobody. I made it up." Yidarica laughed as the two sat on the couch together. "Sometimes I like to sound like I know what I'm talking about, you know?"

"A modern day philosopher, for sure," Muiren played along as their father made his way back to the kitchen. "Thanks for coming, by the way, especially on such short notice. I'm still re-adjusting to living with my folks, so it's nice having someone here to talk to who's not them or a child."

Yidarica frowned in confusion. "A child?"

"You've undoubtedly heard the racket back there," Muiren pointed toward the back of the house. "Those are my younger siblings. Bunch of hellions they are. I suppose they can be cute sometimes too. But…"

Muiren folded their legs under themself in their seat on the couch.

"I was an only child for the longest time, but then, I moved out and I guess my parents decided to fill up the nest again when they got lonely. I still don't know how I'm supposed to feel about that, you know? Until I moved back in, I had never met any of them. The oldest is only five; how am I supposed to speak to a human that small? So my parents and I, we… the youngsters don't know I'm their sibling yet. We don't know how to explain it to them in a way that a child could understand."

"Ah." *This was like what had happened when Nini was born, but like, on turbo mode. I do wonder if she knows our older siblings though? I've never asked.* "I'd at least hope the young ones will be better at knowing how to refer to you."

There was the vaguest semblance of a frown on Muiren's face. "They will be. As disconcerting as it may be to hear my parents misgender me, though, I promise they've never been anything that's not accepting. It's just hard to change habits after twenty-seven years, you know?"

Wasn't Muiren twenty-seven now? "You only just recently told them?"

"Yeah, when I moved back in. Never had a reason to before." Muiren shrugged. "I never initiated a conversation about my gender or pronouns or any of it. I wasn't physically around them, so I didn't need to perceive how they referred to me, you know?"

That made sense. "Yeah. I follow."

"They'll get there. Amidst everything, I'm glad I have parents who care about me. I know not everyone is that fortunate." Muiren reached for the bowl they'd sat on the coffee table, and held it out toward Yidarica. "Popcorn?"

"Yeah, thanks," she replied, taking a handful.

"So." Muiren smirked. "How did things go yesterday with August?"

Yidarica almost choked. She had forgotten that her "let an outside person know your whereabouts in case of emergency" contact had been Muiren this time. It was usually Gracia, but she hadn't wanted to worry her, or give her extra reasons to use her vocal chords.

"Would you believe me if I said I don't know?" Yidarica confessed. "It's probably really obvious at this point to everyone who I've told about yesterday that I like August. I like him a lot. Yesterday was fun, amazing even, but... I didn't feel as though he was returning the energy I was giving, you know? If it wasn't for the few times I made him laugh, I'd be convinced that I bored him. So it was nice, but as much as I'd want it to be the case, I don't think we'll be going out again."

"You're sure of yourself." The tone with which Muiren said this conveyed an air of skepticism.

"Is there a reason I shouldn't be?"

"I don't know. The impression I've always had of August is that he's just like that. Reserved, gentle-natured, you know? A little shy, even. I'd never tell you that your feelings are wrong, but if you're expecting him to return your level of enthusiasm, wouldn't that be a bit out of character for him?"

This is true. Even when August gets really into something, like when he was studying the code we were working on, I don't think he gets as exuberant as I do. With the exception of when he got really excited over making that code work, you can hardly tell, if you're not as familiar with his mannerisms.

"Makes sense," was what Yidarica said out loud. "Maybe I'm just nervous about the whole thing."

"And that's warranted, since as you said, you do really like the guy," Muiren replied. "It's a good thing you have friends you can lean on in times like these, to help you view things rationally."

Friends. There it was again, and with it, that warm feeling, almost like a hug. Yidarica was now committed to not making the moment weird, which left her unsure of what to say next. Should she thank Muiren for being a friend? Try to present an easygoing facade, so that they didn't catch on to how unfamiliar she was with the concept of having successfully made a friend on her own?

"Now I wish I had August's number so I could ask him about it," Muiren chuckled. "No reason other than I'm curious. Could you imagine how adorable it'd be if he's just as nervous as you are about the whole thing?"

She could, actually. Imagining August at home, reminiscing on their day out and wondering if he should be the one to reach out but getting nervous, was so darn adorable that Yidarica could barely stand it. Even more adorable was the idea of him having the trademark butterflies in his stomach as he thought about it. *I should at least send him a text, right? I wouldn't want him agonizing over this whole thing.*

"Should I text him?" Yidarica asked then.

At this suggestion, Muiren's face lit up. "You should *absolutely* text him! And what better way to do it than for both of us to workshop what you're gonna say to him, together? If we work together, we can get this done before it's time to eat. What do you say?"

The fact that Muiren was so invested in this felt strange, but in a good way. "Okay, sure," Yidarica nodded. "Why not? We've already established that we work well together. Now, where do we start?"

Muiren thought about this. "Did the day end on a good note?"

"Yeah, I'd like to think so," Yidarica replied. "He said that he enjoyed himself, and that it was a pleasure to have me."

"And you're still not sure if he likes you?" Muiren asked teasingly.

Yidarica shrugged. "It's more that I don't know if I should believe it. Part of it is, admittedly, my low self-esteem. But also, it's just, you know how men are."

"I most certainly do *not* know how men are." Muiren laughed. "The whole 'being a lesbian' thing makes it so I don't have that kind of access to them. Elaborate?"

I didn't think I'd need to. "Well, you know. Men have kinda built themselves a reputation of lying about everything. How old they are. Their employment status and living situation. What time they'll be ready. If they're even single. So, it's not entirely out of left field to assume they'll also lie about whether or not they enjoy your company, as a means to some nefarious end... is it?"

It was clear that Muiren needed time to think about this. "When you say it like that, I suppose not. And I guess it doesn't help that both of us have otherwise only communicated with August in a work setting, so we don't definitively know his true character– but even so, why don't we give him a wee bit more credit than that? Not only him, but also you. Let's assume you're a good enough judge of character that you wouldn't go out with someone who you think would lie to you."

I mean, when you think about it, every person I've been on a date with or have otherwise crushed on in the past has been soberingly honest about not wanting to date me, so maybe I do have that kind of discernment going for me.

"Okay. So he enjoyed the time you spent together yesterday, and we're choosing to believe he's telling the truth. In that case…" Muiren thought. "Can I borrow your phone? I can type something up."

"Sure." Yidarica handed her phone to Muiren. This worked; they could type up a draft, and then the two of them could amend it until it was a suitable message to send. Truly, the two of them becoming friends was one of the best things that could have happened to Yidarica.

Surprisingly quickly, Muiren handed the phone back to her. "There you go."

Yidarica glanced at the phone for a second, and was about to thank Muiren before needing to look again. "You already sent it?!"

"If there's one thing I've learned from working with you, it's that if I didn't, you'd agonize over it for hours," they explained. "I've seen how many times you rewrite your emails."

The message read:

> Good afternoon, August! Not sure if I said so yesterday, but I had a great time with you. I'm glad we could spend some time together outside of work. Gives us a greater breadth of topics to talk about; and more freedom to admire your cute face :)

"Muiren." Yidarica sighed.

"What? You do think his face is cute, don't you?" they countered.

I do, but you can't just say that! According to what I've observed from other people, complimenting people so directly when you've only been on one date is a major instance of overstepping!

"Well, it's been sent, so I guess there's nothing I can do about it," Yidarica admitted in resignation. "I still can't believe you did that."

Muiren gave her a supportive pat on the back. "Hey, it's gonna be all right. The worst he could do is not respond, but I'm pretty sure he will."

"But what makes you so sure?" Yidarica asked.

Asking this earned her a confused stare. "Are you *that* convinced that your attraction to August is one-sided? Is there not a single part of your mind that believes he's admiring you every moment he can? I refuse to believe that, or else why agree to go out with him in the first place?"

They had a point. Of course Yidarica wanted to believe that August was fond of her; but there was always the chance that he wasn't and this was all a play to get her in bed… or worse, that this was some sort of elaborate joke. And as long as those possibilities existed, she had to be wary of them.

On the couch between the two, at least one of their phones vibrated, which caused Yidarica to let out a surprised yelp.

"You're so dramatic," Muiren laughed. "That's probably me; I was texting someone while I was waiting for you to get here."

"Oh." Yidarica nodded, picking up her phone. To her surprise, August had also texted her:

> Hi, Yidarica! I think you did say that, but it never hurts to hear it again. I'm glad we both had a good time! If my memory serves me correctly, things in town are about to get much busier, but maybe after that all calms down, we could make plans for another round? There's plenty of other places I've been wanting to go to with someone.

"See? Told you." Muiren nudged her, having read the message over her shoulder. "It'll be fine, I promise."

Being friends with Muiren fills me with a certain type of warmth. Like I always say, they have this older sibling presence that feels comforting. I wonder, is it so farfetched to believe that, even if I don't find a significant other, this type of love is enough to keep me alive? I would be just fine with that.

As one of the Tierney parents called for everyone to come to the table, Yidarica felt a sort of warmth. It was always nice when things turned out well like this, and it was even better when she was able to work through her issues with a friend. Now, she could concentrate on what smelled like it was going to be an amazing dinner.

Chapter Seventeen

The time was nearing for the Firefly Migration.

Yidarica hadn't been to the associated festival in twenty-one years; she distinctly remembered that she'd been ten years old the last time she'd gone, because Runiala had been a tiny infant, being held in their father's arms. After that year, things kept happening around that season that rendered her unable to go, things that were usually her parents' fault. And by the time she was an adult, it felt more normal to stay at home than to brave the outdoors and the crowds.

"It is often a lot," Celosia said in response when Yidarica explained this to her. "And it does cause its problems both socially and here at work, but at the same time… not many of us can resist pretty lights, you know?"

"Yeah." She had a point there.

"The Weather Department will be its busiest at this time." Celosia turned to Yidarica. "There is a lot of demand for weather predictions and accommodations for firefly watching, so we work hard to make sure we disappoint as few people as possible. All of this to say, I may be a little harder to reach for the next few weeks, so I've asked Shiori to help me supervise August for a little while since he's working with you all, and I'm going to send you the contact information to report to Legal directly, in my place."

The last part was what worried Yidarica. Report to Legal? Directly? Her?!

"Uh, it's– it's Dahlia, right?" she asked, her voice wobbly. "We've communicated once or twice. She might recognize my name."

"Oh? Then you probably already have her email address and Slapdash username," Celosia replied. "That's good! I've already let her know of the change, but you may want to remind her on your end. Those Legal folks are always so busy, I wouldn't be surprised if she forgot."

Yidarica nodded. Maybe she'd make this a group project with Muiren and August. They'd make sure she didn't embarrass herself.

Unless the goal all along was to make me embarrass myself… but I'll try to not think about that.

"Yeah, uh, thanks for that, Celosia," Yidarica said, hoping the wobbling of her voice wasn't as obvious to anyone else as it was to her. "I'll reach out when I get settled in."

Celosia smiled. "Of course. Fortunately, this change comes at a time where you're almost done with your project, so there should be very little to worry about, if anything."

Oh, if only you knew how good I am at worrying about the tiniest details.

Arriving at the area that she, Muiren, and August currently called home, Yidarica still wasn't certain of how she would word her email to Dahlia. She had never communicated with anyone so important. The language she used for the email had to be absolutely perfect, or else she could potentially ruin the grace they'd been given for the project taking as long as it had.

Muiren and August were both seated, in conversation, when Yidarica sat, and they both turned to her when she entered the room. "Is everything okay?" August asked.

Do I look so distressed that he feels the need to ask? "Uh, yeah, everything's good," she replied. "But I do have another fun group task for us."

"Oh?" Muiren asked. "On top of all the other tasks, huh."

"This one's a nice one and done, at least," Yidarica replied as she turned to face them both. "Since the Weather Department will be swamped with all of their duties related to the Firefly Migration, Celosia won't be able to send Legal the updates they asked for anymore. She's asked that I send them in her place, and I need help drafting the email."

August and Muiren exchanged a look. "Well, sure, but…" Muiren started, picking up their tablet. "Isn't it… give me a second, I'm trying to find the email I'm looking for to make sure I don't make a fool of myself when I ask this. Okay, yeah– did Celosia never give that responsibility to Eira? It was supposed to be their duty to begin with, but because they were so new, it went to Celosia in the interim."

Wait. That does sound familiar. We got an email about that at the beginning of the project.

"That… is a really good question," Yidarica admitted. "I'll reach out to a few people to get some clear guidance on that."

She composed a Slapdash message to Celosia:

Good morning! Upon review of all the communications we've ever gotten about this project, I noticed a mention that the report to Legal was to be made by an Eira Daschen once her permissions cleared. Is that no longer the case?

"What would be really fortunate is if we could make this next update our last," August was saying. "We're really close to being done, after all. We just need to figure out the finishing touches."

The familiar notification sound alerted Yidarica to look at her tablet.

```
New message from Celosia Ramura
You're absolutely right! We've all been so
frenzied with the restructuring that all of us
forgot! I'm sending a message to Eira now, and
will also visit their desk; you should come over
as well, so she'll be able to place names to
faces when the reports are finalized.
```

Yidarica looked up at Muiren, then August, and said, "I guess this fun project has become a field trip."

***

Eira wasn't new to the company, but she was new to this building, so Yidarica couldn't conceptualize what she should be keeping an eye out for once the group was in the Weather Department's area. She didn't even remember where exactly Celosia's desk was, because (partly due to how much work she took on within the department) Celosia was rarely actually at her desk. Yidarica turned to August, with the intent of asking him where it was, but before she could get the question out, she saw him wave.

There was Celosia, dressed in her usual cozy aesthetic (this time involving lots of greens), standing with and presumably speaking to someone Yidarica could only describe as ethereal. There was no one factor that gave her this impression, it was the sum of their appearance: the icy blue hair in a layered cut draping over their shoulders, their deep brown skin, the cerulean blue eyes that seemed to sparkle just as the stars did. Even being dressed in a white blouse and black pinstripe slacks, there was something about them that simply felt otherworldly. Yidarica could stare at this person for hours, if that was socially acceptable; but she knew it wasn't, so she attempted to regulate her gaze.

"You all got over here at the perfect time!" Celosia greeted the trio as they came into earshot. "These are the three who are doing the work on this project: this is Muiren, Yidarica, and August. Now, this one," she gently placed a hand on August's arm, "sits with us usually, and will continue to once this crossover event has concluded, so it's probably a good idea to get to know him well! And, everyone, this is Eira. She has been granted the position that Iris vacated, so expect her to have a wealth of knowledge about everything that Iris knew about!"

"How *is* Iris doing, by the way?" asked Eira. Even her voice felt ethereal, like a crisp morning's wind on an otherwise sunny day. "She was one of the first people I met when I transferred to this office, but I don't think I've seen her recently at all."

"That's because she's been at an offsite congregation for the past couple of weeks," Celosia explained. "She'll be back soon!"

"Oh, okay. That makes sense." Eira hummed. "Well, it's nice to meet all of you. From what I've learned about the project you're doing, I'm led to believe that it'll actually be better the less we get to work together, huh?"

That was an interesting way to phrase that… but it was entirely true, so Yidarica nodded. "It's our hope that we don't have to reach out to you too much more."

"And I'm sure Legal has that same goal too," agreed Muiren. "Are you going to be as busy as Celosia is during this whole firefly season?"

As Eira answered that question, Yidarica thought about how it was interesting that– despite not being very high up in terms of the department's hierarchy– Celosia seemed to not only be able to take on a lot of responsibility (and at times be expected to, even, like the day she had almost fainted), but actively command the sort of presence that someone with a much higher position would. Even with Yidarica knowing that Celosia had been with the company a long time, she couldn't understand why, for all the time and effort and respect, she was only one level higher than she, Muiren, and August.

"And I'd assume we'd probably get answers to any questions we have sooner if we ask you?" August was asking then.

Celosia and Eira exchanged a look. "It's probably about equal," the latter replied. "I would imagine I'm a little busier because of the nature of my position, especially if nothing goes wrong for the Project Biome, but either of us will be slower to respond than usual. Oh! Speaking of delayed responses, we have a meeting to get to, Celosia. We should get going."

Instead of following along, Celosia held her hand up, as if to tell Eira she was stopping. "If you need to be there urgently, could you go without me? I wanted to speak to Muiren for a brief moment."

"Oh." Eira nodded. "Sure, I'll meet you there; we'll be over in Tartine. And it was a pleasure to have finally met you all. I look forward to reading your updates!"

"Of course," Yidarica agreed. "Have a nice meeting!"

Why did I just say that?! Nobody says that! Great, it hasn't even been ten minutes that I've known Eira and I embarrassed myself in front of them.

As the group adjourned, August paused for a moment. "Can I meet you back in our little area? I want to pick up some things from my permanent desk first."

"Yeah, of course," Yidarica nodded. "Come by anytime."

Yidarica didn't want to head back by herself, but fortunately, Muiren caught up with her fairly quickly; and so, the two of them started the walk back.

"Before we began working more closely with the Weather Department, I never thought about how busy they must get this time of year, but it makes sense," Muiren said as they walked. "I guess it's kind of like how we tend to get more projects whether a holiday is coming around that has an emphasis on food. Are you headed to the migration, by the way?"

I shouldn't tell them that my band is performing. That'll sound like I'm bragging. Humans usually hate that. "Eh, probably not," Yidarica shrugged. "I haven't been in years. Since I was a kid."

"What, does that not make you excited to experience it as an adult?" Muiren asked. "I won't pressure you, but as a person who's been going more or less every year since they were a wee tyke, the child and adult experiences are vastly different."

"Hm." Yidarica had to admit to herself that that made sense. "So you're going, then?"

Muiren nodded. "I was on the fence myself, but I was convinced by being asked along as company– I'm going with Celosia."

Yidarica stopped what she was doing, staring at Muiren.

Technically, that wouldn't be violating any policies, would it? Celosia might be at a higher level than Muiren, but they're in completely different departments; she's a manager, but she's not their manager. Besides, I'm getting ahead of myself. What if it's just a friendly hangout?

"Oh," was what Yidarica said out loud. "I didn't know you guys were that close. As friends?"

"If I received her invitation the way she intended it: definitely *not* as friends," Muiren winked. "I can't tell for certain what her endgame is, but I wouldn't mind if it ended at her place, is all I'm saying."

I can't say I agree, because the thought of someone taking me back to their place has implications that make me feel sick. But I can understand. Celosia's really pretty. She has the sort of cuteness that I aspire to.

"Well, I… hope for the best outcome then," Yidarica said, wondering if that was the correct response. Her studies of humans indicated that they didn't always appreciate this kind of reaction, believing it distant from the communication. "Wait, is that what she wanted to talk to you about just now?"

"Just now? Oh, no, she asked weeks ago," Muiren replied. "She wanted to ask me if I had any food allergies, probably relevant to what we're going to pick up to eat while we're out and about on the day of the migration festival."

When August arrived back at the work area, he brought with him a thick book about climate. He explained, "To put the finishing touches on what we've got going on, I wanted to be sure we had alerts for every single type of inclement weather, *and* that they display in the appropriate regions. If any book I was given for this role change would help, it would be this one."

"Smart." Muiren nodded. "Will I need to draw any new graphics, then?"

"Unlikely, since we researched that before you began drawing at all, but I'll be sure to take down any ones we don't have yet," August replied.

As they all worked, Muiren cleared their throat and turned to August. "So, August. Heading to the migration festival?"

He hesitated. "I'm not sure."

"Really? You too?" Muiren laughed.

"Well, you know I'm not native to this area," August defended himself. "If I go to this kind of thing that a lot of families and friends go to, while I don't have that option, I think it'll only make me feel lonely."

"You guys are so gloomy." Muiren laughed even more at this. "Why don't you just invite some of your family and friends and have them crash at your place when everything is over?"

August paused here. "I mean, there's a good chance none of them will bite, but I guess I could at least extend the invitation. I think I'd be willing to go if someone went with me. I assume, based on Muiren's choice of words, that you're not going, Yidarica?"

She shook her head. "Similar reasons. Haven't gone in ages, so I just don't know if I feel like it's worth the effort."

"Oh." August went quiet, fidgeting a bit with his hands. He slightly opened his mouth, as if he had more to say, but soon closed it and went back to studying his book.

"Well, you know, if neither of you have anyone to go with and that's what's deterring you, you could always make plans to go together," Muiren pointed out, heavily hinting that this was the better outcome.

Yidarica thought about this. *I can't, because the band... but even if we don't, I doubt August would want to go with me. I'm not a very fun person, and I won't have the stamina to hit any of the afterparties, which is the biggest pull for people around our age. He'd have more fun going alone than with me.*

"I wouldn't want to intrude if she's already decided she doesn't want to expend the effort," August replied. "Will you be in attendance, Muiren? Maybe we'll see each other there, if I go; potentially make plans to have a drink together after the main event, even? My treat."

Muiren gave him a look, hesitating before speaking. "I, uh, I'm already accounted for in that regard, but I appreciate the offer. Maybe save the complimentary drinks for when we've officially concluded this project? We could make plans to hit a nearby bar after work that day. It'll be well-deserved."

"I couldn't agree more," he replied. "Yidarica? It wouldn't feel right if you weren't in attendance for that."

She turned, feeling warmth from her coworkers wanting to include her in their plans. "Of course. I'd love to celebrate with you both."

***

Every year, when the flowers began to bloom at their highest ability, and the trees began to sprout fruit, one of the hallmarks of the season was when the fireflies would return to the city in droves, ready to make roost in the grass and trees for the next eight months. Aside from the obvious benefits of a harvest season, the migration was believed to also bring good fortune and health; and aside from even that, seeing all the lights in the sky was pretty, so there was always a festival to celebrate the occasion.

In the days that preceded the migration, the festival's location and its vicinity would be decorated with lights, streamers, and many other themed adornments. Local businesses would decorate their storefronts as well, and advertise any deals they had running at the time. This year, the festival was being held at the Park of the Center; so named because it was located directly in the middle of the city. Of all the possible locations for the festival to take place, this one was the most common; in fact, Yidarica was pretty sure that this was where it was held the last time she ever went, but she wasn't certain. Like most of her childhood memories, that one was foggy.

The location of the festival meant that, of everyone in the band, Cérilda lived the closest to the venue, so everyone met at her house. Being the youngest in the band and only having recently graduated, Cérilda still lived with her parents in an ample-sized house just outside of the city limits, in a sleepy suburb. She was the youngest of her siblings, so while the house had obviously been bought back when her older siblings were of an age that precluded them living with their parents, it felt a bit too large now that there were only three people in it. But this had its perks, as well. It was the best place for the band to practice due to all the space, and since the impending reality of empty nesting was now looming over Mrs. Sueche's head, she often fed the band while they were over.

After convening, the band began to walk the decorated streets near the Park of the Center, minus one. Landen had refused to come for reasons everyone else was still a bit unclear on. It would have been fine if he had just said he couldn't come because of prior commitments, or whatever other reason, but it was the way he had said it that continued to dampen Yidarica's spirit.

> **Why does it matter if I don't have time to walk around the park with you guys? Nobody says**

> a word when Yidarica cancels on practice for the hundredth time, but this is a problem?

Gracia had swiftly defended her with some rather colorful language, but at that point, the damage had been done. Part of the reason Yidarica was always so hesitant to cancel on practice was because she'd felt this way exactly: that her health was causing secret resentment within the band. And although she'd been reassured multiple times that it wasn't the case... if that were true, where had this come from? It was a very specific thing to say unprompted.

In the end, Cérilda had gently, but firmly, stated that she would not welcome anyone into her home that would bring any hostile energy. This made sense because her father often had to utilize very complex spells to maintain his health in his old age, and probably couldn't risk such pointed negativity throwing off the balance of the atmospheric magic, but also because Cérilda herself had always been a calm, reserved person. She was, after all, the perfect foil to Gracia's boisterous positivity, and Yidarica's anxiety.

"When will the city hire us for the design work for the festival?" Gracia was saying, referring to her place of employment. "I've wanted this project for *ages*. Every designer they've chosen since I've been going to the festival has done a great job, as far as I can remember, and I'm practically dying to get my hands on that type of work. I can only imagine the types of things I could design with such an amazing theme!"

"Why don't you come up with some prospective ideas with some of your coworkers, Gracia?" Cérilda suggested. "I think the designer is chosen through some level of self-advocacy, right? If you sent them a well-curated portfolio of what you're all capable of, that would probably at least get your foot in the door."

Gracia's face lit up at this suggestion. "How did I never think of that?! You're a genius, Ceri! I will do exactly that the minute I sit at my desk tomorrow!"

"Cérilda, are you giving Gracia ideas?" Walchelin asked, in the exact tone a disapproving parent would use.

Gracia nudged him in response. "Stop trying to dull my shine."

"I'm not! I'm just a little worried for the sanity of your coworkers," he continued to tease her. "If you're gonna do this, at least try to remember that they'll need food and water to survive long enough to decorate for the city."

As the group continued to talk, they reached one of the entrances to the park itself; here, there were three people working on building one of the entry arches for the festival. They seemed to have just started, because the only visible evidence of the arch was the foundation and a few lights. Beyond this, the park itself was also largely not yet decorated. In time, this would be a sparkling, busy haven of festivities, but at the moment it was still an ordinary park.

"Excuse me," Walchelin approached one of the people working on the arch. "Would you happen to know where the stage is being built?"

The person, with black hair sleekly pulled into a ponytail and wearing some type of construction safety gear, stared at the group of four for just a bit longer than was comfortable before turning to the other two people working on the arch. "Stage?"

One of their heads shot up. "It's closest to the East Gate and past the stone bridge."

"Excellent. Thank you all," Walchelin waved before heading in the direction of the correct gate. "Come on, guys; it's this way."

The walk to the East Gate would take a considerable amount of time, so conversation started up again. "So, what does your cousin do, again?" Walchelin asked Gracia. "You've probably told me at some point, but you also have more cousins than I have people in my entire family, so you can't expect me to keep them all straight."

Gracia laughed. "You're not wrong! This particular cousin works for the city's entertainment bureau. He gets to rub elbows with a lot of prolific musicians because, if they're doing a concert in this city, they've probably communicated with him at some point. So, when it's time for the festival, he's usually one of the people picking out potential acts."

"So, what happened to make him turn his attention to us?" Cérilda asked.

"Apparently, one of the bands that booked had to cancel. I didn't get all of the juicy details out of him, yet, but it apparently leaves a pretty big gap in the programming. So big that they're attempting to get three acts to fill it," Gracia held her hands far apart to signify the gap. "So we won't be the only newly brought on act, but it'll be probably the best opportunity for us to start booking bigger and more frequent gigs, right?"

"Exactly!" Walchelin agreed. "But I'd be lying if I didn't admit that there's an aspect of this that also feels a little scary. It's such a big crowd, and it's not like any of them will specifically be coming to see us, you know? I think I'd be crushed if we started and I kept seeing people leave because they weren't feeling our vibe."

Gracia hit his arm. "Stop it, you're gonna scare Yida."

Oh, that was happening way before this conversation.

"You *have* been pretty quiet this whole time," Walchelin noticed then, turning to Yidarica. "Is everything okay?"

Everything is exactly the opposite of okay, Walchelin. You're exactly right. None of these people who will be at the festival want to hear us, and seeing evidence of that in real time would do more than crush me; I don't know that I'd survive it.

"I'm just…" Yidarica trailed off. "It's not the highest of energy days, for me."

"Oh," all three of them immediately seemed to understand.

"Well, don't be afraid to let us know if you need a little rest," Walchelin added. "There's no rush, and the weather is lovely today, so we have plenty of allowance for a little plop into the grass."

"Thanks, Walchelin." If no one else understood Yidarica's health problems, he would; and she was always grateful for that, especially now when she couldn't find a lot of words to explain herself.

I hate having moments when I feel like I can't be completely truthful with my friends, but at least this way, I don't have to worry about them telling me my feelings are stupid. They never have, but I would not be able to deal with that if it started today.

Walchelin had been right about the weather being lovely; there wasn't a cloud to be found in the sky, and the cool breeze that occasionally blew by felt wonderful. There weren't any impending showers, either, so the air was free of humidity– but not to the point where it felt overly dry. They were now nearing the stone bridge, which was Yidarica's personal favorite part of this park. There was something about the cool grayscale cobblestone and the wild plants that surrounded it– brilliant in all of their green, pink, orange, yellow, and white hues– that felt almost poetic. She didn't come here often, but when she did, her journey always merited a stop here. Sometimes, looking down at the stream that the bridge flowed over, it was possible to see small fish swimming with the current.

Today, however, there were no fish to be seen.

THE ABSENCE OF COMPLETE DARK

"We should be coming up on the stage soon, if the park workers are to be believed," Walchelin said, beginning to look around. "I see something that I think might be what we're looking for; but from here, there are so many trees that I can't really tell."

This is exciting. To think that we'll be making this walk as a band soon.

Drawing close to the stage– which, at the moment, was little more than a raised platform and a couple of sturdy beams– everything began to feel so much more real. This was where history would be made. This was where the members of Half Past Haberdash would be standing when the lights came on with a commanding whoosh of electricity, and they saw everyone in the crowd, hopefully cheering and waiting for them to go on.

This was where everything could go wrong.

Yidarica sat in the grass then, behind her friends, unable to bear the weight or the thought of somehow ruining such a large stage. Whenever she had these thoughts, she always reminded herself that it was never just about her, but in this instance, that worked to her detriment. Truly, it was not just about her. It was also about the rest of the band, people she cared about, whose reputations would be ruined if their performance was bad enough. It was also about the people who would be at the festival; it could ruin the entire event for them if the performance fell short, and the thought of ruining such a culturally prominent event for so many people was…

It was too much to bear.

If everything went well, then everyone would have a good time. But there was so much to lose if it didn't.

At this point, everyone had noticed Yidarica sitting on the grass, so they went to join her. She was too mired in her thoughts to speak, and this seemed to go unnoticed by everyone else.

"This is gonna be *so* exciting," Gracia said as she pulled a water bottle out of her bag. "When I get home, I'm going to start mixing all the dried herbs and fruit I need to make the herbal teas I like to drink before shows. If any of you want to have something like that on hand, let me know. Another one of my cousins is really into herbal therapy, so she sends me a ton of information about tea mixtures and a bunch of other stuff too."

"Oh, now this cousin I do remember," Walchelin said, happy to be able to recall them. "She's the same one that helped with the tea I currently drink to keep up my immune system, right?"

"The very same!" Gracia beamed. "I'll call her later tonight and ask her if she knows anything about a recipe for good fortune; not that we'll need it, of course. Oh! I also wanted to contribute a few ideas about the outfits we'll be wearing on stage, too. I know we don't have a lot of time– or money– to come up with anything that's too extravagant, but I do think it would be cute to put together semi-matching ensembles that are connected to the event theme, which makes it a good reason that we came here! Now that we've seen the color palette of the decor, it should be easier to match it."

"We could!" agreed Cérilda. "We could also come up with something that signifies flowers in general, since that seems to be a pretty heavy emphasis this year. Personally, I'm always a fan of glowy effects."

As everyone spoke, Yidarica could only be pulled into further despair about things that could go wrong at this concert. About half of this band was chronically ill; who was to say they could make it through an entire set? Their shows so far had been so small and short. The chance of injury was palpable. Wardrobe malfunctions were always a possibility. And then there were things completely out of their control, like lighting and stage issues. And then, even if everything went exactly as planned, who could be certain that people on social media would be kind? They could get dragged across the entire internet for performing at all.

She couldn't do it.

"I can't do it," she whispered.

Everyone turned to her, having heard her say something, but having been unable to distinguish the words. "What was that, Yida?" Gracia asked.

"I can't. I can't!" Yidarica all but yelled. "I can't do this. I can't do it. I can't do it!"

She was in tears now, shaking her head. Before anyone else could speak, she was running away.

"Yidarica!" Gracia called after her, before tossing her bag onto the grass and pursuing her. She gave it a minute before realizing that, even with her best friend not being a good runner, she'd never catch up in the shoes she was wearing; the heels dug into the grass every time her feet touched the ground, which slowed her down immensely. Stubbornly, she pulled her shoes off– but by the time she got them off completely, Yidarica was nowhere to be seen.

***

Her friends would try to contact her for the rest of the day, but Yidarica would not answer.

She turned her phone to silent, hiding it under the throw pillows on her couch before curling up in her bed and letting herself cry as hard as she'd been wanting to ever since Zaya had left. She'd been holding all of her emotions in for so long that her body trembled with the intensity of her sobs, and it wasn't long before her eyes stung and her nose became stuffy.

This is it. This is the final straw. If there was ever a time where I was certain my friends would finally get tired of me and drop whatever obligation they felt to continue putting up with me, it's now.

I wish I was sadder about that than I am. But I knew this day would come. Someday they'll see that the way this happened was for the best; they're finally free from me, and they did it without having to embarrass themselves in front of the entire city. They'll understand in time, I'm sure. They're rational people.

The sun had still been up when Yidarica had arrived back at home, but to no one's surprise, she didn't feel like eating. She remained in her bed and cried herself to sleep.

The band tried the next day to reach Yidarica, as well. Still, she would not answer.

She worked from home, explaining to Shiori that she was in agonizing pain– she may have played it up some, but between all of her emotional anguish and how weak she felt from missing a total of three meals once lunch passed, there was some truth to that. None of the people that she regularly spoke to at work sent her any messages over Slapdash, so she assumed they weren't too worried about her, like she'd always suspected. There was the possibility that Muiren or August had texted her, but she refused to retrieve her phone from where she'd left it the previous day.

The next day was more of the same. At this point, because of the proximity to the date of the performance and the fact that no one else in the band knew how to play bass, Gracia had to call her cousin and tell him to cancel their set. She said as much in the band's group chat, which was the one message Yidarica let herself read once she finally built the resolve to fish her phone out from those pillows.

That was it. She had officially ruined everything– as she always did.

***

On the day of the Firefly Migration Festival, walking around the park grounds where it was being held only filled Yidarica with more guilt. Things hadn't had to be this way, but ultimately, her ability to ruin the things she touched was working in overdrive lately. She continued to reassure herself that this was for the best. She knew that, in some way or another, she'd saved the band from terminal embarrassment.

There was a violinist on stage now, and the music they were playing felt calm, which was interesting; acts at this festival usually played fast, up-tempo, riveting music to match the general energy in the air, but this… this was a welcome divergence from the norm.

Yidarica placed her black leather jacket on the grass and sat, picking out an area far away enough from the festivities that she wouldn't– or shouldn't– be approached, but close enough that she wouldn't appear strange from sitting so far away. She made sure to sit in a way that wouldn't accidentally expose herself; she was wearing one of her favorite one-piece dresses, a light blue three-tiered lime print dress with puff sleeves, and it was just a bit shorter than the dresses she usually wore, so she always had to be conscious of the manner in which she sat.

The first thing she did once she had settled: let out a long, drawn-out sigh.

What am I going to do with myself?

Her gaze turned to the sky, its blue hues beginning to shift purple, pink, and orange with the coming of night.

The hardest part about being a person who ruins everything is figuring out how to come back from it. What could I say about squandering our big chance that could ever be meaningful? Will any of them want to hear it? I'd imagine— I'd like to hope, at least— that Gracia and Cérilda would make time to hear me out. But I know I'm on thin ice with the guys. As I should be. Why should they be kind to me? They barely know me. I haven't earned that.

She drew her legs closer to her chest, resting her chin on her knees.

Is there anything I can say? Or am I right to assume I've burned every bridge we had? It's a little presumptuous of me to think that it's even possible for me to come back from this,

I need the Dark to come for me already, I'm tired of having to mitigate my massive fuck-ups.

There was a rustling sound near Yidarica then, followed by an approaching shadow. She mentally scrambled to try and remember one of her defense spells, but relaxed when a familiar tall, brown-haired figure sat beside her on the grass.

"Not exactly prime real estate," August said, smiling just a bit, but the smile slowly faded when he realized how down Yidarica looked.

"No. It's not. But it's what I deserve," she said softly.

His expression softened, wanting to extend a hand to comfort her, but immediately taking it back. "What's going on?" he asked gently.

She let out another of those heavy sighs.

"My band was supposed to perform at the festival today."

This made August turn to Yidarica. "You're in a band?" he asked, surprised.

"Yeah, I'm the bassist." She drew her legs up to her chest again. "I don't even understand why I got so scared, but I pulled out four days ago. I haven't spoken to my friends in the band since then. They probably hate me."

"Hm?" August raised a brow. "What makes you think that?"

"Why wouldn't they?" Yidarica asked. "The Firefly Migration Festival is one of the biggest gigs in the world, and it was a miracle that a band as small as ours was given the opportunity to perform here at all. Not only did I ruin that, I've probably ruined our standing with the festival by withdrawing so late. If none of them ever talk to me again, I'd understand."

August took some time to think about the situation. "I guess that makes sense. But these are your friends, right? I'd like to think they'd give you some grace."

"Yes, but August, this isn't the first time I've fucked things up for our band. The first time we were looking to find a venue for a show, I sent our comms so late the venue POC didn't even remember who I was by the time I asked about the opportunity. I've had to do at least half our practice sessions via projection because my body was too weak to leave my place. I've canceled a couple of them for that same reason. All I've been doing is giving them reasons I'm a horrible friend."

There was a moment of silence before August looked over at her, leaning over so that he could look directly at her face. "What... do *you* think, Yidarica?"

The question obviously confused her. "What do I think?"

"Yeah. Do you think you're a horrible friend? Do you never want to speak to yourself again?"

"I *really* don't think you want to hear my thoughts on those two questions."

With this, August nodded. "Got it. So, is it that because of that, you expect everyone to feel the same? Which is, you know, sensible and plausible, but when you consider how diverse and unique we are as people... a little silly."

Maybe so. The source of much of my agony when it comes to interpersonal interactions is that there aren't specific codes or procedures that work for all humans. We're all so different. It's impossible to predict our thoughts and behaviors at a perfect rate. Even with how much I rely on my studies of humans, I'll be the first to admit that those studies aren't absolute.

"After all... I like to think we're friends, and so far, I've liked all of the interactions I've had with you."

Yidarica's eyes zoomed to where August was sitting beside her. "Really?"

"Yeah." He nodded, a very cute smile on his face, before standing up and offering her a hand. "Come on, let's go for a walk. We still have a little time to find a good spot to watch the migration."

The two began to walk then. The sun was closer to setting now, which meant there wasn't a lot of time left before the migration began, and most of the people present had already set into their positions. "So why are you here alone, then?" Yidarica asked. "I thought you weren't interested in coming unless you had someone to accompany you."

"Well, I thought I could use the fresh air and– as previously discussed– since most of my family and friends are back home, I knew I'd have to come alone," August replied. "The trip from home to here is one of those trips that's far enough away that it's bothersome to make it. Although it's probably for the best that I don't see my family for a little while."

"Oh, why is that?" Yidarica asked.

August sighed, trying to think about how he would present this information to someone who had no idea about any of the dynamics in play. "Are you sure you want to know? It's kind of a long story."

Yidarica looked around at their immediate area, and immediately got excited when her eyes caught sight of a large box a few feet away. She hurried toward it, hopping on top and sitting down with only a little bit of a struggle. "Okay. Perfectly ready for a long story."

This made August laugh. "I guess I can't dispute that logic. Well, you're comfy, so I've got no reason to refuse any farther.

"Three years ago, my father died. He was unanimously liked in our family, and I had always been really close to him. As if losing him didn't cut deeply enough, my family– my mother, especially– decided basically overnight that it wasn't enough for me to be a part of this family, I had to be responsible for the family line continuing. It's really wild to me because the fact that I'm not interested in being a father is anything but news to anyone in our family, but she seems to have conveniently forgotten that. My older sisters enable her, so I can't ask them to help me explain to her that she's driving me up a wall.

"So, recently, she texted me as she always does, asking if I'll attend some work event with her and included the fact that someone she knows has a relative around my age. I responded that I couldn't make it, and in that same message, let her know that I'd like to hear from her without the pretense of her setting me up with somebody. I like to think I was kind with the language I used, but…"

He paused here, gathering his thoughts. "According to my sisters, she freaked the fuck out."

"Oh!" This surprised Yidarica for two reasons. She couldn't recall a time where she'd ever heard August swear; but, mostly, she had been expecting to hear something more similar to the situation with her own mother. Although, one could probably classify that as flipping out too, depending on what the criteria were. Curious, she asked, "How so?"

"Well, she…" August paused again. "Let me get the chronology of all of this correct. The night that I sent her that message, both of my sisters were texting me so much that it woke me up in the middle of the night. They were like, 'August, you gotta apologize to Mom,' and at that point I'm really confused because I have no idea what's happening, what I did to Mom, or even what planet I'm on, because it's 4 am. So then one of them starts a group call, but I'm still completely disoriented and I'm not able to fully digest any of what they're saying. When it was finally a decent hour, I called one of my sisters back, and I couldn't get any words in before she started screaming at me– telling me I'm a horrible brother and son and that our mother has been threatening to hurt herself for pretty much the past twenty-four hours. Which I obviously don't want to happen, but I know she's trying to manipulate me, because she does things like this whenever someone does things she doesn't agree with; and I just want to know how long any of us are supposed to go along with this before we call it out. So, I haven't said anything since then, but it's not because I *want* to give them the silent treatment. I just have no idea what I'm supposed to say to a group of people who are upset with me for… finding this incredibly irrational? Being my own person? I don't even know anymore."

And Yidarica didn't know what to say in response to all of this. She obviously knew that there were other people who had familial issues, but she would have never guessed that one of them was August. This sweetheart? It made no sense!

"I probably can't say anything to make the situation feel any better, but what I can do is reassure you that you're not alone in having a family that seemingly gets mad at you for existing," was what Yidarica settled on. "If you ever want to commiserate, I'm here."

The sky seemingly began to hum just as August smiled. "Thanks. I'd like that."

And so, the fireflies came into view; bringing with them their warm and awe-fulfilling light, bathing the surrounding areas in a yellow-orange glow. At this moment, everyone in the immediate area looked up at the sky to see the cloud of tiny lights overhead; the fireflies tended to fly high up enough that most people didn't have to worry about accidentally smacking them out of the air, but close enough that their light was powerful and vibrant. Yidarica stood up on top of the box she had been sitting on, deciding that being as close as she could to the sky would make this wondrous event even more breathtaking.

There's a part of me that's glad I'm here experiencing this. It's been so many years that I forgot how beautiful the migration is. I guess there is a pretty great reason there's so much fanfare surrounding this event.

"This is amazing!" August was grinning again, like the day he'd made his coding work. "I'm so glad I decided to come after all."

"So am I. It's like all my problems begin to fade away when I look at these little guys going on their way," Yidarica said then, turning from the sky to August beside her; but not without a great deal of effort, for looking away from the beauty and wonder of the fireflies was a struggle. "It's beautiful, isn't it?"

With his gaze fixed not on the sky, but on the woman beside him, August replied: "Yeah. Very beautiful, in fact."

An indescribable sound left Yidarica's mouth before she could stop it. What did he mean? What was he implying?!

Many of the fireflies from the first wave had passed the area at this point, and the area began to dim with the influence of the night sky; it would become bright again during the next wave, which would be more yellow-green than yellow-orange. While waiting for that next wave, August stepped closer to the box that Yidarica was standing on. There was a tense pause between the two, as if the world was standing still.

Although there was still a considerable difference between their heights, standing on that box meant that this was the closest that Yidarica had ever been to August, and it filled her with a sense of longing; one of necessity. For his touch, and– as she glanced at them for perhaps the first time– his lips, that today, for some reason, looked more kissable than they ever had. When she felt one of his hands on her waist, pulling her closer, she was certain that nothing before this moment had ever felt so satisfying. Their eyes met, both full of wonder and another emotion that was impossible to explain. Neither spoke, but both felt the invisible force between them; the force that drew them together, closer and closer still– until finally, their lips met in a tentative, gentle kiss.

It was perfect. It was exhilarating. It was everything Yidarica could have ever asked for, the soft, warm sensation of August's lips against her own. And even with the kiss only lasting a few seconds, when they separated, it still felt like she was walking on air.

I never noticed before, but August's eyes are so beautifully blue. They're like the sky right before sunrise, or the waves of the ocean, on that night I thought would be my last.

"Um…" August said softly, getting her attention. "Was that… okay? I mean, I probably– I *definitely* should've asked you first. I'm sorry. I don't want you to think I'm some kind of–"

"I don't think that at all," she replied, smiling and shaking her head.

"You don't?" August asked softly.

"I don't." Yidarica smiled again, in an attempt to reassure him.

August nodded, showing he understood. "Then… I'd like to, if it's okay with you, I mean–"

"Okay." Yidarica knew what was coming, and fortunately, her soft but audible agreeance was all August needed before he gently lifted her chin, and bent down to kiss her once again.

This time, it wasn't simply walking on air; it was like floating through the clouds, without a care in the world. Feeling satiated at the reciprocity of something she'd wanted for a while now, with the certainty that it was something he also wanted. She could imagine herself reaching out and touching the fluffiest of cumulus clouds, like she'd always wanted to; one hand sampling all the different forms of clouds, and the other holding on to August's, never wanting to let him go.

I can't believe it. This is really happening. And I'm so glad it is.

When they separated this time, August placed both of his hands around Yidarica's waist, holding her steady. "There's a part of me that cannot believe I just did that… but an even larger part of me that's so glad I finally did."

Finally? "So you… you've been thinking of kissing me before now, then?" Yidarica asked.

"Oh, have I." August laughed. "But every time I would have the thought, I'd remind myself that we were at work. Or, if we weren't, that it wouldn't be right. I couldn't assume that your kindness meant you were interested in me, but at the same time, my heart ached to know if that was the case. I was so nervous for a litany of reasons that I'd work really hard to not think about my growing feelings for you, but on a night like tonight, where you looked this beautiful but also so sad… I could no longer hold it in."

The second wave of fireflies began to fly overhead then. It was usually the largest of the waves, which meant it was the brightest, and the loudest. It had been Yidarica's favorite as a child because of its slight green tint, but she'd never noticed before just how bright it got. For a moment, the surrounding area was almost as bright as it was during the day.

"So, do you… have any plans after this?" August asked.

"Going to bed, probably," she replied. "This was enough for me. I'm too old for after-parties."

August laughed. "I see. Well, I had some loose plans to go to one of the bars around here a little later, so I'll be making my way there. I won't try to convince you otherwise, but I am really glad we were able to spend some time together today. It was probably the most amazing evening I could ask for."

He was blushing now, and Yidarica loved the slight rosy tone of his cheeks; it made him even cuter somehow. "I feel the same way," she agreed softly. "I'll get going, while there's still a little bit of natural light left. If you're going to be out late, August, please take care of yourself."

"I will." He nodded, using his thumb to gently brush Yidarica's cheek. "And you take care of yourself, too, all right? I'd be distraught if I never got to see this beautiful face again."

I could say the same. "Of course. See you around."

Chapter Eighteen

The next morning, a text message from August greeted Yidarica upon her awakening for the day.

> **Good morning, Yidarica. The sunrise is beautiful today.**

Attached was a photo of the sunrise, which was indeed beautiful. The vibrant hues of orange, yellow, and blue merged together like citrus within blue waves.

> **I have some errands to run at the start of the day, but if you're free and interested, I'd like to take you to dinner this evening. I'd like to see you today, regardless, but I'd like it even more if we could make it a date, you know? If you can't make it though, my apologies for being forward– forget I asked**

She could easily read this in August's voice. Between knowing his relationship history and now also the dynamics between him and his family, though, it had become more clear to Yidarica why he apologized so much. But she did want to see him again, especially after the events that had transpired yesterday.

It would be amazing if we could kiss again, too– or am I getting too ahead of myself?

She picked up her phone again, intending to reply, but not knowing what to say. August was always so sweet and intentional in his communications that it was kind of hard to follow it up, especially this early in the morning. The previous day had been such an amazing time, even if it had started out on a rough note. How would she ever be able to convey her level of eagerness in a text message? Or her gratitude? Or–

Maybe I should take a page from Muiren's book. When they messaged him for me that time, they didn't spend a lot of time pondering over the correct language to use. And now that I think of it, they don't do that at work, either. And yet, most people seem to like them just fine still.

Yidarica picked up her phone.

> Good morning, August. There's no need to apologize; I'd love to see you again today. Did you have something in mind?

Sending short text messages wasn't something she usually did, but it said all it needed to right there, so she sent it. There. No agonizing. No over-explanation. Just her feelings and vibes, even if she felt slightly uneasy at how incomplete the message had felt.

The speed with which August replied meant he had to have been waiting for her to reply.

> That's great! If you don't mind a little venture, there's this 24-hour breakfast diner near my place that I've been dying to try out. Also, I haven't been to the botanical gardens at all since I moved here, and I feel like that's a bit of a silly oversight on my part. Do either of those sound okay?

Both sounded amazing, but the more Yidarica thought about it, she probably wouldn't have the stamina to make it around the botanical gardens, and she didn't want to worry August when she inevitably collapsed. Besides, she also had the perfect outfit befitting a diner, so she sent a message letting him know that was her choice; and with that, flopped out of her bed, ready to get dressed and start another day.

★★★

It was strange, how breakfast was such a versatile meal. One could eat it alone, or with someone. At its designated time in the morning, or at dinnertime. And, somehow, all of those situations would feel different, even if the food was exactly the same.

With the advantage when it came to proximity to the diner, August arrived first– which meant, when Yidarica arrived about fifteen minutes later, he was able to be surprised by her outfit for the day. The ruffled white blouse and knit sky blue cardigan with white ribbons was very Yidarica-like, but the fun part was that her blouse didn't have sleeves– before now, August wasn't certain on if he'd ever actually seen her arms, or if his mind had just filled them in– and the print of her skirt, an overall blue gingham check pattern with a blue ruffle hem. About an inch above the hem was a repeating pattern of painted toast, orange juice, and sunny side up eggs.

"I can't say I've ever heard of a breakfast coord," he said when she came into earshot. "You look lovely, though."

Yidarica smiled, performing a small curtsy in front of where August was standing. She was thankful that he probably wouldn't be able to see the blood rushing to her cheeks. "Thank you. I'm surprised that you know that term, coord. Where'd you learn that?"

"I know a thing or two about fashion," he replied elusively. "How else would I be able to compliment people adequately, when the way they're dressed is pleasing to the eye?"

He had a point. "Yeah, true," Yidarica agreed. "I'm glad you picked this place out. The exterior and interior design is just darling."

Although this was a modern building, it had been modeled and decorated to look like an old-fashioned diner, and inside of an abandoned train car, at that! Most of the furniture in the place was either wooden or chrome-plated metal, which added to the antiquated aesthetic. The design called for the usage of black and white with the occasional primary color, and plenty of checkered and chevron patterns. This was as much a place to eat as it was a moment of time.

"Let's go get seated," August suggested, gesturing toward the check-in desk.

Once seated and looking at the menu, Yidarica suddenly remembered why she didn't often go out to restaurants for breakfast: it was impossible to settle on just one dish. How was she expected to only choose one thing with all of these delicious options in front of her? Curse her stomach for not being able to eat seven separate plates.

"How was the trip here?" August was carefully examining the menu. "Nothing too stressful, I hope."

Yidarica shrugged. "Regular Comtran commute. You know how it is."

"Yeah," he affirmed. "I do feel horrible that, so far, we've ended up at places that require you to commute. That hasn't been very considerate of me, and I apologize for that. Next time, I'll do some research and choose a place near where you live, and I can be the one that commutes. Or, if you'd like, you can choose the activity and place."

This left Yidarica speechless. They'd only just arrived at this outing, and he was already thinking toward the next one? How could he be so certain that he'd want to see her again, outside of work? Or even *at* work? Wanting to speak, Yidarica was suddenly overcome by a strong spell of dizziness; one so strong that it blurred her vision and scrambled her thoughts. Even when the effects lessened, she found herself needing to squint to focus.

"Are you okay?" August asked, noticing her squinting. "If you're having difficulty reading the menu, I can read it to you."

No, August. You don't need to do that. I can see fine. Usually. I promise.

But when Yidarica tried to say this, she found that her lips wouldn't move. She struggled against the invisible force keeping her quiet until she was able to get out, "Dizzy…"

"Oh, but that's… that's not good, is it?" he asked, concerned.

Yidarica shook her head, but realizing that this could be misconstrued as her saying it was a cause for concern, she followed up with, "It's… normal. Don't worry about–"

The next thing she knew, she was opening her eyes, lying down on one of the benches at the front of the restaurant. August was at the counter, speaking to the hostesses. "I hope that's enough for the trouble," he was saying. "Thank you for your kindness. I'm going to take her to the emergency room; hopefully they'll be able to figure out what's happening. You've been incredibly helpful."

Please don't take me to the hospital. They won't be able to do anything. It's a waste of time; I already know what's wrong.

Seeing that Yidarica was now alert, August smiled, releasing the tension that he had been holding in his shoulders. "I'm so glad you're awake!" he said, hurrying to close the gap between them, and hugging her tightly. "I was so scared when you passed out. Are you feeling okay now? Have you eaten?"

It was then that Yidarica realized why she was in such a bad way today. *I was up so late, and then I didn't bother to eat before I came here. Even with me not being able to sleep, I probably should've eaten something.*

Noticing her silence, August was able to surmise that she indeed hadn't eaten. "Well, I, um... you need to rest while we figure that out. If it's okay with you, we're close by my place, where I don't mind you resting for a moment. If that's too forward of a suggestion, please don't feel obligated to agree. Actually, forget I–"

She shook her head. "Should be fine."

"If you're sure, then okay. I'll lead the way, and you let me know if you need to stop at any point," August replied, helping Yidarica off the bench and assisting with getting her footing. Once she was stable enough on her feet, the two set out.

★★★

"You can make yourself comfortable."

Yidarica had expected, for reasons she no longer remembered, the place that August called home to be incredibly minimalistic. Maybe a plant or two on the counter, wall paintings with a lot of white blank space– that kind of thing. What a surprise it was, for her to enter his home and be surrounded by seemingly endless greenery. From the time one entered, they were smacked with rows and rows of leaves, flowers, so many vivid and fascinating plants. It was amazing.

"Did you grow all of these plants yourself?" she decided to ask, as she hung her jacket on the coat rack by the door.

"Not all of them, but I would say a good 90 percent of them, yeah," August replied. "Why do you ask?"

She shrugged. "This isn't what I expected when I'd imagine the place you call home. I don't know– I'd pegged you as more of a minimalist."

"A minimalist?" August made a face, one that made it clear he was feigning disgust. "Also, you've imagined my home before?"

"Yeah, doesn't everybody?" Yidarica asked without missing a beat. "Haven't you imagined what my house might be like? Or Celosia's? Or Muiren's? Or, like, anyone you've ever met whose house you've never been to?"

August regarded her with a look of curiosity. "No, I don't think I have, but now I'm probably going to. Where would you like to sit?"

The two walked further into the living room. The greenery swirled around the walls and ceiling enough that the room felt like a living, breathing greenhouse. Even so, the furniture in the room was set up just as any other living room was; a couch, an end table, a coffee table.

"So, the plants…" Yidarica was careful to not step on any leaves, stems, or branches as she sat on the couch.

August followed suit, taking a seat beside her, while giving the leaves of one of the nearest plants a pat. "Yeah. Um, sorry. I didn't think about the fact that it's probably a lot for people who aren't used to them."

"That wasn't what I meant. I like plants as much as the next person, but with as many as you have, I figured there's probably a story behind all of this, right?"

"Oh." August nodded. "It's not a very elaborate story, but my dad really loved his plants, so I took over taking care of them after he died. And then, once they were stable, I figured they probably wanted some new friends. I had done fauna maintenance magic very rarely before he passed, so I didn't think I'd be able to keep them alive, much less all of this, but…" he gestured around the room. "I guess there's something about all these little guys that makes me feel closer to my dad. I don't know. I hope it's not a problem," his eyebrows furrowed.

"The opposite, if anything. You have some lovely colors here," in particular, Yidarica was referring to some of the flowers blooming on the ceiling, in all their yellow-orange ombré glory.

"I'm glad you said that! I think so too. My favorites are the ones over there, the ones that go from blue to purple in the most beautiful marbling I've ever seen," August replied. "I'm also really fond of the tulips and the bluebells, particularly because they were so difficult to contend with that it felt extremely rewarding once I got them to cooperate. Oh, and that tiny micro shrub over there– I don't know what it's called, and the berries it produces are far too bitter to be enjoyable, but they're so pretty! Even for the plants that don't flower or bear fruit, the variance in greens is always so wonderful!"

August, then, realized that he was going on about his plants longer than a normal person would. "Well, now that we've got you off your feet, are you feeling any better?"

Of course she was. She was now in the home of the man she'd fallen head over heels for. And having him ask about her wellbeing only endeared him to her even more. "I'm not dizzy anymore, if that's what you're asking," she replied. "I do feel an overall sense of exhaustion, though. I guess I was more overwhelmed than I thought."

August nodded. "Okay. I'll get you some water and a pillow. Stay here; I'll be right back."

Before Yidarica could say anything, he'd hopped off the couch to go and retrieve those things.

I realize now: in addition to August being cute and incredibly sweet, I find that I can relate to him in a lot of ways. The way he immediately got up to get something for me feels the same as me dropping everything for other people. Maybe that's why he's been so easily able to understand me.

"I brought you an ice pack too. I don't remember you having a fever, but I thought it might help with grounding you if you still feel a little unnerved. Also, I can't find any of my extra pillows, so I hope this folded blanket is okay. It's nice and fluffy and soft." August placed these on the table and handed Yidarica the glass of water he'd retrieved.

She took a sip, but then frowned. "Room temperature? Ew."

August stared at her, as if this sentence didn't compute.

"I'm really appreciative of everything you're doing for me, August. But really, more than anything, I think I just need a quick nap. No more than a half-hour. I think I'm good to go home, so I just–"

"But you live so far away," August reminded her. "I'd worry about you. Here, you can… my room is right around that corner. You can take a nap there."

This suggestion automatically put Yidarica on guard. She liked August a lot, but not enough to be oblivious to the dynamics at play. She wasn't at 100% at the moment, and even if she was, August was more than a foot taller than her and could (likely) easily overpower her. And while she felt safe around him, she worried that her feelings would be her undoing.

"I–" August must have realized how that sounded, because his next words were, "No, I– I promise that I'll leave you alone. A half-hour isn't a long time, so I can knock some small chores out while you're asleep. I won't lay a finger on you unless you ask, all right?"

The inclusion of "unless you ask" was enough to render Yidarica unable to speak. She could only nod.

I like to think I'm good at discerning people's character at this point, and I trust August. He's never given me a reason not to, and I've never felt any discomfort when I'm with him.

I hope I don't end up regretting this decision.

"I'll show you to the room, then," he replied. "Follow me."

The bedroom was the first room so far that wasn't filled with plants; the only one in here was a young bird of paradise seated on the windowsill. The walls were still painted green as if to emulate a greenhouse, and the bed's headboard and footboard had beautiful, floral intricate wrought iron designs. The bedspread itself, though, was a simple dark green set.

As Yidarica settled under the covers, her only thought was how this was possibly the softest set of sheets she'd ever felt.

***

A certain cacophony of undistinguishable noises caused Yidarica to wake from her sleep, about forty minutes later.

She felt an initial panic from waking up in an unfamiliar place, but as the events of earlier this evening returned to her, she felt relieved that all of her clothes were still on, and exactly the way they had been before she'd fallen asleep. It was an immense comfort to know that August had stayed true to his word.

Movement in her peripheral vision caused her to quickly turn; August was on the other side of the room, folding laundry and putting it away; the noise had probably been him opening one of the drawers.

"Oh, you're awake!" Even in low light, it was easy to see that August's eyes had lit up behind his glasses. "It's been longer than a half-hour, but when I came to check on you, you were snoring so loudly that I decided it was best to leave you alone."

Well, she'd never live *that* down.

"It was loud enough, actually, that I thought you wouldn't hear me if I came in to put my laundry away, but I guess I miscalculated there." He finished folding the white shirt he was holding and placed it in the open drawer, before heading toward the bed. "Are you feeling better now?"

"Yeah, I–" Yidarica sat up, and was taken over by a moment of intense dizziness, but luckily, that subsided quickly. "Lots better. I'm sorry, August. I don't know what came over me today, but I promise I'm not always this frail."

"Well, yeah. I know that. We've been out together before and you were fine. You don't have to apologize," he replied, sitting beside her on the bed. "Even though we weren't out for long, I still had a good time, 'cause I like spending time with you, and… there's probably something to be said about the fact that now, I'm spending even more time with you than I would've if you hadn't needed to rest."

This was true. "Yeah. Sorry. I guess I just feel personal responsibility whenever the reason for plans falling apart can be traced back to me in some way."

"I can empathize, but don't worry about it. You feel better now, and that makes me happy too, so we both benefit from the way things have gone."

August smiled then, and it was then that Yidarica knew she wouldn't be able to resist anything else he said; nor the familiar force that seemed to be drawing them to one another, once again.

Their lips met, so soft, so gentle, but with an underlying sense of necessity. It hadn't been mere curiosity for either of them this time; both had needed this kiss more than anything else at this time. And even though this was only the second time, it was as if it was natural for them both by now. Gone were Yidarica's worries about accidentally knocking August's glasses off of his face, or bumping into his nose, or anything like that.

They separated then, but not very far– both smiling at almost the same time, taking a breath. This was perfect. Moments as small as this one, being in such close proximity with someone she adored: this was what Yidarica had yearned for all her life, and the feeling was better than she could have ever imagined. And when August kissed her again, with the gentleness of a summer wind, she wondered how she'd survived this long without this. Without him.

"This is okay, isn't it?" he asked softly, to which he received a nod in reply.

It felt natural for him to gently nudge her back onto the bed as they kissed, he beside her, his arm resting at her waist to pull her in ever closer. His hand was so gentle as it slowly traveled from her waist to her face, holding it tenderly so he could place gentle kisses on the other side; her cheek, then trailing down to her neck, settling at a very specific spot where the tickling of his facial hair startled her a bit, mostly because she didn't think it had grown in enough to feel it. But there was something about it that felt satisfying, as well, and her body began to melt into his, her hand instinctively moving to brush his hair back so it wouldn't get in the way.

His hand moved then, finding a resting place at her chest.

The warmth of the moment began to fade as Yidarica became conscious of the natural progression of things: *it won't be long before we start taking our clothes off, will it?*

The idea… did it scare her? Did it make her uncomfortable? She struggled to sort out her feelings, as their lips met again. She knew she was extremely fond of August, and loved the way it felt when he kissed her and held her close. Didn't that mean she was supposed to also love the idea that they would eventually have sex? She thought she did, but here she was, in a position that precluded that, and… it didn't seem very enticing at all. If anything, the idea was closer to discomfort.

But what did that mean?

As August again placed kisses at her neck, she was filled once again with feelings of euphoria, ones which dampened the feelings of discomfort, giving way to a certain sense of pleasure. There was some level of trepidation as he reached under her shirt, gently grasping one of her breasts; and in no time, Yidarica absolved to move her clothing out of the way so he could touch her freely.

Where did that come from? I was so undecided about the whole thing, but him touching me here… oh, that's just heavenly.

A kiss on the cheek and a brief peck on the lips happened before he trailed kisses down her neck and collarbone, traveling to her nipple, kissing it gently before taking it into his mouth, slowly sucking in a very gentle way.

This is paradise. I thought I liked this when it happened with Zaya, but August is… dear Mother, he's amazing. Is this what people mean when they say they're "turned on?"

However, it wasn't long before she was suddenly filled with a strong sense of dread. *As wonderful as it feels, I don't think I can do anything further. I don't want anything else. I can't. I can't take off my clothes. I don't want to be touched down there. The thought of it makes me feel sick.*

Yidarica was sure she'd never forget that August had rested his hand on her breast, before interrupting their kiss and saying, "I'm sorry, I don't think I can do this."

Thank the Mother he'd had *that* epiphany.

"And I– I don't mean that I can't do it right now. I mean…" August let go of her then, and turned to his back. "I don't… think I want to do this at all anymore."

This made Yidarica sigh the biggest sigh of relief. "I am *so* glad you said that."

"What? You are?"

"I am. This is new territory for me, so I guess that because of that, I've never been in a position where I needed to sort out my feelings about sex, because I wasn't having it anyway, right? But here, now, where the possibility was lingering in the air and over my head… I think the realness and proximity of the situation made me realize that it's not something I've ever particularly *wanted* to do. It just always felt like something I would *have* to do, if I liked someone. And right now, I was very nervous about the whole idea; because I like you, August, and all the times we've kissed have been amazing, but I really would be perfectly okay with not having to think about sex anytime soon, or even at all, because all it does is make me panic and feel gross."

August had that look on his face again, that face that made it impossible to tell what he was thinking. "This has been on my mind lately: that, the more that I think about it, I don't think I've ever been in a situation where I was in bed with someone because it was what I wanted. I– that sounds horrible. Uh, what I mean to say is that all the times I've had sex with a partner, it's been kind of like what you just described: something I felt I had to do because I was enamored with them. And don't get me wrong, it does feel fulfilling to give someone I love that satisfaction, but sex has never been something I've actively wanted, and at this point in my life, I'm kind of weary of pretending that I do."

Yidarica's expression probably mirrored the indistinguishable one August often used at this point. "So… what you're saying is, you don't think I'm weird for not wanting you in my guts right now?"

"I'm honestly relieved that you don't," August replied. "I mean, I– we could always revisit the idea later. If you're that interested in me, that is."

"Of course I am." Yidarica smiled. "I would never sit here and make out with someone I didn't truly like. Who has time for that?"

August smiled back. "I'm glad you feel that way. So, what are we doing about dinner?"

"Dinner?" Yidarica repeated.

"Dinner. Remember, we didn't get to eat before you started feeling weak," August reminded her. "I know you said you feel better now, but you'd probably feel even more better with some food in your system. I'm not the best cook, but… I'll try, for you."

As endearing as this sounded, Yidarica didn't know how she felt about potentially eating food made by someone who seemed to be acutely aware that they didn't know how to cook.

"Or... we could order out," August added then, noticing how silent she had gotten.

★★★

Minutes later, the two were seated on August's couch with takeout noodles, and August had been right: Yidarica certainly *did* feel much better with food in her system. These noodles weren't the best ones she'd ever had– but for some reason, the sweet, slightly tangy sauce they were cooked with, and the tender slices of beef within, felt like a homecoming meal.

"This is good stuff," August said softly, to himself.

"Yeah," agreed Yidarica, which took him by surprise.

"Oh! I didn't realize you'd... heard me. Sorry, it's just that there's so many restaurants around here that I'm still discovering some of them, and I've never eaten from this one, so I didn't know what to expect. It's a pleasant surprise," he explained.

The two continued to eat, Yidarica taking another look at all of the plants around the living room. She wasn't sure why, but she wanted to ask about them... without really knowing what it was she wanted to know. August had already explained why he had so many, and it was clear that they were well-cared for. What else was there to know?

"You know," August said then, placing his folding noodle container aside. "Part of the reason I like having plants here is because, when I first moved in, the high ceilings and white walls and halogen lights made this place seem eerily sterile. Until I got my couch and everything, it almost felt like I was living in a hospital. Even after it was furnished, there was still this weird feeling, like this wasn't really a home, you know? I like to think that having so much life here now feels much more warm and inviting. Although, I do admit: this is probably why I went a little overboard with their life spells."

"I could never get those to work right," Yidarica confessed. "Even with water, sunlight, and magic, I'm lucky if I can get a plant to live longer than a month."

August tilted his head. "Would you like me to teach you?"

"Teach me what, plant life spells?" Yidarica asked.

"Yeah." August nodded, smiling. "If you want to. I figured, if you're open to learning and I'm the one with the knowledge, then it only makes sense... but if you don't want to–"

"No, it's okay. I very much do." Yidarica sat her food aside as well, folding her legs under herself and turning to August. "Where are we starting off?"

August took a moment to think of the best point to start at. "Well, to start, why don't we see how you usually cast? Here, give me your hands, and start whenever you're ready."

Yidarica carefully placed her hands on top of August's– taking a brief moment to note how well they fit together, and how soft his hands were, and how lovely it was that her brown skin so contrasted his fair skin– before closing her eyes and, as always, beginning the spell.

How did the plant life spell begin, again? It had been so long. The last time she'd used it, she had still been living in her dump of a dorm.

Now concentrating on the dark canvas of her mind, she carefully took hold of the pieces of magic that appeared there, piecing them together, one by one– *oh, that's right!* She suddenly remembered:

the magic particles needed to be woven together, braided, like the way her mother would do her hair as a child; or, more accurately, like a plant's stem. Yidarica had never been good at braiding herself, though, so while she knew the strand of magic she was weaving was too loose, she lacked the knowledge to make it any less loose.

Oh no. I don't remember how to end it. You don't throw it... that I do know, but there has to be an ending action; if there wasn't, I'd be braiding forever. But what is it?

She opened her eyes. "I'm sorry. I forgot how to conclude the spell."

"Don't apologize. You did your best." August was thinking again, giving both of Yidarica's hands a gentle squeeze of reassurance. "Oh! I know! I'm going to show you the first spell my father ever taught me. It's not as complex because it's usually taught to children, and it's not so strong that my apartment will get even more overtaken," he chuckled. "But it doesn't work unless you physically have a plant in front of you. I should have a younger one around; I'll be back."

After searching the other rooms, August returned with a tulip so young, it had barely grown a flower bud. Yidarica also noticed that its leaves were a bit wilted. "Here we are. This little guy was hiding, so I haven't had much time with him. He will be perfect for our demonstration. I want you to try your best to focus on how I'm casting, but you should also try to keep an eye on what I'm doing, because one of my hands has to go here," he touched the top of the plant's structure pole. "Ready?" He asked, holding his hand out.

"Ready." Yidarica nodded, taking it.

First, she closed her eyes. The warmth when August began casting was intense, so much it almost hurt, and she almost let go of him; this was when she opened her eyes.

The same shimmering, glittering golden and green magic that August was currently consciously controlling in his mind, was also swirling around the structure pole itself; curling, climbing like the vines and leaves of plants were so inclined to do. It wasn't long before the plant itself recovered from its wilting.

It was, in a word, amazing.

Even more interesting than this, was the fact that even though the intensity of August's magic was such a sensory onslaught that it had caused Yidarica discomfort and almost pain, there was a part of her that wanted to feel it again. August was usually so reserved and shy that it was a stark contrast to feel him so passionate in this roundabout way.

"What do you think?" he asked, bringing her back to reality.

She nodded. "I think it's a lot more doable since it doesn't have the technical aspect of braiding. I was always really bad at the motion, even with my hair."

"Really? But I've seen your hair in braids before. They're very pretty," August replied.

"That's because I paid somebody's auntie to do it for me," Yidarica laughed. "I am a horrible braider, I assure you. These hands are simply not skilled enough."

"Well, you still have the technique down. It's just the tightness. I always struggled with braiding spells; mine are always lopsided." Almost instantly, it was like a lightbulb had lit in August's mind. "We can try to cast together! It'll be good practice, and we can focus it right on this little guy here."

Yidarica agreed instantly, curious about how the end result would turn out. "That's a great idea!"

"Now, I haven't cast with a partner in a very, very long time," August warned her. "So I encourage you to be loud and clear about it if I'm being too aggressive, okay?"

"Okay." She nodded, placing her hands in August's again. She would just be braiding again. Nothing difficult, right?

When her eyes were closed, and she began gathering her pieces of magic, before long she felt August casting with her, assisting with gathering all of the magic in the air. Immediately, she noticed that he was better at recognizing which pieces of magic were best for plant spells. She also noticed that he didn't pay much attention to the thicknesses of the strands of magic, which was probably why his braids were always lopsided. She tried to gently encourage him to keep them even, until she got frustrated and physically grabbed his arm. "Keep them even," she whispered, afraid that if she talked too loud, the pieces would disintegrate.

He must have heard her, because the distribution gradually became more even, and she returned her hand to his.

When the braiding began, Yidarica led the motion, August usually following up behind her to tighten the strands when she'd leave them too loose. This meant that they were working more closely together, which meant that she could feel the intensity of his magic again. He stopped at one point, trying to inspect the braid so far, but unable to backtrack very far; he paused before realizing what it was he needed to do, and let go of one of Yidarica's hands, his fingers gently traveling up her arm, progressing to a full caress by the time he reached her elbow. She could feel the intensity, but this time, it almost tickled. She had to put in great effort to not laugh reflexively.

When the braid was sufficiently long, August held Yidarica's hands tight, showing her the correct way to end the spell: by *braiding it into itself.*

Damn it, that makes so much sense. Why couldn't I remember that?!

Now that the spell had concluded, she could feel the plant had grown because one of the leaves was tickling her thigh now, but she kept her eyes closed, savoring the feeling that was now resonating through her body. Magic had never felt that amazing. She could count on one hand how many times she'd had a casting partner, but it had never felt this exhilarating.

August was still holding her hands. "Would you like to cast together again?"

"Please," she agreed.

"I'm not very good at magic that's not plant or tech based, but…" he trailed off. "This next spell always intrigued me. I've always thought this one had great potential if I could cast it with someone with a higher aptitude for magic, which you definitely have… and more kindness in their heart."

He began to cast again, and Yidarica noticed the difference in the strength of this one. She also noticed the colors in it: pink, purple, blue.

"I wouldn't say it's high difficulty, but it's nuanced, so it can easily hurt its casters instead of its intended effect," he explained. "It, um… I hope you're okay with me explaining to you how I know it, because it involves my ex-boyfriend. I won't go into it, if it makes you uncomfortable."

"No, tell me," Yidarica insisted. She could tell that this was one of those things that needed to be talked through. "I'm fine with it. Also, am I supposed to be doing anything?"

"Just repeat the same actions you feel me doing," August replied. "You see, the intended outcome of this spell is to, in a sense, become closer to your casting partner; it creates a sense of clarity between everyone involved, so it's often used in corporate settings, in schools... in relationships."

August paused his casting, and gently placed a hand on Yidarica's shoulder so she would do the same. "Before I go any farther with any of this: do you trust me, Yidarica?"

Did she? The fact that he was asking made her second-guess herself.

"Is there a reason I shouldn't?" she asked.

Now August was the one who needed a pause. He explained, "I don't want to accidentally hurt or upset you, and I'd feel a lot more confident in my ability to not do that, if you were to reassure me that you trust me to have your best interests in mind."

That made sense. "Then, yes. I trust you, August."

And so the spell resumed, continuing its intricate weaving. "I wasn't familiar with this spell at all until my ex-boyfriend taught it to me. He initially said it was because he couldn't understand me, in the sense that apparently, the words and actions I used to describe things confused him; that he could never be certain what I meant. And I do think it helped in that regard, because sometimes, I didn't understand him either. Small things, like he'd mention it being a rainy day and I was supposed to know that meant he wanted to cancel our dinner plans, or he'd say he was cooking breakfast and I was supposed to know that he expected me to do the dishes afterward. But remember when I said this spell can also hurt sometimes?"

Yidarica nodded. "Yeah."

"Whenever we cast this spell together and it hurt, it felt like he was punishing me; even when the spell itself was beneficial, there was always this uncomfortable feeling that varied in subtlety or outright pain whenever we cast together, and he always brushed it off whenever I brought it up; insisting it was my fault, sometimes. But the more I think about it, I don't think it was. I think it would only be soothing to cast such a spell with someone who is kind, and gentle… and hopefully, who cares about my feelings."

The jury's still out on me being kind or gentle, but I care about you, August. I care about you so much.

Yidarica didn't notice until August reacted to it, how intense she'd gotten with her magic. He adjusted quickly, though– matching the amount of effort she was putting into this congregation of energies. And after a while, she could feel the effects; she felt closer to August, which came with a side effect of wanting to be physically closer to him.

Tentatively, she let go of his hand, placing it instead on his arm. The spell didn't break, and he didn't stop the contact. She felt vindicated when he did the same for her other arm, testing the waters to see if it was okay to make the spell even stronger. She almost jumped at the chance, wanting to feel all of the–

All at once, the spell collapsed as Yidarica fell back onto the arm rest of the couch, intensely dizzy and disoriented. She also couldn't see anything, but not in the way she'd always feared. If anything, this was the opposite; there was a blinding light, so intense that all she could see was whiteness, and it hurt. It hurt so much she squeezed her eyes shut, waiting for it to subside.

When it did, thankfully pretty quickly, she was met with August's concerned face. "Are you okay? What happened? I wasn't too forceful, was I?"

"No, it wasn't you. I'm pretty certain I overexerted myself." Yidarica sat up, but felt dizzy again; this time, August caught her before she could fall over again. "Sorry. Dizzy."

August regarded her with even more concern. "I'm about to ask you something, but before I do, I want you to understand that I'm asking it because of your health and out of concern for it, and for no other reason. Okay?"

She nodded just a bit, too weak to do much else.

"Would you feel comfortable staying here for the night?"

Yidarica didn't balk at this as much as she wanted to (mostly because she physically couldn't). Realistically, she'd never be able to make it home like this. She would probably collapse before she made it out of the building. Even if she managed to make it home, she didn't have the stamina for those three flights of stairs, so it would be no use to have August request her a ride. And she trusted him. She'd trusted him earlier, and she could trust him again now.

"Except… I don't know where you should sleep," August continued. "It's just that I can't sleep on the couch because I'm too tall, so I have to stay in my bed; and I don't want to put you in a position you're not comfortable with."

Oh, shit, that's right. This is a nice couch, but I don't know that it's suitable for sleeping. It's not very wide, for one. What if I fell off in the middle of the night?

"I trust you." The dizziness was subsiding now, but Yidarica still felt so very weak. "I slept here a little while ago and you respected my boundaries then. Is it wrong to assume you'll do the same overnight?"

"I won't be doing much of anything other than sleeping," August replied with a laugh.

"Then… I just ask that you lend me something that's a little more comfy to sleep in."

This made August smile. "I can certainly do that."

Yidarica motioned to get up, but was taken by surprise when August picked her up, carrying her the fifteen feet to his bedroom. "I could've walked," she insisted.

"You also could have hit your head on the way, and made yourself feel worse," August pointed out, as they reached the room. "If you just end up hurting yourself more, what's the point of you staying here in the first place? Here," he placed her gently onto the bed. "Wait right here."

He walked over to his dresser, rummaging through its drawers and the contents within, before settling on something. "Here we go. Are you coherent enough to catch?"

"Why wouldn't I be–" before she could finish, the shirt that August had picked out for her narrowly missed her face. It was a dark blue, and had intricate patterns of triangles and swirls all over, in varying tones of purple. The fabric was a satisfying texture, too. Not the softest, but soft enough; and the grain of the weaving was nice and straight. "Cute shirt."

"Thanks." August smiled, picking up a pajama set that had been sitting on the top of the dresser. "I'll give you some privacy."

Changing clothes, Yidarica had been of the mind that August's clothes would be huge on her because of how tall he was. And this shirt certainly was long, but she had never considered how thin he was, so she was surprised at how fitted the thing became around her chest. It made sense, though, when she thought about it more. August didn't have to worry about breasts, so of course she'd take up more space in the chest area.

I can't complain, even so. It's still comfy. Wonder what kind of fabric this is? I should've looked at the tag.

Moments later, August returned, dressed in a very cute black and white pinstripe pajama shorts set. Seeing him in such casual, cozy wear made Yidarica's heart skip several beats. *He's so adorable. I never thought of how he must look when he's about to sleep, but I could have never prepared myself for this.*

She must have stared longer than usual, because August asked, "Is something wrong?"

"I don't–" Yidarica laughed a little. "I'm sorry, it's silly. I don't think I've ever seen your legs before now."

August looked down at his legs, which were pretty emblematic of the rest of his body; pale, thin, and peppered with enough brown hairs that they were just visible enough from a distance. "Oh. I... I just realized I could say the same about you. Even with all of your dresses and skirts, I noticed that you are a frequent wearer of hosiery."

"Yeah, because my legs are–" *When was the last time I got rid of the hair on my legs. Oh no. August is gonna know that I have hair on my legs now. Even if he doesn't see it, he's going to feel it if our legs touch–*

"Please forgive me if it's presumptuous to assume so, but I get the feeling you're worried about whether or not you have hair on your legs at the moment," August said then. "It's okay. I don't really– well, truthfully, I don't much care for non-head hair at all, but I also doubt that you're as hirsute as any of the men I've shared beds with."

Oh, Mother, that bisexuality is really coming in clutch here.

"Are you sure you're okay with this arrangement?" he was asking now. "I can sleep on the couch. Really. It's no problem."

"August, it would absolutely be a problem if I made your beanpole self sleep on the couch. You'd be so uncomfortable. You'd wake up in pain. Would you be able to stand after that? Would you even be able to fall asleep?"

He must have pondered this, because soon enough, he climbed into the bed. "Maybe 'no problem' wasn't the best way to word it, but please tell me if anything about this makes you feel uncomfortable, all right? I mean it. I don't want you to feel like you have to be on guard all night."

"I trust you." Yidarica turned so that she was facing August. "I'm getting the feeling that something's happened to you before in a situation like this. Is it something you want to talk about?"

For a moment, August stared into space, before shaking his head and removing his glasses, placing them on the nightstand, and settling under the covers. "I'm sorry. I'll do better at not projecting my insecurities onto you."

"It's fine. I like knowing that you care so much about my well-being." Yidarica smiled, but realized, "You probably can't see it; I'm smiling at you."

"Oh," this made August smile as well, with a small chuckle. "You're right that I can't see it, but I'm sure it's beautiful. Your smiles always are."

It was still so surreal, for Yidarica, that August was looking right at her and yet couldn't see her. She could only see the outlines of his face because there was such low lighting in the room at this time of night from this angle, but even so, she could still see the general shapes of his nose and eyes. Those beautiful eyes that she could get lost in if given the opportunity.

The circumstances aren't ideal, but I'm glad I'm here.

She snuggled close to where he was, resting her head in the space between the bed and his chest. Moments later, she felt the soothing motion of his hand on her back, rubbing, gently coercing her into sleep.

Chapter Nineteen

When Yidarica awoke the next day, she did so because it felt like she had been falling.

Where am I? What is this place? Did I somehow fall through the floor of my... wait. No. This isn't my building.

Her senses returning to her, it was a relief that August had given her the opportunity to rest here overnight. The thought of having to commute back home, especially at that time of night, sounded exhausting; but here she was, as rested as ever, cozy in his bed without having had to do anything that made her uncomfortable.

Was this the good life? It certainly felt as such.

She turned at the sound of August softly grunting in his sleep– *oh, Mother, he's so cute like this*– before he shifted, kicking some of the bedsheets off of himself. As he readjusted, Yidarica noticed that, in the area where his shirt had moved enough that it exposed some of his stomach, there was a small scar, about three inches long. It was very obviously fully healed, so it had to have happened a long time ago, but the positioning suggested that it wasn't a surgical scar. She was curious, but decided it would be in poor form to ask him. She'd wait until he brought it up, if he ever did.

With another soft grunt, August slowly opened his eyes. When they had focused, he gasped, a shocked look on his face.

Immediately, Yidarica felt rejected. *That's horror. He's disgusted. He regrets having me here.*

"No, Yidarica, that's not–" he immediately said, seeing how hurt she looked. "I can see you!"

She was confused now. "What are you talking about? Of course you can see…"

His glasses. He's not wearing his glasses!

"You can?!" she gasped.

"Not perfectly, I mean, there are still details that are fuzzy. But mostly, I can see you; the overall pattern of the shirt you're wearing. Your sparkling brown eyes. Your beautiful smile."

August gave her forehead a gentle kiss.

"This is amazing. I… I don't know what to say."

Yidarica didn't, either. She couldn't put into words how happy she was– not only because August was able to begin fighting the pieces of the Dark that afflicted him, which was probably beneficial for her own silent affliction– but because she was probably the reason for it.

But it never hurt to be sure. "That… that's because of me, right?"

In response, August grinned, laughing. "Yes. Yes, it's because of you. I really… don't know how long it's been since I felt this content and safe around someone. Or if I ever have, and it's– I can't possibly describe how exhilarating it feels to have my feelings returned by such a beautiful person, mentally and physically."

He paused for a moment. "You– you *do* return these feelings, don't you?"

Yidarica smiled, extending her arm just enough to be able to pull August close and kiss him. He reciprocated, pulling her in, one hand holding her close and the other gently stroking her hair. She wondered to herself if last night was a fluke, and if she felt differently about sex today... but, reaching into the very corners of her mind, there was no part of her that felt the desire to go that way, once again. Being close to August was always euphoric, even more so if it was while they kissed, but... that seemed to be the extent of her desires at this time.

I think I'm realizing that I don't need to worry about all that at this very moment. I'm happy with anything that transpires, as long as it's with August.

As she rested her head on his chest, he asked, "Um... potentially awkward question."

"Yeah?" She looked up at him.

"How are we handling work, exactly?"

Amazingly, Yidarica had not once considered the fact that the idea of dating her coworker meant that they'd also have to work together sometimes. It would be fine, right? No one had to know. They'd just have to resist the urge to hold hands.

An urge that will probably be nonexistent with our project ending. Remember, August has moved to a department that's farther away, so he probably won't walk past as often, if at all.

"It'll... be easy, won't it?" Yidarica asked aloud. "With our crossover project ending, we probably won't see each other very often at work anymore. We just need to be normal around each other when we do."

In response, August lifted one of her hands to his lips and kissed it. "I don't know if I can."

A feeling of warmth bubbled up inside Yidarica's stomach, spreading through the rest of her body, as she again rested her head on August's chest. They could let all of that wait until the time came, couldn't they? Right now... right now she just wanted to enjoy being this close to him. His chin rested on her head for a brief moment as he held her tight, almost squeezing for a second; then loosening the hold again as one of his hands gently stroked her back.

"I think this is the type of intimacy I've been missing this whole time," he softly confessed. "I've never been able to have this because my previous partners would always be so focused on sex as intimacy that we'd never have the chance to just… cuddle like this. I guess I'm partially at fault for not explicitly saying that it was one of my needs, but that brings further questions to mind about whether or not I've ever dated anyone who actually liked me, and I'd *really* prefer to not go down that road."

"Then don't," Yidarica said softly, also not wanting to consider how much those interactions must have hurt him.

August could only smile, snuggling even closer to her.

"If I could make a humble request," he said then. "Would you be okay with me taking you home? I want to be sure you get back okay, but I'm also a little curious about what the place you call home looks like, now that you've seen mine."

This immediately caused Yidarica to panic. Compared to this place, her apartment was a dump. "Y-you're sure?" she asked.

"Yeah. If you'll have me, it would be an honor."

He gave her another quick squeeze then, and another kiss on the forehead.

It's amazing that someone this tall is so gentle, but I love it. I would stop time here if I knew how, but I guess I'm gonna need to go home and change clothes at some point.

***

"Oh, ow, I– I'm gonna need my glasses," August realized the moment he tried to step out of his bedroom without them. He squinted, hurrying back into the more dim bedroom, searching for his glasses. "I got too ahead of myself without them. I'll be back! Give me five seconds, it won't…"

He re-emerged then, wearing the pair of black-rimmed glasses Yidarica was used to seeing him with. Almost immediately, he smiled.

"I like that I can mostly see you without my glasses now, but… it doesn't compare to being able to see all of the beautiful details you're made of," he said then. "It's fine. I didn't expect to have perfect sight immediately."

Plus, he's still very cute with them on.

"So, breakfast." August clasped his hands together. "You can sit here and make yourself comfortable. I won't be long. How do you like your eggs? Fried? Scrambled? Poached?"

It had been so long since Yidarica had made her own breakfast, she didn't immediately remember. "Uh, scrambled is fine," she said, taking a seat on the couch.

"I am *so* glad you didn't say poached, because I have no idea how to do that," August replied, giving her a dual finger gun pose before heading into the kitchen.

Yidarica laughed just a little as he disappeared into the kitchen, and then she began to observe the living room, wondering what she should do to keep herself occupied until the meal was done. The plants in the room curled up and around the many bookshelves, which surprisingly didn't have many books on them. This was when she noticed that this room didn't have a television, which was practically unheard of, especially for this age group.

Oh, right. Might be hard with all the plants. He probably uses a projector, or some other visualization spell.

I don't know a lot of flora spells, but I wonder if I can figure out how to communicate with these plants. I'm sure there's a way to. I bet August knows how.

But before she could call for him, Yidarica stopped herself. She wondered if it was worth disturbing him over– after all, if he had to stop cooking to show her how to cast a spell, it would take even longer for him to finish cooking– and, realizing that, she curled up on the couch, not quite certain what to do with herself. In the kitchen, she could hear the sound of something frying, and something being mixed in a bowl. After a few minutes of listening, she could hear the frying get just a little louder, and what she was pretty sure was August swearing under his breath at the food being cooked.

I hope he's doing okay.

Yidarica picked up her phone then, noting that her messages were still empty, and sighing just a little bit. It was what she had expected; but there had also been the tiniest part of her that was hoping otherwise, that one of her friends would reach out first. With this not being the case, she knew she'd have to eventually go into the group chat and basically beg for forgiveness. She'd do that later though, when she'd gotten some food in her stomach and was more coherent.

Even so, she missed talking to everyone in the chat, especially Gracia.

Placing her phone face down on the console table behind the couch, amidst the plants, Yidarica noticed a picture frame. In it was a photo of August and a group of men who all looked to be around his age, if not slightly older. The photo appeared to have been taken at some sort of restaurant, or possibly an unusually well-lit bar. August, though grinning in the picture as he held a glass of what Yidarica assumed was either beer or some kind of wine, seemed out of place somehow. She couldn't place why she felt that way, but the longer she stared at the picture, the more she felt it.

"Breakfast is served!" August announced as he entered the room carrying two plates and two cups of orange juice. "I hope it's edible. Oh, you noticed that picture! That was a good day."

He placed everything on the coffee table, and sat on the couch, cross-legged. "Back home, one of my friends has this big ranch home that he lives in, with his wife and their kids, that he bought a little while after I moved away. This is from around when they first got it, and a lot of us visited. It was such a fun time. That drink I'm holding there is strawberry melomel; he makes it in their backyard sometimes, can you believe that? It was deliciously sweet, but I did end up having to stay the night after drinking it. Deceptively strong drink, that."

Yidarica nodded, not sure what to say in response.

"Well, I've rambled long enough. Let's get to the food before it gets too cold," he said then.

Turning to the food, and seeing it for the first time, Yidarica had to double-take. The sliced fruit looked fine. The eggs looked… edible, probably. The breakfast sausages looked off somehow, in a way she couldn't quite place. The pancakes… the pancakes were a lumpy mess, but they at least looked fully cooked.

As she found out upon her first bite, they were definitely *not* fully cooked.

August regarded her curiously, before taking a bite of his own pancakes. He was silent for a long while, before gently placing his plate back on the table. "Yeah, I probably should've ordered breakfast."

"It's not bad! The eggs look delicious," Yidarica exaggerated as she decided to try those next. The difference between this and the pancakes were like night and day, as she ate another forkful. "Can I share an opinion with you that usually makes people look at me like I've lost my mind, August?"

"Yes..?" he said, confused.

"You know how the widely accepted way to make scrambled eggs is to have them be at least a little wet and mushy? Personally, I hate that. It feels gross. I like it when my eggs are dry and a little browned, like what you did here. The cheese addition is a nice touch, too." Yidarica smiled. "I'm sure other people would say these are overcooked, but I love this."

August was beaming at the compliment. "Thanks! I never thought about it before, but maybe that's why I can never finish my eggs unless I make them myself: the texture. Hm. I'm going to be thinking about this for a while now."

"It always shocks me that there are people who don't think about the texture of their food," Yidarica confessed. "It's something that I pretty much obsess over, so the idea of people not giving it a single thought is surreal."

"Really." August said this as a statement and not a question, in a tone that made it clear he was thinking about things. "I think that I'd love to talk to you more about this sometime, because now I'm realizing that there is a non-zero amount of foods I dislike that are probably because of their texture. We could maybe continue to discuss it while we're at your place, even."

At the mention of visiting her place, Yidarica was once again overcome by a feeling of inadequacy. "Are you sure you want to come to my place?" she asked then. "I mean, I- it's not a lot. For you to take the whole trip just to see it, I'd feel guilty for wasting your time."

"It's not a waste. I promise." August closed the gap between the two, giving her a brief peck on the lips. "It's never a waste to spend time with you."

I'm glad he's so optimistic. But I'm pretty sure I still have clothes on the floor and dishes in the sink.

***

Walking up the three flights of stairs and opening all three locks on the door, Yidarica didn't feel any more confident in showing August her place of residence by the time she pushed her door open, but at this point, there was no turning back.

"Well, this is it. Welcome to paradise."

She turned to study August's reaction, but was surprised to see that he looked more curious than anything, taking in the surroundings. He stopped walking when his eyes fell on the couch, and gasped, clasping his hands together gleefully. "Your couch is so cute! I love it!"

"Do you really?" Yidarica asked, shocked that this was the first thing that had come out of his mouth.

"Yeah! I love the colors," he replied. "I wish I had thought of getting a couch like this. You've seen mine now, it's so boring."

Yidarica had been so afraid of August seeing where she lived and judging her, but here he was, admiring her couch. *And he's so cute when he gets excited about things.*

THE ABSENCE OF COMPLETE DARK 295

"Would you... like to stay a while?" she asked then.

August smiled. "As long as you'll have me. Can I sit here?"

"I mean, it's a couch." She shrugged, trying to play off how relieved she was that he already seemed to like it here. "Designed perfectly for sitting. Can I get you anything? Water, snacks?"

"Um, if water isn't an imposition," he replied. "I'm a little thirsty after the walk up the stairs."

"Sure." Yidarica first hurried to her bedroom, though. She had to change clothes before she felt normal, but after that, she made her way to the kitchen to grab water.

Returning to the living room, August was reading one of the books that had been on one of the end tables, one leg crossed over the other. Amazingly, given the short amount of time that had passed, he already seemed to be engrossed in whatever he was reading. Yidarica tried to remember what books she had sitting there as she approached the couch, but she couldn't think of what they were. Damn brain fog was rolling in once again, it seemed.

She sat on the couch with August, which caused him to turn to her. "Do you read travel books often?" he asked.

That's right— I was reading my book about Dochram the last time I moved my books around in here, because I missed Gracia so much. Funny how that's happening again. "I don't think I'd say often, but at times," Yidarica nodded. "I bought that book to learn more about the place my best friend was visiting at the time. She'd been gone for a while, so I missed her."

"I see." August placed the book aside, and moved his body so that he'd be fully facing Yidarica. "What do you usually read, then?"

This wasn't the conversation she had been expecting to have. "Uh, it depends on my mood I guess," she replied. "All of the books I have here are vastly different, because sometimes I want to laugh, sometimes I want to cry, sometimes I want to learn something, et cetera, et cetera. Are you a reader?"

August started to nod, but then stopped himself. "Well, yes, but not recently. When I moved into the apartment I currently live in, I couldn't bring any of the books I had because I couldn't get my head around how I would get them here. Weight versus volume, all of that. So they're currently still in a storage unit back home. Since then, I've been trying to find new books until I can regain access to those, but nothing seems to appeal to me lately. I guess I'm in a bit of a reading slump."

That explained why his bookshelves were mostly empty. "I could probably recommend you something, if you're open to that," Yidarica suggested. "I've read a lot of books over the years. Even if I can't think of exactly what you need, I could probably come up with an author whose work you'd like."

"Really? That would be amazing," August agreed. "Let's see… how would I describe my taste in literature? I think the perfect book for me would be at least three hundred pages long, with a bit of a science fiction feel, but that doesn't take itself as seriously as most books in that genre do. I like a plot that's mostly easy to follow, but not overly simplistic; the kind of plot that, if I decide to read the book a second or third time, I notice details that I hadn't during the first read. And then, so far as the characters go, I like to have an assortment of appearances and personalities; and it never hurts for most of them to be somehow queer too," he winked.

Yidarica smiled at him in response. "Taste," she replied, nodding. "It's so weird; that sounds a lot like what I usually read, but I can't think of a specific book to recommend. Let me consult the spreadsheet of books that my best friend set up for me. I'm really bad at maintaining it, but it should still have a decent amount of books I've read–"

At this point, Yidarica had been picking up her phone, but hadn't had a good hold on it, so when it vibrated she dropped it in surprise. A large part of her was hoping this was finally someone from HPH calling her, but when she finally got a chance to see the screen, she became even more shocked.

"This is… this is my sister," she explained to August. "Do you mind if I–"

"Yeah, of course," he immediately agreed, nodding.

"Thank you so much." Yidarica smiled, making sure to give his hand a squeeze before answering the call. "Nini! Hi! What's been going on? Um, is everything okay?"

There was a laugh on the other end of the call. "That is *such* a Riri way to answer the phone."

It's true, but she doesn't have to say it. "Did you call me just to roast me?"

"That would've been the funniest reason to call you, but no," Runiala responded, with another small laugh. "I realized it's been a long time since we talked, so I wanted to make sure everything was okay with you. It gets a little hard to be sure when you go silent like that."

But I wasn't silent. I spoke to you. You were the one who left me on read! "I'm alive," Yidarica said out loud. "But I did speak to you. You didn't answer."

"What? You did?" There were a few sounds of movement on the other end, most likely the sounds of Runiala picking up her phone so she could check the text messages between her and her sister. While this was happening, August pointed to the bookshelves across the room and mouthed something Yidarica didn't catch, probably asking if he could peruse the selection since it was relevant to the conversation they'd been having. When she nodded, he got up and walked over there, so she'd presumably guessed correctly.

"Ohhh. You did. You definitely did. What is wrong with me?" Runiala said. "I am so sorry, Riri. I wasn't trying to ignore you! I just, I genuinely thought I replied to this. Wow."

"Happens to the best of us, right?" Yidarica downplayed how upset the silence had made her. "Don't worry about it. You've probably been so busy with school that you didn't notice. I've been to university before, so I know how hectic it gets."

"Right. Yeah. About that…"

Amidst this, Yidarica watched admiringly as August was reading one of the books from her shelves. At a point, his eyebrows raised, and he hesitated before closing the book and putting it back, searching for a new one. "Is everything okay at school?" she asked then.

Another moment passed before she finally responded, "I'm not in school right now."

"Oh!" This was a shock. Yidarica didn't know how she felt about this. On one hand, as someone who flunked out of school herself, she understood that the environments of university weren't for everyone. But she also remembered what the familial reaction had been when that had happened, and the mental state that had left her in.

She decided to ask: "Are you okay?"

The call went silent for a few minutes before Runiala responded. "I don't know."

This answer was enough to set off the big sister sirens in Yidarica's mind. "Well, you– do you want to talk about it? In person maybe?" It pained her to think of leaving August, but when it came to the only member of Yidarica's family that actually liked her, her priorities always were with her. "If you'd rather hash this out over the phone, that's fine too, but I know that sometimes these things are easier in person."

There was a bit more hesitation before Runiala spoke again. "Could you meet me at the pier in a couple of hours, then? Maybe this *is* something that we need to speak about in person."

"The pier. Sure. Of course." Yidarica nodded. "See you in a bit."

When she hung up, August had just grabbed another book off of the shelf. "Hey, uh, August. I am deeply sorry, but my sister has had some life things happen and wants to speak to me about it in person. I really have been enjoying the time I've been spending with you; it's been amazing. But this is my baby sister."

"I understand." August nodded. "You were going to go to the pier, right? I can head there with you as moral support, if you'd like."

"Really? I don't want to impose," Yidarica said. "I feel bad enough having to bail on our time together."

August waved it off. "It's fine. This is more important. There's no point in both of us making our siblings hate us, right? Besides, I haven't been to the pier since I first moved here. It'll be nice to reacquaint myself with all of the shops there."

★★★

It had been years since Yidarica had been to the pier, too. This was mostly because there hadn't been any major reason for her to go, but there was also a small part of her that felt slightly uncomfortable around the area; the wooden boardwalks and crashing waves brought up memories of her tumble into the ocean. There was a certain level of comfort in seeing that the area had only minimally changed, in that there were some shops and small attractions she didn't recognize, but she was certain that the pier would mostly always be the same. All the shops. The marina. The Ferris wheel.

As her feet touched the ground, August not far behind her, he said, "Text me when you're done, all right? We can split the cost of a water taxi, and I can drop you off back home."

This made Yidarica turn to him. "You don't have to do that, August. Dearest Mother, you've already done so much for me; I don't want you to think you have to."

"I don't understand your reasoning with things like this. Do you think I'm supposed to do one good thing for you and then have a cooldown period?" August asked. "I wish I could help you understand that it's perfectly normal for people who like you to want to do nice things for you. Look, regardless of how I go home, I have to pass your building to get back to my place, anyway. Why wouldn't I take you?"

A good point, Yidarica had to admit. "Yeah. I don't mean to give you a hard time. I never do mean to. It's just… it's hard, you know? I'm so used to good deeds being transactional that I feel a lot of guilt over not having done any nice things for you."

"I understand that sentiment. But if we're ever gonna get you to a point where your feelings surrounding the acceptance of help are more healthy, we've got to start somewhere." August smiled as he added, "We can start as early as today, even. I need you to not think of repaying me for taking you home later today. All right? Thanking me is fine, encouraged even; but I will not be accepting any gifts or acts of service as a result of offering you transportation."

"But that's…" Yidarica sputtered a bit, unsure of how to make her point. "What am I supposed to do, then?"

August shrugged. "Enjoy having someone in your life that wants to do things for you, maybe?"

Yidarica lowered her chin in thought. *Is this common? There's nothing in my studies of human interaction that mention this, but I guess that's probably because I've never been in this position before, have I? There's a subtle difference between when my friends do something for me and when August does something for me, that I can't quite put words to. Does that make me a selfish person? Or have I been convinced that I'm inherently a burden, so no one should ever go out of their way for me?*

"I think I can try to do that," she finally said.

"Good." August smiled. "Where are you headed? I'm going to go over to the mall area to see what's happening. I'm kinda hoping there's some good food over there too, since we both know today's breakfast left a lot to be desired."

"Oh! Actually, could you text me the restaurants that are over there?" Yidarica asked. "I'd love to have that information since I'll probably need to pick something up to take home with me for dinner. The whole… expending energy to come here makes dinner dubious."

August began to reply, but Yidarica noticed a figure in the background dressed in a black and white checkered dress that felt familiar for some reason, and her attention went there. As the figure drew closer, she was able to realize why she felt this way. The different hair color had thrown her, but this was none other than her younger sister.

"Riri! There you are," she said when she came into earshot, causing August to get startled a bit, and turn to her. "Something about you looks different, but I can't put my finger on what. Have you let your hair grow out more since the last time I saw you?"

"Probably. And yours is a whole new color!" As the two hugged, Yidarica admired the new red tones of her sister's shoulder-length hair. It was easy to tell the two were sisters because of their similar height, skin tone, and facial distribution, but Runiala had always been the thinner of the two. The difference felt even more pronounced now, though. *I've been gaining weight recently.*

At this point, August was still standing where he had been, but very uncertainly. He felt that he should go, but he didn't want to leave without letting Yidarica know he was leaving, because he didn't want her confused as to where he went. As he tried to think of what he should do, he stood, rather awkwardly.

"Who is this gentleman, by the way?" Runiala asked then, turning to August.

Finally, an opening. "Oh, this is August," Yidarica replied. "He came this way with me, and will be going back the same way, so we were trying to configure the logistics of that when you first caught my attention."

"Oh." Runiala nodded. "So a friend, then. Hi. I'm Runiala; Riri is my older sister. I hope you've been looking after her. She needs help with things sometimes, especially when she gets sleepy."

Yidarica sighed. "Nini." *Once again: it's true, but she doesn't have to say it.*

August merely smiled. "It's a pleasure to meet you. We had actually just finished contemplating the specifics of when we leave, so I can give you two some privacy. Text me when you're ready to go, all right, Yidarica?"

"Of course." She waved, watching August as he walked toward the doors to the shopping area. When she could no longer see him within the crowd, she turned to Runiala. "Okay. Where do you want to go, to make this easy on you?"

"Somewhere nearby would be great," she replied. "Maybe right near the edge of the pier?"

Why is it that whenever I give people the option to choose things, they always choose the worst one? "Somewhere else, maybe?" Yidarica suggested.

"Sure. There's also this seating area not far from where the Comtran station is. Not many people go there, so it'll be quieter."

The two walked there, and sat down at one of the tables that had been placed in the area. Not certain on how the subject should be breached, Yidarica started with, "So, what's going on?"

Runiala's response was to let out a long, drawn-out sigh.

"School got to be too much," was what she finally decided to say. "Especially with me having to also work. I tried so hard to make it all work somehow, but there were so many moving parts involved, it got to a point where I just… couldn't do it anymore. I was exhausted, and miserable. So I came back home. And even though I was little back then, I still remembered what it was like when you came back home after dropping out, so I was expecting something like that when I got back too. Imagine my shock when it didn't happen."

Yidarica frowned. "What do you mean?"

"I mean, I was expecting to be told I'm worthless and a disappointment, but so far, Mom hasn't done that," Runiala explained. "She's been eerily quiet. Part of me is glad, but there's also a part of me that's kinda scared of what will happen once she decides to break her silence, which we both know she will."

I had to get my inability to shut up from somewhere, after all.

"Is the house tense at all?" Yidarica asked.

"Yeah, absolutely," Runiala nodded. "Because I still have friends here, I was really lucky to find a new job quickly. It's only part-time, and the pay isn't great, but it does also get me out of the house for hours at a time, so I can't complain too much. I just… I really wish things were different."

That was a feeling that Yidarica was all too familiar with. "And Dad?"

Runiala shrugged. "You know Dad. Stoic as ever."

When I was younger, I used to think our father being so silent and withdrawn was the Mother's blessing, in contrast to whatever our mom has going on. But the more I think about it, it kind of sucks. He didn't stick up for me any of the times his wife called me everything but a child of the heavens, and he's not supporting Nini now.

Does he care about us at all? I've never experienced anything that indicates he does.

There was a silence before Runiala asked, "Riri, do you think that if you talked to Mom–"

"No," Yidarica immediately rejected whatever her sister was about to say. "No, I don't."

"You didn't even listen to what I have to say."

"I know that," Yidarica said, as firmly as she could. "There is nothing in the world that will make me speak to that woman ever again. I've told you this before. It's very frustrating when you don't listen to me, Nini. I don't expect you to agree with me about everything, but this is a subject I've very clearly stated I have a stance about, and I'd really like it if you could respect that."

"Well yeah, of course I do," Runiala mumbled. "But how can you be so sure? It's been so many years since you guys stopped talking, you don't know if Mom's changed."

"I don't care!" Yidarica immediately regretted how loud she'd said this, so she took a breath and tried again. "I do not care. Unless she does some sincere soul-searching so that she can understand and take accountability for all the hurt she's caused me, I want nothing to do with her. Why are you defending her when she's got you in such a dire state now?"

"Because!" Runiala pointedly sighed. "As much as I hate the way things are, I try to understand where she's coming from. This is the woman who raised us, so I can't sit here and believe she has absolutely no regrets about how things happened between you two. How can she make amends if you won't talk to her? She is our mother, you know? The only one we'll ever get."

Yidarica stood up then, as calmly as possible– she tried to not make too much noise, but the chair she'd been sitting on did screech when it moved. "I'm not doing this."

"Riri, why are you always so stubborn?!" Runiala asked, also standing. "You're the only person I know who's ever been in the position I'm in now. What am I supposed to do without your help?"

"Figure it out," she replied. "Maybe ask your mother, since you're so convinced she's able to give a damn about anyone who's not herself, and then tell me how that worked out for you. Even if you discount everything I've gone through because of her, don't you ever think about the fact that we have two older siblings that want nothing to do with her either? We never even got to know them because she's the way she is. I need you to be a little more reasonable about these things. What are the odds that the three people who refuse to associate with that woman are wrong, rather than her herself?"

Runiala was silent before she said, "I know, you've got a point. But when you two got into that screaming match the last time you talked, you weren't exactly a perfect angel, either."

Hearing this, it felt as though Yidarica had been stabbed through the heart with a hot knife. This was her sister, who she loved and trusted and confided in so earnestly over the years. As she'd said earlier to August, Runiala was the only person left in the Verbestel family that even spoke to her, let alone was kind to her. And now she was here, telling her that their mother calling her a worthless piece of shit– which was hysterically ironic given that woman only continued to live because she leeched off of others– was somehow *her* fault?

Yidarica turned to her sister; looking her straight in the eyes, trembling with a mixture of anger and sadness. "Stop pursuing me. I refuse to continue this conversation. If you ever fix your mouth to say *anything* like that to me again, that will be the last time that you, your mother, or anyone in this damn family *ever* hear of me, do you understand me?"

She walked away then, upset, tense. This wasn't how she'd pictured the conversation between herself and her sister going, but she was less surprised at it than she wanted to be. Youngest child privilege had done its damage to Runiala, in many ways, one of them being always wanting to believe in the goodness of their parents because they had been so kind to her in the past. As long as that tie persisted, the relationship between the sisters would be rocky.

Once she was back on the pier proper, Yidarica stood next to one of the stands and texted August.

> The meeting didn't go as well as I'd hoped, but it's over now. Can we head back now?

If she concentrated on how delicious the stand next to her smelled, she didn't have to think about everything that had just happened.

***

Despite having lived in Sonusia for twenty-eight of her years, Yidarica had never ridden on any of the water taxis that helped transport people around the city via the rivers that flowed through the city, and the ocean beside it. She would see them sometimes, but she had never had a reason to utilize them since her living and working arrangements had always been inland. So, today was the first time she'd be riding one, and as the vehicle progressed down the coastline, she wished she could enjoy the gentle mist more than she currently did.

Today was also August's first time on a water taxi, and aside from occasionally needing to wipe the accumulated droplets of water from his glasses, he was enjoying the experience. He placed a hand on Yidarica's back when he realized she hadn't said a word for the duration of the ride so far, and mere seconds passed before she began to cry.

"Whoa, hold on," August kneeled down so he could see Yidarica's face. When he confirmed that she was indeed crying, he immediately extended a hand to wipe the tears from her cheeks. The faintest smile appeared on her face because she liked the contact, but her somber mood didn't fade.

"Do you want to talk about it?" August asked softly.

This was a question Yidarica had to ask herself first. She didn't want to rehash everything, because that would require her to go into the history between her and her mother, which she definitely did not have the energy to do right now. But she also didn't want August to worry about her.

"My sister and I... our relationship is complicated. My relationship with my entire family is complicated, but with her specifically, it's always been strenuous to maintain a relationship with her. The simplest way I can describe why is that our mother dotes on her, but has always hated me for reasons outside of my control. I haven't spoken to that woman in almost a decade, but my sister seems to hold on to some type of hope that we'll get along someday or something, even when I've stated multiple times that's not what I want. So I... we got into a dispute of our own, which ended with me telling her to not speak to me again if she can't respect my boundaries."

"I see." August stood now, the kneeling position having become uncomfortable. "I can understand why that's upsetting you. It never feels good to feel as though you're not being heard, and I can only imagine how much harder it's hurting you because of the circumstances. If there's anything I can do to make the situation hurt less, all you need to do is ask, okay?"

Yidarica looked up at August, who was again cleaning his glasses. "Thank you, August. I appreciate that more than you know. And, as much grief as I gave you about it earlier, I'm really glad we're making this commute back together. Having you here with me is... I don't think I'd be holding it together as well as I am, if you weren't here with me. The combination of the movements of this boat, and your comforting presence, makes it easier to believe things will be all right even if they're not right now."

She rested her head on August's arm, holding on with both of her hands, which elicited a smile from him as he looked down.

"My dad used to say something to the effect of, we experience lows in our lives so that the highs feel ever higher," August said then. "It's one of those ideas that feels silly at the time, but in time, it's brought me comfort. I hope that, by sharing it with you, it brings you some too."

What would that mean, in this case?

Yidarica reflected on everything that had transpired in the past few months, since the last time before today that she had spoken to her sister.

My relationship with Nini has always been tense, but part of the reason I clung to it so intensely was because I didn't have anyone else, really. I've had Gracia for a while, but my mindset has always been that Gracia isn't bound by a familial tie, so she could decide my friendship isn't worth the cost of having to deal with me as a person, and leave at any time. I always assumed my sister wouldn't do that because she's family. But in the time since she last spoke to me, I became friends with Muiren, and only now am I realizing I don't feel that fear of desertion when I'm with them. Is it because we work together? Or is our friendship more secure? Heck, even with my fear that no one in HPH will ever talk to me again, being friends with them has been way less stressful than meeting Nini where she is.

Maybe I should have re-evaluated our relationship before now. Maybe I should've been more firm on my boundaries, and sooner. Maybe my sister and I aren't meant to be close. And maybe... maybe that's okay.

"I think I understand what your father meant, August," she finally spoke. "Thank you for sharing his wisdom with me. It's helping me put some things into perspective."

"I'm glad it's helping. It does that for me too," August replied. "Even more so now. With everything I've been through in regards to relationships, it makes me appreciate you so much more," he smiled at her again.

The two stepped off of the water taxi then, which had left them at a small marina, not far from the trademark rails of a Comtran route. Yidarica wasn't quite sure where exactly they were, as she looked around to try to see any landmarks that would signify their location. "Oh, the clock tower!" she said, pointing to the beige-bricked edifice. "I know exactly where we are now. My building is this way."

"Then that's the way we're going," August replied, as he took her hand, and they set off.

Chapter Twenty

When Yidarica awoke the next day, she did so with the idea that today would be the day she finally mustered the strength to speak to her bandmates. She wasn't sure of what she should say, but she knew she should apologize at the very least. This all changed when she checked her phone and noticed that she had a voicemail from Gracia.

This was uncommon. Gracia knew to never leave Yidarica voice messages because of the difficulty she had understanding the words, but occasionally she'd have so much to say that a voicemail made more sense than contemplating over a paragraph to send. This, apparently, had been one of those times; and so, Yidarica listened before she even got out of bed so that she could devote all of her energy to processing the words.

"Hi, Yida! Um, I… I'm sorry for all of the silence, first of all. I figured I should leave you this message because I only just now found out that Ceri and Wally haven't spoken to you either, and I didn't want you to think we're all ignoring you, or making some kind of conscious effort to shut you out or anything. I'd never do that. But I do have a lot of really big emotions that just don't feel right to express over text or on the phone. I'll be over in Piersica Park tomorrow afternoon to enjoy the weather, and it'd be great if you came over so we could talk. Let me know if you can, or you could also just show up since it's so close to you. I don't know. I've rambled long enough. But even if you don't come around, I want you to know that there's no malice between us, all right? I could never hate you, Yida. I hope I'll see you soon."

The park wasn't far, so there was nothing stopping Yidarica from going there. It was so accessible that all she did before leaving out was get dressed– today in a dark green dress with a pink and orange flower print and short puffy sleeves– and pull her hair into a half-updo that made her look more put together than she was. There was no time for a balanced breakfast, which would be bordering on brunch at this point; right now all she needed was to be able to talk to her best friend.

Stepping outside, it was easy to see why Gracia had mentioned getting out and enjoying the weather today. The still air was of a pleasant warmth, with the occasional cooling breeze. The sun shone brightly, but the sky was speckled with the fluffiest white cirrus clouds, one of which drew closer to the sun as Yidarica made her way to the park.

Shockingly, the park wasn't as busy as one would expect it to be on a day like today. There were a few children on the swing set and a few more running around the garden area, but it was entirely possible to find quieter pockets, which was something Yidarica hadn't expected. After walking around, surveying the area for a suitable place to sit that wasn't too far away from the main paths, she took a seat on one of the benches near the pond, which was empty today. The ducks appeared to have had prior commitments in other locations.

With a small sigh, she pulled out the book she'd brought along just in case she got here before Gracia.

If I wasn't such a coward, I would've asked her what time she was coming around, and if she wanted to configure a particular meeting spot. But even with the reassurance that she doesn't hate me, the idea of asking anything of her doesn't feel right.

"Yida?" She turned abruptly to see not Gracia, but Cérilda, with a wicker basket in her hands. She was dressed appropriately for the weather today; the breezy orange sundress gave Yidarica a moment of height envy. She could never wear sundresses unless they were tailored because of how short she was– they would drag on the ground and be a tripping hazard– but Cérilda was tall enough to not have that problem.

"Hi, Cérilda." Yidarica waved, taking a moment to appreciate the frilly scrunchie holding her hair in a neat ponytail. "Cute outfit."

Cérilda looked down at herself, as if she needed to remember what she was wearing. "Thank you. What are you doing here? Oh, wait, don't answer that; you live close by."

She nodded. "Sure do. What brings you to these parts?"

Cérilda held up her basket, which looked like it had seen better days. "I was hoping I'd be lucky enough to be able to harvest some choice peaches today. My brother is visiting soon, for the first time since I graduated, and I was hoping to bake peach pie for the occasion."

"Maybe you will. It's a little early for the best peaches, but it's not unheard of to be able to get appetizing ones ahead of schedule," Yidarica replied. "You did well to get here before all the kids start knocking them down just 'cause they can."

"That is always a good thing to hear." Cérilda sat on the bench, placing her basket in her lap. "How are you, then? Are you doing okay?"

Yidarica sighed. "Do I look so pitiful that you'd ask?"

"I spoke to Gracia last night and mentioned that I hadn't heard from you, because I figured that she must have, since you're both so close," Cérilda explained. "But then she said that she hadn't. Which meant that of course I had to text Walchelin to make sure he'd heard from you. And when he said he had not... honestly, I was planning on stopping by your place after I got my peaches to be sure you were okay– and offer you some, of course. I don't know what took me so long to feel that I needed to check on you, and for that, I apologize. That was not very friendly of me."

Why is she apologizing to me when I'm the whole reason the band missed out on our big chance? I'm the one who ruined everything.

Just when Yidarica thought she'd found the words to ask, she was interrupted by Gracia's arrival, as she sat between the two. It was a bit of a tight squeeze because of the basket on Cérilda's lap, but fortunately Gracia was thin enough to make it work.

"Having a friendly get-together without me?" she teased.

"Yeah. It's quieter that way," Cérilda teased right back.

"Oh, you." Gracia nudged her, but then, the area grew quiet.

What should I say to them? These are my two best friends. How can any apology I give them ever be enough for jeopardizing what could've been a life-changing opportunity for them? And at the last minute, too? And it not being the first time I've had to last-minute cancel something? There's so much talk about giving others grace, but all things considered... how much grace do they have left to give?

"Do you remember when we weren't able to play Roundhouse?" Cérilda was the first to speak.

That was the place I fucked up the booking on because of my horrible time management.

"I know that you blame yourself for that, Yida. But for some reason, I never connected the dots on something else that happened around that time until recently." Cérilda shifted into a thinking position. "I realized that Walchelin sprained his ankle two days before that, the day we would've performed, at work. We wouldn't have been able to play that show regardless, the only difference was that we were spared the abrupt cancellation. And because of that, we're still within the good graces of management there."

He sprained his ankle because someone else at his job had quit a few days before, and he was forced to do the work of two people. I guess that's not my fault. I couldn't have made the person not quit. I didn't even know them.

"Yeah, and then there was the time we had to block off a whole month of shows during peak season because I lost my voice screaming at Ceri's graduation," Gracia said then. "But I don't regret it. We had to let our girl know we're proud of her!"

"I appreciated it so much, Gracia," Cérilda added. "You were louder than my family was!"

She really had been. There's a reason she's our singer. Those vocal chords are unmatched.

"Actually, it took everything within me to not cry when I heard you," Cérilda continued. "My family's always been so reserved when it comes to showing emotion that, even on the rare occasion that my parents told me they were proud of me, it was always so cut and dry that it felt difficult to believe. Hearing someone be so exuberant and forthcoming of their pride for me was… it was amazing in ways I still cannot articulate to this day."

Gracia smiled at her. "Well, yeah. I'd do that for any of you. You're like family."

She turned to Yidarica then. "Family doesn't just give up on each other, especially when the things that are happening are out of their control. We talked a lot about this idea the other day, which was when we realized none of us had successfully spoken to you since the day you pulled out of our gig, and that was kinda shitty of us; to give you all that time to let your thoughts go to the darkest places."

"As expected, we were all initially mildly-to-moderately upset about missing out on our prospective festival performance," Cérilda picked up. "But from there, it's become obvious to us that we weren't ready for a performance of that scale, anyway."

"When we say that, it's not about our music– that's always class– but more so us, as a band," Gracia added. "We did a lot of talking. Some arguing. A lot of arguing, actually. And we've decided it's for the best if Landen and us parted ways."

Yidarica had stopped breathing for a moment, but when she realized it wasn't her the band was parting ways with, she nearly choked, coughing from the lack of airflow.

"You seem surprised," noted Cérilda.

"Well, yeah! That's who you decided to get rid of?!" she asked, confused.

Gracia held up a hand. "Now, hold on. We didn't want to get rid of *anyone*, but believe me when I say that the way our discussions were going, he forced our hand. You're the backbone of this band, Yida, and I don't just mean that in terms of you being our bassist. None of this makes sense without you being part of the band, no matter how many practices you have to miss because of your health. I know that, Ceri knows that, and anyone who can't see that is full of it!"

A bird flew off at the volume of Gracia's voice.

"Also, Wally said he'd bring you some of your favorite bread to next practice as an apology for the silence," she finished. "We won't be seeing or hearing from him for the next few days, though. His mom's visiting."

"Oh…" Yidarica and Cérilda said in unison. Both had heard enough stories of Walchelin's mother to know that he'd be tied up until she left. No one could complain, though, given everything she had gone through to raise him, and ensure that he would make it to adulthood. He still had the least antagonistic mother of the four, except maybe Cérilda's.

I can't believe this is how things are turning out. Why are they forgiving me, when I haven't had a chance to prove to them that I'm worthy of their forgiveness? I'll never understand this.

"You've been so quiet, Yida," Gracia said then. "What's going on in your mind?"

She froze at being put on the spot, struggling to form her thoughts into coherent words, but she couldn't leave her friends in suspense, could she? After a moment more to conceptualize what she was going to say, Yidarica spoke.

"I'm shocked that you guys aren't incensed with me and cutting ties. This is the latest in a string of ways I've proven myself to be unreliable, but this one was catastrophic, monumental. I really, *really* don't think that I deserve your grace. I'm not a person worth being this kind to. It makes sense that I'm not, right? That's why the Dark is gonna come for me any day now. I'm not a person that anyone can love."

Gracia and Cérilda's faces were blank, unreadable, as the silence permeated the bench. The air stood still for an uncomfortable amount of time. It was as if the air itself was so thick and humid that no one was able to breathe.

Finally, Yidarica felt Gracia's hand holding hers tight.

"Do you really think that none of us love you? That I don't… love you?"

And it was that rawness; the tininess of Gracia's voice, bursting at the seams with sincerity and emotion and possible hurt, that made Yidarica wonder why she'd ever believed otherwise.

"I just, I always thought…" she struggled to put her words together. "So you guys don't keep me around out of some sense of obligation?"

"Why would we do that?" Cérilda asked, in a tone that indicated sincere confusion.

"Why *wouldn't* you?" Yidarica countered. "It's not like I bring any value into any of your lives. All I do is take up space, without any benefit, or doing anything to show that I've earned that."

"So…" Gracia, meanwhile, was still processing everything she'd heard. "All this time, when you would say you're afraid of the Dark coming for you… you didn't mean it in the 'I'm over thirty and unmarried' panic way? You've spent all this time genuinely believing *none of us* loved you?"

"Yida." Cérilda asked gently, "Do you believe that, or is that what you were told?"

This was, somehow, a question that Yidarica had never asked herself. Although she was aware that her opinions of herself drew heavily from her observations of others and their interactions with her, she didn't think to consider how significantly observational data could be affected by the environment in which they were studied. And considering that the bulk of her life had been spent figuratively locked away in a home with people that didn't seem to like her very much…

I've always thought that, if my own family didn't like me, it would be that much harder for anyone else to. But is this… was I wrong to think that way?

Do I still have my sight not because of some fault or oversight of the Dark, but because... because all this time, I've been loved after all?

Before Yidarica could speak, she was interrupted by the sensation of a hand touching her shoulder. She turned quickly to see a figure sitting on the little bit of bench left beside her; to her surprise, it was August.

"I went to go see my optometrist about an appointment to hopefully update the prescription for my glasses, so I was in the neighborhood," he explained. He added nonchalantly, "Hi. Beautiful day, isn't it?"

Yidarica could only laugh. "Yeah, it is. Hi. Um, these are my best friends, Gracia and Cérilda. They're also in the band I play in, the one I told you about the other day. Guys, this is August. We, uh..."

What are we, exactly? Should I have already asked that? I should've asked that by now. I can't just call him my boyfriend without us confirming that that's his intention. That'd be weird.

"We work together," she decided to say, it not being lost on her that August's brow furrowed ever so slightly.

"Oh! So you also work in that really big impressive building!" Gracia realized. "Yida tells us about it sometimes, and I got an opportunity to see it for myself not very long ago. It was amazing, especially the garden. I work in an office downtown too, but it's nowhere near what you guys have going on!"

"I'm sure whatever you do is just as important," August said in that gentle affirming way of his. "But so that we can all make that judgment for ourselves... what *do* you do?"

"What do I do?" Gracia repeated. "I work at a design firm. So, unlike you guys, who work with optimization of your own product, I work with a bunch of different products from a lot of different companies; it is our goal to make their projects, applications, et cetera look the prettiest they can."

August held out a hand toward her, "See? That's super important!"

The girls all laughed then. "Is everyone you work with so kind?" Cérilda asked.

"As I'm told, not everybody," Yidarica replied. "And, unfortunately, as I got to experience a little while ago. But I've been fortunate enough to not have to regularly deal with those who aren't. Even so, I can't say everyone is quite as nice as August is." She turned to him and smiled, "He's a bit of a cream puff."

"Wow. I can't tell if that's a joke about how pale I am, or me being queer," he replied, which made everyone on the bench laugh again, much louder than before.

It was neither, but I'm glad I didn't overstep with that joke.

"Well, this is lovely, but I should be getting the peaches I came for if I want to finish that pie today," Cérilda said, standing and picking up her basket. "Would any of you care to join me?"

Gracia stood and stretched, before turning to August. "We could probably use this one."

"Yeah, sure," he agreed. "It is my duty as a tall person to be constantly helping those of lesser altitude reach things. I'll be along in a few, if that's okay?"

"Sure. We'll be at the north end of the peach trees," Gracia nodded. "See you in a bit, Yida."

Yidarica waved, trying to remember which area of this park was the north end. As she tried to recall its layout from memory, August lightly cleared his throat beside her. "So, your friends call you Yida."

This startled her. "Uh, yeah," she nodded. "Actually, it was more that Gracia started to, and after a while, everyone else gradually started doing it too. She gives everyone nicknames once she gets close to them, like Cérilda is Ceri, and our other bandmate, Walchelin, is Wally."

Now that I think of it, Gracia never gave Landen a nickname. I guess there is a point to be made about the closeness and dynamic of the ensemble. Gracia and Walchelin immediately liked Cérilda, and I've always been fond of Walchelin, but I can't say that anyone was particularly close to Landen. I don't think I ever even had a one-on-one conversation with him.

"That's honestly really endearing, in its own way," August replied. "I have friends, but I've never had any that had those fun little quirks like giving out nicknames. Unfortunately, I've mostly been exposed to boring people."

"Boring people have their positives too, though! They're usually really grounding, for example." Yidarica could only think of the people in college that fit that description then, recalling that hanging around them was usually when she would get her best work done. There was always something about the no-frills existence of boring people that made her feel like she needed to be more productive.

"Yeah, absolutely," August agreed. "They're good people. Good friends. Just… boring, you know?"

Yidarica nodded, and grunted in effort as she stood, offering a hand to help August up. "I don't know where the north end of the peach trees is, but are you up for finding out?"

August hesitated before replying, "I think that the singular navigation spell I know could help find that, actually."

He held his hands out, conjuring a three-dimensional model of the park. Before long, a pink dot appeared. "That's where we are," he explained. "Now we just need to find out where the trees are."

The problem was that the model of the park was vague enough that it was difficult to tell which trees were part of the peach grove, and which ones were cedars or oaks. August realized this as well, and sighed. "This is what I meant when I said I'm not very good at spells that aren't plant or tech related."

Yidarica smiled. "It's okay. If we get back onto one of the trails, I'm pretty sure there are signs that will direct us to the peach grove. That'll get us the majority of the way, and then we can worry about which way is north."

"An excellent plan," August agreed. "Glad we thought of it. Why don't you lead the way, since you're more familiar with the terrain?"

"Sure." Yidarica took a precautionary look around to see where the paths were. Once she remembered where they were, and began to walk, she felt August's hand gently touch her back for a few seconds, as if to guide her, and for that moment, her body felt just a bit lighter.

I wonder if that's magic, or if I'm really that deep into my feelings for him. Maybe a little of both?

Thankfully, the walk to the peach grove wasn't far, and it was easy to find where Gracia and Cérilda had gone off to. At the time that Yidarica and August had arrived, it looked like Gracia was about to attempt to climb the tree they were near, so it was a pretty well-timed arrival; Cérilda looked as though the color returned to her face once she saw the two approaching.

"It certainly does look like you could use my help," August said then, holding his hand out, wordlessly asking for the basket. "Which of these lovely peaches are catching your eye? I'll grab them for you."

As Cérilda pointed out which peaches were optimal for pie-making, Gracia stood with Yidarica, waiting for them to finish their harvest. "So. Coworker, huh?" Gracia asked.

"Yeah." Yidarica nodded. "He's one of the very lucky people that works with our Weather Department."

"I see." Gracia gave her a nudge. "He's cute."

Yidarica gave her a look. "You, calling a man cute?"

"Leave me alone." Gracia laughed. "I mostly meant that his mannerisms are what's cute, the way he's so nice with that little touch of awkwardness; but I guess he's easy on the eyes too, for people who are into that kind of thing. Well put-together, seemingly hygienic. This would be the perfect time for me to wingman for you, if he wasn't. You know," she flicked her hand, letting her wrist go limp.

For a moment, Yidarica was confused as to why Gracia thought that, but she then remembered the conversation they'd all had at the pond. "Oh, that's– he didn't mean queer as in gay. August is bisexual."

"Oh!" Gracia gasped. "Genuinely shocked. It's just that, you know, he has a certain… candor? Demeanor? There's a certain air about him that made me think that he's all about the men, but hey, I'm glad to be wrong! And hey– you probably are too, huh?"

"Gracia." Yidarica gave her the most exasperated look she could.

"I can tell there's more than just friendly coworker stuff going on between you two, Yida. It's all in the body language; I can tell that, at the very least, you're attracted to him, so spill. What's the story?"

★★★

A few days later, on a day in which August worked from home, he invited Yidarica over for dinner; most likely ordering in, since he'd made it very obvious that the goal was to spend time with her. He'd been proactive in asking her to bring along a change of clothes as well, because of the chance she might get too tired to go home again, especially after a hard day at work.

This also meant that August was frantically freshening up his apartment, making sure the floors and furniture were clean, and that his plants looked the best they could. He was busy gently singing to one of them while casting a restoration spell, when the intercom buzzed.

"Are you expecting a visitor?" The doorman's voice came through.

"I am. Please let her in," he replied, looking over the apartment, and himself, to see if any last-minute changes were necessary before his visitor made it to his residence.

When Yidarica arrived with a courteous knock on the door, she was holding her work bag as well as a brown paper bag with no branding on it, which was unusual. There was also a third bag over her shoulder, presumably where her extra clothing was.

"I got you a gift," she said, holding up the bag.

"A gift? For me?" August stepped aside to let her in, but the idea of receiving a gift on a normal day like this was already consuming his thoughts. "I appreciate it. What is it?"

"See for yourself." Yidarica handed him the brown paper bag.

He carefully opened the bag, pulling out what was possibly the softest blanket he'd touched that wasn't a comforter. One of its sides was pure white fluffy material– some kind of fleece, he noted– and the other was a pink and black plaid pattern. "I noticed you don't have a throw blanket for your couch," Yidarica explained. "I also brought that in case I end up sleeping on the couch, so."

"Would you... prefer that you did?" August asked.

Yidarica looked up at him. Truly? No, she didn't. The last time she'd been here and shared a bed with August, she had quite liked the ability to be near to him; to cuddle up close to him and rest her head on his chest, and then wake up beside him. But she was also aware that sharing a bed meant less space, and didn't want to intrude on his sleep routine like that.

"Does it matter what I prefer? It's your house," she replied, hoping her tone didn't come out too dismissive– but judging by August's falling expression, it definitely had.

"I don't want you to feel that way," he said softly.

Now, she was confused. "Feel what way?"

"Like your opinions don't matter," August replied. "I invited you here because I wanted to spend time with you. Why would I expect you to disregard your comfort for a few hours at a time just to see me? It wouldn't make sense to do that."

When Yidarica didn't speak, August used his free hand to grasp her own. "Let's have a seat. I'm sure you're tired of standing."

The two sat on the couch then, at first sitting on it as one regularly would, a touch of awkwardness in the air. *Should I let him know it's okay to touch me? Should I let him know that I'm hoping he does, even? I would love it if he held me.*

"Um..." August said after a while. "So, what are we thinking for dinner? I was hoping we'd either go somewhere or order in, especially after, you know, breakfast that time."

Yidarica smiled. "It wasn't that bad, August. You've gotta stop beating yourself up over not being the perfect chef."

I draw the line at those lumpy pancakes, though. I don't have it in me to try and stomach those again.

"Okay, I'll try not to do that so often," he replied. "But I don't think I have enough of anything here to make a coherent meal, so prowess notwithstanding, we should probably order something anyway. What do you have a taste for?"

"Hm." Yidarica thought. "What's nearby? I'd love to make an informed decision based on the places that you tried and liked."

At this, August hopped off the couch and hurried to his bedroom. "I have the perfect thing to help us with that! I started writing a–" He stopped talking here, probably realizing how far away he was and how difficult it would be to hear him. He picked back up when he emerged from his room: "I started writing a log of all of the restaurants in the neighborhood I tried, what I ordered, and my thoughts on the flavors, textures, serving sizes, and presentation."

This amused Yidarica. "You really are better suited to a project team than whatever you used to do before at work."

"Really?" August smiled bashfully. "I *have* been told by multiple people that it astonishes them how meticulous I am. But to me, it just makes sense to organize my thoughts about things in a centralized location so I can reference and share them if I need to."

Relatable content… or at least, some of it is. My studies of human behavior make me feel this way; but I don't think I'll ever be so organized that I think to write them down. And I'll definitely never be so organized that I would remember where I wrote them.

I think August will get along really well with Gracia. This seems like something she'd do.

August sat beside Yidarica then, and opened the notebook he'd brought with him, noting that the cover was made of a few different fabrics, all of which felt satisfying to the touch. "So, where the notes start is not where I started logging these, because I bought this notebook after I had already gone to a few restaurants. This is a really nice notebook, isn't it, by the way? I found it at this really cute stationery store when I first moved here, and I bought it because it has tulle crash, which is one of my favorite overlay fabrics. Oh, but that's not– sorry, I got sidetracked. You can interrupt me if I do that. So, let's take a look at what I've got in here."

As August continued to talk, Yidarica rested her head on his arm, trying to read what he'd written in the notebook, with varying levels of success. He had the type of handwriting that toed the line between neat and illegible, so some sections were as clear as day, and the others looked like aesthetically placed lines with no real meaning.

When August was almost at the end of his notes– and Yidarica was heavily considering the rice bowl place he'd given a glowing review– the doorman buzzed the room again. August stared, confused, before turning to Yidarica. "That's the doorman. He usually buzzes the place if there's someone at the door for me, but… you're already here. I have no idea why else he'd call the room."

"A package? Or an accident?" Yidarica suggested.

"I haven't ordered anything lately." August stood, heading to the intercom controls, but clearly still confused. "And he's never accidentally called the wrong room before, but I suppose it's not impossible. Hello?"

When no one answered, August turned back to Yidarica, even more confused. "I guess it really was a–"

There was then a knock on the door. This was even *more* confusing, but at this point, August was too invested (and intrigued) to not answer the door.

He had barely unlocked the locks and pulled the door open when an older woman, average height, with graying brown hair came barreling through, followed by the doorman.

"This woman claims to be your mother," he said. "She–"

"August Sostrin, who the *hell* do you think you are?!" She yelled, dramatically turning to him and pointing a finger. "For weeks. *Weeks!* You haven't returned any of my calls or messages! You're ignoring your sisters as well. Do you think you can move to the big city and forget about family?!"

August could only sigh as he turned to the doorman. "Yes, she is. I'm very sorry for the trouble. If there's anything I can do to make up for her behavior, please let me know."

The doorman nodded, and took his leave.

"Mom, why would you come here and cause trouble in the building I live in? Security is one of the most important aspects of this place. Are you *trying* to get me evicted?" This was the most annoyed that Yidarica had ever heard August sound.

"What was I supposed to do?" She asked. "It's not like you'd answer if I called you, clearly."

"I wasn't answering because you'd call me while it's the middle of the night here, or while I was at work," August explained, more calmly than expected. "You haven't been showing any respect for the life I've built here."

"Respect? It is *so* rich of you to be bringing up respect! Where is your respect for me and my feelings? My well-being?!"

August gestured to the length of her body, "You seem perfectly well and existent, or else you wouldn't have made it here."

This clearly stupefied his mother for a moment, as she sputtered, unable to speak. Finally she said, "I did *not* raise you to be such a sarcastic and disrespectful person! You wouldn't dare speak to me like this if your father was still here, now would you?"

At the mention of his father, August tensed, clenching his hands into tight, mangled versions of fists; not quite as compact, but every bit as filled with anger. "No, I wouldn't, because when he was still here, you were still treating me like a human being instead of some vehicle to fulfill your own wishes," he said firmly. "And I don't appreciate you bringing Mareille and Haviera into all of this, either; it has nothing to do with either of them."

"It has everything to do with them! How do you think they feel, seeing their baby brother shirk the responsibilities they'd probably kill to have–"

"Probably? So you admit you're projecting," August cut her off.

Again lost for words, this was when August's mother finally noticed Yidarica sitting on the couch. She froze, startled, but quickly recovered. "Why didn't you tell me you had company?"

"When did I ever get the chance to?" August pointed out.

"You need to leave. My son and I are–"

August placed his arm in front of his mother, stopping her from getting any closer to the couch. Firmly, he said: "*She's* staying. *You* need to at least try to be kind of decent toward my girlfriend."

Girlfriend? Me?!

Yidarica would never be able to explain the feeling that transpired within her when she heard August use that word to refer to her. It felt strangely close to when her heart would lurch forward, thundering as if to escape from her chest; but less pointy, more warm, bubbling to the surface with feathered edges. It was similar to the feeling she felt whenever there was perfect weather outside– sun, intermittent clouds, low humidity, and a cool breeze blowing–

but even that wasn't the same as this new emotion. This one was so much more powerful.

"I'm so sorry you were here to see all of this. This is my mother." August turned to her, "Mom, this is Yidarica. I'd appreciate it if you were nicer to her than you've been to me so far."

The air was so awkward that Yidarica could practically feel the plants in the room recoiling; and if she could feel that, she knew August could too. "I-it's, um, it's a pleasure to meet you, Mrs. Sostrin. August has told me–" *and none of it has been good.*

"August has spoken of you," was what she settled on.

Saying nothing, August's mother instead took his place on the couch, staring at Yidarica an uncomfortable amount; particularly her clothes, then grabbing her hands without asking, and examining her nails as if she were looking for something. Finally, she said, "Why?"

Yidarica struggled to tell if this statement was directed to her or August. "Why…" she repeated softly.

"I don't like this. August, I don't think this is a suitable woman to carry your children. Look at how she dresses, and she's much too frail."

"Mother. I already told you I don't want children. I've been telling you that for the past fifteen years." It was easy to see, at this point, that August was struggling to keep his composure.

"Yes, yes, I know you *said* that. And I've been incredibly patient with you about it, but that phase is dragging on for far too long. Now, I was patient with you during that phase where you thought you loved other men, but this is–"

"So dating a woman who abused me was okay?" August asked. "She'd yell at me every day, Mom. She'd hit me. She stabbed me because I said I couldn't grab something for her right that minute! Are you saying all of that was better because she was a woman?!"

At this, Mrs. Sostrin's face softened. "August. I didn't know—"

"And you sure as hell didn't ask! None of you did! All you cared about was the fact that you wouldn't have to tell people that your only son was some kind of deviant, right?" August sat, not on the sofa chair near him, but on the floor beside it, curling up into a ball as best as someone of his height could. "Mom. I can't do this with you right now. I don't have the strength. Please leave."

The weight of the conversation was fully hitting her now; she was lost for words, and her body language was indicative of someone who knew they had crossed a line, but wasn't aware of how to go back to the other side of it. "I mean it, August. I would have never…"

Not looking up at her, he replied: "You say you wouldn't have, but that doesn't change the fact that you did. I'm not in the right mind to have this conversation, right now. I'd like you to leave before I say something I'll end up regretting. Please."

If August had the strength, at this point, to look at his mother, he'd see the hurt in her eyes; that she was barely holding back tears, and was trembling ever so slightly. But she did as he said: stood up from the couch, and left the apartment without another word.

Yidarica wasn't sure how to process this.

I don't know if I can, even. I'm not familiar enough with August's mom, or even the concept of her, to be able to tell if her emotions just now were genuine, or if that was also a part of the manipulation he's been telling me about. I'm unfortunately extremely familiar with having a mother who can fake emotions to get her way.

But she was familiar enough with August himself to know he could probably use some reassurance, so she sat beside him on the floor, placing a supportive hand on his back. "I'm so sorry that happened, August."

He was silent, unmoving, for an uncomfortable amount of time before replying: "It had to."

"Hm? What do you mean by that?" Yidarica asked curiously.

"Whether it's about my family's expectations versus my plans for my life, me moving away, my orientation: I seem to constantly exist in a space that puts me at odds with them, so a difficult conversation had to happen at some point. And it'll probably only get worse from here. Honestly, I wish I had stood up for myself sooner, but I… I just wanted to give grace to the people I love."

"Yeah. That's who you are." Yidarica nodded. "Someone who always wants to be kind. But I'm starting to get the sense that it comes at the cost of you being unkind to yourself. You know, in the sense that you kinda have to negate your own boundaries to be so kind to others, sometimes."

August shifted, resting his head on Yidarica's. He didn't speak, but he grasped her free hand, intertwining his fingers with hers. His hand was clammy and tense still.

"It's hard," he finally said. "When my family– minus Dad, who supported me– found out I was in love with a man, we didn't talk about it. When I moved in with him, we didn't talk about it. But there was always something different about the way my sisters and mom spoke to me, after that. When I first started wearing my glasses, and when one of my sisters saw the bruises I had, I know she told the other women in our family because they got distant. But when I dated a woman, they acted like none of that happened; that we'd been best friends the whole time. It's hard because– because I really do love my mom and my sisters, Yidarica. I'm certain of that. But it's been a long time since I was so certain that they loved me."

"Then…" Yidarica was confused. "Why are you so sure you love them?"

This, in turn, confused August; he sat up, turning his attention to her. "What do you mean?"

"I don't understand why you continue to hold space in your heart for people who don't seem to be doing the same for you," she explained.

"Hm." August sat, quietly, pondering what she had just said. "I don't entirely disagree with the idea, but there is something just a little bleak about the line of thought that, in order to give your love to someone, they have to give it to you first. Who starts it, if that's the case?"

"No, that's not what I– I think I explained myself badly," Yidarica replied. "That's not what I meant. What I mean is, I'm assuming it's been years since your family learned about you being bisexual, and there's been multiple occasions on which they've been hurtful toward you for it, right? I guess I'm not understanding why you continue to give them more chances to hurt you."

August nodded here. "I understand. And you may have a point. The calmest points in my life have happened when I was barely speaking to my mother. Now that I think about it, maybe it's not a coincidence that everything in my life began to get better once I limited our communications. I got a new job, and through it, I've gained so much more confidence. My plants are thriving. I met you."

Yidarica smiled up at him then. "Well, you know, I certainly hope I've been a good girlfriend for all the…" she checked her phone, "eleven minutes I've been aware I had that title."

This made August laugh, a hearty laugh that Yidarica was glad to hear from him. Minutes ago he'd been more upset than she'd ever seen him be, and she had felt that vicariously. How relieving it was to hear his laugh now.

Surely, this must be what it's like to love someone; to feel their emotions as if they're your own.

"I'm sorry if I caught you off guard," August said then. "But I thought it was fairly obvious that that was where my intent lied. We've been to each other's houses, shared a bed. As a matter of fact, I was surprised that, when you introduced me to your friends, you just introduced us as coworkers."

When he puts it like that, it makes me feel dumb for not realizing sooner. "Yeah. It makes a lot more sense in hindsight," she agreed. "But, uh, for the future: I don't really do well with gray areas. Direct, clear communication is ideal."

"Okay. I'll remember that."

Yidarica froze. "What?"

This, in turn, confused August. "What do you mean, 'what?'"

"I– I asked you to communicate directly with me and you just… you just *agreed*. You're not going to give me any pushback on it? None whatsoever? Make fun of me? Tell me you're not going to do that because I'm not a child?"

August looked horrified. "Why would I do any of that?"

Dearest Mother, I really do think I love this man.

Unable to explain why this was so emotionally overwhelming, Yidarica threw her arms around August, holding him as tightly as her arms would allow. Seconds later, she felt his hand on her head, gently stroking her hair as he held her close, as well. Neither spoke, but there was a general understanding of each other that meant they didn't need to. They remained this way until August's stomach growled, and he immediately let go. Yidarica could see the profound redness of his cheeks as he turned away, embarrassed.

"That's right, we were going to get dinner," he recalled. "We should do that. Do you want to do that? Are you still hungry?"

As much of a bad taste as the encounter with August's mother had left in Yidarica's mouth, it wasn't so bad that it dissuaded her from food. "If that rice bowl place is still available, then absolutely!"

"Then let's go. The night is still young, and there is much food to be eaten." August lifted her hand to his mouth, giving it a soft kiss, before standing and offering a hand to help her up. She took it, the sudden change in resting position to her feet causing her to get dizzy, slumping over onto August. He caught her, supporting her weight.

"Sorry! Stood up too fast. I'll be fine, I just need a moment," she explained.

"Or… I can go pick up our food," August suggested, steering Yidarica to sit in the chair behind her. "You can stay here and rest. The restaurant isn't far, so I should be back soon."

"That's– no, you don't need to do that. I'm fine. Really," Yidarica insisted, and yet, made no effort to get out of the chair. It was extremely comfy, after all. It was almost like she was being enveloped in the fluffiest cumulus clouds, but in a material way.

"Don't say that. You're not fine. You need to rest, and that's okay. You don't always have to keep pushing yourself," August said. He kneeled to the level of the chair then, so that he could make sure Yidarica's eyes were able to focus and she didn't have a fever. "Good, you're coherent and not feverish; and also, beautiful."

He smiled then, before leaning in for a kiss. Yidarica smiled as well, as they continued to exchange small, sweet little pecks of affection.

"On second thought…" August whispered. "If someone delivers the food to us, I can stay here and kiss you until they arrive, and that sounds like a lovely itinerary for the evening."

Yidarica grinned at this suggestion. "I couldn't possibly agree more," she said, as both neared each other for yet another kiss.

Chapter Twenty-One

When Yidarica handed the physical copy of the notes for the Weather Project to Shiori and Celosia, with Muiren and August at her sides, she was certain that she had never felt more proud of herself. There had been numerous setbacks, the project had gone on longer than anyone had anticipated, and their solution wasn't completely foolproof, but in this world, what was? The feedback that Eira had given was that the product's conclusion was above satisfactory, so there truly wasn't anything else the three could do, other than be proud of themselves.

"Wow, this is hefty," Shiori noted, seemingly weighing the notes in her hands. "I'll have to get around to reading it someday, when our other projects aren't as demanding. Speaking of which: take it easy for the rest of the day, Yidarica and Muiren, but be ready to get back into it tomorrow. I'm sure that Hadiza and Nanda will be overjoyed to have you two back on our regular workload."

Muiren gently nudged Yidarica's arm. "The gang's all back together."

It's been so long since all four of us have been together in the office. It'll be nice to get back to the way things were, in that regard.

"As for you, August: now that we're in post-migration times, our workload becomes its slowest unless a major storm is projected," Celosia picked up. "I'll be reading those notes first, since I'll have the time. Why don't we use today to help you get to know everyone else in the Biome? You didn't get very much time to, before."

"Yeah, true," he agreed. "Can I do that after lunch? If we have the time, I'd love to fit in a heartfelt farewell to my comrades here."

Celosia smiled. "Yes, of course. You know where to find me."

When everyone adjourned, Yidarica stopped at her desk to place her bag under it; no one else on her team was around at the time, so she decided to take a walk around the office to kill some time. Not long after she grabbed a bottle of water, she found Celosia reading at one of the meeting tables in a quieter area of the office. As she read the notes, Yidarica noticed that her hands would tremble whenever she reached to turn a page. Seeing this made her realize that, ever since she'd met Celosia, there had always been something that felt slightly off about her, physically, but it was impossible to explain why she felt that way. Even disregarding the day where she had almost fainted, something about her physical state always felt different than everyone else's.

"Too excited to make it back to your desk?" she asked, taking a seat across from her.

She looked up, startled. "Oh, Yidarica! No, it's just that if I sat at my desk, I'd never find the time to read this; I'd keep getting interrupted by people coming up to my desk and speaking to me, so I figured I should sit somewhere far enough that it would be an imposition to walk over here to ask me anything. You are welcome, though, so don't worry about that!"

"I see." Yidarica nodded. *It's very kind of her to reassure me that way.* "Can I ask you something, Celosia?"

She hummed affirmatively, as she turned another page.

"You've been with the company a long time, haven't you?" Yidarica hoped this was a suitable way to start this inquiry. "I'm a little surprised that, for all the time you've been here, you're in a position that's equivalent to Shiori's. You'd think someone like you would be higher up the ladder; somewhere with a little more prestige, at this point."

"Prestige." Celosia repeated the last word Yidarica had said. She then looked around, before her gaze centered on the meeting room nearest she and Yidarica. "Would you like to discuss this in a meeting room? I think the capabilities there will help me best explain what it is I want to tell you."

Yidarica would never say no to a fun meeting room display. "Sure."

"This way, then." Celosia stood, making sure not to forget the book of notes on the table.

In the meeting room, Celosia was uncharacteristically quiet as she concentrated on putting in the necessary codes for the meeting projection. After she was done typing in all of the necessary information, her hands glowed with the casting of a spell, one which was unfamiliar to Yidarica, but brief. She then turned to her, and smiled; but this smile was, noticeably, smaller than the usual Celosia smile.

"Let's go back. Back to when the Weather Department was first founded, nine years ago."

The two women walked up to the projection that appeared: a group of five people sitting at a table together, in a deep discussion about something that seemed important. On the table were a multitude of notes as well as one tablet, which was projecting what appeared to be a mockup of an application. Celosia stopped beside the only woman at the table, her brown hair pulled into a sleek ponytail. Judging by the cozy dress and shawl in earth tones (emerald and forest green plus a medium brown, to be exact), this had to be her.

She smiled again when she realized Yidarica had figured it out. "Yes, this is me. I was a fresh-faced twenty-five year old woman, just out of university and ready to take on the world. I was the youngest person at this table. The only woman. The only immigrant. I wonder now: is this why they were so impressed with me? That they expected less of me, because of who I was? But there's no reason to think of those things now. It's in the past."

Wait a minute. Celosia graduated at twenty-five? That's three years later than usual.

The projection disappeared then, and in its wake, left a new one of a group of people standing beside a display modeled to look like a giant phone. Yidarica was familiar with this apparatus: it was used whenever a new major development was made at MFI, to show it off.

"After we all worked tirelessly for almost two years, we finally made it: the Weather Aggregation, the optimal plug-in for all other MFI applications. At this time, we didn't yet have the resources to make our own application. That was a future goal, but in that moment…in that moment, we were so proud of ourselves. Overjoyed, that we were able to create something that functioned. This projection you see, here, was our launch party. If I close my eyes and remember, I can still see how happy everyone was there. We were elated, ecstatic. Drunk. Oh, I got *so* drunk," she laughed. "But it was okay. My friends in the office helped to make sure I was okay, and they made sure to call my husband to carry me home."

Husband? Celosia is married?! But didn't she and Muiren…

"Yes, I was married." Celosia giggled, noticing Yidarica's visible confusion, but then her smile faded. "Yes… I was. But life happens, and we, as humans… are powerless to stop it."

Now, the projection in the room was of a younger Celosia and a taller, thin man with blond hair, in front of a modest house; judging by the skies and the plant life surrounding the house, this appeared to be the same time of year as now, post-migration. The two shared a hug and a kiss before heading in opposite directions, presumably going to work.

The lighting in the room shifted to night, the moon rising in a crescent shape, and stars spackled across the sky. In the distance, a few clouds gathered. Celosia returned, alone. As time passed, she eventually made her way to the living room of the house, sitting in a particularly comfy-looking reclining chair, one that had been upholstered with a seafoam green corduroy. She sat in that chair for hours, well into the wee hours of the night, a crocheting project on her lap left long untouched.

The man did not arrive.

The sun rose again. Celosia remained in her chair, still awake, with barely any movement. As the sun poured into the living room, highlighting the redness of her eyes and general lack of rest, two uniformed men knocked at the front door. Her husband was not with them.

The projection disappeared.

The next projection was unmistakably a hospital; the white walls and sterile environs gave it away. The view in this hospital shifted from a lobby to a room. Celosia was in one of the beds, hooked up to a few machines.

"Ten years before…" Celosia's voice startled Yidarica, as the projection shifted to fill in more hospital details: a tray here, a book there. "When I was seventeen years old, I got very sick. We never found out why. It took a couple of years before I was able to resume my life because of it. But once I did, and was living a normal life again, I thought that was it, that my illness was behind me. But the stress of losing my husband…"

Celosia, in the projection, in the hospital bed, began to lose her hair as time passed. She also visibly began to lose weight. "I got sick again, severely so. I lost my hair, a chunk of my memories, my fine motor skills, and struggled to understand things that happened right in front of me. My speech suffered, too. I became a wisp of a person. I found out, after I lost my hair, that I had been carrying a child. But that was gone too. My husband and child were dead, and my family was so far away. I couldn't take it. Any of it. I went on extended leave from work. Most of that time, I remained in the hospital."

Now, the projection was of a particularly wispy Celosia, with her hair beginning to grow back; still in a hospital, but in an inpatient unit. She was seated in a circle with vague, shadowy figures of other people, assumedly participating in some kind of group therapy. One of them was handing her a slice of strawberry cake, assumedly brought to the meeting by another member, and she was clearly happy to receive it. There was something about a fully grown twenty-seven year old woman clapping in response to someone being nice to her, because she couldn't speak well enough to thank them, that was so chilling that Yidarica couldn't move.

"For a time, I had to stay here. It had its ups and downs, but it was what I needed to be certain I could regain my independence, and wouldn't hurt myself. And during this time, I gained clarity. I was still alive; I had a chance to continue on, and so, I decided not to squander the rest of the life I had been graced with. When my physician determined me well enough to be released, I sold my house. I got a tiny studio apartment. And I asked to be demoted at work."

"You *asked* to be demoted?" Yidarica asked. *Unheard of!*

"I did. I knew that I wasn't the same person anymore. I couldn't do what I did before I went on leave anymore," explained Celosia. "I knew that, if I ever reached that capacity again, I would be able to work my way back up; I hadn't done anything to break the trust of management, so I knew they'd be in my corner. But at the time of my return, I was still recovering, mentally and physically, and I knew that if I overexerted myself too much, I'd just get sick again. And during this time, I was… not necessarily happy, but I was relieved. I could rest. Focus on recovery. And from there, things got better."

The projection, then, initiated a montage of a few moments: of Celosia accepting her new position as the equivalent of Yidarica's position in the Project Garden; to her moving into an apartment with a woman who looked so much like her that Yidarica didn't have to ask, she knew it had to be her sister; to moving again on her own, and her promotion to her current position as Project Biome manager.

"And now, I'm so happy." Celosia was holding back tears. "Everyone here has been so patient with me, and respectful of what I've been through; and the fact that I was able to maintain the level of respect I had when I was at a much higher level within the company, it fills me with nothing but joy. And as much as I will always miss my husband, these days, I feel hopeful for the future as well. It is truly as though I was given a new lease on life."

The room began to power down then.

So much makes sense about her now. She's experienced things that some of us could never survive. If I didn't already have a ton of respect for her, I definitely would now.

"Thank you for sharing this all with me, Celosia," Yidarica said sincerely. "You've been through so much; I'm flattered that you feel comfortable enough with me to bare your soul like this."

Celosia smiled. "Maybe I'm naive for being so open, but I trust you. Muiren thinks very highly of you, and I trust their judgment of people more than my own. Besides, I have always been fond of you. You're so cute!"

At this, Yidarica smiled bashfully. "You calling me cute is a *huge* compliment, given how cute *you* are. I mean, look at you! Everything you wear is so cozy. Whenever I look at you, I feel calm and warm."

"Cozy. I think I like that word." The expression on Celosia's face now seemed as though she was reminiscing about something. "I'll get back to managing now. I think I've shirked my responsibilities long enough. Shall we walk together?"

The two began to walk in the direction of the Weather Department's seating. "By the way, how did you know that I've been here so long?" Celosia asked. "Did August or Muiren tell you?"

"Neither, actually." Yidarica had never thought about how embarrassing it might be to explain to Celosia that she'd studied her and her cohorts, but the reality was certainly hitting her now. "I have a kind of intense fascination with the weather, and it's led me to study the inception and accomplishments of you guys' efforts. I noticed your name came up a lot when I'd read about the history of the Weather Department. Got kinda excited knowing a woman helped cultivate the area of work I aspire to."

"Oh!" Celosia grinned, but her gaze quickly became confused. "You've been here a few years; why haven't you introduced yourself before now? Or at least sent an email? I would have loved to mentor another woman in tech!"

Mother, why is that saying about hindsight constantly being proven true? "I don't know, I didn't want to be too overzealous and make you uncomfortable, or anything," Yidarica confessed. "One of the things I've learned from working in a corporate environment like this, is that the way your cohorts feel about you is just as important as the quality of work you can put out. Sometimes more so, and I didn't want to accidentally burn a bridge somehow."

"You're cautious." Celosia nodded in understanding. "That's resourceful, but given how bright you are, I hope that doesn't overcorrect by pushing you into subconsciously making yourself small. You deserve to be proud of your skills. Well, from here on, feel free to speak with me if you want to learn anything about the Weather Department that you don't already know. There aren't many people still employed here that would know more about its inner workings than myself."

"Celosia, I don't think you understand what you just volunteered to do." Yidarica laughed.

"Perhaps not. But it is always a good thing to share one's knowledge," she replied.

They had reached the Project Biome's area now, and Celosia greeted the person whose desk sat beside hers before turning back to Yidarica. "Whenever you all send August this way, could you let me know? He's been so lovely so far; I want to get everyone else in the Biome excited to work with him!"

They should be very excited. He's amazing. "Yeah, of course. See you around!" Yidarica waved before heading back toward her desk.

Returning to the Project Garden's area, Yidarica could see August chatting with everyone else on her team; he and Hadiza were sitting, and Muiren and Nanda were standing, and they were all listening to Shiori speak. Based on her body language, this wasn't something that required her to be overtly businesslike. It was always nice to see coworkers having casual conversations.

As she arrived at her desk, she could hear Shiori speaking: "…which can run anywhere from a few hours to a few *months*, so if you haven't already learned how to section off and color-code your calendar, now would be a great time to do that." She then held out a hand, "Yidarica is really good at organizing a calendar, if you want to see how it's done."

This made everyone turn to her, which immediately put her on guard. "Yeah, I… guess I am," she replied nervously. "What's happening? What did I miss?"

"Oh, we're just priming August for the daily life of someone on a project team," Muiren explained. "He's got to learn that this past undertaking was the exception, and that we're usually juggling a bunch of small things at once."

She nodded. "Yeah, absolutely. Being able to devote as much time as is necessary to all your active projects is the secret sauce to bring a good contributor to the Biome, I'm sure, because that's definitely the case here in our Garden."

"I see. Well, that doesn't sound impossible, so I'm looking forward to it," August smiled. "Celosia has a lot of faith in me, so I'm hoping to live up to that."

"You're lucky to have such a cool manager, too," Nanda told him. "She literally helped create that entire department! She's been here like, forever, and yet she's still so sweet and down-to-earth. On my first day back, she shared some of the dessert with me 'cause

I was bummed they sold out before I could remember where the cafeteria was."

"You know, they ought to bring more desserts for the lunch service," Shiori said then. "I can't remember the last time they didn't run out. It's been months! Ridiculous, really."

Now that I think about it, same; it's been so long since I was able to get my hands on any of the desserts. You'd think they'd want to keep up with demand, right?

"It has been a while since I was able to secure a sweet treat here, now that you mention it," August agreed. "What's up with that? I want the fun of baked goods, but I don't want to have to get into a fracas for them."

"What, not willing to throw hands for a brownie?" Yidarica gently teased him, giving him a soft nudge. "No one here would judge you if you did. Those are really good brownies."

Everyone in the area agreed, beginning to discuss how good the brownies usually were.

"At any rate, I think I'm going to place my things down over at my desk and then head to lunch," August said then. "You didn't hear this from me, but I have been hearing talk of there being iced oatmeal cookies today. I'm going to try my hardest to get my hands on some of those."

As everyone else seemed to be enthralled by the idea of the cookies, they were too busy to notice August's gentle touch to Yidarica's back before he walked away, and the small smirk he gave her before setting off sent the best kind of tingles up her spine.

★★★

Later that day, on her way home, Yidarica received a message from Zaya. It included a photo of a plant almost identical to the one she had helped Yidarica raise, positioned on a high rise balcony. The sun was setting in the background, so it was likely a photo that had been taken not very long before it had been sent.

> I hope your girl is doing as well as mine is. And I hope you're doing equally as well. Things are great here, but I'd be lying if I said I didn't sometimes long for Dad's nursery and seeing you, sometimes.

Yidarica smiled. She missed Zaya too, even if the kinda sorta relationship between them had fizzled so quickly.

She texted back:

> Mine is, yes. Any day now, the flower buds it grew should be opening. I'm really excited to see what they'll look like, and I can send you pictures too. That is a beautiful view, by the way. Your living situation seems to be way better than it was here.

In some ways, Yidarica envied that; she had a lot of love for her modest apartment, but she'd adore having a place that was ground level and had ample outdoor space, if nothing else. She wouldn't have to constantly worry about having the strength to get up her apartment stairs, and she could have the opportunity to maybe start her own garden; one which she was sure August would be happy to help her with.

Zaya sent another photo then, this one of her hand intertwined with someone else's, most likely a woman based on the accessorization of her fingers and wrists.

> **Well, it helps that I don't live alone. As it turns out, there is no shortage of nice, flourishing girls in my life.**

This was something that, initially, Yidarica felt a bit hurt to see, wondering what Zaya's intentions had been with her if she had been able to get into a relationship with someone else so quickly after moving. But that lasted for only a moment, when she quickly realized that it didn't necessarily matter. After all, she would have never had found the courage to speak to August if anything else had transpired there, between the two of them. Maybe disappointments were necessary in the path to find those who would stay in one's life for a long time; and maybe, just maybe, Yidarica was finally at a point in her life where she was willing to accept that.

In response, she looked through the photos in her phone for a little while, trying to decide which photo of herself and August was a good one to send. It was hard partly because they didn't have a lot of photos together just yet, and also because taking selfies together often left one of them at an unflattering angle due to the height difference. There was, however, a very cute picture that Gracia had snapped of the two of them that day they gathered peaches, so that was the one she decided on.

> **I'm glad you're finding your happiness, Zaya. We both seem to be making progress, in that way.**

Yidarica put her phone back in her pocket so she could disembark from the rail car and continue home, but not before she saw Zaya react to the picture she'd sent with a heart emoji.

Walking home, Yidarica was happy that Zaya had found the time to message her again amidst all of her busy communications work, but this did also remind her that she still hadn't heard from her sister. This felt different from the last time their chats had gone silent, because it came on the heels of a disagreement. How could she know whether or not her younger sister would ever speak to her again? Her older siblings already didn't, so it didn't feel like a stretch to assume it could also happen with Runiala.

If for no other reason, and even if it is petty, I don't want our birth giver to succeed in driving a wedge between us. I have so much love for my little sister, and I refuse to let it end like this. I just wish I knew what to say to her, to get this train of thought across.

Realizing then she knew someone who was in this exact predicament, when Yidarica got home, she absolved to call August. If anyone had sage advice about rocky sibling relationships at the moment, it would be him. After all, it had been a while since he'd said anything about either of his sisters, so things had to be either better, or so, so much worse.

Lying in her bed, Yidarica initiated the call between herself and August; as the phone rang, she hoped she wasn't disturbing him. Was it too late to hang up–

"Hi, Yidarica. Is everything okay?" Well, it was too late *now*.

"Hi, August! Yeah, things are fine. But while I was on my way home, a train of thoughts made me realize that it's been a while since you mentioned your sisters. I hope everything is okay between you guys."

The sigh on the other end of the phone clearly indicated that it was not.

After a few more moments, August spoke again. "I don't really know how to describe it, but at the moment, family is…"

"Complicated?" Yidarica suggested, when it became clear that August didn't know what to say.

"Yeah. Complicated is a good word." Somehow, it was easy to assume that August had nodded here. "My sister Mareille, who is the eldest, has a couple of kids. Good kids. I'm always happy whenever I get to see them, but the rest of my family has always been kinda weird about them. Like, they're obviously loved, but I've been a part of multiple conversations in the past that indicated that my niblings are seen as, I guess, inferior because they came from a woman in the family, and not a man. You'll need to remember this, because it becomes an important part of what's currently going on.

"Anyway, after that day when you were over and my mother forced my hand in kicking her out of my house, she ended up staying in a hotel before heading home the following day. At this time, if you'll recall, both my sisters were firm on hating me for the time being. It's easy to assume that when our mother got home, she was easily able to add onto that. But after a couple of days passed, Mareille was the one to realize there was probably more to the story than she was told. She mentioned that she believes me getting so upset that I kick someone out of my house is extremely out of character for me. She told her husband to think about it: if I had formerly been in situations where my partner was literally abusing me and I continued to put up with it, what was it that would cause me to tell someone to get out?

"So, she sat on this for a few days before deciding she wanted to talk to our mother about it. Now, my sister's always had a gentle nature, even when touching on situations where she knows the subject matter is probably going to start an argument. I say that to say, there's no way she would've approached this tactlessly. She's very good with words, so I know she was able to curate them in a way that doesn't assign blame or shame to anyone involved. Even so, when trying to have this conversation with our mother, she freaked out on her for daring to question her, is how I understand it. They both got really upset at each other, and my sister called me that night to tell me everything. She also apologized to me, which was nice.

"But the next day, our other sister contacted her and they got into a disagreement over how our mother took that conversation. I don't dislike either of my sisters, but Haviera is… it's easy to tell that she's the one who's most wrapped around our mother's finger. I was spared the details, but I'm told that the conversation got really heated. I'm led to believe that the context of how my niblings are regarded came up, because the day after *that*, Mareille reached out to me and told me that she still won't be in a place where she's comfortable with speaking with me for a while because of how our family is about nonexistent heirs. So, while everyone in my immediate family still seems to be mad at me for existing, they're also all mad at each other now."

He took a breath before adding, "Sorry. That was a lot."

"No need to apologize," Yidarica reassured him. "But it is a lot. I'm so sorry, August. If nothing else, hopefully, with none of them wanting to speak to each other you can have some peace."

"Yeah, of course," August agreed. "I blamed myself at first, because I thought I was the catalyst for all of this, until I thought about it more. It really is our mother causing chaos because she can't stand to be questioned or contradicted. I swear I don't remember her always being like this. She used to be so kind, but I guess not having Dad anymore really has taken its toll."

Yidarica thought back to when she had met August's mother, and he had first asked her to leave; the hurt within her expression, and wondering if it was genuine. It was something that had resonated with her because, in all of her memories, she'd never seen a show of emotion quite that potent from her own mother. Something about the way Mrs. Sostrin had looked felt so raw, but the fact that she was still causing problems for her children, especially August, left Yidarica uncertain on how to feel about her as a person.

Even if she isn't intentionally causing problems, she needs to accept that she is, and take responsibility for all the fallout. That's something my own mother would never do. I hope that isn't also the case for her.

"I realize now that you're probably asking me this because of the situation with your own sister," August said then. "Has there been any change since the last time you two spoke?"

Yidarica was always impressed by how intuitive August was. "Well, no, we haven't spoken," she replied. "But what's been on my mind is, I don't want this to be the end of us. We have two older siblings that have never wanted anything to do with us, and I'm sure that's our mother's fault too. I don't want her to succeed in driving me apart from the one sibling I ever got to know, but Nini is so under our parents' influence that I don't know how to convey that in a way that she'll be receptive to. I'm afraid that, when I do finally speak to her, I'll end up driving her further away."

"May I suggest that you tell her that?" August asked. "It's very difficult to bare your emotions over text, but I think it's important that you do: taking the time and explaining it to her should get the point across that you believe your relationship is worth fighting for."

This made a lot of sense. "Yeah. You're right, August. If you don't mind, I'm gonna type up that message now."

"Of course. See you soon, my beloved."

Yidarica took a moment to smile, basking in the warmth of being beloved to someone, before composing (and revising) the message to her sister. After about twenty minutes of editing and deliberation, she decided it was good enough to send.

> Hi, Nini.

> I hate that we left our last conversation the way we did. The silence between us since then is not one that I ever want to be permanent, so that's why I'm reaching out now.

> I am very sorry if I upset you during our last talk. I know I got very emotional for reasons you're probably unable to empathize with, but I also need you to understand that the way you suddenly switched to condemning me wasn't okay. I'm trying to be understanding of the fact that you have a different relationship with our parents than I do, but I cannot do that if you can't extend the same grace to me.

> Who you want to keep in your life is your decision to make. If you've decided that I crossed a boundary and you cannot forgive me for it, I will respect that. But I didn't want to have that be the case without a fight, so to speak.

> You're not obligated to reply, but this will be my last message unless you indicate you don't want that to be the case.

> Whatever you decide, please: take care of yourself.

★★★

"Legal sends their regards. Even though they were very clear about how much they hate how long it took, they're also apparently very impressed with the way you all decided to go about the application revamp."

Yidarica stood in a meeting room with Muiren, Shiori, August, and Celosia. Currently, there was a simple outdoor park projection playing so it wouldn't be dark in the room. Shiori had been the one to speak, and so, she continued.

"When you all get back to work– Yidarica, Muiren, August– you should be seeing an email from them thanking you all. I think there might be a gift involved, even, which is why Celosia and I gathered you here," she winked.

"A gift?" August asked, verbalizing what the other two had been thinking. "Wonder what that could be."

Knowing how office work goes, it's probably just some special email highlight or something. Yidarica refused to let herself get too excited.

"Scale from one to ten, how excited should we be getting about this gift?" Muiren asked, seemingly reading Yidarica's exact thoughts.

"Definitely not a ten, but... satisfactory, I'd like to think," replied Celosia. "Maybe a six? What do you think, Shiori?"

"I think we shouldn't be playing this game with our direct reports," Shiori replied firmly, completely overlooking the fact that Celosia's only report here was August.

"Oh. Right. Sorry." Celosia overlooked this as well. "Well, at any rate, you all should let yourselves be proud! This kind of collaboration project, on this large a scale, has never been done before. If anything similar happens down the road, your work will be used as the blueprint. You are all officially part of MFI history!"

Muiren smiled. "Well, when you say it like that, I guess it is kind of cool."

"Very cool," August agreed.

It wasn't how I expected to immortalize myself here, but I suppose that everyone starts somewhere.

"Speaking of which, it looks like your gift has arrived," Shiori said, tapping a few buttons on her tablet so she could project what was on her screen to the room itself. When the projection appeared, in all of its sparkly glory, it appeared to be an e-mail. Glancing over it, it seemed to be a thank-you email regarding the project and a few details about what it had entailed.

"I'd invite you all to look here," Shiori highlighted the "to" and "from" fields. "This email wasn't only sent to our teams, or departments. With this, the entire company now knows that you three did an amazing job that will benefit all of us."

That's cool, but… am I ungrateful if I feel like it's a bit lackluster?

"Also, I have just been informed that there will be pizza later!" added Celosia.

Still lackluster, but pizza does make everything better, especially when it's free.

***

At the day's end, Yidarica felt tired enough that she worried about having enough stamina to get home. There was less riding than walking, but still, she didn't want to miss her Comtran stop and end up lost somewhere. In moments like these, she always cursed her weak body.

"Hey." She was nudged by Muiren, who was standing opposite her. "You okay? For a moment there, it looked like you were gonna tip over."

"Yeah, I'm fine," she lied. "Just a little tired, but I'll be peachy once I can get home and shut my eyes for a little while."

Muiren nodded. "Okay. Well, if you need anything later, just remember that I'm not too far away, all right? I don't mind you coming over. Celosia is coming over to have dinner and possibly stay the night, but I know she wouldn't mind seeing you. Quite the opposite, if anything. She's been telling me she'd love to talk to you about where you get your clothes."

"Oh." Yidarica raised an eyebrow. "You two have been hanging out together a lot recently, huh?"

"Yeah. Well, she met my parents this past weekend," Muiren explained. "They like her. My parents always say they've known I'm a lesbian since I was in primary school, but my mother still definitely had a Mom Moment when she learned her age. I think it went well once they got to talking, though. You know Celosia, she's a sweetheart."

Honestly, yeah. There's a reason she's so well-liked, unrelated to her legacy here. It almost feels impossible to be angry when she's around. "I guess it's a good thing we're not working with her anymore, then," Yidarica lightly teased. "I'm sure you're tired of talking to HR at this point."

Muiren laughed, giving Yidarica the lightest of nudges. "Hey, I don't want to hear it from *you,* of all people."

If they were going to say more, they were interrupted by Celosia's sudden appearance at their side. "Hi! Ready to go?" she asked exuberantly.

"Damn it all, woman. You've got to stop being so quiet when you walk. Scared the life out of me," Muiren complained, their face slightly red from the scare. "But yes, I'm all packed up. And you?"

"There's a reason I'm here," replied Celosia. "If you don't mind, I'd like to stop by the convenience store near your place. One of my direct reports told me about this ice cream I've never had, and it sounds amazing. We can share it!"

"You will never hear me say no to ice cream." Muiren checked their space once more, before beginning to leave the area. "See you farther up the road, Yidarica. I mean it– text me if you need me."

"Bye!" Celosia added, waving, before both started on their way out, Muiren holding the door open for Celosia before putting their arm around her shoulders.

Yidarica knew it wasn't a good idea to head home when she felt this weak, but she also didn't know what else she could do. She didn't have the option of calling someone to come get her. She concentrated her hardest to try to think her way out of this predicament, but her thoughts scattered when she felt an arm around her shoulders.

"Come on, let's go home," August said, with a warm smile.

She looked up. "August, you– no. I don't want you to think you have to–"

"I don't think I *have* to, but I know that I *want* to," he reassured her. "I want my girlfriend to feel safe and rested, and to cook for her tonight to be sure she can regain some energy. And if she's up for it, some cuddling sounds nice too."

Yidarica laughed at this, but honestly, cuddling did sound nice. "You drive such a hard bargain, August. I guess I have no choice but to accept."

The two left the building then, Yidarica holding on tight to August's arm, leaning on it a bit so that walking didn't feel quite so taxing. He gave her hand a squeeze, his way of reassuring her that he wouldn't be leaving her side.

About the author

Michelle Rivera is an Afro-Latina author from Chicago, IL, who began writing at a young age in an attempt to bring all of the vast, vivid worlds in her imagination to life. What started as quick short stories scribbled in school notebooks or on spare loose-leaf paper quickly grew into earning their own notebooks as aspiring full-fledged novels. In time, this expanded even further into long, detailed works saved electronically. Her long dreams of becoming an author were given life in July 2022, when she published her first novel, *Revolution*, the first book in the *Revosaga* series.

In addition to writing, Rivera also enjoys crafting, traveling, and video games. She draws inspiration from the daily happenings in her life, as a queer, neurodivergent woman working in corporate America.

Milton Keynes UK
Ingram Content Group UK Ltd.
UKHW010749190724
445797UK00004B/126